THE

Prospering

THE

Prospering

Elizabeth George Speare

HOUGHTON MIFFLIN COMPANY BOSTON

The Riverside Press Cambridge

1967

FOREWORD

In the year 1734 a young Yale tutor by the name of John Sergeant accepted a call as missionary to a remnant of the Mahican Indians living along the Housatonic River in western Massachusetts. The committee of clergymen responsible for this mission had conceived a plan at once bold and reasonable. On land granted by the General Court of Massachusetts to the Indians "to their use and behoof forever" there was to be an Indian town, with a meetinghouse and schoolhouse; through preaching, education and the responsibilities of franchise the Indians were to learn the English way of life. Three years later the clergymen selected four English families to settle in the town and to serve as models for the Indians, the first of these settlers to arrive being Ephraim Williams with his six youngest children. *C, 2*

The story of the Stockbridge mission has been many times retold, for the experiment was fruitful in diverse ways. The Mission House, built for John Sergeant in 1739 and restored in 1928, remains as one of the most beautiful of America's historic houses. Williams College owes its founding to the will of Colonel Ephraim Williams, son of the first settler. The theological writings of Jonathan Edwards, which were to dominate New England thought for a hundred years, were completed during his ten years in the mission.

Yet inexplicably it was not one of the famous but Elizabeth

Williams, youngest daughter of the pioneer family, who spoke from the Berkshire chronicles directly to me. Of the eighty-two years of her life there are only two witnesses — a chair cover embroidered in her youth and the conventional eulogy delivered at her funeral. From this scant testimony her story began to take form in my imagination. In the telling of it I have no way of knowing how far I have missed the truth or where I may have come close to it. To the recorded facts I have been, to the best of my knowledge, scrupulously faithful. The personalities of the men and women of Stockbridge, revealed by their own writings and by the judgments of their contemporaries, I have attempted to convey accurately. For the undocumented history of mind and heart I alone am answerable to Elizabeth Williams.

E. G. S.

CONTENTS

THE

Prospering

PROLOGUE

1784

IN A FEW MOMENTS the service will begin. This is a day the
town of Stockbridge has long anticipated, for a new meetinghouse is a symbol of many things. Chiefly, as Stephen will point
out in his sermon, it is witness to the faith that was brought to
this continent by our fathers and nurtured in the wilderness.
Yes, I am almost certain he will use those very words, though I
suspect he is not the first to speak them. Also, as I am sure he will
remind us, this handsome building in which we have gathered is a
sign of the great goodness of God toward us in this pleasant valley.

For we have indeed prospered. I counted nine carriages before the door as I came in. We have lived through two wars.
The devouring monster has passed so close to us that we could
feel its fiery breath but we have been left unscathed. Would we
have flourished so without God's favor? Why must this day be
shadowed for me by the thought of the wicked who flourish like
the green tree? And who am I to ask, sitting here in my new
gray silk? Would I give up willingly even the smallest measure
of my own prospering?

Abigail does not doubt for a moment. What an entrance she
made today! Always has made, for that matter, but the new
building is more fitting for it. Past sixty, and that magnificent
back and the lift of her head in its high pleated cap as imperious

— some say arrogant — as in her twenties. Mother was a very old woman at her age, but Abigail will be handsome at eighty. Her hands, in the exquisite gloves from France, lie so enviably still against the lavender silk; Abigail has never fidgeted. In a sense, it is her day, even more than Stephen's. She is the one who rightly belongs in father's place, and I must allow her the pride that should, had he lived, be his.

Because they can say what they like of him, in their hearts they must admit how much of their prospering they owe to him. They — or their fathers — came here at his invitation. They sought his advice when they would increase their acres, they elected him to deal with the surveyors while they looked the other way, and in the end they let him be the scapegoat for them all. Say what they will, not one of his grandchildren possesses his quality. The raw thrusting strength has been schooled and polished out of them. Perhaps it will never be required of them in this prospering town.

My father's day is long past. What is there about this dedication that has caused the old aches to stir like weeds deep under water? Is it the sight of Abigail surrounded by three pews full of children and grandchildren? No, truly I rejoice with her in these. I am proud of them all, and proud of her too, sitting like a queen in their midst. Will any of them, I wonder, sit like that at her age? Joseph Dwight's children all favor Abigail, as though in fathering them he merely underscored the pattern she would create. John's children have another stamp, perhaps only the shadow of loss laid upon them too young. Yet this burden may have made Erastus the dependable physician he is and given Electa her gentleness. Neither one has inherited Abigail's charm, nor the steel beneath it. And young John, who has no trace of these qualities? Ah — I cannot think of John impartially.

He sits not with the others but on the far side of the house with his Indians. We have grown unaccustomed to seeing them at meeting, for it is some years since they have worshipped with us. Are they impressed with the dignity of this dedication service? At least they are all wearing their best beaver hats, so incongruous atop the blankets. Some of the women have decorated theirs with fresh flowers. What do they think of our new meetinghouse? None of us, after a whole lifetime, has ever learned to interpret that gaze, leaden as water cupped in rocky hollows. Abigail, I know, still sees only stubbornness or craft. Stephen saw only indifference, and he soon gave up trying. I try, but often I wonder if I see reflected in their dark gaze only my own thoughts. The dullness that seems to have closed over their faces in these last years — is it only the lengthening shadow of my own uncertainty?

Stephen is mounting the pulpit. Dear Stephen! His shoulders are rigid under the new coat. He is so anxious. All that fuss about his white bands having to be relaundered when any eye but his would have found them perfect. But he is right to feel proud; he is precisely the minister for this increasing parish. They have come to expect the word of God spoken in thunder. A lion in the pulpit, they like to say, and though it should be absurd, for Stephen is lightly built and shorter than average, it is somehow not so. When he stands there with his eyes glowing and his head thrown back, that slight figure of his seems actually to tower over us. But they want something quite different at their tea tables, and there he pleases them too, innocently I think, for he is completely without guile. It is the immaculate white bands of fine lawn, so exactly folded, and a sort of elegance when he sips his tea that makes it seem worth while to have opened the best bottle of Madeira. And in sickness and despair, who should know better than I the blessing and courage in that thin hand?

But — how can I warn him? — he is not alone there in the pulpit. They have mounted the stairs behind him, or perhaps they were already there and I did not see, and now they stand behind him staring out at us, three lean silent wraiths. They do not frighten me, but I would like to cry out in protest. Of what fault can they accuse Stephen? It is unfair that they should hold him accountable, that they should stand there waiting for the words of a language he cannot speak. It is unreasonable that there should be ghosts at all today in this place filled with the fragrance of fresh-sawn timber.

Has anyone but me observed them? Certainly not Stephen; I need not have feared that he would look behind. He is already, before he speaks, assuming the lion. The little rustlings and scufflings have quieted, every eye is on him, and the service is about to begin. He will preach a fine sermon, and I must try to keep my mind on it.

But there are so many ghosts. When did they come in? A moment ago I was aware only of the living, the prospering, and now, one by one, these others have taken their places among us. I see now that they are all here; how could we have thought to hold a dedication without them? My father, solid and ruddy-faced. Eph, his legs crossed in their smooth white leather breeches, studying Stephen with that amiable smile. Konkapot in his red blanket. Catharine. Timothy Woodbridge. Sarah Edwards, and Jerusha, whom I never saw in life. And behind Stephen that gaunt figure with burning eyes. No, I am not afraid, even of him. This day belongs to them more than to us. But how can I listen to Stephen when they press upon me like this?

Indian Town

1737

I. I MUST GO BACK forty-seven years to the beginning, to the time when we came to this town. I was seven years old, and I remember the journey chiefly as the occasion when my father first took notice of me. I think I sensed even then that I had won his favor undeservedly, that it was due less to my own merits than to the others' default, but I remember my smugness and my childish scorn at the knowledge that of the entire family he and I alone shared the joy of this adventure in the wilderness.

The powerful figure pushing ahead of us through the forest had been transformed in my eyes. The very characteristics that had terrified me at home, the massive shoulders, the thick red neck thrusting up from his shirt, the hard jaw, the wiry hair that sprang from his hands and arms, had all become reason not for fear but for trust. Beyond question he could look out for us. Unseen Indians, the wolves whose distant howls sometimes chilled us even at midday, or the nameless things that thumped and screamed in the dark tangle on either side — my father was more than a match for them.

It would never have occurred to me to bid for his attention. I was rapt in my own delight. The journey, leading further every hour from the restrictions of chores and books, had the entrancing aspect of a prolonged holiday. My sturdy body scarcely noted discomfort and fatigue; instead every sense had been re-

leased. The forest trail was a constant novelty, winding for
hours at a time through a perpetual twilight, then merging
briefly with a traveled road and coming unexpectedly upon
a cluster of houses and a village green, straying again and nar-
rowing so that a single horse could scarcely pass between the
branches, obscured in places altogether by fallen trees, dipping
into rank-smelling swampy stretches or climbing to heights
treacherous with half-concealed rocks and snaring roots. It was
inconceivable that the world we would discover when finally we
reached the end of this trail could have the slightest resemblance
to the town we had left behind. We were traveling toward
Housatonic, and the strange Indian name filled me with excitement enhanced with a peppering of foreboding by the fact that
the others could not endure a mention of this place that lay ahead.

For the first time in my life I understood my father's impatience; I was as irked as he at the dragging and complaining. We
traveled slowly because the horses were heavily loaded, in a
straggling halting line, and father, who had impressed on us the
necessity of staying close together, had to eat his own words in
hourly frustration. On the whole he submitted to this unfamiliar
diet with better grace than I would have expected, resigned perhaps to paying this price for the migration he had forced upon
his family.

Josiah, Elijah and I shared the horse just behind my father's.
He had fastened two big wicker baskets one on either side of the
saddle, and in these Elijah and I were enthroned, none too comfortably. The first day we sat with our knees jolting against our
chins, but Elijah complained so loudly that my father cut holes
in the bottom through which we could dangle our legs. Josiah
sat in the saddle, cuffing us when my father's back was turned if
we so much as shifted our weight. It was a relief when he chose
to walk ahead and jerk the horse along by the rope. Elijah, who

hated sitting still, kept begging to get out and walk with Josiah; then in no time he was whining that his legs were tired. He was only four years old, and he expected that at any moment we would come out exactly where we had started and find the old house waiting there for us.

Just behind rode mother holding two-year-old Enoch, and behind her my sister Judith, eleven months older than I, like my mother timid of horses and only accustomed to riding out in the riding chair for an afternoon's visit. Judith could never have made the trip at all without mother's waist to cling to and a shoulder to bury her face in at every fresh terror. Behind mother came my uncle Josiah with a musket across his saddle in front and Abigail on the pillion behind somehow managing even there to look as though she had no part in us all. Trailing them came the last horse, with packs almost scraping the ground on both sides, and with mother's little rocking chair tied to a roll of feather beds behind.

On the second day we halted for one of our recurring delays. Usually little Enoch was to blame, for frequently, to ease our mother, he had to be shifted about. Sometimes he rode in Elijah's basket while Lijah walked. Sometimes his damp restless little body was deposited beside me in my basket, and on occasion even my father had to carry him for a spell. This time Elijah had a stone in his shoe, Judith had a headache, and my uncle shouted up that the pack horse was limping. My father, in the hope of forestalling a later stop, insisted that we all dismount and walk into the bushes whether we wanted to or not, and he stood slapping at flies impatiently while we all fussed with straps and buttons.

Crouching behind a cedar bush, I peered into the awesome dusk of the forest. Among mottled greens and browns I had caught a flicker of motion. Not far away rose the gray hulk of a dead tree, riddled with holes, and from one of these holes was thrust what had to be the head of a bird, though I had never seen one so large. As I watched, a montrous feathery body pushed free, spread wing and slid soundlessly off through the trees. Years later my brother shot down a great horned owl, and when I saw its wingspread I realized that the mythical creature of my memory had indeed been an actuality; I had thought it an apparition from a fairy tale. Then, where the empty hole yawned, there suddenly appeared, one by one, three soft puffs of heads. Forgetting all orders, I gathered up my skirts and picked my way through briar and root to the foot of the tree. Three pairs of perfectly round eyes stared down at me.

When my father came crashing through the brush behind me, I was too enraptured to be afraid. Before he could touch me I broke in. "Look!" I whispered. "Sir — up there."

He looked up at the tree and gave a grunt of surprise. Then he scowled down at my face. For the first time in my life I think he really looked at me.

"Liza," he said slowly, "damned if you're not enjoying this." I stared back, unsure.

"Tell me something. Do you think your father is dragging you off to exile in Babylon?"

"I — thought it was Housatonic." I did not understand that he had attempted the first joke he had ever made with me even when he let out one of his sudden terrifying brays of laughter.

"Same thing to some people I know." He scooped me up, not roughly but not with much dignity, and carried me back to the path.

"At least there's one of my family with a little spunk!" he said loudly. "Doesn't behave as though the end of the world had come."

Too young to recognize that his praise was no more than a

reproach for the ones who waited on the trail, I saw only that for some reason I did not understand I had been singled out and approved before them all. Then, as I dangled in mid-air over my basket, he did the simple impulsive thing that was to change forever the course of our relationship. He swung me instead up to the vast height of his own saddle and heaved himself up behind me. I clung to a ridge of leather and braced my feet against the pack, every muscle rigid with delight. The horse's back seemed as high as the ridgepole of our barn at home, the swell of it was hot and prickly against my bare legs. I could not remember ever being so close to my father before. He seemed enormous; the immense hard thigh pushed against my back, the broad chest loomed over my head. I was choked with a smell of leather and sweat and wool and an almost unbearable pressure of maleness and power. I had never been so happy.

Presently he began to talk to me, or rather, I think now, to himself. He talked about Housatonic, and if to my childish mind the word was filled with mystery and infinite potentiality, I know that for my father that day it held the same magic. His voice was exultant. One hundred and fifty acres of the prettiest country in the whole province, he gloated. A town spick-and-span new to make what we wanted out of. And we were the first.

This reminded me of my one uneasiness. Abigail had said there were Indians, I questioned timidly.

Certainly there were Indians, he boomed, but I wasn't to listen to Abigail. These were Praying Indians who wanted to live like Englishmen. There was already a meetinghouse and a school to which we children would go with the Indian children.

"Wouldn't you think any reasonable soul would jump at a chance like this? Wouldn't you think a man could expect a little gratitude from his family, instead of this weeping and carrying on? You wait, Liza. A year from now they'll change their tune. You'll see."

As easily as he had lifted me on his horse he swept me to the level of his anticipation. I did not understand half of what he said, but I drank in his eagerness. I wonder now if anyone but me ever heard my father talk like this, or if he ever talked so again. In the years of our growing up no one of us would have called him a dreamer. The very thought would have been laughable; the word, when he himself uttered it, was twisted with scorn. It is only after all these years, remembering, that I realize that on the journey to Housatonic this plain practical man was possessed by a dream and had no one to share it with but a seven-year-old child.

Before long I saw that my time had run out. Elijah, who had endured my triumph long enough, was whimpering for his turn. My father, still goodnatured, dismounted, lifted me down, plunked me into my pannier, and took Elijah up with him. I was content. He had asked me first, and he had not even thought of asking Judith. From now on I would do anything he asked of me, and never, no matter how difficult the demand might be, would I weep or carry on.

2. EVEN IN my new complacency I think I recognized that the others had more reason to weep than I, that they all had more to lose. Especially Abigail, who ever since her sixteenth birthday had had three beaux coming to sit with her every Sabbath night, and all day long other girls coming and going, flicking their skirts and giggling and whispering and raising their eyebrows to make it plain there were plenty of things a seven-year-old didn't know about. With so much to relinquish I might not have wanted to leave either, but I would never have dared to stand up to my father as Abigail had done. Abigail had pleaded and screamed that he was ruining her whole life. When he had ordered her to her room she had slammed the door and stayed there all day, and when he had made her come to the table at night she had sat with red eyes and clenched teeth, refusing to eat.

Josiah, also sixteen, had tried to run away. Abigail had egged him on and helped him pack up his things. But two days later he had come home, even though he knew well enough what would be waiting for him, with that quavering insolence that never failed to provoke father's wrath and that made it impossible for the rest of us to be really sorry for him. If Abigail had been a boy she would have run away and stayed. Josiah hadn't tried it again, and now here he was, scuffling along beside the horse, not bothering to push the hair out of his eyes.

And our mother? She had never said, one way or the other. She had silently gone about packing our things into the saddle bags, and giving away the furniture we couldn't take, and seeing to it that we all had strong clean clothes to start out with, and at the end she had closed the door of the house and climbed into her side saddle with Judith. And I had got so used to seeing the tears spilling over and running slowly down her cheeks that I could hardly remember her looking any other way.

It seemed to me reasonable that mother should be afraid of my father, for we children all feared him, except Abigail. I am sure that he always thought of himself as a kind, even an indulgent husband and father. It was simply that he was not one to be moved by helplessness, which was the only defense my mother possessed. At the same time, I do not mean to paint a tragic picture of mother. I think that for much of her life she was content, even happy in her own way, having two great compensations. The first was a true vocation for ministering to the sick. At a bedside all her hesitancy and vagueness dropped away and she moved with astonishing confidence. Once relatives and neighbors had witnessed this metamorphosis they took it for granted, and my father grumbled that they imposed on her. Most often, of course, it was Enoch, frail from his birth, or Judith, falling abruptly into one of her spells of asthma, who claimed mother's unsparing solicitude.

Mother's second recompense was her eldest daughter, whom she looked upon with awe. Such a gift as Abigail could be repaid only by constant weaving and bleaching and sewing and ironing. Small wonder that she had scant time left over. It often seemed to me that when Mother turned to the rest of her children a veil of abstraction clouded her eyes.

I understood that I had little claim, for I came early to the knowledge that I was a very plain child. Where Abigail's hair was dark and sleek, mine was the color of dried winter leaves. I had neither Abigail's clear blue eyes, so startling over the indigo-dyed dresses she loved to wear, or the wistful faded blue Judith had inherited from mother, my own eyes being no particular color, like water over pebbles. Abigail and Judith and Josiah were all slender and quick-moving, as Enoch promised to be. Elijah and I had our father's wide shoulders and stocky legs and his plump apple-red cheeks. At seven all this did not trouble me; the heartache was to come much later. But I had long since learned that I must give mother up to the others.

One of my clearest memories is the severe attack of measles which occurred the year before we left Newton. I can recall the headache and the hot itchy bedclothes, and my mother's face filled with tenderness and her cool sure hands. I remember lying in bed, my eyes tightly closed, sometimes even holding my breath, trying by sheer force of will to prolong the fever and the rash which were all the while slipping away from me. In the end my child's body made the choice for me; inactivity was too great a price to pay. I think it was the only time in my childhood that I was ever ill.

As a result I enjoyed a rather shocking independence. I was alone a great deal, for although girls sprang up wherever Abigail moved, there seemed to be none at all of my own age. Judith was useless for the active sort of play I craved. I tagged after Josiah and his friends till finally they turned on me, though I could throw and catch a ball or swing into a tree or bait a fish line as well as any of them. After that I amused myself till Elijah was old enough to tag after me. I spent long days in the fields behind our house, coming in at night to eat what was set before me and to crawl into bed, scarcely noticing whether Judith shared it with me or had been removed to the special cot near the fire. Sometimes my mother's eyes would focus on me momentarily and she would murmur that she must do something to make a young lady out of me. But there was always a new dress to fit for Abigail, or a kettle to heat for Judith, and at the time we went to Housatonic I had still happily escaped any such fate.

3. I CANNOT TELL how many days we spent on that journey from Newton to Housatonic, nor the roads we followed nor the ordinaries where we stopped for the night, though I know that the taverns must have been as painful a trial for mother as the days in the saddle. There was one where we did not even have a room to ourselves but had to sleep on matting behind a curtain hung across a room, our beds only a few feet

removed from the boots of the strangers crowded around the table. I remember being told to eat a plateful of something that looked and tasted like mud from a river bottom, rich with rotted fish, and how we were kept awake half the night by an argument on the other side of the curtain, and how I woke after a short sleep with three fresh bites, stinging as nettles.

At each of these stopping places my father took on added dimension. At home I had taken for granted that everyone who knew him, tradesmen, neighbors, even the minister, should speak to him with a glaze of respect in eye and voice. But here, when he walked into the room a stranger, I saw the same look spread instantly over every face. The landlord himself always led us to the best room in the house, and fussed about at the table asking if the roast were cooked to his liking. When, after the meal was done, father pushed back his chair and went to knock out yesterday's ashes from his pipe against the fireplace bricks, the men scraped and shifted their chairs to make room for him. As we children followed mother out of the room, I would look back and see him lowering his wide hips into a chair, and marked that the others watched him silently, passed him the tankard with respect and waited for him to speak first. It came to me that in any room, anywhere, his was the commanding figure. To my seven-year-old eyes he was larger than life-size.

There was one night's stopping that I was never to forget. We came out of the woods, past a row of good frame houses with farmland stretching behind, to a crossroads and a substantial inn. Inside, at the further end of the raftered hall, a fire glowed, and a mouth-watering fragrance of roasting meat drew us all closer. In a mammoth fireplace, twice as big as the one at home, a whole sheep was turning, the juice dripping slowly into the sizzling-pan below, missing occasionally to provoke a hissing leap of orange flame. I stood bemused by the homely comforting sight, till I noticed a strange contrivance. On a low platform at the edge of the hearth was a wheel with two rims and steps between like the paddlewheel of a mill, which an ugly stunted short-haired dog with black patches was vainly trying to climb. Whenever his front paw touched the next step, the wheel slipped down from under his feet, and he lifted them another step just in time to have it sink from under him again. The dog did not scramble or even raise its head. Patiently it went on lifting its feet to the next step, and suddenly I understood. The wheel was attached by a long rod to the spit, and as the wheel turned, the spit with the roasting meat revolved. I had often enough taken a spell at turning a spit; it was a hot tiresome chore considered by adults to be proper for children. But this spectacle, the stumbling rhythm of those short legs reaching and reaching, struck me as altogether different, and it filled me with horror. I clutched at Abigail. "Look!"

Abigail watched dispassionately. "He's trained to do it," she said.

"It — isn't fair. He's chained."

"Don't be silly." Abigail jerked me away. "He's a dog. He doesn't know the difference."

Later in bed upstairs, between Abigail and Judith, I came cold awake. The meat — for I had eaten it despite its manner of cooking — was a heavy lump in my stomach. In the dark the wheel began to turn. He *does* know, I thought. They make him do it and he can't ever stop. I could not bear it that the dog would climb those stairs tomorrow and the day after that and the day after that, on and on forever. For the first time in my life it came over me that things happened that I could not bear, and that they would go on happening. Things I half-remembered came back to me — the worn earth around the whipping-post at home, the unnamed, unimaginable things that people whispered in corners. Pinned under their formless weight I lay helpless and watched the wheel in the darkness, till at last its relentless turning dragged me down into slumber.

In the morning the dog sat in the sunshine just outside the inn door, tied with a short length of leather thong. As I came through the door it got slowly to its feet, the ratlike tail weaving uncertainly. I bent down and touched the short wiry hair. The brown eyes looked up at me, expectant.

Across the yard my father was tightening the straps of the pack horse, and at the sight of him the new confidence gained in his saddle rushed over me. How I dared put it so soon to the test I cannot imagine, but I ran across the yard and tugged at his coat.

"Father! Will you buy the dog? Please will you, sir?"

"Let go of me, Liza," he snapped. Then his hand slowed on the harness. "What is it you want?"

"The dog. Please, sir. Can we take it to Housatonic?"

I waited to find out whether anything had really changed, and willed him to remember. My astonishing behavior must have puzzled him. He looked across at the forlorn creature pulling against the thong. "You call that a dog?"

I stood silent, having no adequate words.

"Look here, Liza." He shook off his hesitation. "When we get settled I'll get you a real dog. Or a kitten maybe. Confound you, can't you see I've got my hands full?"

Staring up at him I saw that nothing had changed. Uncomfortably he looked back at me, some realization perhaps stirring in him because he reached down and gave me an awkward pat. "Run along now and have breakfast."

The moment they let me leave the board I went to sit on the doorstep. The dog and I looked at each other with yearning. My father, relaxed from a hearty meal, stopped on his way past.

"Can't see much in that to take a fancy to," he commented. "Ugliest critter I ever laid eyes on."

"I don't care if it's ugly. I want it!"

The landlord, following my father through the doorway, caught my passionate words and laughed. "Can't have that one, my girl. He's the spit dog."

Instantly I saw my father bristle. The amiable blue eyes froze to ice. "How much you want for it?" he demanded.

"I told you, sir, he's not for sale."

"And I asked how much." My father's voice had dropped to that flat quiet level I knew very well.

"Takes time to break in a new one, sir. You got no right to ask after a man's spit dog."

The coin flipped so abruptly into the air that the landlord could not even reach out his hand before it struck his chest and dropped to the ground. He blinked down at the silver glint of it in the dirt, and then bent and picked it up, rubbing it with one finger. He stared at my father, his eyes popping like an alarmed rabbit's. Then he shrugged and bent and untied the thong and put it into my hand. My father, without a word, was halfway across the yard.

He could not so easily shake off the indignation of our assembled family.

"You bought a dog for *her?*" Josiah's voice broke in an ascending squeak of outrage.

"You watch your tongue, sir," my father roared. "When did I ask your advice what to buy? If you want to know," he flung out as scornful explanation to them all, "I bought it because she's the only one of the lot of you who hasn't been puling and balking ever since we left Newton. If she wants a fool dog she can have it. Now hang onto it." He vented his irritation on me as he hoisted me into the pannier. Picking up the dog by the scruff of its neck he thrust it into my arms. "If it runs away we don't go chasing after it, understand? And if it makes a nuisance of itself we tie it to the first tree and leave it there."

I had no doubt he would do exactly this. I nodded, hugging the squirming body tight against me. His name is Adam, I decided. It was the first name that came into my head.

I did not have another moment of comfort. The dog was restless, lumpy and flea-ridden, constantly struggling against my constraining arms to reach up a wet tongue to lick my chin. Cramped and hot and anxious, I was still as near to heaven as it is possible to be, I think, choked with feelings as unmanageable as the burden in my arms. Nothing that happened in all the years to come could ever crush out the love for my father that rooted itself that day in my child's heart. I have often wondered that there is not more love in the world, knowing as I do how it can take hold in the smallest patch of soil and thrive without tending. I marvel it does not push up everywhere as common as chickweed.

4. IT WAS HARD to see, when finally we dragged into the settlement in the late June afternoon, why we should have come so far for this. It was not a town, not even a village such as those we had passed through. The trail came out abruptly upon a cleared stretch of meadowland and became a meandering dirt path along a nondescript little river. Just ahead, like heaped-up piles of brush, squatted a row of dome-shaped huts covered with bark, which must be Indian wigwams, though they were not much better than the beaver house in our pond at home. Here and there a thin waver of smoke rose from an open hole in a roof. In front of the nearest wigwam two motionless figures sat hunched in faded blankets. On the path four dark-skinned children, almost naked, were playing some game, throwing small javelins at a marker in the grass. Far beyond, at the end of the

row, was a square flat building of rough boards, and beyond
that one ordinary frame house, very small and plain.

I was bone tired, stiff and chafed and scratched; loyalty alone
kept me from bursting into tears. There was crying enough going on. Abigail had taken one look and flung out, "I knew it
would be a hateful place like this. I'll never forgive
you — never!" Judith was sniffling, and mother's features had
dissolved into the familiar blurriness.

"It's a good place," I said, loud enough for them all to hear.

My father did not notice. He stood looking ahead along the
path, squinting up at the hill that rose on our right. "Good
land," he said, to no one but himself. "I haven't made any mistake. And it won't take long."

The instant we moved out of the shadow of the woods the
Indian children whisked like chipmunks into a doorway. The
two men did not stir. Then a dog yelped sharply and my own
dog's legs went stiff, a ridge of hair rising along his spine. Forgetting my weariness I wrapped both arms around him and clung.

A man came bounding out of the small timber house at the far
end of the row, a white man, not an Indian, though his hair and
features were dark. He came rapidly with firm young strides,
and before he was near enough to shout he raised an arm to us.
We could see that he was smiling, grinning actually, his teeth
very white.

"Mr. Williams, sir! You are exceedingly welcome."

"Mr. Sergeant. Happy to see you, reverend." My father's
hand clasped his. "We're glad to be here, no doubt about that.
Reckon by the state of that rabbit trail you called a road there
aren't many ahead of me."

The young man laughed. "I hope you met no real trouble. In
time there'll be a —" His voice faltered, as though it had slipped
from his control. He was looking past my father, including us all

in his smiling welcome, and for an instant he looked as though he could not trust his own eyesight. Then he caught himself and hurried on. Looking back, child as I was, I understood. No one, I saw, had told him about Abigail. Even then, at the end of a day's travel, with the tears still in her eyes, Abigail could take a man's breath away.

"Meet my family," my father was saying heartily, unaware that one meeting had taken place. He introduced us with his Sabbath manners. Uncle Josiah walked forward and shook his hand, explaining that his own family would follow in a month or so. When it was my turn, Mr. Sergeant reached over the edge of the basket, and seeing that my hands were occupied, gave Adam a pat instead. For the first time I saw that his left hand, held against his body, was stiff and misshapen.

From that moment he remembered all our names. "Madam," he said, bowing to mother, "this will be a happy day for Mrs. Woodbridge. It's not been easy for her here since the young one came."

He had said exactly the right thing. Another woman — and with a baby! Mother's drooping shoulders lifted.

We followed along the path. From the doorways of the wigwams dark faces peered fleetingly and disappeared. "You will get to know them soon," Mr. Sergeant explained. "They have looked forward to your coming, and they will meet you in their own way."

"That's the meetinghouse." He waved his hand at the low square structure. "The first building we attempted, and it's no architectural achievement. But it serves our purpose."

In the doorway of the frame house a tall young man with unkempt sandy hair waited to meet us. This was Mr. Timothy Woodbridge, the schoolmaster, and we children, appraising him, exchanged a quick approval. He did not seem delighted to welcome us, but his plain speech was disarming, and I thought there could be nothing terrifying about going to school to him.

It was already dark inside the house. Mr. Woodbridge hurried ahead of us, stirring up the fire and lighting a candle, shoving aside a clutter of books and papers to place it on the table. There were two leveled-off stumps for seats and only one proper settle, into which my father lowered himself with a loud sigh. From the back room came a young woman, really a girl scarcely older than Abigail, with a bundle in her arms. Her pale brown eyes looked shyly at us from a thin sweet face.

"This is my wife Abigail," said Mr. Woodbridge. He began to introduce us all methodically, but the girl saw no one but mother.

"Oh," she whispered, "I'm so thankful you've come." She began to sob like a little girl, both hands taken up with the baby so that she could not even wipe her nose and eyes.

Mother thrust Enoch upon Abigail and her hands reached out. "There now. Don't you mind. Let me take the baby. Poor child, you must have been frightened to death with no Christian woman to turn to."

"I don't know much about babies." Mrs. Woodbridge sniffled like Judith. "I couldn't — I mean I've had to give her goat's milk and it doesn't set on her. She cries all the time."

"Why, she's a little beauty," mother crooned, peering into the bundle. "Looks just like her mother, only maybe a little mite peaked. You just stop worrying. We'll have her fat as a pigeon in no time."

"Well," said my father, with such obvious relief that I realized he must have been concerned after all. "If that isn't a piece of luck. All my wife needs is a baby to fuss over."

Our own Abigail was staring about the room with a wrinkling of her nose. It was a poor sort of house, I had to admit. The walls inside did not look as raw as the outside, having darkened to a dubious gray that even I recognized as due to a faulty chimney. The long plank table had not known a scrubbing for a long time, nor the unwashed pewter mugs and plates a scouring. The huge iron kettle in the fireplace, slung from a crude wooden lugpole, looked much too heavy for little Mrs. Woodbridge, so perhaps she could not be blamed that it was crusted with baked-on spillings.

My father was working off a heavy boot. "Plagued long trip and a slow one," he was saying. "Thought we'd never get here. Another time I'd come ahead by myself without the whole family. Where you reckon on putting us up, parson?"

Mr. Sergeant hesitated. "I had hoped my own house would be ready," he answered. "It has gone a little slower than I planned. At the present this is the only house we have. It will be cramped for you, I'm afraid, but you see how welcome you are, and I think you can manage. As soon as you've chosen a site for yourself we will suspend all other work until your house is built."

My father nodded affably. "Shed like this shouldn't take more'n a day or two to raise," he said. "Then with a roof over our heads we can take our time. I aim to have a house finished by winter."

He did not notice the look Mrs. Woodbridge and her husband exchanged. Mr. Sergeant did, perhaps, for he turned to mother. "We should not keep you standing here," he said. "Have you had supper?"

Mrs. Woodbridge looked about to cry again. "Please excuse me, ma'am," she quavered. "I can't seem to think. Of course you're hungry. If I'd only known, I'd have had the board all laid for you."

"Don't you fret," mother assured her. "You aren't going to wait on us, not with three big girls to help. Now you just tell us where we can wash up and then we'll help get the supper on."

Clearly Mrs. Woodbridge was not prepared for a family of seven or for a man with my father's appetite. However, we made do with a meal of cold beans and corncake that was tasty enough, and afterwards we children stood quietly about the table while father answered questions about the journey and about the news from Boston that Mr. Sergeant was eager to hear. In the warmth of the fire my muscles were beginning to crawl with a longing to sleep. Behind me on the floor, Adam, with a clean-scraped bone under his chin, gave a long tremulous sigh of content. It was all I could do not to lie down beside him and put my head on his warm rump. Then I was startled wide awake by a sound I had never heard before. Through the open door drifted a soaring sweetness that spread till it filled the room like fragrant apple smoke.

"Listen," said Mr. Sergeant. "They are singing to welcome you."

Even now, when it has become a part of my life, I don't know how to describe this singing. Indian voices are true and mellow, with no hint of English twang. They make of our common English psalm tunes something strange and unearthly, half pagan yet still sacred and beautiful. To this day I cannot listen without an ache in my heart.

On this first evening we were all captivated by the sound, especially my father, for there was nothing he enjoyed more than singing, he himself having for years led the psalms every Lord's Day with his firm clear voice. But I am sure he had never imagined such singing as this.

"Remarkable," he commented, as the sound died away. "Surprising that they sing in parts. Did you teach them, reverend?"

Mr. Sergeant looked like a proud parent. "They have a natural gift for it. I believe God intends that we should use it to open their hearts to his word." Then he rose to his feet. "They are waiting for you," he said. "You and your family."

Father pulled himself up. "By all means. I'm curious to see them."

But Mr. Sergeant had moved swiftly between him and the door. "Just one thing, sir. It is their custom to offer presents. You must accept whatever they offer, since this is most important to them."

"Certainly. I understand."

Mr. Sergeant still blocked the doorway. "They will also expect presents from you, sir," he said.

Father bristled. "Money?"

A groove of anxiety showed between Mr. Sergeant's eyes. He hesitated. "For several reasons that would not be wise," he said finally. "What they need most is tools, knives of course, almost anything metal. They have so little."

"So have we," said father shortly. "We've brought next to nothing."

"I realize that." Mr. Sergeant looked miserable. "It is my mistake. I should have warned you. I don't suppose you have a musket to spare?"

"A musket!" Muttering some word under his breath, father went to poke into the bundles on the floor, jerking out our belongings every which way. "Trinkets is what they like," he said, turning his irritation on mother. "Haven't you some gew-gaws or other?" Mother could only stare at him helplessly. I'm sure she had never had a trinket in her life.

Hastily he assembled a little pile of oddments — one of the two frying pans mother had brought, a small comb and a length of scarlet ribbon that drew a mortal gasp from Abigail. Uncle Josiah added a battered hunting knife, and father grudgingly laid down a pouch of gunpowder. Mr. Sergeant looked at these objects for a long moment and then quietly stood back from the door.

I can recall to this day the shock of fear that shot down

through my body. The Indians sat on the ground a little distance from the cabin, so many of them it was incredible that we
had not heard them approach, more than a hundred men and
women and children all facing us in silence. We had been unpre-
pared by the timid figures that had melted into the wigwams as
we passed; assembled they had a fearsome strength. Here and
there unearthly faces, hideously streaked with white and crimson, floated disembodied in the twilight, and everywhere there
was a quivering of feathers. I had seen few Indians in my life,
but I had heard tales aplenty of scalping and torture. Even
without the tales this spectacle would have been terrifying. I
could feel the fear in the others as we huddled in the doorway.

Two astonishing figures stepped out of the assembly and
moved toward the house. Unmistakably Indians, with their dark
skins and hooked noses, they were dressed like English soldiers in
buff-colored breeches and scarlet coats, cocked hats set atop
their long black braids. As they stood before us with dignity,
unsmiling, the tallest one began to speak, the unintelligible words
giving off the deep solemn vibrations of a minister praying in the
meetinghouse.

When he had finished speaking a third Indian came forward,
naked above his leather breeches, his chest banded with black
and white. He spoke to us in a warped but understandable English. "Konkapot he has spoken," he said, and then proceeded to
translate for us. They welcomed us as brothers, he told us, the
tribe of Muh-he-ka-neew, people of the ever-flowing waters.
They had invited us to move our fireplace. They rejoiced that
we had come to sit down with them. They prayed that the
Great Spirit would look with favor on our new fireplace. They
promised that the new chain of friendship between us would be
kept bright and shining. In proof of this friendship between us
they had brought us gifts.

There was now laid on the ground before my father what

seemed to me treasure enough to welcome King George himself. There were nine beaver skins, thick and lustrous, and as two young Indians laid them down, one by one, the interpreter made a motion toward each of us in turn, to show that there was one for each, even for Enoch. Then on the top of the pile he placed a wide band of white and purplish beads sewn into an elaborate design.

Next there was brought to Konkapot a pipe with a long slender stem. The chief set it to his lips till the coals in the bowl made a bright crimson spot in the half-darkness; then he held out the pipe to my father. Though any of us children could have said at once what was expected, it was not till Mr. Sergeant made a tentative motion that my father took the pipe into his own hand, put it to his lips and coughed out an abrupt puff of smoke. Perhaps the smoke actually choked him, for when he cleared his throat and opened his mouth no sound came for a time that seemed to me unbearable. I had never before seen my father at a loss for words.

"I thank you," he said finally. His voice sounded thick and unfamiliar, and he cleared his throat again. "On behalf of all my family I greet you." This was not my father's way of speech; he was aping the pattern of the Indian and he spoke much too loudly in the still evening. "We have come on a long journey to make our home in Housatonic." He hesitated, then abandoned this unnatural form and went on more confidently. "We mean to make a fine town out of this place. If you and your tribe are willing to learn and to work with us, before long, I promise you, you'll be the envy of every Indian in the country."

He looked back at his own presents on the doorstep, and I saw that he was remembering that Konkapot had not stooped to touch the gifts he had given. Then he jerked his thumb toward Josiah in a way well known to us all. Josiah, rearing his head at first like a colt, stumbled to obey. Scooping up the objects he took two shrinking steps forward, dropped them in an untidy heap at Konkapot's feet and backed clumsily into our midst again. The objects looked shabby and shrunken.

Not a wrinkle of the Indian's face changed; it might have been carved from dark polished wood. Again he made a long speech which was interpreted for us, thanking us and repeating everything he had said before. Then he turned and the other Indian with him and walked away. Almost without perceptible motion the whole assemblage was blotted into the darkness.

Inside the house no one had anything to say. Then in a burst of emotion I did not understand I suddenly rushed at my father and put my arms around his hips and hugged him. Puzzled, for I had never done such a thing in my life before, he looked down and patted my head.

"Well," he said, looking around at us all. "I must admit that took me by surprise."

"I told you they would welcome you in their own way," said Mr. Sergeant. "Perhaps I should have explained, but I was not sure just what they intended. I try to discourage their painting themselves, but one cannot root out all their heathen practices at once. One must go slowly. On important occasions they insist on their own ceremonies, and provided they are kept within bounds I allow them."

"Humph," said my father. "Where'd they get hold of those uniforms? Stole them, I suppose."

"No. The uniforms are their own. Konkapot, whose Christian name is John, is a captain. Umpachenee, who has been baptized as Aaron, is a lieutenant. Four years ago Governor Belcher gave them commissions as a reward for services they had rendered and also, I suppose, to cement their friendship. Konkapot is chief of his tribe, and Aaron, though he is less powerful, also

has much influence. They are exceedingly proud of those uniforms."

"Humm," said my father. "Who'd have expected it? That
young fellow — how'd he learn to speak English like that?"

"His Christian name is Ebenezer. He was the first Indian I
baptized out here. He lived for a time in his childhood among
white people, and I've found him invaluable as my interpreter."

"Pretty highfalutin language he uses."

John Sergeant smiled. "If you could understand Konkapot's
speech you would find it even more surprising. The Indians are
natural orators. The speeches they make at their own councils
are worthy of Parliament."

"Well, I don't mind saying I was surprised," my father repeated. "All that talk about the Great Spirit. Thought you said
that chief, whatever his name is, had been baptized."

The minister's smile faded, and a red flush came up behind his
natural ruddiness and showed in his ears. "It is not easy," he said.
"As I told you, one has to go slowly. Even though they still
speak of the Great Spirit, I think they are beginning to understand. I believe that they worship the true God, but there is still
much that they must learn. That is the real purpose of this mission, to bring them here where they may be taught.

"When I am tempted to discouragement," he went on, against
my father's silence, "I try to remember how very much we have
already accomplished. The fact that they are here, living in one
town, is a very great step forward. When I first came here, they
moved, whole families together, with every season, according to
the time for planting or hunting. The first year that Mr. Woodbridge and I began to teach them, we had to follow them out
into the woods and live there with them in deep snow for six
weeks while they made sugar from the maple sap. It has not been
easy for them to give up their habit of wandering. The men

would still prefer to spend their lives as hunters. And any form of government is new to them. Even the children are given every sort of freedom and almost never punished for anything."

My father had long since lost interest. He was lifting the edges of the beaver skins. "Excellent pelts," he commented. "What do I do with this thing? I've no use for wampum."

"You may well have," said Mr. Sergeant. "Out here it often serves as good negotiable currency. That belt has six strands. In terms of exchange it's worth several English pounds."

My father shot him a glance from under his bushy eyebrows and did not ask any more questions that night.

5. NEXT DAY, though Josiah and Elijah went about their own exploration of the Indian village, we girls did not leave the cabin, for it was Saturday and there was scant time to make ourselves ready for the Lord's Day. All day long the kettle was filled and heated and emptied and filled again as we washed our dusty clothes and took prolonged turns in the wooden tub scrubbing even our hair. On the Sabbath morning we emerged from the Woodbridge cabin in a state suited to our exemplary role and self-consciously walked behind our parents the short distance to the meetinghouse.

Inside, as out, there was no paint to relieve the raw jagged boards. There was a rough table for a pulpit, and set before it were rows of splintery planks laid on cross pieces. The Indians had already assembled, courteously leaving the two front benches for us, and we took our places, mother and we three girls on one side, father, Uncle Josiah and the boys on the other. I sat with a horrid prickling up my spine, knowing how the

Indians must be staring at us, unable to look at them. Mother and Abigail sat as serenely as though they were in the meeting-house at home. Being a child I could risk a cautious squirm and managed at last to look over my shoulder. What I could see was disappointing. Here in the meetinghouse the Indians had lost their advantage over us; they were divested of the romance that paint and feathers and twilight and our own awe had lent to them on that first evening. Now they looked shabby, the men in dirty cotton or leather trousers and shirts, the women in long skirts of faded blue or green cotton decorated with wampum beads and porcupine quills. In the summer heat most of them had dingy blankets over their shoulders. As the service pro-gressed, a horrid stench swelled in the small building. Abigail put her handkerchief daintily to her nose and held it there through the entire sermon.

The morning was interminable, far worse than the Sabbaths at home, because between every line of Mr. Sergeant's long prayer and longer sermon we had to wait for Ebenezer to slowly trans-late his words into the Indian tongue, the strange sounds grating unpleasantly on our ears. The novelty of this was soon ex-hausted. The only relief was when we stood to sing, though I could have wished that father had done so less wholeheartedly. At the close of the service, to our surprise, Mr. Sergeant himself offered a prayer in the Indian language.

"Yes, I am learning slowly," he admitted at the noonday meal. "It has been far more difficult than I anticipated. Latin and Greek came quite easily to me, but Indian dialects are not only confusing, but the guttural sounds almost impossible for an Eng-lishman to pronounce. I have to write out the prayer and memo-rize it, syllable by syllable. Before long I shall be able to do the same with an Indian sermon."

"Is that necessary?" my father inquired. "From now on you

have an English congregation to consider. Speaking for myself, a good sermon is the high point of the week. I don't relish the idea of having it dished up to me in some gibberish I can't understand."

Mr. Sergeant looked across the table in surprise. "Of course that would be unreasonable, sir. I shall preach two sermons at each service, one in English and one in Mahican."

A happy prospect, I thought, my heart sinking at the approach of the long afternoon service still to be endured. I am certain my father had exactly my thought, and that as long as he lived he chafed at the time he was forced to waste every Lord's Day sitting through two Indian sermons.

Up till the Sabbath the Indians had stayed at a respectful distance. Now we were dismayed to learn that they walked in and out of Mr. Woodbridge's house without ceremony. The men, that is. The women and girls were out before daylight bending over short wooden digging sticks in their vegetable gardens, and they seemed to labor all day long. Apparently they did all the work, leaving the men free to loiter about the village, to argue, and to besiege Mr. Sergeant with demands and questions. He answered them with endless patience, in an abbreviated and practical combination of English and Mahican, and he seemed never to resent their inconvenient arrivals. I don't think he realized in the least how this continual coming and going distressed Abigail Woodbridge, not to mention my mother and our Abigail. I could see that there was an open door not only to the Woodbridge cabin where Mr. Sergeant lived but to his mind and heart, from which no Indian would ever be turned away.

The morning after the Sabbath my father and Uncle Josiah set about finding a home site. I think my father had determined to build on the hill from the moment he first set eyes on it. At supper, after the second long day of tramping through brush and thicket, he reported that he had found his spot, a stretch of natural meadowland at the highest point of the hill. "High land is healthier," he assured us, when Albigail protested she would die of loneliness. "This river bank is good enough for the Indians, but you notice how the mist settles in here at night. Mark my words, it won't be lonesome up there for long. Your uncle Josiah is building there too, and we're staking out lots for the other two families. There's a magnificent view — hills in every direction."

Certainly we could not continue much longer to accept the Woodbridge hospitality. Even though the men were gone most of the day and had taken to sleeping out under the stars, we women were continually in each other's way. The cabin was hot and stifling, hazy with pent-up smoke and never free from the smell of grease and of babies' napkins. Yet I was loath to think of moving far up on the hill. For once I agreed with Abigail, having found the cabin a perfect vantage point from which to observe and listen. Up there I would be cut off altogether from the Indian village which fascinated me.

My father insisted on hiring some of the Indian men to cut and plane lumber for him. He could not understand Mr. Sergeant's reluctance, and finally, in his usual direct fashion, he intercepted Ebenezer on the path. He came back furious. Ebenezer had told him to his face that only women worked with their hands at building houses. However, Mr. Sergeant must have persuaded them, for next morning five young men with sullen faces were waiting outside the door. That night and the next my father came to supper fuming that Josiah, for all his puny size, could finish more boards in a day than the whole batch of Indians together. The third night he sat down to his meal without complaint and tucked his napkin between his coat buttons with a satisfied air. We had scarcely taken a bite when Mr. Sergeant came striding into the house, cheeks flushed and eyes blazing.

"I must ask you, sir," he said, without greeting, "never again to give the Indians spirits to drink."

My father, looking up from his plate, cocked an amiable eye at the young man. I think he was surprised to see that the minister had so much spunk. "Well now," he said, "didn't seem to me such a bad idea. I got as much work done in four hours as in the three days since we started."

"You don't understand." Mr. Sergeant's lips were white with the effort to speak reasonably. "Drunkenness is their worst weakness, the one thing that defeats everything we try to do. It reduces them to the lowest state. It —"

"Come now, parson," my father interrupted. "No need to carry on about drunkenness. I didn't have that much to spare. What each of 'em got out of it wouldn't intoxicate a flea."

"It was all they needed to whet their appetites, and they have excited all the others. I can't make them listen. Everything I have told them — everything we have done — is useless."

"They want more? They can have it if they're willing to work for it." My father was still amused.

"They already have more. They always have some hidden somewhere. They know that I know it, but they had promised not to touch it. Now —"

"Where'd they get it?"

"From traders. Mainly from the Dutchman, Van Valken-burgh, above the mountain. Some of them are on the way to him right now."

Behind Mr. Sergeant Mr. Woodbridge came through the door. At the minister's quick question he shrugged. "Might as well eat some supper," he said. But before coming to the table he turned back and shot the bolt of the door, and at the sight his young wife burst into sobs.

"I can't stand it again," she wailed. "I don't care what you say. I just can't stand it."

Mother went round the table to put her arms around the distraught girl.

"I can't help it," Abigail Woodbridge kept saying. "They frighten me to death, and I'll never get used to them. When I was nine years old my grandmother and four cousins were killed outside Deerfield. Dragged out of bed and scalped. Timothy says it isn't fair I should hold it against these Indians here, but you can't forget. I wish they didn't know we had a baby. I wish I could hide her and never let them see her."

We girls looked at each other with curiosity. Was there really something to be afraid of? Mr. Sergeant looked directly at our Abigail.

"There's no reason to fear them," he told her. "Their wives will have hid all their weapons by now, but there's no real danger anyway. They will very soon drink themselves stupefied." His anger had died now; he looked weary and discouraged. "It's a weakness peculiar to the Indian race," he explained. "A very little strong liquor crazes them and they will sell everything they have to get more. The only cure is to persuade them never to touch it at all."

He turned back to my father. "The traders take advantage of their weakness," he said. "I relied on you, sir, to help them."

My father's high color darkened to an alarming red. His eyes had taken on that blue iciness that silenced any argument. It did not fail now; Mr. Sergeant met his look, rose from the table without a word and went out, and my uncle Josiah got up to bolt the door again behind him.

"Van Valkenburgh," my father said in a low voice as my uncle sat down again. "Don't let me forget that name. My own supply is running pretty low."

Mr. Sergeant did not come back for his supper, though mother kept it warm for him. Through the night there were bursts of horrid screeching and wild singing, but no one came near our cabin. In the morning the Indian women were silently at work as usual, but few men were about. Sprawled in the middle of the path was one of father's workers; we peered out at him in horror till Elijah reported that he was snoring. The other four were nowhere to be seen, and father and Josiah and my uncle went off up the hill to finish the house alone.

True to my father's prediction, the one-room plank house was raised in less than a week. It would serve for a barn later on, he said, and he began at once to lay out the trench for a permanent house. Cramped and remote as it was, our family moved into the new shelter with relief, everyone I think but Abigail and me. I was wild with envy of Elijah, who would be escorted by Josiah down the hill every morning to Mr. Woodbridge's school. And Abigail was in love.

From the moment that Mr. Sergeant first welcomed us at the edge of the clearing, we never heard another word from Abigail of protest or despair; it was obvious to us all that she walked in a dream of waiting. It was as though in that first encounter she had turned her back on everything she had cherished in Newton, and I think she never looked behind again or knew a moment of regret, accepting on the instant the destiny that had been waiting here in exile for her coming. I have always envied Abigail this sudden sure recognition. It has never happened so to me; knowledge is always withheld from me and seeps into my heart, filling it imperceptibly from hidden springs. Love rushed visibly upon Abigail, and without question she plunged to meet it.

She never spoke of it and she would not have tolerated that anyone else should do so. Perhaps, had I been older, she might have taken me into her confidence. Between her and mother there existed an unspoken complicity. But Abigail confided in no one, and all of us, even my father, respected her silence.

I wonder now how it would have been for them both had John asked for her hand in those first days that we spent in the Woodbridge cabin. No one would have been surprised. We needed only to look at his face, at the dazzled look that barely brushed Abigail's, retreated and continually returned, to know that sooner or later he must speak, and surely he could not have doubted the answer. But he kept silent.

6. MY FATHER had told me that day on the trail that I would go to school with the Indians. For one day only he kept his promise. On the day after that first Sabbath, Judith and Elijah and I followed Mr. Woodbridge to the schoolhouse. Josiah, still in a black mood, had refused, and father, who had never been a scholar himself, was of a mind to be lenient. Josiah was sixteen, he had had a respectable schooling in Newton and he was competent at figuring. The truth was, with land to clear and plant and the house to raise, father needed him. So Josiah put his schooling behind him, though he was certainly no happier working under my father's orders.

I have never forgotten those first moments when the three of us stood in the schoolroom face to face with forty Indian children, Judith hanging her head and refusing to look, Elijah and I staring back at them. There was an expression in the dark eyes that I could not interpret, not that day or at any time since. Not hostility, certainly not friendliness, not even the curiosity which must have showed rudely in our own faces; merely a sort of waiting and a measuring. Before the judgment of forty pairs of eyes I knew that in an indeterminable way we fell short. I still know this.

Mr. Woodbridge tested each of us to establish our rank in the
school. Elijah recited from the Primer scornfully, conscious that
he was the youngest in the school, already puffed up from listening to some of the big Indian boys stumbling over ABC. Judith
stood mute and tearful, her whole body drawn inward, till Mr.
Woodbridge gently told her to sit down. I did not know which
one had embarrassed me most; in consequence, when my turn
came I rattled off the words as rapidly as possible to have done
with it, and only after I sat down realized that I had shown off
even worse than Elijah. To my relief, some of the Indian boys
read reasonably well, but with an odd flat tone that gave the
syllables an unfamiliar sound. Elijah told me next day that they
did not understand a word they read. But they brought to their
work an intense, almost desperate concentration I had never before witnessed. I wondered if Mr. Woodbridge had some secret
and terrible method of punishment, but throughout the morning
he displayed nothing but patience.

If we were complacent about our reading, we were humbled
by the singing lesson. Even the youngest of the Indians could
sing a part; their voices were clear as running water, and I dared
not make a sound. When Elijah joined in with no caution I saw
two of the Indian girls look slyly at each other and one of them
giggled. I prickled with embarrassment all over again, for I had
been watching one of these girls all the morning. She seemed to
me almost as lovely as Abigail, slender and smooth-skinned, with
dark braids and soft black eyes. Around one arm she wore a
band of the same beads that had been given to my father, an
unsuitably valuable thing, from what Mr. Sergeant had said, for
a child to wear to school. Once she turned her head and looked
directly at me with that unsmiling gaze I could not read. Was she
acknowledging my admiration, or was she wishing I had not
come?

Next morning Judith refused to get out of bed. "I feel sick," she protested, hunching tighter as I tried to yank off the quilt, and producing alarming symptoms under mother's solicitude. I was not fooled. "She doesn't want to go to that school," I told mother.

Mother appealed to my father. " 'Tis no place for little girls like Judith and Elizabeth," she said, her words crumbling at the edges. "Judith is frightened to death, and no wonder, brought up the way she's been. They'll get nits in their hair and goodness knows what worse. They're too old anyway to be going to school with boys."

"But ma'am," Mr. Woodbridge interposed, much distressed, "your purpose in coming here was to help to civilize the Indians. I had counted on having your children as examples for my pupils."

"I don't see why my girls should be taken advantage of. Isn't it enough the way they all stare at us every time we go out of the house?" Mother could be bold enough when Judith's health was at stake.

Father, impatient to be off up the hill, gave in with a shrug. "My wife is right," he told the schoolmaster. "You don't have many girls in your school anyway. It's the boys who matter, and Elijah can be an example to them, he's quick at his letters."

At this I came rushing out of the back room. "You promised!"

"Nonsense," said my father. "I didn't know the circumstances. Your mother is quite right."

"Why can't Judith stay here and I go with Lijah?"

"Schools aren't intended for girls, and you know it. Mind you," he added, as Judith, quite restored to health, came through the doorway behind me, "this doesn't mean you skimp your lessons, either of you. Mr. Woodbridge will set out the copying

for you mornings and I will hear you read after supper every
night. I don't intend any daughter of mine should grow up an
ignoramus."

That was just what we'd be, I knew. Mother was too busy
and father would never think of it four nights out of five. But it
was not the lack of learning that troubled me, it was the prospect
of being cooped up with Judith all day. I had liked the school, I
hadn't minded the hard benches or the smell or the strangeness.
Now it would all go on without me; I would never hear the
singing or see the girl with the beaded armband. I went out and
sat on the ground beside Adam, and pressed my face hard against
my knees, and he snuffled in my hair and licked my ear till I had
to play with him.

As the only English pupil in the school Elijah took on an importance and independence all out of proportion to his years.
After the first few days he scorned the protection of Josiah, who
was supposed to take him down the hill. Within a week he knew
all the games that the Indians boys played, and he came home up
the hill only in time for supper. He had found a new masculine
world, and I was left behind in a world of constant feminine
chatter. Judith could not understand my restlessness. When the
long morning hours of copying and reading were over, she
worked lovingly at her sampler or was content just to sit on the
doorstep or to hang about listening to mother and Abigail. She
never knew my aching need for running and jumping. I would
have been a very miserable child had I not soon found a way into
Elijah's world.

7. ELIJAH could never forbear boasting. When the Indian boys promised to show him the caves in the woods, he had to come bragging to me. I was a gratifying audience, for he knew I would be envious and also that I would not tell. But this time I spoiled his pleasure by an instant undiscourageable determination to see the caves myself. At first scornful, then stubborn, Elijah surrendered at last to a bribe; I offered to make him the sling he was longing for. I made a good strong one, for I could work well with my hands, and he agreed to wait for me next day when school was out.

It was unthinkable that mother would allow me to go into the woods with the boys. I had no choice but deception. I asked her permission to pick blueberries on the slope west of the house, made a great show of choosing a basket from the kitchen, and even accepted without protest the sunbonnet she tied under my chin. It seemed cruel to set off without Adam, but he had a bristling English suspicion of the Indian dogs and I dared not risk an encounter. I left him sleeping, tied by his rope behind the house, and the only remorse I suffered was at deceiving him. The moment I was out of sight of the house I hid the basket and the sunbonnet, took a roundabout path through the brush and ran down the hill.

Behind the schoolhouse Elijah was waiting with two expressionless Indian boys, and I saw at once that he repented of his bargain. "They don't want you," he greeted me, his blue eyes imploring me to go away.

"Tell them you promised." I was not going straight home to be punished for nothing. "Indians know you have to keep your word."

Though Elijah had picked up in a few weeks a fair amount of

Mahican, such a concept was beyond his powers; his disappointed baby face must have pleaded for him. The boys communicated in grunting syllables and finally, with something like a shrug, they turned and set off, looking back at us with a gesture we took for permission to follow.

We had to scramble to keep up with them. They led us along the river path to where two logs were thrown as an unsteady bridge from bank to bank. They stood and watched as I teetered across after Elijah, and though their faces did not change I felt that I had passed the first test. From the opposite bank we struck into deep woods and began to climb sharply, so rapidly that we were both soon out of breath. We did not drag; I would have let my heart pound straight through my chest before I asked to stop and rest. Not far up the slope we came abruptly into a monstrous tunnel. Rocky walls towered on either side, veiled with tangles of bush and vine and topped with pines and oaks and maples that showed fragments of sky infinitely small and far away. The floor of the tunnel was a heaving tumble of boulders, scattered as though flung in some titanic battle of giants. They were cold to my hands and feet; all day long the sun could not have touched them. It was the dwelling place of demons, and I stopped, feeling the dark chill of it in my stomach.

"Ask them how far the cave is," I told Elijah, filled suddenly with distrust.

He called after them and they looked back, pointing briefly. I saw their scorn and knew that I was behaving exactly as they had expected. I pushed after them, clambering, sliding, hitting away branches, for there was no sort of path, only rocks heaped one on another, jagged and slippery with moss. Without a thought Elijah and I had both come away barefoot; we were unaccustomed to shoes in summer save on the Sabbath. Engrossed in finding a bearable footing, we lost sight of the Indian boys. For

a time we struggled faster to catch up, and then Elijah sat down
with a howl of pain, clutching a stubbed toe. When his howl
died away I noticed the silence.

"Call them," I demanded. "Tell them to wait for us."

We both called, confidently at first. We clambered on, up
and down, in the direction we thought they had taken, stopping
every few moments to call again. Our voices, shriller now, sank
into the stillness like drops of water into sand. I realized before
Elijah that they had left us alone. I knew too, long before he
thought of it, that they had intended all along to leave us, that
they had played this trick on us because I had insisted on tagging
along.

"We've got to go back," I said, sick with disappointment and
chagrin. It took some time to convince Elijah, and just as I had
almost persuaded him it occurred to him that it was all my fault.
Finally I turned and went away from him, and looking back I
saw that he was slowly coming after, snuffling. I retraced our
steps carefully. After a time we pulled ourselves up between
two boulders, tugging at cedar roots to keep our balance, and
stopped, breathing hard, to look ahead. Nothing seemed familiar. In every direction there were the same jagged rocks, flung by
monstrous hands for an evil purpose, with no sign that a human
being had ever passed.

"You don't know the way," Elijah accused.

I denied this fiercely, but the bravado which had carried me so
far was trickling away.

"It's getting dark," he said, a few moments later.

" 'Tis always dark in here," I told him. "Look up there, you
can see the sky is light." But not so light as it had been last time I
looked. I shouted at him crossly to hurry. Then in my own
panic I lost my footing and fell. Pain spurted up my leg and
burst crazily in front of my eyes in black and red.

I screamed at Elijah when he tried to touch me. One foot was caught between the rocks at an odd angle. When I moved the pain made me retch. When I could think again I managed, very slowly, to work my foot free. But when I tried to pull myself up I knew it would not bear my weight. "You'll have to go home alone," I told Elijah. "Bring father back here, no matter how angry he is."

"It's too dark," he objected. I saw then that the shadows lay in deep pools under the rocky walls, black and sinister. More than that, I knew it was no use. Behind and ahead the rocks looked all alike, and I could not make out which way the town might be or where to tell Elijah to go.

We both shouted ourselves exhausted. I did not really believe that anyone was near by. There was an emptiness when our voices died away that informed my very blood. Then I discovered something more than emptiness. When Elijah began to cry I suddenly put my hand over his mouth. All at once it seemed terribly important that we should keep perfectly still, that I should prevent him from making a single sound. I whispered to him to be still; I pleaded with him and threatened him and lied to him. I promised that father would come and find us. Elijah was a little boy and presently, because he was used to believing me, his hiccups died away. Worn out, he fitted his body into the hollows of the rocks and went to sleep.

I sat and watched the darkness fill up the tunnel. I thought of mother and Judith laying the board for supper and of Adam watching the path for me to come. I thought of a horse I had seen once in Newton which had fallen into a ditch and lain there with its leg at a queer angle like mine till someone had brought a musket and sent us children away. I knew that though they would doubtless look no one would ever find this place and that we were going to die. I remembered the words from the

Child's Catechism, so often recited, so meaningless till this moment:

> *What must become of you if you are wicked?.*
>
> *I shall be sent down to everlasting Fire and Hell among wicked and miserable creatures.*

I was wicked. God had heard the lie I had told, and he had not even waited for me to die but had begun my punishment already, not with fire but with this dreadful cold and blackness. And Elijah, who did not deserve it at all, would have to be punished too for my wickedness.

After all these years I still believe there was in this place something primitive and clinging and evil, which had repelled me from the moment I came upon it. I am sure that the thing that chained my mind and body that night was more than cold and fear and pain. I think it was sin. All my life the horror of it has come back to me in sleep. I have waked knowing the lostness, the betrayal, the guilt and the despair, reduced again to a quivering child. I have looked at other people and wondered, has there been such a place for them, each of them? Or have I alone been there?

Toward daylight I jerked from a sort of sleep with a spasm of terror. A man towered over us, tall as the trees themselves. I am sure I took him for Satan in person. When he squatted down and brought his terrible dark-skinned face close to mine, I must have come near to dying. Elijah's voice brought me back. He had bounced awake with all his swaggering confidence restored.

"Don't be afraid," he said. "It's just old Konkapot."

I could not believe at first that he meant to help me. I lay like a dumb creature in a trap while the dark hand moved along my leg, the fingers cunningly probing for the point of greatest anguish. Slowly he began to twist my foot straight. I marvel now

to recall how gentle he must have been, but then, barely conscious, my head swimming with pain and fear, I thought only
that I must not cry out or he would do something even more
dreadful. After a time my head cleared and I saw that he was
binding two sticks against my leg, winding them with green vine.
When he had finished, he picked me up, cradling me like an
infant, and carried me through the gray woods with Elijah stumbling behind.

We came at last to a wigwam in the trees, and he bent his head
to carry me through the doorway. Heat and firelight and smell
and color leaped at me like a brilliant stifling cloth flung in my
face. Then I made out two women. They had been squatting
by the fire, and they straightened their backs and looked at us.
One of them was the Indian girl I had admired in the schoolhouse.

The other was a woman with heavy swinging black braids.
When Konkapot laid me down on a pile of fur she came close
and stared at me, reaching to pinch my hair and my dress, making a soft clucking that somehow reassured me. She gave Elijah a
push so that his legs collapsed and he sat down beside me. Silently she took a wooden bowl and dipped out some steaming
mixture from an earthen pot near the fire and put it in my hands,
and filled a second bowl for Elijah, handing us each a small
wooden ladle with a curious animal carved at its top. Courage
was in the smell, and scarcely stopping for breath we devoured
every mouthful.

After this the three Indians paid us no attention. The woman
filled a bowl for the man and he ate it in silence, squatting near
the fire. The fear began to drain out of me, and the hollow that
it left began slowly to fill with the quietness in the wigwam. I
can still remember the feel of it, but I cannot describe it, except
that it was a goodness different from any I had ever known. I

felt the gentleness of these Indians not only toward Elijah and me but toward each other. When the girl moved lightly to take the empty bowl from her father's hand and to refill it for him, something passed between them though they spoke no word and did not even smile. Soon after, with a few grunted words, he got up and went out of the wigwam. Then the woman and the girl ate, and after this the woman lighted a clay pipe and sat puffing at it. The smoke and the warmth had already overpowered Elijah. He had toppled over beside me on the bearskin, and presently sleep betrayed me too.

I woke up to my father's voice, angry and inexpressibly dear, but when I saw his face I did not dare to show my joy.

"What do you have to say for yourselves?" he demanded. "Not a lick of sleep for anyone in the town all night. You know what your mother's been through? You're going to get a hiding you'll remember, both of you."

I was in a panic that he might carry out his promise there in front of the Indian girl. But he hoisted me up, much less easily and gently than the Indian had, and with the familiar jerk of his thumb commanded Elijah to follow. Over his shoulder I saw that the girl was watching me. I could not think of anything to say, and she did not speak, but something was said, nevertheless, without words and it comforted me like the bowl of stew.

Mr. Sergeant said later that Konkapot had made an astonishingly skillful setting of the bone in my ankle. It healed straight and strong, and the very slight stiffness I have always been conscious of has been scarcely noticeable to others. I have often wondered if anyone ever thanked him.

Not so simply healed was the memory of that night. It is with me yet. I have seen that place of rocks many times since; years later the young people discovered it and even Judith went there with them on rambles. They called it the Ice Glen because in early summer the boys found thin trickles of ice still lying like the shed skins of snakes in the deep chasms. When I could look up and see the sunlit sky far overhead, I could acknowledge the wild beauty of those tumbled boulders. But no matter how the others laughed at me, I had to be away before the summer twilight moved up the steep walls. Those others did not know that in the dark God withdrew from this place, and that evil crept out with the damp from among the rocks. Nor do Stephen's pupils know, those earnest young men who have studied geology and tell me that the glen is a marvel of nature. I doubt that even Eph would have understood, though he would have known what to do. Had I ever told him, he would have taken me back straightway in the dark, and perhaps the nightmare would have been exorcised instead of recurring to torment me. But I could never speak of it.

8. I CANNOT altogether regret that misadventure, because without it I might never have known Catharine Konkapot. She came of her own accord to see me a few days afterward. Having begged to be allowed out of the hot cabin heavy with cooking smells, I was sitting outside under a tree to which each day I managed to hop with mother supporting me. Once there I spent my time at lessons and sampler and in long empty stretches of feeling sorry for myself. My injury had saved me from punishment, but with all my heart I envied Elijah his thrashing. When it was over he had gone off down the hill to school, his conscience wiped clean, free as ever to find new adventure. I was doomed to lasting imprisonment, shackled by my own remorse at mother's haggard face. Abigail had given me the

berating my mother could not; Judith had withdrawn into a righteous silence I knew for resentment; for company I could only wait for Elijah to come home.

The slight figure that came up the path was not Elijah but the Indian girl, walking lightly and proudly, her head high and her back straight. When she saw me under the tree she stood still, tensed like a woods animal, till I called out to her. Then she came slowly and gravely. She had brought me a gift, a toy-baby made of braided corn husks with wampum-bead eyes and a scalp-lock of corn silk. I held it in my hands, rapturous and inarticulate; I thought I had never seen anything so beautiful. When I looked up she was smiling, showing perfect white teeth.

How can one explain friendship, which can leap like a squirrel from tree to tree, not needing an ordinary path? Each of us was shy of the strangeness in the other, but we met on some level that ignored the deep-rooted differences. There was little we could say to each other, but we told our names and she sat on the ground near me for a time. When she went away I knew that she would return.

She did so often while my leg was healing, and never without a gift for me, a handful of berries wrapped in a leaf, a lump of the sweet brown sugar made from maple sap, or a little basket of woven grasses. Most of all I cherished the corn husk baby, and though Judith told me we were too old for toy-babies, when she could not hear I talked to it. Next to Adam it was my dearest possession. I was aware that I must give a gift in return, but this had to wait, for I knew already what it must be. I had only one thing that was worthy, a little gold locket on a velvet ribbon which had once belonged to my grandmother and which had been given to me on my fifth birthday, though I would not be allowed to wear it till I was grown. The thought of parting with it was a physical ache, but I had no choice; anything less would be like my father's gifts of that first night. As soon as I could get about by myself I found it, wrapped in a scrap of silk in a corner of my mother's chest, and I kept it concealed in my apron pocket till Catharine came again. At her solemn shining pleasure I forgot my begrudging.

Mother was uneasy at Catharine's visits and Judith refused to come out of the house when she was there. Unexpectedly my father stood up for me.

"She's Konkapot's daughter," he said, "and he's touchy. Woodbridge is always complaining, too, about our living up here so far and not letting the girls go to school. If we let Liza play with this child it may satisfy them. She looks harmless, seems to know her place. Leave them alone."

Father was too occupied that summer and autumn to be much concerned with any of us, being determined that the cold weather would find us in a proper house. In the building of it he had not relied on Indian labor; instead he had ridden to Springfield and brought back with him two hired men who shared our table all that summer. The house that they raised was a good frame one, two stories with a summer beam and a long sloping roof; with our first cabin as an outbuilding and an ell added two years later, it served our family for many years.

One day after we had moved into it I invited Catharine inside, the first time I had made so bold. Mother spoke to her kindly, and I tried to win Judith by showing Catharine her sampler, which was much more elaborate than mine. I wanted to show her everything, partly from a desire to share with her but mostly, I am afraid, from plain smugness. She walked with me from one thing to another, not touching anything, pondering each most commonplace thing. She walked up the staircase gingerly. She looked at the beds with their linen sheets. She stopped at every window, incredulous at the panes of glass, and I wished that my father were there to see her, vain as he was of those leaded windows which had been a vast amount of trouble to bring over the trail. She was fascinated by the brick oven built into the side of the hearth, and by mother's few cooking utensils.

"You ought to see the houses in Newton," I told her. I suppose I had had little occasion for strutting in my life; I was heady with what I took to be her envy. As we went out at last through the door I overreached myself. Leaving her waiting I ran back into the house.

"May she stay for dinner?" I demanded.

Doubt crinkled over mother's face. "I think that would be very nice," she said finally. "I'll fix up a little table here by the fire just for you two, and you can have your dinner early."

I was not deceived. "Why can't she eat with all of us?"

Mother looked helpless. "Elizabeth, I don't know what your father would say. Or Abigail. How do we know if the child has any manners at all?"

When I went back to the doorstep Catharine was gone. I was sure she could not have understood what mother had said. Yet when had she ever needed words? It did not occur to me till much later that not my mother's gentle doubts but my own fierce whispering had betrayed our want of hospitality. Catharine never came to my house again, not that autumn nor in all the years I knew her.

9. MOTHER LABORED from sunrise to bedtime, and that first year was grievous to her. When the other families came, my uncle Josiah's wife and children first, then Timothy Woodbridge's brother Joseph and his family, and last the Browns, it was less lonely. There were three other houses now ranged

along the hill, all filled to bursting with children. Sometimes the
women lightened the heaviest chores by sharing them, turn and
turn about, dipping candles or making soap now in one household, now in another. Still, there must never have been a moment to rest, and my heart aches to think how weary my mother
must have been. And in the first winter Enoch sickened.

Never a buxom child, he seemed to grow smaller before our
eyes. He did not run about as a child going on three years old
should have done, and he was forever whining for us to pick him
up. When we did, he weighed no more than a feather. No
amount of coaxing could make him eat more than a few mouthfuls. My aunt Anna Jones gave advice, as did the other women,
but neither their remedies nor my mother's seemed to benefit.
More and more often, though she could ill afford the time,
mother sat in her rocking chair and held him in her arms like an
infant to soothe his fretting.

One morning she laid him on her own big bed upstairs, and I
carried up from the hearth some milk and some linen towels she
had warmed. Gently she unwrapped his woolen quilt. All at
once, as the cold air touched his body, Enoch went into a sort of
fit, his hands clawing, his thin legs rigid and shuddering. Mother
seized the towel and fell frantically to rubbing his hands and feet,
but after a moment she stopped and slowly straightened, a great
fear on her face. Enoch had ceased his jerking and the dreadful
whimpering coughs, leaving a silence that closed down over the
room and reached into my stomach. Then mother screamed at
me, "Go get your father!" I ran, but before I reached the doorway she had given a terrible cry and flung herself across the bed.

That night she came upstairs and bent over the bed I shared
with Judith. On a wooden platter she carried a candle and her
best silver mug. I sat up, sniffing the rich rare fragrance of chocolate.

"You must eat something, Liza." In the candlelight her face

looked ghostly. "It isn't good to go to bed on an empty stomach."

Then she put down the platter and sat on the edge of the bed and pulled me onto her lap. "You're only a child yourself," she said, rocking me back and forth as she had Enoch. " 'Twas not right you should have been there."

I could not understand what she meant. If such a thing could happen, what did my being there matter?

"How could he die?" I whispered, shivering. "He hadn't grown up yet. Couldn't you stop it?"

"I've tried everything. The poor little thing never seemed right from the start and maybe it's a blessing he should be taken. It is God's will, Liza."

She wanted to comfort me, but instead she filled me with horror, for I glimpsed for the first time in my life our utter human helplessness. I fought to escape in wild sobbing.

"He was our baby! Why should God take him away from us?"

Mother held me against her, and I felt her tears trickling cold down through my hair. Words came hard to her, but she found some at last. "God knows best. Perhaps he needed the baby. There can't be all old people in heaven. There have to be children too, even babies. Or why would he take so many of them?"

Did she find some easement in her own words? For Enoch was not the first baby she had yielded back to God; there had been another Elizabeth, for whom I had been named, who had lived only a little longer than Enoch and died the year before I was born.

God needed them. A straw in a whirling current, a sugared comfit for a mortal hurt. What did the well-intentioned say in all the centuries before they could fall back on the divine will?

What did they say to Pharaoh's wife the night her first-born was
stricken in Egypt? All these thousands of years — is there still a
need in heaven that is not satisfied? *Rachel weeping for her children and would not be comforted because they were not.* Years
later I came on these words, and I remembered, as clear as
though it had that moment ceased, the first time I had heard Rachel's voice. No, my mother's words do not suffice. But that
night they brought me comfort. I drank the chocolate and
slept.

IO. WITH THE COMING of spring I achieved my independence, for the same reason I had enjoyed it in Newton; no
one knew quite what to do with me. I did not fit the pattern of
little girls. The ceaseless work in mother's life flowed in over the
empty place Enoch had left, and there seemed to be no change in
her. She was distracted still by the old claims. And in justice, I
believe now that many times when I thought she was indifferent
she actually denied herself my help when she allowed me to go
off down the hill to join Catharine.

In the Indian town I found no lack of welcome. Had I been
only a few years older or more securely rooted at home, I might
have missed altogether, as did Abigail and Judith, the delights of
Catharine's world.

Partly my joy was in Catharine, for I had never before had a
friend of my own. I lived through the day only for the moment
when I could join her at the schoolhouse door for the brief hour
or so that was allowed me. On holidays I sometimes spent all day
with her, and she introduced me to a world of inexhaustible
novelty. I loved the smoky bark wigwams lined with bright

mats and hung with strange garments and weapons. I admired the Indian women, chiefly I suppose because, after the first few visits when they wanted to stroke my hair and clothing, they accepted me with matter-of-factness. Even my uncritical eyes could not find them beautiful, but I envied their strength. At planting time they could stand all morning in a field swinging stone hoes as wide as trenchers and so heavy I could scarcely lift one, sending them back over their heads in great arcs time after time, while the children, and I among them, followed to drop the dried kernels of corn into the cleft-open earth.

The babies enchanted me most, staring solemnly from their cradleboards. These boards, each one different and as eloquent a labor of love as an English christening robe, were intricately carved, the belts worked in elaborate patterns of beads and quills. At first I was troubled that small arms and legs should be so bound into rigidity, but Catharine met my protests with amusement. I observed that newborn babies were rarely separated from their mothers, almost never out of actual touch, for the women carried them in their boards, the weight supported by burden straps across their foreheads. For strenuous labor they hung the boards on a nearby bush, pausing now and again to call out in universal baby language which caused the little brown watching faces to wrinkle up in toothless smiles.

As soon as they were out of their cradleboards, the babies were underfoot, and mischievous and annoying as they were I never saw one cuffed or even shouted at in real anger. There was very little quarreling or anger among the children themselves. Only once I saw a small boy go into a rage, kicking and spluttering at something that had been denied him; his mother picked up a jar of water and dashed the contents in his face, and in a moment she was hugging him, wiping his eyes on her sleeve and glaring over his head at the other children who dared to laugh. Indian children, especially boys, cannot endure to be laughed at. As they grow older I think the fear of it keeps them in control more effectively than any punishment.

I envied their freedom from the ordeal of mealtime. When an Indian man came home at any time of day, his wife served him; when the children were hungry they helped themselves from the earthen pot. I was well acquainted with the monotonous fare that pot contained, for it was impossible to enter any wigwam without accepting the food that was offered. This early training has held me in good stead, as have the Indian words which Catharine taught me. Even now they make it possible for me to sit down in a wigwam without constraint, and sometimes to bring a smile into eyes long dulled.

I suppose I must also have seen the filth and the indecencies. No English child, even one so enamored as I, could have been blind to them. There were many things I forbore to mention at home. I remember cringing against a doorpost one day unable not to watch as a mother cut open a still-wriggling snake and rubbed the bloody fat across a child's colicky stomach. Once I saw a woman pick up the three pups of a litter and put them, one after the other, to suck at her own breast. They were a good hunting breed, Catharine explained, and their mother had been bitten by some wood animal and died. A week later I was coaxing them to lick soup from my finger.

Catharine's mother taught me to make twine, not at all shocked as my own mother would have been when I pulled my skirts high to roll the twisted bark fibers along the calf of my leg. At other times we plaited baskets of fibers from the swamp ash. When we tired of the work, we watched the old men at their endless games, liking best the one which they played with smooth elk-horn buttons shaken in their hands and rolled out on a blanket. I could not understand why Mr. Sergeant disapproved of these games. Sometimes when the game was over one old man or another would play for us on a wooden flute, a thin sweet sequence of notes never quite a melody.

And without Catharine how empty the forest and fields must have been. For I would not dare to tell Stephen that sometimes even now they are peopled with spirits. I cannot look out upon a summer field astir with corn stalks and not remember with gratitude the three beautiful sisters, spirits of the corn and squash and beans, who dwell together and bless the earth with their bounty. When I tremble beneath the Thunderer I must still remember to thank him for his gift of rain. The maple tree outside my window has its own spirit; through most of my life it has offered to me its wise and gentle wisdom. These are all red men's spirits I know, but long ago they whispered to a white child, and I would have them know that she has not forgotten.

II. WHAT I DID or owned seemed of so little consequence to my family that it did not occur to me that my gift of the locket would ever be discovered. Yet one morning Abigail came to the table where I was copying my lesson and asked if she might borrow it to wear. I could only answer no.

"Please, Liza. Mr. Sergeant is coming for supper. It's exactly right for the neck of my new dress."

I scowled at the verse I was tracing.

Mother spoke from the corner where she was shaping dough. "Liza, it was considerate of Abigail to ask you. Run and get it for her at once."

"When your turn comes I'll let you wear my things," Abigail promised generously.

I felt hot all over. "I don't know where it is."

"Of course you do. It's in that little carved box in the top drawer of mother's chest."

"It's not there any more."

Mother wiped the dough off her hands. "Perhaps it has slipped down under the linens," she suggested, going to look.

Judith had been bending over her copybook, and something in her pursed lips and downcast eyes caught Abigail's notice. Questioned, Judith kept a stubborn silence till Abigail accused her of taking the locket. I knew that this was far too great a strain on sisterly loyalty and that I would have to confess, but before I could open my mouth Judith had blurted out the truth. She had seen in meeting the velvet ribbon concealed under Catharine's shirt, and all these weeks she had kept her jealousy to herself.

Mother was dumfounded. "Catharine? Why Elizabeth — you gave your grandmother's locket to an *Indian?*"

Their indignation broke over my head. "I told you she was too young to have it," Abigail blazed. "You can see how much it meant to her."

How could my simple gift carry such a multiple load of guilt? I had been stealthy and deceiving, I had given away what was not really mine to give, I had belittled my grandmother's memory. In giving the locket to an Indian I had done something dishonorable, more unforgivable than if I had carelessly lost it. Mother was incapable of dealing with such wickedness. "We will see what your father has to say."

I sat blinking my eyes to make the letters come straight, resolved not to add to my sins an unfinished lesson. Adam came and pushed his nose against my knees, and as I reached down to scratch behind his ear the feel of the bristly fold of skin brought a reminder that turned me weak with relief. My father had bought Adam for me in defiance of them all. He had allowed me to have Catharine for a friend, and he would listen to me now. That was all I asked, that he would listen. The punishment that must be meted out was of no consequence.

My father, when he had heard my mother's account, was not angry; his response was far more terrible than I could have anticipated.

"Nothing to make a fuss about," he said reasonably. "Comes of giving a child something she can't appreciate. You just go straight down to that school, Liza, and get it back again."

He cut off my first stammered words. "You heard me. Tell Mr. Woodbridge I sent you."

"She brought presents to me —"

"Elizabeth!"

At that I broke into noisy rebellion and he pushed back his chair. I stood my ground, prepared to be beaten, but he did not touch me.

"Either you do," he roared, "or I'll go down there and pull the damned thing off her neck myself."

Halfway down the hill I sat down by the path. I could only weep with a child's total grief. Behind the shame of my errand there was something more terrifying. It was as though my foot had suddenly encountered a bog, and I drew back, unwilling to test the ground again. If they had not all been listening, if Judith had kept silent, if Abigail did not always have to have whatever she wanted — I hated Abigail and I hated Judith, and I lay on the grass and wept the harder because I did not want to hate my father.

I must have stayed there for a long time, for I could see no way to go, either down the hill or back. I was still in the same spot, tearful and undecided, when the man came riding up the hill on a gray horse, pulled in his reins and sat looking down at me.

"Are you hurt?" he inquired.

I shook my head and looked down at the grass, not shy but ashamed of my soggy countenance.

"Lost?"

When I shook my head again, he swung his leg back and dismounted with a thud of boots. "You haven't by any chance run away?"

I looked at him then, surprised that he should read my mind.

"I'd advise against it," he said. "Those woods impressed me as mighty lonesome even for someone my size with a horse under him."

Though he was a big man, with shoulders as broad as my father's, he was young. His hair was thick and fair, gathered in a ribbon at the back of his neck. His face was pleasant to look at, full and red-cheeked. The amusement that crinkled the corners of his blue eyes had no hint of condescension. He sat down, seeming in no hurry.

"Would you care to tell me about it?" he asked.

All I had hoped for was a chance to explain. The words I had had ready for my father spilled out now to this stranger, and after he had heard me out he sat without speaking.

"There's nothing to gain by running," he said finally. "Considering the circumstances, I'd say the only thing to do is to get that locket back. Now wait a minute! I think it can be done without hurting your friend."

I waited hopefully. He stood up then, unstrapped one of his saddlebags and rummaged inside. "You might make a trade," he suggested. "All Indians love to trade, and she might like this even better."

From his fingers dangled a string of blue glass beads, scattering azure fire in the sunshine. They were much more beautiful than the locket and instantly I coveted them passionately.

"I bought them in England for a young lady," he said. "But while I was gone she up and married. So you see, they're no use to me." He reached down and took my damp hand, dropped the beads into my palm and closed my fingers over them. As I looked down at them, dazed and tonguetied, he swung himself up on the saddle, very lightly for so heavy a man. I watched him ride away, too confused to thank him or to wonder what he might be doing on the path that led only to my father's house.

Catharine listened to my explanation; she took the locket from around her neck and gave it to me, and accepted the blue beads in its place. I could see in her face no sign of disappointment or hurt or anger or pleasure. But where she had worn the locket every day, she never, to my knowledge, wore the beads. Later I discovered that they hung on the wall of the wigwam over her mattress, where they caught sometimes a glint of sunlight through the open door or leaped to blue life with the flames of the cooking fire. I don't know whether their being there had any meaning or whether they had been forgotten. Looking back after all these years, I can still see them hanging there. Sometimes it seems to me that they sum up my whole life, and Eph's as well.

When I came back up the hill there was the gray horse tied to the post in front of our house. From within I heard voices, higher-pitched than usual, and a trill of laughter from Abigail. I went slowly in the back way.

"Here is Elizabeth," mother exclaimed, in the company voice I had not heard since Newton. I saw that my crime had been forgotten. "Liza dear, come and make your manners. This is your half-brother Ephraim, come home after all these years."

The stranger sat in the best chair. Now he rose and walked across the room toward me, holding out his hand. "Elizabeth and I have already met on the road," he said. "But I didn't recognize her. I expected a child and she is a young lady, as pretty as her sisters." He made me an exaggerated bow, and his quick look sought and found the locket clenched in my hand. One blue eye closed in a wink.

Never before in my memory had our family spent such an evening. Father was at his best, indulgent, proud and fond of us. Abigail, in her new dress with the locket at her throat, had never looked lovelier, and her laughter held a tremulous excitement, as though this stranger who turned every remark he made to her into a compliment were not a half-brother but a new beau. Mother was pink-cheeked and flustered at his praise of her cooking, and Judith was lured from her shyness into little bursts of nervous giggles. Even Josiah was surprised out of his sullenness into an occasional stare of real respect, for Ephraim had gone to sea as Josiah himself had merely longed to do. He had traveled to Spain and to Holland and with his own eyes he had seen King George riding on his horse through the streets of London. As he talked I turned over and over, like a precious coin, the encounter on the path. A few hours ago I had feared to lose the only friend I had ever had. Now it seemed that a second friend, a champion, had come to live under my very roof.

I think something of the same incredulous gratitude came close to overwhelming my father that night. Several times I was astonished to see tears flooding his eyes. Perhaps he had missed this son by his first marriage more than he himself had recognized. At the death of his first wife he had sent his two boys, Ephraim, then only six months old, and Thomas, a few years older, to be raised by their grandparents. Now they were both grown men. Thomas, who lived in Deerfield, had visited us infrequently, a spare, scholarly man, completely unlike my father, a graduate of Yale college and a physician. I had always thought of him as an elderly uncle rather than a half-brother. Ephraim had never visited us within my memory. Now suddenly he had appeared, in answer to a letter none of us had known my father had written, and in doing so he had put the final seal on the Housatonic venture. I am sure that for my father, as for me that night, the cup was running over.

12. MORE THAN ANYONE else I have ever known, Eph possessed a natural touchstone which led him at once, without any of our common sorry fumbling, straight to the best in anyone he met. The years that he lived at home with us were the happiest for us all. He and father got on well, though for all father boasted that this son was the spit and image of himself, their likeness was only in their fair corpulent handsomeness. Certainly Eph did not inherit my father's ambition, nor his impatience to achieve it. If Eph had a goal in life I think it was that everyone around him should find life as agreeable and amusing as he himself believed it to be. Though people speak of him as a soldier, I remember him best as a peacemaker. He disliked argument, and he had a way of seeing both sides that disarmed opponents and blunted — though it did not always settle — a conflict. All of his life — with one exception — he seemed to be confident that left to itself almost any matter would work itself out reasonably in the end.

Yes, Eph wanted us all to be happy, and effortlessly as he had dried my tears with a string of blue beads he wrought a change in all our lives. He brought mother the little Canton teacups that were her dearest treasure to the end of her days. He did not seem to notice that Judith was what mother called "not very strong," and many a time, when he came home from a trip, I have seen her scramble up out of a sick bed to come down to supper. As for Josiah, before he knew what was happening to him Eph had set him a course of military exercises, and then won his everlasting devotion with the gift of the first flintlock musket ever seen in this town. He even taught Elijah some wrestling holds that secured his place among the Indian boys. He soon called the Indian men by name, and he was willing to listen, sincerely listen, to John Sergeant's endless earnest hopes for the mission.

He was closest to Abigail. They had many traits in common — gaiety, charm and a fondness for small luxuries. Eph was the first to recognize in Abigail the sharp logical mind from which most people were distracted by her beauty. From his frequent trips outside he brought her back books instead of ribbons. He talked with her about politics and colonial affairs till she could hold her own in a man's discussion far beyond her years or station. At the same time he was unimpressed by what he called her Queen of Sheba manner. I think Eph was the only man Abigail ever knew, except the great Mr. Edwards, whom she never succeeded in wrapping round her little finger.

As for me, from the moment I first saw him on the path I worshipped him.

Abigail

1739

I. It was apparent to us all that Abigail's waiting was over-long. John Sergeant had, to be sure, no home to offer her. In the first weeks he had often labored with his own hands on my father's house, while the small house he had been building on the Plain was neglected. But even after the other Hill families were long settled, he seemed to find no time to work for himself; the small structure stood for weeks at a stretch without so much as a nail being driven. Barely in time for the first snow his roof was finally fastened down and the oiled paper set into the tiny windows. And still he did not speak.

Perhaps it was shyness; he was never entirely at ease with any of us, certainly not with Abigail. His awkwardness and his solemn formality were evidence of his rearing to a plainness and poverty she could scarcely have envisioned. He bore the token of pain and humiliation as well in the shriveled hand which only gradually I came to look upon without cringing. It was revealing of his nature that he regarded this handicap with gratitude. God moved in mysterious ways, he told us one evening. If the scythe had not slipped that day in the meadow and cut the tendons of his left hand, he would doubtless have been a farmer all his life; instead he had turned to books. In college he had perceived his vocation, and once he had received the call to serve his God among the Indians he had never wavered.

From the beginning Abigail had nothing but dislike for the Indians. She was not afraid of them, as Judith was, but her muscles involuntarily stiffened whenever one approached. Everything about them offended her; she told me once that when she as much as sat in the same room with an Indian the nausea began to crawl in her throat. It is quite true, the smell of them was repugnant. Even the little children, so appealing with their soft brown skins and doe's eyes, were smeared with bear's grease to keep the mosquitoes away or with rancid beaver oil to cure some malady. But I think it was more than that, perhaps a recognition even then that the contest between her and this dark race was deeply personal and hidden, never to be joined in the open, and therefore never to be subject to her will.

As soon as John was established in his own house, Abigail and mother admitted a concern for his well-being. As poor a cook as the other Abigail had been, they said, while he boarded at the Woodbridges' there had always been something on the table; left to himself could he be sure of even so much? At least once a week Abigail went down the hill with some offering, a fresh-baked loaf of corncake, a bowl of rich venison stew, an apple pie flavored with maple sugar. I marvel now how mother, with a family of seven to feed, contrived so frequently to have these delicacies on hand. In addition, regularly on the Sabbath night there was an invitation to Mr. Sergeant to have supper at our table, a custom we were to continue all of his life.

So, though no words were spoken, when Abigail walked down the path, her hair freshly washed, her eyes alight, I am certain she understood well enough that she carried with her not only a "taste of supper" but mother's blessing. Rarely she allowed Judith or me to go with her, deliberately I am sure to indicate to Mr. Sergeant that her offering was but a neighborly gesture. Even so early, my place in their lives was established, a ubiquitous child, useful at times, for the most part scarcely to be noticed.

Late in November the first heavy snow came, wrapping the hill in great swaths so that the house might have been floating free of its foundations on a white sea. On the Lord's Day we woke to an almost intolerable brilliance. The house was once again firmly settled on the hilltop, and far below us the settlement had reappeared, dwarfed by the drifts that almost obscured the wigwams. There was no thought of going to meeting, no chance that Mr. Sergeant would come for supper. The Hill was removed from the Plain by many days of labor.

My father had prepared for this isolation and had laid in provisions to make us self-sustaining for weeks if need be. He and the boys were out early tunneling their way to the barn to feed the animals, and I soon joined them, glad to be free of the cramped house, of Judith's sniffles and Abigail's impatience. For three weeks we were alternately curtained from the Plain or allowed to look down upon it over impassable wastes of snow. It was the middle of January before Abigail and I, well muffled and burdened with many cautions, made our way down the narrow path which the boys had broken and packed. Abigail carried a basin of English plum pudding, she wore for the first time a blue woolen hood edged with rabbit fur, and her face was alight, almost reckless, with expectation.

The Plain was smothered in quietness. A single path staggered from wigwam to schoolhouse, and the criss-crossed patterns of snowshoes were stamped on the white surface like the tracks of giant birds. A drift of smoke quivered against the sky above Mr. Sergeant's rooftop. Abigail picked her way daintily, and I followed after, knowing well enough that I was not wanted, yet somehow like her expectant and happy.

At her knock the door swung open. Not Mr. Sergeant but a

stocky Indian woman stood in the door frame, her small eyes glittering like bits of jet. Abigail stumbled back, almost losing her balance in the snow. Then, before she had recovered herself, we heard Mr. Sergeant's voice, and his eager boyish face appeared behind the woman.

"Miss Williams!" he stammered, surprise and joy, all she could have anticipated, unmistakable in his eyes. "Come in out of the cold. How very good of you." And as we stepped into the house, "This is Weenkeesquoh, my new housekeeper."

Beyond his welcoming figure the little room heaved with life. Indian boys sat on the benches, squatted on the floor, leaned against the walls. There were books open on the table; obviously we had interrupted a lesson.

"We are a large household you see," Mr. Sergeant said happily. "Finally I have my boys." Then, as he at last realized Abigail's bewilderment, he explained. "You didn't know about the boys? You see, the money was sent to us last spring by our generous friend Mr. Hollis in London. Twenty boys, he specified, but actually there was only enough to support twelve, and we have had to wait till the house was ready."

"You mean — they live here?" Abigail's voice had a flattened quality.

"Of course. That is the whole benefit of the plan. We all learn so much more, so very much more than ever before. I encourage them to speak in English, and they help me with Mahican. We have family prayers in both languages morning and evening. You would be amazed at our progress." His face glowed and his eyes, like a fond parent's, begged her to share his pride.

Abigail looked down in confusion at the little basin of pudding that had suddenly dwindled to foolishness. John reached to take it out of her hand. "This is good of you," he said. "But your mother need not worry about me any longer. Weenkeesquoh is an excellent cook." The woman, not understanding but knowing herself included in his warm smile, responded with a toothless grin.

To my disappointment Abigail left at once, refusing the tea he suggested. Almost pushing me in her haste, she hurried me out and our visit was over before it had begun, though being always curious and usually hungry I would have liked to see what he had to offer us. Bewildered, I hurried after her along the path and up the hill, and presently, when she did not answer me, I caught up with her and was taken aback by her face, scarlet, thin-lipped, with blind blazing eyes.

"Abigail — ?"

"The fool!" she burst out. "Standing there and grinning and acting so pleased!"

"Why shouldn't he be pleased?"

"An excellent cook, is she? Why doesn't he marry her then and eat well for the rest of his life?"

"She's an Indian," I said practically. "He couldn't —"

"Oh, hold your tongue," she snapped at me, and I dropped behind her again, abashed and uncomprehending. Inside the house she went straight up the stairs to her room and she did not come out again till the next morning.

I wonder, as I have so often, would it have been better if John had spoken sooner? I suppose that this moment must have come, that nothing could have kept it from coming But Abigail changed, I think, from that day, though none of us recognized it then, least of all John himself. On the day he finally spoke, on a late summer afternoon filled with the sunshine of goldenrod, I am sure he never suspected that the woman whose hand he asked for was no longer the girl whose heart he had taken that day on the trail more than twelve months before.

I remember they came wandering up from the meadow hand

in hand, and Abigail busied herself with laying the table while John went into the parlor with my father and the door shut behind them. Afterwards, at supper, we were very merry. Mother's eyes shone a bright wet blue, and father poured out for us children a few mouthfuls apiece of his best wine while he proposed a toast. I could not take my eyes from Abigail's face; I did not wonder that John worshipped her.

He told us that night that he was planning to build for her a new house here on the Hill within sight of her parents' rooftree. "I am forced to be away so often," he told my father. "Abigail is still young, and it would be unfair to take her far from her family." Furthermore, he would not ask of her that she take any Indian boys into their house, nor any Indian housekeeper. "She is delicate and naturally timid," he explained. "When she comes to know the Indians she will cease to be afraid of them, but I understand how they must appear to her now. And at the beginning it is right that we should be alone."

I was confused, remembering his happiness and pride on that snowy winter day, and all his plans for teaching the boys to live together. When had he changed? Now, so many years later, knowing her as I do, I am still incredulous that any girl so much in love as Abigail could have so kept her head in that long-awaited moment there in the meadow. Yet it must have been accomplished then. Somehow she had won her terms so adroitly that only a few hours later he spoke sincerely, with no thought that his arguments were not his own.

I think that the year of her engagement was for Abigail a time of unblemished content. She immersed herself in preparation, spinning and weaving and spreading her exquisite handiwork on the grass to whiten. She dipped candles in the brew made from the small gray bayberries on the hillside. Day by day as she worked she talked of the house that was taking shape in her

mind. She had chosen a piece of land a little to the south of my
father's house, and she planned to build there a house quite
different, she told us, from her father's or from any she had ever
seen. It was surprising how accurately she seemed to recall the
houses she had known in Newton, and how from her memory of
them she selected the details she would use. It seemed to me that
she could actually walk about in her imagined house, and that
already she loved every mantel and cupboard.

John, enraptured by this domesticity, as he was by everything
about her, would look indulgently at the sketches she had made
for him. "It looks very handsome," he agreed. "But very costly.
You can't expect too much of the Indians. A doorway like
that —"

"Dearest," she would say, reaching to smooth the rumpled
band at his neck or to twist her fingers in the dark hair that
curled over it, "do you think I'm going to trust the building of
our house to the Indians? I know of course they will want to
help, and so will the men here on the Hill. But father has the
name of an excellent builder in Connecticut. He can board with
us while he is here."

She charmed away his every scruple. "Father is sure you will
get a grant from the General Court. They can't expect you to
build a house out of your salary alone. And you forget, dear,
that they know perfectly well how much this whole mission depends on you."

In the summer of 1739 the builder from Connecticut arrived,
and the house began to take the shape that Abigail had devised,
to the astonishment of the folks on the Hill who watched it rise.

"Planned every inch of it out of her own head," my father
boasted. "Can't figure where she got her ideas, girl her age.
Who'd of thought setting those two chimneys back behind the
ridgepole would give all that extra room inside?"

I do not think that Abigail was ever surprised. I believe she moved through each room with recognition, having always known it would look exactly as it did.

2. ABIGAIL'S WEDDING, in August of 1739, was the first real social event of our new settlement, and in its preparation my father spared no expense. Abigail had made a good match, and he was proud of her. Though the Housatonic mission could scarcely be considered an important parish, its founding had attracted much notice, and influential clergymen from all over New England had been present at John's ordination. From now on, when the commissioners came to observe his progress it would be Mrs. Abigail Sergeant who would entertain them. And as wife of the minister she would take unquestioned place as first lady in the society of the growing town.

The road to Housatonic was no longer a "rabbit trail." Prominent Williamses were planning to ride in for the wedding from Longmeadow, Hatfield, and even from so far as Wethersfield in Connecticut, and it would be an opportunity, my father reminded us often, to impress on all their minds that our town, now officially incorporated under the name Stockbridge, was no backwoods outpost. His own house needed no apology and would comfortably welcome a goodly number of guests. The smaller houses of the other three English families ranged along the Hill were scrubbed and polished to take the overflow.

One unpredictable and distressing factor intruded upon the orderly plans. There would be a number of Indian guests, probably a very large number, and here Abigail surprised us all. "We have to have them," she insisted. "It is John's wedding too, and he is their minister. It would break his heart not to let them come." Now, after all these years, I know that this was her wedding gift to John, and that none of us, least of all he himself, ever suspected the struggle it must have cost.

"But suppose —" my mother quavered. "You know how they behave with even the slightest drop of spirits. It would be so dreadful."

"We are not going to serve spirits," Abigail told her. "Just fresh apple cider."

"No wine at a wedding, when your father's people have ridden so far? What will they think of us?"

"You can have a party here inside the house after the Indians have gone, with all the wine you please. Outside, with the dozens of cakes and pies you've planned, no one will miss it. It has to be this way, mother. John has made them promise to behave themselves. If we made them break their promise he would never forgive us."

So the Indians were present, ninety of them overflowing the meadow where the boards were set. They brought wedding gifts, wooden trenchers and bowls made from maple knots, rubbed smooth as the inside of a shell, spoons of white spoon-wood, soft deerskin moccasins embroidered with perfect quill-work. Each Indian, as he laid his gift before his minister's bride, made a short speech, unintelligible, grave and stately, such as a Peer might address to his queen. They stood by themselves and there was no mingling. I saw Catharine with her father, and we smiled but made no move toward each other. I was held back by some constraint, a sense not that my mother would object but that Catharine herself did not want me to approach. The Indians stood rigid as statues while my father, Justice of the Peace, pronounced the marriage lines. They partook of the feast sparingly; only when food was pressed upon them did they accept it with dignity. The visiting Williamses were impressed. "Remarkable," they said. "Shows what Christian influence can do."

Smiling, John Sergeant denied this. "We can take no credit," he told them. "It is their true nature. If you visited them in their wigwams they would show you the same courtesy. Often their tact puts me to shame." He scarcely noticed their English skepticism. His look, dwelling on the dark faces of his children, was radiant with pride and affection, so that Abigail must have felt well repaid for her sacrifice. Moreover, she must have been aware that the Indians, far from being an embarrassment, added the distinctive touch to a wedding the aristocratic cousins would never forget.

I can see it all still, every detail preserved for me forever in a honey-tinted light, and my heart aches to look upon it. We were greatly favored that day, we Williamses, and bound close in our awareness of it. My father, vigorous, genial, so masterfully the squire and host in this world of his own creation. My mother proud and happy and untroubled. Eph in an elegant suit of yellow damask, handing out the cider with such an air that the fluttering aunts and cousins probably mistook it for some rare import. Judith and I heady with excitement yet mindful of our stiff white muslin dresses. Josiah reconciled, Elijah strutting before the admiring aunts, an Eph in miniature. And Abigail — the jewel for which we were all the setting, her pure beauty misted with happiness, moving by John's side, these two set apart for me even yet in some inner temple which only the few and privileged may enter.

I can remember too the Hill on that day. Beyond the sloping stretch of meadow, flashing with satins and laces and Indian headdresses, the land dropped away into peace and stillness, far down to the thin glittering line of the river, to rise again in a splendor of hills stretched in a golden haze under the western

sun. I believe I had never really seen it all before and I was all at
once overwhelmed with love and gratitude. How wise and good
my father had been to bring us to this place. I will never leave it,
I thought. I will live here on this Hill forever.

The Indians kept their promise. For much of the night I lay
awake in my bed while voices shrilled through the house, but
from the Plain below there was no sound. Abigail and her husband had left us long before, and the paneled door of the new
house shut them away from both the celebration and the silence.

3· IN THE MORNING, when it was long past time for breakfast,
mother sent me to Abigail's house with a loaf of new-baked
bread, and I carried it carefully along the path, feeling important
that I should be the first to visit the bride. I had been told not to
stay and bother them, but John threw open the door with a smile
of welcome that canceled out such caution. In the kitchen Abigail was laying on the table the shining new pewter plates, and
the brilliance of the day before still lighted her eyes.

"Did the cousins enjoy themselves?" she asked me.

"I guess so," I answered. "They sent me to bed, but they made
such a noise I couldn't sleep. Most of them aren't awake yet."

She laughed. "Did you like the wedding?"

"It was beautiful!" I told her fervently.

She stood looking at me, her eyes dreaming, not seeing me at
all, a smile moving at the corners of her mouth. "Yes," she said
softly. "It was quite perfect, wasn't it?" Then there was a silence, in which I was suddenly aware of the two plates on the
table and of my mother's warning, and I backed uneasily toward

the door. Then I saw that, early as it was, there were other callers.

"Yokon and his brother are waiting to see you," I told John from the threshold.

"Oh!" Abigail's voice was sharp behind me. "This morning?"

John too made a wry face as he peered through the window at the two Indians. "If they have come," he said reluctantly, "then I will have to let them in."

"Couldn't they have given us a few days? Or just this one day?"

He sighed, reaching to take his coat from the peg. "I am their pastor, my dear."

Slowly Abigail folded the bread back into its white linen napkin. "Then tell them to go round to the side door," she told him. "They can go directly into your study from there."

John looked back. "The side entrance? But they have always come in any door they pleased. They won't know what to think."

"They will understand," she answered him. "It's different now you're married. If they never come in here from the very start, then they just won't expect to."

He waited, his boyish face puzzled, and I think I understood before he did that this was the reason for the door in the side wall and for the narrow passageway leading from it. How many times had my father commented that they seemed to him a waste of space and labor? Now, after a few moments, John too saw her intention.

"You mean they are not to come into this part of the house at all?" he asked slowly.

She went to help him button his coat. "Why should they?" she asked. "This is our home, John. Ours. We have a right to that much. And you must understand, dear, that I couldn't be left alone here, I couldn't go about my work, always thinking that any minute an Indian could sneak in behind me."

"I did not think of that," he said, bewildered.

"Tell them we planned this little hallway especially for them. We will leave the side door unlatched so that when they have to wait for you they can come inside out of the cold. They'll be flattered. You'll see."

She bent her head and rubbed her cheek against his coat, and there came over me for the first time the feeling I would have so often in this house, that I was of no more account than the settle or the broom that leaned against the wall, but that I had less right to be there. Then John touched her hair briefly and went out to meet his Indians. Abigail stood looking after him, and I saw that all the happiness had been wiped from her face, as though a hand had passed over it. Then, as the sound of guttural voices came through the walls, she started and moved quickly across the room to fasten the heavy bolt on the door to the passageway. "Thank mother for the bread," she said. "And run along now, Elizabeth, like a good child."

4. EVERYTHING I ever dreamed of marriage in later years I learned as a child in Abigail's house. Those four walls held an enchantment for me, filled with Abigail's beauty, her happiness, the new softness in her nature. Through the years of my growing up, we never had a work of fiction or drama in the house, scarcely I imagine in the town, nor any pictures other than those of ministers and martyrs. I would be a grown woman before I would discover that a love story could exist between the covers of a book. What need did I have of one? Not that I ever

believed for a moment that all this could ever be within my own reach; it was an idyl that belonged only to Abigail. But it was more than enough to fill my dreams.

Nor was it an illusion. I believe that in those early days of her marriage Abigail was happy as only a few are allowed to be. John worshipped her, and in return, bringing to her task all her love and her talents, she created for him the sort of home a man must dream about, a place of order and warmth and beauty. She had a way with simple objects, a knack of placing the Delft bowl just where it would catch the shaft of sunlight falling through the clean woven curtains. She worked swiftly with skill and grace, humming to herself. It was a joy to watch her at the wool wheel, her arms lifting as her foot stepped back, her whole body delighting as in a dance. Her house was filled with fragrance, of fresh flowers and grasses in summer, of bayberry and dried herbs in winter, and the good smell of fresh-baked bread and of supper bubbling in the kettle. And in this serene and lovely place she waited at dusk with shining eyes for John's return.

How could it have been that all this was not enough, either for him or for her? Is it only imagination, only hindsight, that tells me that almost from the beginning Abigail recognized how small and vulnerable was this world she had created? I am certain that John Sergeant never remembered that he might once have had some hope that was not richly fulfilled, but I believe that in Abigail's very striving for perfection there was an acknowledgment of it. Abigail has always demanded far more of herself than others have required of her.

I asked her one day to walk down with me to the Indian village.

She gave me a quick sharp look. "Did John put you up to this?"

"Of course not. Why should he? I was just thinking —"

"Then stop thinking. I have no intention of going, and John understands that now."

"But they want you to come," I told her. "The women are always asking me about you, and they're too shy to come up here."

"They see me in meeting."

"That's not the same thing. They want you to visit them."

"I wouldn't go into those filthy wigwams for anything. I can't understand how mother lets you, Liza."

"What's the matter with them?"

"You know yourself they're crawling with lice and fleas. I have to pick them out of John's clothes. And I'd be expected to eat some revolting food."

"It's not so different from our food."

"I can't bear to think how it was prepared. It's a wonder you haven't got some sickness from it."

I persisted, childishly. "You could just stand outside on the path and talk to them. You don't even need to talk. They just want to be friendly."

"The way they were with you after meeting last Sabbath? I saw them feeling your dress and your hair. It made my skin crawl."

I was puzzled. The Indian women loved pretty things, and I had been flattered that they had noticed my new dress. No one else had.

"My place is right here," Abigail said now, with more warmth in her voice than was needed to convince only me. "When father goes to Court he doesn't expect mother to ride off and sit there with him. A wife's business is to make a home for her husband, and when you have a house of your own you'll see it's more than enough to keep your hands full."

I never asked her to go again, and I tried not to speak about the village at all, for fear she might somehow put a stop to my going there. But a week or so later I found her sewing on a small dress, much too small for me or Judith.

"It's for that miserable child who waits outside with her father," she explained. "She was coughing her head off this morning, and it's too cold for her to go half naked like that, not to mention the shame of it."

When John came in at noon and saw what she was doing, there were actually tears in his eyes. Abigail bundled her sewing away, and hurried to take the loaves out of the oven, looking embarrassed and annoyed. I think now that his disproportionate gratitude must have somehow canceled out her purpose. Had the little dress been a penance? I never knew, but throughout that winter I noticed that every week or so another Indian child appeared in meeting in a new garment which was an ingenious patching together of Williams scraps.

5. THAT AUTUMN OF 1739 the mission promised to become a mighty work for the glory of God. On Thanksgiving Day we met in a new meetinghouse, raised with funds voted by the General Assembly of Massachusetts, the solid, two-storied building which, with slight changes, has served us well for almost half a century. Inside we sat comfortably on pews divided by two aisles. Fifty Indian families worshipped with us in those days, almost all of them baptized by John. Every Sabbath day he preached to them, as he had once promised to do, in their own tongue, without an interpreter, and they listened with joy on their faces, and sometimes tears. Scarcely a week passed without a new sign of God's favor — some Indian long indifferent came

humbly to inquire about the gospel, some stranger from a distant tribe traveled through the forest in search of the Word. The school under Timothy Woodbridge was flourishing.

Yet the old enemy was still at work. Despite the fact that the Indians themselves had voted that no rum should be brought into the settlement, mysteriously it would appear, and John's converts, even the most promising, frequently lapsed from grace.

"You don't realize what it means," John explained at our table one day, when father tried to make light of his concern. "This drunkenness can destroy everything we have done. The moment they give in to it they go straight back to their foolish wicked ways, and then I see how little, how shamefully little, we have actually accomplished."

"Nonsense," said my father. "What harm does it do? They sleep it off in a day or so."

"Yesterday two of the men dug up the winter supply of dried corn their wives had buried and disappeared with it. The poor women came to me in despair, a whole summer's work gone. The men will come back, yes, but the corn will have been sold and there will be no food for the children, and soon the men will need more rum to make them forget their guilt."

"Isn't there some way you can keep them from getting it?" Abigail demanded. "Why is it so easy for them?"

John sighed. "There has to be a thorn in the flesh," he said. "Van Valkenburgh is mine. He has resented the mission here from the start."

"You've done your best to ruin his business," my father reminded him.

"What sort of business?" John answered him with indignation. "A business based on evil and human misery! How low can a man fall? These traders have no conscience whatever. All these years the Indians have watched the way they behave, listened to their vile language, seen the way they lie and cheat even one another. What can I say to an Indian when he asks me why, if our religion is true, it hasn't made the white man good?"

My father looked at him, saying nothing.

"Van Valkenburgh makes a great show of being their friend," John went on. "When they have no money he gives them rum anyway, to keep them coming to him. Then he deliberately stirs up their suspicions, telling them we are only trying to deceive them, that we really mean to make them our slaves and put them in chains."

"Shows how ungrateful they are," my father said. "They know well enough it's the English, not the Dutch, who gave them this town."

"Some of them have never understood *why* we gave them the land," John said. "They are still watching for some trick, and realizing how so often they have been defrauded, one cannot blame them. The traders take advantage of our past mistakes. They taunt the Indians and tell them they are already our slaves, so that the Indians have to buy rum just to prove that they are still free men. What can I do? How can I convince them that it is drink that is making slaves of them? This is where I have failed."

Abigail leaned toward him, instantly defending him. "What a foolish thing to say," she protested. "How can it possibly be your failure?"

"It must be," he said. I was startled at how tired he looked, his usual bright color gone from his cheeks, and two lines I had never noticed before drawn deep between his eyes. "If I cannot make them see, then I am at fault."

"Oh, John," she burst out. "What makes you think you can ever change them? They don't understand human kindness. They have no sense of gratitude. Why should you go on spending all your strength on them? There are so many other places and people who would appreciate what you do. Couldn't you accomplish more — ?"

"Abigail!" His shocked voice stopped her. "Surely you don't realize what you are saying. It's not a question of gratitude. God has sent me here. He knew that the soil was barren, no, not even barren but overrun with weeds and pricking thorns. Yet this is the place he chose for me. How could I refuse? I should be ashamed to call myself a Christian, or even a man."

He pushed back his chair. "Don't expect me for supper, my dear," he said more gently.

Abigail watched him go, chastened, close to tears. "I shouldn't have said it," she whispered, as the door closed. "It was only for his good, but it makes things worse. Do you know what he meant? He won't *eat* any supper. He means to fast again."

"No use wasting your breath," my father told her, comforting her after his fashion. "You've got a good man, but he's set and you won't change him any more'n he'll change the Indians."

"I don't want to change him," Abigail said, her head coming up. "I just want people to appreciate him."

"We all do, dear," mother said earnestly. "Why just the other day your aunt Anna told me she didn't know how she'd get through the week without John's sermons."

My father sat pursing his lips thoughtfully. "He's right about one thing," he said finally. "The Dutchman's a nuisance. He owns some of the best land in these parts. Furthermore, I've thought for a long time it's a mistake to let the Dutch monopolize all the trade. We ought to be able to take care of our own town. As it is, I'm handling most of the orders that go out from here, just as a personal favor. With a little added investment we could have our own trading post, convenient to everyone. But first Van Valkenburgh's got to go. You leave it to your old man, Abby. I'll put my mind to it."

6. By the new year everyone on the Hill knew that Abigail was pregnant; the prospect of a birth in the new town, and to the minister's wife as well, was too happy to be kept secret. Had she had any wish to hide it, Abigail's bouts of morning sickness would have betrayed her. As I look back over the years, I realize now that Abigail's high spirit, her will and pride, always obscured for us her actual frailty. She has always been too thin, and often, I am convinced, more delicate than Judith, but her whole life has been a fierce denial of it. At any rate, she did not take her pregnancy easily. And as the most expendable of our household I was sent often to help her. I went joyfully, work in Abigail's house being altogether different from labor in my own; I felt important to be waiting on her and more able to bear with patience the long months ahead before I could look upon a baby of our own.

Eph came often as well, dropping in frequently in the late afternoon at the time Abigail found most tedious. He was good for her, but I think his reason for coming was rather that he found in her house something that met a need of his own. They were honest with each other, these two. Eph responded with a chuckle to the barbed wit that left John so bewildered and uneasy, and I think that nowhere in the narrow Stockbridge circle could he himself speak so freely. At ten years all this meant for me was that, unlike most grown-ups, they did not send me away when they talked, and that in their presence I could comfortably be myself.

Abigail would pour a cup of tea for him, using her best Canton china, and he would settle himself in John's chair, with that deliberate satisfaction that was so like father's. Watching him, I would think that with a few added years and pounds Eph would indeed be fathers' spit and image. Yet I hoped that in some ways they would continue to be unlike.

"Sit down now," I remember his saying to Abigail one wintry afternoon. "Have a cup with me. If you don't mind my saying so, you're looking frazzled."

Abigail, who most certainly would have minded anyone else's saying so, perched obediently on the edge of the settle, tucking back a strand of hair. Out of habit she reached for her knitting, then, apparently changing her mind, let her hands drop idle in her lap. "I'm glad you've come," she told him. "It's been a tiresome day."

"As I remember," he said, "the Hebrews put cleanliness *after* godliness, not before. Are you trying to outdo your husband?"

"A house doesn't take care of itself."

"Maybe the house needs less caring for than you do just now. Haven't you a right to spoil yourself a little?"

"I don't enjoy behaving like Judith," she told him crisply.

Eph studied her, his blue eyes not sparing her, but respecting some boundary he dropped his teasing, and pouring out his tea sipped it from his saucer, with a flick of appreciation for the sprig of dried mint she had brewed in it.

"Don't know as I'd stay in Stockbridge, Abby," he said mildly, "if it weren't for the way you make tea."

Why did he stay? We all wondered. None of us, even Abigail, ever really knew what went on behind Eph's shrewd, affable smile. For all he could talk by the hour, he seldom said much about himself. He had built himself a small house, where he lived alone. He never worked hard at anything that we could see. He always had plenty of time to enjoy whatever was offered, be it a cup of Abby's tea, or a glass of father's lime punch, or, if the rumors were true, a noggin of cheap flip at the tavern over the mountain. Every now and then he left for Boston or Albany, having no urgent business that anyone knew of, and returned unexpectedly to everyone's delighted welcome. There was talk that he would be elected the town's first representative to the General Assembly, but that was scarcely a job to fill a man's life.

"I've been through a spell of housecleaning myself," he said now. "Stocking up my larder at least. I'm entertaining some of the sachems who are coming to Stockbridge for the conference."

"Sachems?" Abigail questioned sharply. "You're having Indians in your house?"

"It's important we make a good impression on them."

"On the Indians? Are you jesting, Eph?"

He lifted one eyebrow. "John hasn't told you about the conference?"

Abigail flushed. "John has been too busy to tell me much of anything."

Eph must have known that John would talk about his Indians to anyone who cared to listen, but he did not remind her of this. "I'm sure Elizabeth could have told you," he said, with a nod to where I sat.

"I know they sent out five belts of wampum for invitations," I put in, much too readily.

He nodded. "The Stockbridge Indians hope to persuade the other tribes to stay neutral in case of war with the French," he told us.

"Is there going to be a war?" John would have kept any such hint from Abigail, I knew.

"Not right away," Eph answered calmly. "Bound to be sooner or later. The old treaty didn't really settle anything, and both France and England are biding their time."

"What does it have to do with the Stockbridge Indians?"

"Don't forget the French are in Canada," he reminded her. "There's nothing between us and Montreal but two or three hundred miles of forest swarming with Indians. Our skins may depend on the Six Nations staying neutral. If our Mahicans have any influence, we'd best do all we can to encourage them."

"What makes you think you can trust them?" Abigail demanded. "Why should they be allowed to invite strange Indians here? You can't believe a word they say. No matter how much you do for them, they haven't one spark of gratitude."

Eph looked at her reflectively. "That's not altogether true, Abby."

"Look at that Aaron for example. He missed meeting yesterday, and when John went to his house he was too drunk to pay attention. After all his promises."

"Aaron has good intentions. And I know he's grateful. He has a weakness."

"They all have. And John takes all the blame on himself. He fasted again because of Aaron, and he stayed up all night praying. I know because I came down twice and saw him on his knees, and he didn't even hear me. Sometimes I think I can't bear it, Eph."

Eph considered. "What you don't seem to have gotten through your head, Abby, is that you're married to a saint."

"I know that without your telling me."

"When I first came home I'd have said you were about the unlikeliest girl I'd ever known for this job. But I take it back. You've done surprisingly well at it."

"I haven't been able to change anything."

"No, and you won't, either. That's a hard thing for a Williams to accept, isn't it? Whatever it is, first thing any Williams wants to do is do something about it."

"Even you, Eph?"

"Even me, though you may not believe it. I just don't go at it as hard as the rest of you."

"Then what would you do in my place? Just sit by and let the

Indians bleed John like leeches? I still don't see why he couldn't be a saint in some respectable church where they'd be proud of him."

"Don't ever make that mistake, Abby. Besides, what makes you so sure he's not appreciated now? You should hear what they say about him in Boston."

"Do they have any idea in Boston how much it costs? A little money, they think, and they begrudge him even that. Do they know anything about the nights without any sleep? Or the hours and hours wasted straightening out some stupid squaw's quarrel? Or just trying to keep the men from going to Van Valkenburgh's place?"

"Well, at last we're getting rid of the old Dutchman. You can thank your father for that."

"Father?" Abigail was surprised. "I thought he'd forgotten. In fact I suspected he patronized the Dutchman himself."

"He probably has. But he's persuaded some of the ministers in Springfield to go in with him now and buy up Van Valkenburg's property. Only way we can get rid of him, and none of us could afford it alone."

"Father's paying actual money to get rid of him? I didn't think he cared that much."

"He cares where there's land involved. Part of the agreement is a trade. The Indians will get the Dutchman's good cleared land, and the English families will take some of the forest land in exchange, land the Indians have no use for."

"What use does father have for it?"

"None just at present. Frankly, it's an investment. One thing I don't believe your husband has faced, Abby, is that we can't keep good unused land like this fenced off forever. Question is whether we even have a right to try. Land properly belongs to those who can use it. The Indians aren't farmers by nature, and they're slow to learn. Take this obstinate notion that they won't use manure. They complain that the same soil gives them a smaller crop every year, yet they don't take to clearing new fields either. It's going to be years before they can cultivate half of what they have here. And meanwhile there's people hungry for land like this. One way or another, the English are going to come in here, whether John likes it or not."

"John thinks there are too many here now. I think in some ways he's sorry he asked the four families to come. He had an idea that everyone, English and Indians, would be one happy family."

Eph laughed. "Isn't it too much to ask a saint to be practical as well?"

"You mean you agree it will never work?"

"I don't say that. Just that it's pretty hard to change human nature. For men like father, no, it won't work. They've seen too much, and an Indian is an Indian, whether you make him a selectman or not. Perhaps the next generation. Elijah and Elizabeth seem to get along well enough with the Indian young ones."

"Is that a good thing? Liza knows perfectly well I don't approve of it."

"She knows that I approve," said Eph, smiling at me. "Leave them alone, Abby. She and Catharine are good for each other."

Abby sniffed, but I could see that she felt better. The tea, the speaking her own mind, Eph's very matter-of-factness had lifted her spirits.

"Stay for supper?" she asked, as he pulled himself out of John's chair. "Josiah brought us a partridge."

"No," he said. "No thanks. Come along with me, Liza. These two have little enough time to themselves."

7. IT HAD BEEN nearly thirty years since the Treaty of Utrecht had been signed, two years before Eph was born, and of the Stockbridge men only my father could have had any clear memory of the last war. As for their wives, a lifetime of peace had lulled them with an illusion of permanence. With consternation now we all watched as onto our quiet Plain there flowed an alarming tide of war paint and feathers. The Iroquois chieftains who came to the conference, attended by retinues of braves, were a different breed from our docile Stockbridge Indians. Arrogant, flint-visaged, defiantly savage, they brought to the town a restlessness that, borne upward on the wind, caused the white families on the Hill to shiver behind their bolted doors.

The English boys were unmanageable with excitement. In spite of the icy January wind, they hung about outside the meetinghouse all day and dared each other to open the door and peep inside, though the rash ones who did were bewildered by the Sabbath-like quiet and the endless sonorous speeches. In the evening, when it was rumored there would be entertainment and dancing on the Plain, every household had to deal with rebellious young ones.

"It would do them no harm," John Sergeant interposed for us. "Our Indians have given me their solemn word there will be no intoxicating drink, and it will not be a war dance. Remember, this has been a conference of peace."

But the Hill women, nurtured on fearsome legends, sent their children to bed early. Toward darkness, when the beat of drums pulsed clearly through the closed shutters, some of the men, Josiah with them, went down the Hill to witness the spectacle.

"It warn't much," he reported next morning. "Mostly talk. They wrestled some and threw javelins and played that betting game with peach stones. The dancing was no more'n a sort of walking round and round, not worth freezing your feet to watch."

John, uneasy as a parent who yearns to have his children put their best foot forward, came wearily up to breakfast after a sleepness night. "They kept their promise," he said. "I was proud of the way they conducted themselves. This whole conference has been providential. It was evident that the chiefs were impressed to find our Indians so content and prosperous, and when they saw how well the boys were doing in the school, some of them asked if they could send their own sons. It may well open a whole new field for the Lord's work."

Eph, stopping by at Abigail's house that afternoon, was optimistic for a different reason. "Too soon to tell," he said. "But it sounds very hopeful. These tribes at least have no interest in war. They've agreed to sit by and smoke their pipes while their white brothers fight it out between themselves."

"Is that all? They wouldn't help us?" Abigail inquired.

"They're not committing themselves. What they've tried to explain in these long-winded speeches is that when white men go to war they can make an armistice at any time they choose. When Indians take the warpath there is no stopping till one tribe has destroyed the other. The tribes of the Six Nations have no desire to fight. In my opinion they'd like nothing better than to watch the English and the French kill each other off. But I think we can breathe easier for awhile."

"I'll breathe easier when they've left town," Abigail told him. "Are they staying much longer?"

"Just this night. They'll be off before dawn. And meanwhile there's something I'd like to ask you. You see, I was lucky enough to draw the Chief Sachem of the Mohawks as my guest. None other than King Hendrick himself.

"The name doesn't impress you, I see," he went on, as Abigail made no response. "It ought to. He's not a man to take lightly. Probably has more influence over the entire Six Nations than any other Indian alive. He's a born king. Elizabeth can tell you that."

I shuddered. I still thought Konkapot the born king, but the majestic savage I had seen on the Plain, with his stony scarred face and flashing eye, inspired more terror beyond a doubt.

"The thing is, Abby, I've been a little embarrassed by his reception here in Stockbridge, at least by the English. He might go away with a better opinion of us if you'd allow me to bring him up here for a cup of tea."

"*Tea?*"

"Oh, he'd know what to do with it. This is no ordinary redskin. He was one of the chiefs taken to London by Colonel Schuyler, and he was received by Queen Anne herself. From what he says, I gather they made a lion of him in London society. Even had his portrait painted."

For a moment I could see Abigail was shaken. Queen Anne! But it would never do, and I held my breath. Then, "No," she decided quickly. "He may be an exception, but the Indians here won't understand that. If he comes, before you know it Konkapot and that miserable Aaron will be here every day in the week. No, Eph. They could afford to make a lion of him in England. They weren't taking any risk."

"You're pretty set for a person your age, Abby. You might at least consider what this man could do for John's mission." Eph stalked away, as close to anger as I had ever seen him.

Abigail slammed the door. "Tea!" she muttered. "What your brother needs is a good wife to rid him of some of his notions."

8. In APRIL THERE was a softness in the air and a warmth at noonday. The lacework of branches against the sky was intricate with buds and alive with redwings. The ice was gone from the river, and in the still water close to the banks the wild duck lighted. The Indian women slid through the trees like wraiths, searching for the tender purple shoots of red root.

As soon as the trails were dry enough for travel, John Sergeant decided to pay a visit to the Indians at Kaunameek, about twenty miles to the west of us. Convinced that the Kaunameek Indians were ripe for salvation, he was hoping to persuade the commissioners to establish a mission there, but in the meantime he could never refuse an appeal. He would be gone for a week, and I was invited to stay with Abigail, not so much on my own merits, I knew, as because there was no one else, and perhaps because Adam, who followed me everywhere, was fervently protective, often to the point of awkwardness.

To make him feel at home, I carried the old shirt of Josiah's on which he always slept and patted it down at Abigail's hearth, and he sniffed at it, wriggling his plump rear with recognition, then settled down with a thump and a sigh. My own things I spread out in the spare bedroom, my long linen nightrail, my wooden comb, a clean shift and petticoat and my tattered copy of *Pilgrim's Progress*. It was the first time I had ever been a guest for the night, and the fact that my own bed was just across the field did not rob the occasion of its importance.

Abigail, unwontedly quiet and prone to sighs during the day, apparently decided in the end to make the best of it. After supper, as we sat outside on the doorstep to watch the spring evening come on, she made a sisterly overture, inquiring, "Did you bring your sampler to work on?"

I made a face. "I thought this was going to be a holiday."

"When I was your age," she said primly, "I thought a holiday the best time to work on my sampler. I used to spend hours pondering the colors for every new flower."

"I haven't got to the flowers," I explained. "I'm still making the alphabet. I'd like to put an Indian picture on it, like a sunrise or mountain, but mother won't let me."

"It would look a little odd, don't you think? Did you ever see a sampler with Indian pictures?"

I let the matter rest. "A sampler isn't good for anything," I told her. "I'd just as lief work on something sensible. If I knew how, I'd like to sew something for the baby."

Abigail must have been truly concerned about my lack of feminine graces, for the words were no sooner out of my mouth than she was on her feet, hurrying inside for her work basket. Perhaps she had wondered what to do with me in the week ahead. In short order I had my first sewing lesson, and I think I surprised her, for I have always been fairly good with my fingers. For a few days the little biggin I fashioned kept me from missing Catharine and the Indian village. My visit was quite uneventful except for the incident of the rosebush.

"Look at those witless Indians out there," Abigail said on the third morning, pushing back the window curtain. "They know perfectly well John is away, yet they'll probably sit there and wait all day just the same."

"They probably will," I agreed. "Aaron's wife is very sick. They're afraid she will die before John gets home."

Abigail did not conceal her annoyance. "How do you know that?"

"Catharine told me. I saw her on the path before you were awake." I did not mean to keep from her that I had twice talked with Catherine in the woods at the edge of the clearing.

Abigail tightened her lips and made no comment. "So if John comes," she said instead, "I suppose he'll have to go straight down there without any supper. And when will he get his sermons done? No matter what happens, it never occurs to him he could use a sermon he's given before. As if the Indians would know the difference."

"They would," I told her, carefully drying a cup. "They like his sermons, and I do too. Better than the English ones, at least."

"Because you don't have to listen to them?"

I was never sure when the sharp edge of Abigail's tone meant a reprimand and when she was merely teasing; it was best to answer seriously. "No," I said. "I listen."

"Now don't tell me you can speak Mahican."

"Not very well. Lije can because he's with them all the time. But I can understand. It's not very hard if you try."

"There's no reason why you should try," Abigail said, no longer amused. "There are too many things a girl needs to learn if she's to have a house of her own. You could find better use for your time than hanging about in the village with Catharine."

I did not answer, and Abigail's increasing irritation turned back upon the Indians outside. "They make me nervous," she fussed.

"I'll go out and talk with them if you want."

"No, it would just encourage them. We'll keep the doors and windows closed. I'm sure they've been drinking again. You can tell when they argue like that."

The men's voices had become audible through the closed casement, and there were no polite pauses between one truculent speech and another. Then abruptly both Indians leaped to their feet in a fury of loud shouts, punctuated by a heavy thud against the wall. From behind the curtain we saw a heaving scramble of brown arms and legs.

With a quick intake of breath, Abigail dropped the curtain. "My rosebush!" she wailed, and without an instant's hesitation she ran to the door, threw back the bolt and rushed out, with me at her heels.

"Stop it!" she cried. "How dare you act like this?" As the rolling figures bore down on the little bush, she dashed straight at them, and seizing the first thing that swung within reach, the long black braid of the topmost Indian, gave it a furious jerk.

The two men, frozen in grotesque astonishment, blinked up at her. Awkwardly they clambered to their feet and took, like sheepish boys, the angry berating she poured out at them. When she stopped for breath they shuffled quietly away, making a wide circle around her embattled figure.

Abigail went down on her knees, her tears dropping on the rosebush. Tenderly she staked up the bruised stems, heavy with buds, and bound them with a twist of vine, while I ran to the spring for a gourd of water, then squatted beside her offering sympathy and suggestions. When she had done all she could, Abigail stamped back into the house and shot the bolt behind her. Only then did she suddenly remember, and her hands clutched at her swollen body. "Merciful heaven!" she exclaimed. "I must have been out of my senses. I might have set a mark upon the child!" Her hands were shaking as she wiped off her muddy skirt.

I watched her, unable to keep back my thoughts. "You aren't afraid of them at all," I said.

"What are you talking about?"

"Those Indians. You were just angry."

"Why shouldn't I be angry? Sprawling all over my garden like — like rattlesnakes!"

"I know," I said. "But why do you let John think you are afraid?"

Abigail stared back at me and color flooded her cheeks again. "You mind your own business, Liza," she snapped. "There are a lot of things you just don't understand about."

9. LOOKING BACK on it now, I believe the sewing class must have been, like the first small garment for an Indian child, a penance for Abigail, certainly not of John's imposing, for he would never have acknowledged a flaw, but set by her own stringent self-judgment. There had been some talk in the town of putting the Indian girls into English homes. Very few ever attended the school. The Indian men who could perceive the advantage to their sons of learning to read and write the white man's tongue could see no such necessity for their daughters, and in this they scarcely differed from most Englishmen. John Sergeant understood that the girls needed a quite different sort of education; it did little good after all to encourage the Indians to build English houses if their wives simply carried into them all the slovenly ways of wigwam housekeeping. Remembering his success in teaching the boys who had lived under his roof the winter before his marriage, John reasoned that the girls might be boarded with English families where they could practice the housewifely skills and observe the virtues of cleanliness and thrift. Whether he hoped that Abigail might set the example for the other Hill families I do not know, but each family waited to see what the others would do, no offer was made, and presently John ceased to talk of it.

What Abigail proposed now, to everyone's astonishment, was a sewing class, and for this I secretly took credit, since I

had been bold enough to beg her to allow Catharine to learn
with me. For whatever reason, and I doubt I had much to do
with it, Abigail, to John's incredulous pleasure and pride,
offered to teach a small class of girls for two afternoons a
week. He selected the girls carefully; many were eager, but
no more than seven could fit, and not too comfortably, into
the small study where Abigail insisted the class must meet.
We sat on the floor, with Abigail unnaturally tall above us in
John's chair, and we worked in total silence, for though the
girls came chattering up to her very door, once they were inside nothing could induce them to speak. They learned
quickly, as I had known they would, and this was fortunate,
for Abigail had scant patience, and as the afternoons wore on
her voice tended to sharpen. At one moment full of smiles and
praise, at the next she would swoop down, snatch the cloth
from some faltering hand and jerk out the offending stitches.
Never intending to abuse them, she took offense when they
stiffened in expectation of a blow. Resenting their fear of her,
she preferred to call it stupidity or defiance. I know she
found them all baffling, and that they found her equally so,
and I watched helplessly, torn by a loyalty to both. I noticed
that Catharine often moved quickly to untangle a twisted
thread or to quietly undo a bumpy row before it could attract
notice, and I followed her lead and tried to do the same.

Presently, to further their education and perhaps to ease the
tedium for herself, Abigail decided to read aloud to us as we
worked. She chose from the few books our family had
brought with us from Newton the one book I most despised,
A Token for Children, an account of the "Holy and exemplary lives and joyful deaths" of a number of young children.
John would have approved the choice, because the stories
were intended to promote in young readers a horror of sin and

a longing for piety. Abigail read very slowly, mouthing her words, her voice much too loud in the small room. The Indian girls sat with their heads bent over their work, and when she finished they raised their soft inscrutable eyes and smiled in proper courtesy.

"Do they understand a single word?" she asked me one day, after they had filed out of the room, silently and respectfully, to burst into unrestrained giggles outside the house.

At that age, when I was asked a question I gave a straight answer. "I don't suppose they listen," I told her. "I don't. I think it's a horrid book."

"It's a very wholesome book," Abigail returned, her voice waspish. "I was raised on it, and it would be a good thing if you spent more time on such reading. What's wrong with the book, may I ask?"

"I don't believe any real children ever talked like that. And it's too sad. If they were all so good and never did anything but pray and read the Bible, then why did every single one of them have to die? Besides, I don't think God would send a child to Hell to burn forever and ever just because he told a lie."

"Lying is a sin," said Abigail. "You're certainly old enough to know we're punished for our sins."

But there was an inequity here for which I had no words. Knowing perfectly well that Abigail could not possibly like this book herself, but that she could not now admit it, I said instead, "I wish you'd read *Pilgrim's Progress*, or *Robinson Crusoe*."

"Well, I'm not going to. Those girls are here to be instructed, not entertained, and they need every bit of moral training they can get. If I didn't watch them every instant they'd likely walk off with anything they could lay hands on."

"They would not!" A rush of helpless protest brought tears to my eyes and set me stammering. "You shouldn't say that, Abby. They wouldn't touch anything, not one single thing!"

"Oh, all right, Liza," she said. "Far be it from me to insult your precious friends. I'm too tired to argue about it. Nobody appreciates what a strain it is trying to teach them. I don't see how John stands it."

IO. A TRAVELING PEDLAR had come to town, an event rare enough in itself, this time promising unheard-of entertainment. Elijah, coming up the hill after school, made the most of having been the first to see him. The pedlar had everything you could think of, he boasted, but mainly whips made of real horsehide, with which he could do tricks. He could snap a leaf off a bush, Elijah told us, even letting someone point out any leaf he chose, and then picking off that exact one without touching the leaf next to it.

I was wild to see him. I had seen only one pedlar's pack in my life, and in my memory it poured forth more dazzling treasures than Aladdin's lamp.

"Do you suppose he has indigo?" my mother pondered.

"Elizabeth and I will go down and see," said Eph, divining that I had already determined to go at any cost.

Half the townfolk, both Indians and whites, were gathered on the flat stretch of ground in front of the schoolhouse. Josiah was there ahead of us, walking about with one of the whips in his hand, snapping it over his head in tentative cracks. Under the trees nearby a horse was tethered, and waiting indifferently beside it, as unworthy of notice as the nondescript animal, were a shabby woman and a little girl. In the center of the circle the pedlar was spreading out his goods on the grass, extolling each one in a nasal singsong chant like a schoolboy reciting the alphabet. They were nothing like the bounty I had remembered, only ordinary pins and needles and spools of thread and such commonplace things for housewives, wooden dishes no better than those every Stockbridge Indian made for himself, a few knives and scissors that even Elijah pronounced worthless. The pedlar's prize stock was the whips that bristled from his pack like a clump of saplings with drooping willowy lashes.

"Won't sell many of them things here," remarked Mr. Pixley, who had recently come with his family to settle in our town. "Must be plumb crazy to come all the way over this trail. Said he thought we had carriages. Could of seed for himself the only way a carriage could get to Stockbridge would be to drop right out of the sky."

"Hard luck," said Eph, already taking the side of the stranger. "What do you say, Liza? Should we buy one to have ready? If we keep it long enough, someday there's sure to be a carriage to go with it."

"I'd buy nothing from this one," said Mr. Pixley. "Don't like his looks."

Now that I looked from the wares to the pedlar, I saw what Mr. Pixley meant. The man had a thin sharp face with scarcely any lips at all. In spite of his jocular words, his eyes were as cold and dull as the blades of his knives. But when he was satisfied that sufficient audience had gathered, he selected one of his whips, and I forgot his face for watching the uncanny thing come alive in his hand. The faint cracks Josiah had produced were as nothing to the pistol shots the pedlar could evoke with one quick motion. Wheeling suddenly, he

flicked the lash an inch over the heads of a cluster of fascinated boys. The Indian boys did not move a muscle, but their
faces turned sullen. The English boys scattered, and the men
hooted as the lash neatly lifted the cap clean off the hindmost
scrambler's head.

My stomach tightened and I reached for Eph's hand. The
whip was a like a rattlesnake from which I could not take my
gaze. I remember wishing that my father had not gone to
Court in Westfield and that John had not chosen this day to
ride off to Kaunameek.

When the boys were thoroughly subdued, the man coiled
the lash deftly round his wrist and looked about the circle
with a sneering expectancy. There was some reluctant applause; for the most part the crowd was wary. "You seen
nothing yet," he announced then. He looked behind him toward the trees and beckoned to his child. When the girl hesitated, her mother gave her a vacant push, and she came dragging her feet and stood before her father. He searched the
grass around him with a sharp glance, stooped and picked a
long-stemmed clover. The child opened her mouth obediently to let him thrust the stem between her teeth, then closed
her mouth again and held it there.

"Now keep your eye on this," the man said. He stepped
back, and the crowd shifted behind him. He measured the distance with the squint of a man sighting along the barrel of a
musket. Then with one rapid motion he flicked the lash over
his shoulder. It sang briefly in the air and cracked in the dirt
just before the child's feet. The green stem still stuck out
from her mouth; the blossom was gone. Some woman gave a
gasping cry; one or two of the boys ventured an uncertain
cheer.

"J'ever see anything like that? Watch again now." The
man bent for a clover with a shorter stem.

This time I saw the child's eyes. I can see them still. When the lash came back I buried my face against Eph's coat and took the cracking sound of it on every nerve of my body.

The man was reaching for a third clover when Eph shook me off. "We've seen enough," he said. "I'll buy that one you're using."

While he was counting the money into the man's palm, the child suddenly crumpled and lay sprawled on the grass. A few women broke out of the stupefied ring, and I was with them, propelled by something stronger than my dread.

"Don't pay her no heed," the woman said, coming without haste from under the tree. "She'll be round in a minute." She bent over and shook the girl's shoulder, then, when there was no response, tweaked the flesh of the skinny arm in a sharp pinch. The child's eyes popped open, blank in a white face.

Abigail Woodbridge nervously spoke up. "The child looks sick," she said. "Does he have to make her do that?"

The woman gave her a glowering look. "I done it for him long enough and I never made no fuss over it. Git up now, and help your pa pack up."

Abigail Woodbridge had a courage none of us had suspected. Though her voice trembled, she persisted. "She looks tuckered out," she said. "So do you, and no wonder." She hesitated, then went all the way. "You can come home with me — all three of you. There's plenty for supper and we can find you some place to sleep." I have liked Abigail ever since.

The pedlar, pocketing his coins, shoved his way between the hovering women. "We're not stopping," he said. "We'll git far's we kin before dark. Over in New York they know a good show when they see one." The woman turned her drained-out face toward Abigail and shrugged.

As Eph and I started up the hill, he raised his arm suddenly and hurled the whip with all his strength. It whistled and sank, coiling into the brush with a hiss. I remember that for a long time when I walked past that spot I shuddered at the living thing that still lay there. As we went on I began to cry with great gulping sobs that hurt.

"Damn my fool intentions," said Eph. "I forgot your mother's indigo."

II. ON THE LAST day of August Judith and I sat on the doorstep at noonday, unable to finish our lessons or to think of any play that might distract us from the heat and from the heaviness of waiting. On the afternoon before, John had arrived out of breath to fetch my mother. She had smiled at his white face, moving calmly to put together the little bundle of things she had had in readiness. "No use fretting," she had told him. "The first one is never in any hurry." She had stopped to give Judith and me instructions for dishing up our father's supper, and then had gone down the path beside John, her steps hurrying in spite of her own advice. Late in the evening, and again this morning, our aunt Anna Jones had come by to tell my father that there was no news as yet. It was going hard with the poor girl, she said. Now my father waited too, keeping indoors, and from time to time we heard his heavy tread on the floorboards behind us.

I scratched aimlessly under Adam's leather collar, but when he pranced off to find a stick for me I had no heart for playing, and he flopped down beside me again, puzzled but agreeable as always. I was resentful at being ordered not to leave the house, when in every muscle I felt the pull toward Abigail's. They could have put me to some use, I reasoned. Who would draw water from the well or sweep the floor or remember to water the hollyhocks at the doorstep or to pick off yesterday's Life of Man blossoms?

Suddenly across the field there came a long high scream. Judith and I looked at each other, and Adam raised his head, his ears lifted.

"That was Abigail," Judith whispered, shaking. "Liza — what is happening to her?"

I said nothing. Judith had never watched the cows in our father's meadow. When they started their bellowing she went indoors and stopped her ears. But knowledge moved in my stomach as though I had eaten green apples. A second long cry rose in the still air.

Judith put her hands over her ears. "It must be terrible," she moaned. "I hope I never have a baby, never. I couldn't stand it."

"I'm going to have lots of them," I said. But when the third cry came I clenched my fists to keep from stopping my own ears. Judith burst into sobs and rushed into the house. I sat braced for the next sound.

When it did not come I endured the silence till I could bear it no longer. Suddenly I was running along the path, against orders, against my own will, but running. John Sergeant came bursting from the house as I came in sight of it, and he stood in the sunshine as though blinded, till I almost ran into him.

"It's a little girl!" he cried out, seeing me all at once. He leaped and caught me in a hug, lifting me high off the ground. His face and hair were wet as my arms touched them. "Give thanks to God, Liza! He has been good to us!"

He hurried off down the path, not telling me to go away, and I went to the house and opened the door. The steam and stench of the kitchen struck against my face, and for a moment I could not see after the brilliant sunshine. Then my mother's voice came sharply. "Elizabeth — I told you —"

"Let her look since she's here," said my aunt Anna from the hearth. "Come here, child." On her lap she held a bundle which she was wrapping in yet another layer of linen cloth. She pushed back a fold to show me a red wrinkled face with tight-shut eyes. "Isn't she a beauty?" she crooned. "A little angel. Perfect from head to toe." Indeed, she seemed so to me, this first new-born child I had ever seen.

There was a murmuring from the bed in the corner. "Abigail wants to speak to you," said my mother. "But be quick. She needs to sleep."

I tiptoed to the bed, and Abigail opened her eyes and looked up at me. Her hair was wet like John's, stuck together in long strands, and there was a grayness about her face and lips, but her eyes were drenched with light as they had been on the day of her wedding, and I felt her love welling up, including this time even me.

"Is she really beautiful?" she whispered, and I nodded, speechless.

"John wants to call her Electa," she said drowsily, her eyes closing.

There was something I had to say to her before I could go. "I wanted to come," I stammered. "I wanted to help, but mother made me promise."

"There wasn't anything you could do," she said.

I hesitated. "Was it very terrible?" I asked her.

She opened her eyes again. "Yes," she said. A shadow crossed her face and was swiftly gone. "It doesn't matter now. It doesn't matter at all. Remember that, Liza."

"I knew it anyway," I told her.

"Yes," she said slowly. "I guess you did." And then she smiled. Never in our lives did Abigail and I come so close again. I don't suppose she even realized. People say that sorrow brings us human creatures closer to each other, and I know that it is true. But joy can dissolve all separation like sun burning through mist. It is only that joy is rarer.

12. THE MOMENT WHEN I was first permitted to hold Electa in my arms was the most joyful I had ever known, eclipsing the joy of Adam, even though she was not my own to keep. Knowing this, I was still rapturously possessive, and I must have been a trial, so constantly and eagerly underfoot. Yet I think that Abigail was glad of my help, for her strength was slow in returning.

"Put her down," she would say to me. "You'll spoil her to death if you snatch her up every time she cries."

"I just like to hold her." I was entranced by the warm downy feel of Electa's head against my cheek.

"You've certainly changed," Abigail said, watching me. "To think I worried so about your being a tomboy. Now I scarcely see my own child except over your shoulder."

But there was no sting in her words. It was Abigail who had changed; she was the girl she had been in the first weeks of her marriage, and her happiness and love spilled over and warmed us all. I set Electa into her cradle reluctantly and bent to pat away the first hiccupping threat of a wail.

"Catharine says the reason Indian babies hardly ever cry is because their mothers carry them around so much," I said. "Would you let me carry Lecta in a cradleboard?"

Abigail laughed. "And hang her on a tree, I suppose. It's a wonder to me the Indian children ever learn to use their arms and legs."

"They don't stay tied in all the time. But Catharine says it makes their backs straight." I poked my finger in and out of the baby's soft palm to make the tiny fingers curl and cling. Abigail sat smiling and unwontedly idle, and I gathered courage to speak of something that had been troubling me for a long time. I hurried into words before the possible moment should pass.

"Abby, can people have babies without being married?"

Abigail was surprised. "Why Liza," she said. "I thought you understood about all that. Little young things can't be made without fathers."

"Of course I know that," I answered her, with the scorn of a country child. "I mean, do people have to be *married?* Doesn't a woman who isn't married ever have a baby?"

"Yes, they do." Her voice took on a sternness. "But it's a sin, and all the rest of their lives they can't hold up their heads for shame."

I looked down at Electa, thinking shame a trifle not to be considered.

"Besides," Abigail added, as though she read my thoughts, "it's a monstrous shame on the child. He has to grow up a bastard, and decent people won't have anything to do with him. Even when he's a man he hasn't any right to a proper name, and if it's a girl no one will want to marry her."

I sat dumfounded. This was much worse than I had dreamed. For a child to have to pay! At her terrible words a door slowly closed, leaving me outside, and the hurt of it was too great for me to contain. "Abby!" I burst out. "I don't think I can stand it not to ever have a baby."

Abigail started to laugh, and stopped abruptly. "Why of course you'll have a baby," she said. "Someday."

"Who would ever want to marry me?" I asked her honestly. "I'm not pretty like you and Judith."

Abigail sat looking at me, and then, to my surprise, she got up and came to put her arms around me in a quick unaccustomed hug. "What a worrier you are," she teased. But she did not lie to me. "Just look around you," she said. "All the married women certainly aren't pretty. Besides, you haven't grown up yet. You're only eleven years old." She studied my face for a moment. "You know, Liza, you have very nice eyes."

At this slight praise, only too eager, my hopes gave a bound and the door opened again. "Do you think so?" I wavered.

"There now," she laughed. "You should smile like that more often. Don't be such a serious little grandmother."

But how could I help the way I had been born? And though Abigail meant to be kind, how could she possibly have understood, she who had always known, long before she was eleven and every moment since, that she was pretty? For her the door has always been wide open. I have never learned to watch lightly its random swinging.

13. SHORTLY AFTER Electa's birth, my father sent to Boston for a pair of Africans. He surprised us with the announcement one Sabbath night at table, having always a liking to make the most of an occasion. "I promised your ma when we moved here I'd make it easy for her before long, and I aim to keep my word. Time's come sooner than I expected. I'm

going to see to it now she never has hard work to do for the rest of her life."

We were all taken aback by John Sergeant's reaction. Looking horror-struck, he pushed back his chair and set down his napkin. "I beg you, sir," he said, "to reconsider this." His voice contained a touch of command we could scarcely miss. I saw my father bristle.

"It never occurred to me," John went on, "that there would ever be a question of slaves in Stockbridge. You and the three other English families, if you recall, were invited here to provide the Indians with an example of husbandry. Frankly, I've been distressed for some time at the increase of luxury here on the Hill. If you bring slaves into your household, I am very much afraid you will forfeit the Indians' confidence forever."

"I think you're mistaken, young man." My father turned on his son and minister the ice-blue stare that invariably quelled opposition. "If it's an example you wanted, I've certainly furnished them a prime one. Let 'em see now that sweat and common sense have begun to pay. Nothing to stop 'em from doing the same if they weren't bone lazy and pigheaded. You can't answer that, John. You want an example of what honest work will do, you just show the Indians this place of mine."

"I agree you've made a fine farm of it," said John. "But scarcely one an Indian could hope to obtain by any amount of work. That's not my point. The whole purpose of this mission was for red men and white to live together as Christians. They know well enough that in other towns in New England captured Indians are still held as slaves. Some of them are suspicious even yet that this mission is only a trick to inveigle them into servitude. What can they possibly think if you bring in slaves who are dark-skinned like themselves? Besides, you are their Christian example. How can you justify buying human souls as property like land or horses?"

My father held himself from speaking until he could do so reasonably. "Look here, John," he said, his face red from the effort, "I have the greatest admiration for the work you're doing here. More than that, I came out here to help you, and you know well enough I've kept my end of the bargain. As moderator of this town I give a lot more time than the job calls for. I put up with plenty of nonsense trying to carry on a town meeting with a couple of redskins for selectmen who know's much about running a town as a porcupine. Their votes are as good as mine, and I'm not complaining, but you just might as well understand one thing. Up here in my own house, that's another matter. I aim to run my farm and my household as I please, and no Indian has a vote up here. I don't intend to keep my wife drudging like a squaw when I can do something to prevent it. And you know's well as I do that a farm this size needs a field hand to keep it going."

The two men faced each other across the table, John white-faced and stern, his dark eyes hot, my father red and angry, his eyes like icicles. John swallowed and opened his mouth to speak, and Abigail suddenly put out her hand to him. Before she could touch him, he stood up and left our house without a word, and Abigail, with tears in her eyes, picked up Electa and hurried after him. It was the first time there had been an open disagreement in our family circle.

So Moni and Candace were added to our household, and it very soon came to be the most natural thing in the world to have them there. Though Candace was intended as a gift for our mother, she brought about little change in the life of a woman who could never adjust to idleness. It was we children who benefited the most. Judith and Elijah and I hung about the kitchen, begging small treats that had never before been accessible, and coaxing Candace to tell us, in her soft, almost incomprehensible English, strange tales of her life in Jamaica.

Moni made a pet of Elijah, teaching him how to care for the horses, taking him with him into the woods to hunt squirrels and partridge. Looking back, I cannot imagine how we could have grown up without them. Though they kept apart, having no use for the "heathen," surely the most suspicious Indian could scarcely have missed the smiling content with which they went about their work. But I believe that, though he never spoke of it again, and could have had no complaint about their treatment, John Sergeant never really forgave my father their presence in our midst.

Without a doubt it was watching Candace in mother's kitchen that caused Abigail to abandon her long-standing prohibition. With Electa to tend, Abigail was finding it harder to maintain the perfection she cherished in her household, and she often looked strained and tired. She told us one morning that she had agreed to John's plan and would take an Indian girl into her house to train, that John was pleased and grateful, confident that now that she had taken the lead he could persuade the other Hill families to do the same.

John seemed to do nothing about choosing a girl, however, though I myself heard her remind him several times, and finally one day, when I was in her house to help with the washing and bleaching of new linen, he admitted to her that there had been a delay in the plan.

"Timothy Woodbridge objects to placing any of the girls in our Stockbridge families," he told her. "He thinks the Indians are still too suspicious of our intentions and that such a move would alarm them."

Abigail straightened her back to stare at him, her hands dripping. "How long has Timothy Woodbridge been the one to decide?"

"I believe he's right," John answered. "Though I admit I'm disappointed. As a teacher he knows what is best for them."

"He's not thinking what's best for them at all," she flared. "He's just doing it to spite me."

"Why on earth should he want to spite you?"

Her lips tightened, and I thought she did not want to answer him. "Abigail Woodbridge and I had some words, that's all," she said then. "She's just childish enough to have repeated it all to him."

"Words — about what?"

She flushed. "She had the impertinence to tell me I was putting on airs, dressing Electa too fancy. The way her brats run around in rags with their noses running!"

John looked unhappy. "I'm sure she was trying to be helpful. Aren't you a little hard on her? You don't always understand that other people's talents may be lesser than your own."

"She could try. Most women could keep a house that size with one hand."

"If you could have seen her when she first came here you might understand her better. She was such a shy child — even more timid than Judith. She was the only white woman all that first year, and desperately homesick. I wish you could bring yourself to be a little kinder to her."

"I'm kind enough," said Abigail, plunging her hands into the suds again. "She's just ridiculously sensitive. And now of course he's taken her part."

"I'm sure there's no connection. As I say, in this matter I rely on his judgment. I've already written to Colonel Stoddard in Northampton to ask his assistance in finding homes for the girls."

Abigail glared after him, furious and helpless. "Northampton!" she muttered, as he went through the door. "Do you know I thought of this plan in the first place? And now some strangers get all the benefit while I go on drudging. It will serve him right if I get to look like Abby Woodbridge!" But the thought of this made me laugh outright, so that she kept any further thoughts to herself, only went furiously at her scrubbing.

Within a few weeks, word came that Colonel Stoddard had found a place for two girls, and for others in neighboring towns. John was much gratified; I am sure it never crossed his mind that the Northampton women might benefit. But he had great difficulty in persuading the Indian families. As always, they were wary and needed endless consultations among themselves. Aaron stubbornly refused to send his daughter. Konkapot finally agreed, out of his devotion to John, though Catharine was younger than John thought advisable. Catharine made no fuss about it and uttered no word of disloyalty, but she went about looking so downcast that I attempted to intercede for her with Abigail.

"None of them want to go," I told her. "Catharine says they will just pine away so far from home." I did not think it wise to say that Catharine had told me that none of the girls would stay.

"They are very foolish girls," Abigail said crisply. "Can't they understand when people are trying to help them? This will make them better wives and mothers."

"More likely no one will marry them," said Eph, over his cup of tea. "Not if they get white women's ideas about not doing the men's work for them."

"It would be a good idea," said Abigail. "Maybe the men would have to hump themselves a little."

Eph chuckled. "Aaron has a legend for that," he told her. "Claims the Great Spirit knew what he was doing when he gave the red man a bow and arrow and the white man a plow. Men were meant for war and hunting, women and hedgehogs were meant for scratching the earth. Not a flattering picture. He was too tactful to specify which class he'd put me into, female or hedgehog. Even so, I find the idea appealing. I've always thought English women were overpampered."

"You're as bad as Liza," said Abigail, refusing to rise to his bait. "The Indians are supposed to be learning from us to be civilized."

"Liza has found it can work both ways," said Eph. "It's certain I've learned more from Hendrick than he'll ever learn from me."

Abigail's head went up sharply. "I thought Hendrick was here but three days."

"He drops in to visit me from time to time," said Eph, knowing quite well he was disconcerting her. "It's a friendship I value." Abigail sniffed, withholding her comment.

Within a week Catharine came back. She had walked nearly thirty miles on bare feet, disdainfully leaving behind the English shoes she had been given. Abigail took me to task about it.

"She had to wait on the family at meals," I tried to explain to her. Better not to let her know the indignation and scorn with which Catharine had told me of those days in Northampton. No use to tell her of the indignity of the tasks she had been given to do, of the cruelty of the white children who had laughed at her, of the coldness and indifference she had read in all their faces. "She was homesick," I said instead, the simplest and truest of all the reasons.

"How could any girl be homesick for that miserable pig sty of Konkapot's? Why those girls were given good beds to sleep in with clean linen. They're an ungrateful lot, as I always said."

I could only be thankful it had not been her house that Catharine had spurned, because I knew it would have come to the same end just as surely, and because I could not have borne to have to choose between them.

The grief of the Indian families was short. Within a few

weeks the last of the seven girls had been restored to them. Disheartened though he was, John had no intention of giving up.

"We will have to think of a better plan," he said. "Some of the English women went out of their way to be kind, but I'm afraid none of them really understood what we intended. The girls all claim they were put to work as servants. And though they were well-treated, away from their own people they sickened, and so gave the impression of being stupid or unwilling. We will have to work out a method of training them right here in the town, and I am beginning to perceive how it can be done."

14. THE NEW PLAN John had devised was a Charity House. By the time he and Abigail came to supper on the next Sabbath, he was totally immersed in it, and he could no more have refrained from talking about it than Electa could keep from her happy chirruping.

"It is the logical answer," he told us. "Since the Indians can't abide sending their children far from home, we must provide a boarding school for their instruction here in the town."

My father pushed back his chair, passed his napkin over his chin and pronounced his own benediction on the meal by a satisfied belch. "Perfectly good school already," he said finally.

"This will not interfere with Timothy's school," John explained. "We will take first some of the boys who have already left him and who have nothing to do. The trouble is, the moment they stop learning and go back to their wigwams, they are swallowed up in ignorance and idleness again, and most of what they have learned is undone. It is the idleness that is our greatest obstacle. We must teach them the habit of industry, and to do this we must remove them from their families at an early age."

Couldn't he see, I wondered, that my father had had his fill of
sermons for the day and that mother wanted the table cleared?
Josiah and Elijah, being always more privileged, had already excused themselves and vanished. Judith and I fidgeted, tired of
sitting still. But John's eyes were beginning to glow.

"You see, at this school I would have them learn other skills
than reading and writing, and it would be done by having them
work together to support themselves. The months when I had
the boys in the house with me were in many ways the best time
we've ever had, the most productive. In the evenings I taught
them to do useful things, the simple things a man has to do on a
farm, mending harness and making tools. In the morning there
were the animals to feed and the cow to milk. There was no
idleness, yet they were happy. A pity I ever had to let them go
back to their families."

Abigail broke in. "You found it too great a burden then. Now
when you have a family of your own, would you find it any
easier?"

"Indeed, my dear, I'm not planning to do this alone. We will
engage two new teachers, one to tend their studies and one to
oversee the labor of the farm."

My father briefly raised one heavy eyelid. "What farm?" he
inquired.

"I am certain the Indians will contribute the land, and the boys
themselves can help to erect the building."

"Where's the money coming from?"

"God provides for his own work. There are our loyal friends
in England. I am confident there are many here in Massachusetts
province who will donate funds when they see the great benefit
that will come of it."

"Humph."

"It shouldn't be long before such a school would be entirely
self-sustaining, once they learn how to rotate the crops and we

get a stock of cattle, and with the labor divided so that no great burden would fall on anyone. I've been thinking too that we should include one or two boys from the other tribes, the Mohawks, for example. They could go back to their people and share what they have learned. In that way the gospel might eventually reach even the remotest tribes."

My father opened both eyes and stared at his son-in-law, a flicker of interest glinting behind his stupor. "Mohawks," he said thoughtfully. "Maybe you've got a good idea there, John. But some other time. After supper I like to give my wits a rest."

From that day on John was possessed by his plan. On the rare moments when I saw him sit by his own hearth, his eyes were brooding, his gaze following the leap of flames but failing to mark the glowing cinder that shot from them and blinked a few inches from his foot, so that Abigail had to drop her knitting and jump to stamp it out. At other less convenient times, especially at my father's table, he could not stop talking, his words rushing forth so that any conversation was impossible.

"A year to build the house," he told us. "It will take at least that, though we should be able to occupy it and finish the interior as we find the time. And we must begin at once to look for teachers; the right ones will be difficult to find.

"One reason they make so little progress in our language is that they see no need for it," he explained. "If they live together, if they speak English at table and about their work, then they will learn it naturally. And religion will be the same, a part of their daily lives till they come to love and desire it . . .

"And soon we must include the girls as well. As soon as possible there must be a second house for them, with a teacher of their own, where they can learn to cook and sew and manage a household thriftily."

He had outlined his plan in a long letter to Dr. Colman in Boston. Now he began to write other letters to every man in England or the colonies who might possibly help him. He did not neglect his Indians, nor did he skimp on his sermons; instead he cut into his meager ration of sleep, sitting late in his study, wrapped in his heavy coat.

Draft after draft, crumpled and dropped on the floor, I saw Abigail gather in the morning and use to quicken the smoldering coals in her hearth. No one could accuse him of waste, I thought. Every inch of the paper would be covered with his fine cramped script, and when he had reached the bottom of the page he had turned the sheet and written back again between the lines, so that one had to squint to make out the words. Once I saw Abigail smooth out a letter and read it silently, then crumple it fiercely in her hand and hurl it into the flames.

"How can he humble himself like that?" she cried. "What have they ever done to deserve such gratitude?"

Some of these letters of John's were gathered in recent years and published in a volume. Reading them at last, I was swept once more by his vision. No wonder Mr. Hollis in England put such trust in him. With a few more such benefactors, could the miracle have been accomplished? Yet at the same time my heart ached, remembering the patient hours consumed in their writing. Which was the letter, I wondered, that Abigail had crumpled that day? The one that voiced his hope of raising the Indians "into the condition of a civil, industrious and polished people"? Or the one that assured his benefactors that he had "no expectation of any personal benefit"?

The letters which came in response tossed John like a boy in an Indian blanket. A scant dozen encouraging words from a distant gentleman in London were enough to lift him high. He carried them about with him and read them aloud to us all. Others he pocketed with a sober face. I know that far more letters went out from his study than ever returned to him.

"Listen to this!" He came hurrying up the Hill one spring

morning. "Dr. Colman has had my letter printed and has sent copies to seventy people, even to Governor Shirley. And a Dr. Watts in London has taken up a collection for us." He caught his wife up in a quick boyish hug, bent to tousle Electa's hair, and was off to share the letter with Timothy Woodbridge. Abigail stood in the middle of the room.

"There is no end to it," she said, her voice flattened out.

"But seventy copies!" I tried to cheer her. "Surely some money will come from all that."

"How much?" she answered. "A few pounds at best, and he needs hundreds. At this rate it will be years."

It troubled me to look at her. There was a change in Abigail, and it seemed to me impossible that John could not have noticed. It had come about slowly, perhaps beginning with the time he had devised his plan for the boarding school. Or perhaps, in actuality, much before this time, so far before that Electa's birth, almost two years ago, had only delayed the change and been powerless to stem it.

There were days now when Abigail's eyes were as dimmed as mother's, and all the lightness had gone from her step. She took no pleasure in her work. And though she smiled, the only time the smile ever reached her eyes was when she looked at Electa.

It is the new baby, I thought, for Abigail was carrying her second child. She always feels wretched, and afterwards she will be happy the way she was before.

15. But across all these years, some words come back to me. They were never meant for my ears, and never understood, and therefore, as such things sometimes are, never forgotten.

I was spending the night in Abigail's house, as I was often allowed to do when there was special work on hand. I remember that John came up the hill late for the evening meal, and that he gulped it down abstractedly, speaking little. Afterwards, before the fire, he sat nodding over his book like an old man. Presently Abigail moved softly to shift the candle stand so that the light would not fall across his face, and he opened his eyes and smiled at her. "Don't make me too comfortable, my dear," he said. "There is still work to be done."

She put her hand on his sleeve. "Don't work any more to-night," she coaxed. "You look so tired. Stay here with Liza and me."

He smiled again, but he pulled himself out of the chair nonetheless, and went into his study and shut the door. Abigail sighed and picked up her knitting, and I went back to my book. But through the words I was aware of Abigail's restlessness.

"Why does he have to work so hard?" I asked her finally. "Is he writing letters about the school?"

"It's not just the letters," she explained, glad to talk to someone. "He's making an Indian dictionary. And the commissioners in Boston expect regular reports, and they aren't satisfied with short ones. They have no conception of the time it takes to prepare four sermons a week. The Indian sermons he writes out in English and then translates, word for word."

She was defending him, it seemed, but to me or to herself? She piled his tasks one on the other, like grievances. And then she went back to her knitting, a shadow across her face. She let me stay with her long past my usual hour, and the fire was dying down when finally she sent me upstairs to the icy spare bedroom. I took with me a warming pan, and I left the door open, not wanting to shut out any heat that might find its way upwards.

Much later, how much I could not know, I came instantly awake in the darkness. A sharp sound, a sob or a cry, echoed along my senses, and as I lay waiting to hear it again, John's voice came overloud, almost unrecognizable, from the room below.

"What about me?" this voice cried out, with its strange anger. "Do you think I am not tempted, almost beyond my strength?"

Abigail's words I could not distinguish; they were soft and blurred, and I knew that she was weeping.

When John spoke again, his voice was more his own. "You must try to understand," he said. "God's ways are not easy. This is his manner of testing me. He knew that I was not tempted by money or by comfort. But he knows that I am still weak."

"Why is our marriage a temptation?" she cried out. "Do you mean it is a sin?"

"No," he answered. "Our marriage is of God and he has blessed it."

"Then I don't understand."

"Such happiness can make me selfish. It can make me forget the work he has set me to do. God intends that I must choose, every day of my life."

"Then he is cruel. I don't ask you to choose. I only want a little of your time, just a little. Does God mean that the Indians should have it all?"

"I don't know. I have asked that too. But the answer is that the work is never finished. Sometimes, nights at my desk, I cry out against him. And then I am ashamed. When he has given me so much, how can I grudge the time which belongs to him?"

I could barely hear her voice. I think she said, "I grudge it." And then his ragged voice came again, not harsh now but pleading.

"You mustn't. Abby, you can't. Unless you help me I will fail!"

She sobbed aloud, and then the sound was muffled, as though she had hidden her face. After a time her crying died away. I waited, tense and afraid, but neither of them spoke again. There was nothing but silence, so long-continued that at last I went uneasily back to sleep.

In the morning, though I was fearful to face Abigail, there were no signs of tears. Instead, the shadow seemed to be gone, and she looked pretty and content, humming softly as she ladled water from the kettle. "Go tell John his tea is ready," she told me, smiling.

Had he worked all night? He sat at his desk, huddled in his worn coat, a woolen scarf wound about his head, scraps of old blanket about his feet, bent close over the page to follow his neat small script. He looked up and smiled at me so radiantly that I thought for a moment I must have dreamed those angry words. But I know that I did not.

The Threshold

1742

I. To EVERYTHING there is a season, Stephen reads from Ecclesiastes, a time to keep and a time to cast away. For a child the years of keeping seem very long and the time for casting away can be abrupt and precisely remembered. The year of our coming to Stockbridge had been such a time for me, and after that there was another long time of keeping. In my thirteenth year it was time to shed my childhood, but the casting away was a gradual thing, and I cannot tell the moment at which it took place. Instead, the room I had lived in for a long time rearranged itself, the familiar furniture appeared strange and unpredictable, and the secure enclosing walls dissolved and shifted like walls of ice, now opaque, now treacherously thin.

I think my mother was first responsible, though unwittingly, for she continued to think of me as a child. But that winter there was much sickness both on the Hill and on the Plain and mother's skill was frequently needed. She had a fine stock of remedies. The first summer day that we had come here to the Hill, even before the straw mattresses were laid, she had coaxed Josiah into spading a plot of ground for the seeds she had brought from Newton, and that first late summer there were bunches of fennel and saffron and tansy and wormwood drying along the rafters of our new house. Later the Indian women tried to explain to her the benefits of native plants, but mother was always suspicious of them and swore by the English herbs her mother and grand-mother had cultivated. This year, more than ever before, she was grateful for them.

When she observed from watching me with Abigail's Electa that I had what she called a way with children, she began to take me with her. Her plan was that I should amuse the children and keep them from underfoot, but often several members of a family were stricken at once, and then my hands were needed for fetching and carrying and holding and steadying, and sometimes I proved apter than she at making a child lie still while she tied a bandage or probed a festering blister. Before long I learned to take over these small tasks myself. If necessary I could not only boil the linseed to make a poultice but I could persuade a screaming child to let me lay it against a feverish chest. In the course of that year I stored away much of the knowledge that still serves me, for mother's function has, many years since, fallen to me. No one was to blame that some of this knowledge found me unready; when one opens the door one cannot pick and choose what will enter. Sick and frightened women, needing mother's sympathy even more than her remedies, did not always guard their tongues before her silent unheeded assistant.

There were some things about which mother was adamant. She was forever making me wash my hands with soap so harsh it made my eyelids sting. I have often wondered if there might not be some virtue in such cleanliness, for strangely neither she nor I contracted the maladies we tended. Another rule was that I should have nothing to do with childbirth; I was a grown woman before I was allowed to see a baby not already wrapped clean in its swaddling clothes. Even at thirteen this seemed to me illogi-cal, for I had witnessed birthings in the field and stable, I had no fear of blood, and pain seemed to me a small price to pay for a new life. There were other lessons that year that were far more deeply troubling than this from which I was so carefully shielded.

I learned, for example, that though it was supposed that a woman would not become pregnant so long as she nursed a child, this had not worked for my aunt Anna Jones, whose eighth child had started before her seventh was six months old, and that the herbs her mother-in-law had told her of had not worked either but had only made her so sick she hadn't cared whether she lived or died. Now, remembering my aunt Anna's fourteen children, I can better understand, though still not altogether forgive, the bitterness she did not bother to hide. I learned also that Mrs. Pixley's niece in Connecticut had had her young one six months after her wedding, too soon, no matter what the most charitable might say, and Mrs. Pixley's sister could scarcely hold up her head for shame. The realization that a child could come into the world unwanted jarred the walls of my own childhood and left an ugly fissure which would not mend. It seemed to me — and it still does — an injustice too cruel to be borne.

Other things too I glimpsed through the thinning walls. I knew that Mrs. Willard, no matter how grateful she tried to sound, had not really wanted mother to pull her paralyzed father through his last bout of palsy. And once, as mother hoisted up that stiffened useless body and the gruel I held spilled over and ran down the quivering stubbly chin, I read the same wish quite plain in the old man's eyes. This was knowledge I could not face steadily. Only at times did I wake in the night and know that life, which rushed so gladly through one's body, could come to be no more than the chain that fastened a dog to the wheel of a spit.

I never spoke of these things to my mother, but her conscience may perhaps have troubled her, for when, with the spring, the sickness lightened, she found excuses for not taking me with her. She began to urge me to go with Judith to visit the Woodbridge girls or the Jones girls, or to plan sewing bees or little parties to bring them to our house. I knew this was mainly for the benefit of Judith, who was outgrowing somewhat her childish invalidism and longed now to be a part of the close-knit group of girls on the Hill. Though shy, she soon made a place for herself as I could not. The things they talked about bored me. I had no interest in fashions, nor in brewing tansy lotions to whiten my complexion. Sewing I could tolerate provided it had a practical aim soon accomplished; embroidery was a frustration of knotted threads. The twittering speculation about the few clumsy boys we had grown up with filled me with scorn but put me also at a disadvantage. I preferred Catharine's company; by contrast her gentle acceptance surrounded me with content.

Konkapot had, in compliance with the town plan, replaced his wigwam with an English cabin, though he chose still to keep it remote from the village. Many days I spent more hours in this house than in my own. Sometimes I carried my chores with me and knit a sock or mitten for Elijah while Catharine stitched together deerskin leggings and moccasins for her brothers. She was skilled at beadwork and I loved to watch her. The Indian women, once they had seen them, could never get enough of the small glass beads imported from England; father included quantities of them in every order. The wampum the women had always used was costly, every bead having to be ground and drilled and polished by hand. The glass beads, besides being so cheap that they could be purchased by the handful and clustered lavishly on every sort of garment, were shinier than wampum and made in many brilliant colors. Catharine delighted in them and I delighted in watching the designs that emerged from under her clever fingers.

Contributing to my separation from the English girls was the gift that came to me this year, the second precious gift of my lifetime, in recompense for my first deep sorrow.

Adam, who had been missing all one morning, came crawling at noon to the back door with a hideous bloated face. At first I could not grasp what had happened, till I saw that the bloody bristles that covered his nose and head were porcupine quills. He must have run out his first madness before coming home, for he was exhausted now and could only lie and look at me with eyes almost swollen shut. When I moved to touch him, he pulled back his lip in an ugly snarl I had never heard before. My father, bending over him, barely drew back his hand in time.

"Same thing happened to a hound my father trained," father told me. "Poor critter."

"How can I get them out?" I pleaded.

"You can't, he won't tolerate it." He hesitated. "Only one thing to do, Liza."

I would not let him, I who had never opposed my father in my life. Some of Adam's madness entered into my brain. I would not move from the dog's side, and if my father had brought a gun I think I would have thrown myself against it. They all came, mother and Josiah and even Elijah, and in the end they backed away and left us alone. I sat all afternoon long on the doorstep. Sometimes Adam jerked to his feet and ran in crazy yelping circles, then dropped, his sides heaving, a thin line of foam along his lip. He did not seem to be aware of me, but each time he came back to lie near me, and I was sure he knew that I was there.

At supper time Eph, who had been all day riding from Springfield, stood beside me, and I knew why I had been waiting.

"Liza," he said, not touching me. I pressed my face against my knees.

"Liza," he said again.

I was able to say at last, "Will you do it, Eph?"

"Yes."

I got up and went into the house and up to my room without looking back and stood there with my hands hard against my ears. Later Eph took me to the patch of fresh earth under the black walnut tree and sat beside me there for a long time without saying anything.

The next week on his way to Court Eph stopped by for father's orders. My father dictated his list, and at the end he cleared his throat and added gruffly, "Bring back another dog if you can."

"I don't want another dog," I spoke up.

"You sure of that, Liza?" Eph asked.

"Yes."

He did not bring back a dog. For my birthday two months later he brought me a two-year-old mare, a dainty creature, fickle, capricious, totally unlike Adam, yet in her own way demanding like him my instant love.

"I never heard such damned nonsense," my father fumed. "Isn't a girl in Stockbridge has a horse of her own, or needs one. Who's going to take care of it?"

"Elizabeth is," said Eph. "Just one thing," he said to me. "I want your word you won't ride far in the woods without Catharine." When had he observed how deeply I envied Catharine the freedom of her father's ponies?

I named my mare Nippe, the Mahican word for water, which soon became shortened to a rather unfeminine Nip. All that summer of my thirteenth year I rode with Catharine along the forest trails. I remember it as a period of respite; the matted passageway of the forest enclosed us, the earth thick with moss and fern slowed our steps, all holding us back for a brief time of grace. I wonder if Catharine ever remembered it so, for I know now that such a deferment was for an Indian girl even more remarkable than for me, a privilege made possible only by her father's high position in the tribe and by his indulgence.

The reprieve was short. In August Abigail's child was born, a boy, baptized as Erastus. More than ever she needed and demanded my help. And Catharine's mother died of the consumption to which this tribe has always been so susceptible. With a cabin and garden to tend and two hungry boys to feed, Konkapot could no longer afford to be indulgent toward a daughter.

2. ONE MORNING in February I was dressing Erastus by the fire, dawdling, loath to put him back into the hampering baby clothes. He was a plump, no-nonsense sort of baby, with the Williams blond plumpness and his father's earnest cheerfulness. Abigail was setting the milk to curdle. Neither of us heard John coming till we saw him standing just inside the doorway in his snowy boots. Though he was head of his household, he was still respectful of Abigail's clean-sanded floor.

"Letter!" He waved a bundle of papers at his wife.

So the pack had come in. I abandoned the game with Rata and began to push his wandering arms into the tiny gathered sleeves. On the day the pack arrived I was allowed to help my father to unwrap and record and store away on the shelves the contents of the sacks that were lifted from the horses' backs. But in my haste I still noticed how oddly Abigail stood eying the letters in her husband's hand. I had taken for granted John must have a new gift for his school, and I was surprised when she asked coldly, "From the same old creditors?"

"A letter from Dr. Colman in Boston."

Abigail set down the milk jug so abruptly that a white arc leaped across the table. "They're giving you more salary!"

"No." Some of the eagerness dropped away from John's face. "Not this time. They've appointed another missionary to this territory. Name of David Brainerd. He's going to work in Kaunameek."

Abigail carefully wiped up the milk spatters. When she spoke her voice was thin and cool. "That's something, I suppose. At least you won't have to be riding over and back in all weathers."

"I don't mind the riding," John said. "But it's impossible for me to give them what they need. By the date, he should be coming through any day now."

"He'll have to stay here, I suppose."

"For a day or two at least. He'll be new at all this."

The cloth in Abigail's hand moved back and forth on the table slowly.

"There was another letter," said John hesitantly. She looked up.

"From the County Association. They've invited me to preach at the Association meeting in Springfield in April."

There was a silence so long that I stopped pulling at Rata's sleeve to listen. Why doesn't she say something? I wondered. John looked exactly the way Elijah did when he brought down a grouse or a squirrel and wanted someone to notice. And then, as though John's words had been delayed in reaching her, Abby's face slowly filled with light. "Why John, that's wonderful!"

If he had noticed the hesitation, he forgot it instantly. "We can go together. It will be a chance for you to have a holiday and to see your cousins. That's really why I came up at once. I thought it would give you something to think about."

"You're the one to be thinking. You'll have to give them a sermon that will make them sit straight up in the pews. Oh, John, it might even be published!" She had crossed the distance now from table to doorway and put her arms around his neck. I remember thinking how long it had been since I had seen Abby do that. "I'll be so proud of you.

"It's about time," she went on. "You can preach as fine a sermon as any of them. You ought to be having invitations like this from every county in New England. You will, once they've heard you."

"I couldn't spare the time," he protested, looking enormously pleased nevertheless.

With one corner of my mind I noted how briskly my sister moved about after John had gone back down the hill. I was hurrying now to get Rata's frock buttoned, my thoughts full of the goods being unpacked in my absence. I looked up as the bustle ceased abruptly and saw her standing by the table. "Oh," she said, and sank down on the bench and hid her face in her arms on the table top.

I set Erastus down in his cradle and went over to her.

"I never thought." Her voice was muffled. "What can I wear?"

"There'll be plenty of time to make a dress," I said. "I can mind the children while you work on it."

"What would I make it out of?" She raised her head and her eyes were dry and bright. "We need every bit of cloth I can weave to keep us decently covered. And even if I had any to spare, do you think I could go to Springfield in homespun? Every woman there will have on a new silk."

"Perhaps in the pack —"

"It doesn't make any difference what's in the pack. Did you see those other letters, the ones he didn't talk about? Bills! We owe money everywhere. For the glass in the windows, for that chair, for the dresser and the books John ordered last winter. We'll never even get the house paid for — never! I'm sick and tired of living like a pauper, being humiliated. Just for a parcel of ungrateful Indians, who'd rather be left alone anyway. And now he thinks I can simply pick up and go to Springfield looking like a scarecrow before all those Williamses."

There was nothing I could think of to say. Presently she was aware of me still standing awkwardly beside her.

"Go along, Liza," she said. "Father will be needing you."

I went with relief but no longer with eagerness. The unwonted sight of Abby with her head down had brought suddenly to the surface all the uneasiness of the past months, the vague troubling memories. I had not known about the creditors; it was the first time I had heard that John was in debt. But more than that, the bitterness in Abigail's voice had pierced fully through the dream to which I had clung. I did not want to look through the rift, to see that Abigail's world was flawed or that she was less than perfectly happy in it. So on that day I deliberately outran my thoughts, and I arrived breathless at my father's store, where the new goods piled on the counter distracted me.

3. A FEW IN THIS town still misdoubt my father's store. His rapid prospering in this remote place has been to many, I know, a matter of suspicion. But my father had a sort of precognition in affairs of business. Every venture he undertook turned out to be profitable. He had realized from the beginning, for example, that land in the new town would increase in value, and he never missed an opportunity to acquire more of it. Though

the settlers who came later swore that the prices he set on his acres were outright robbery, they always paid what he asked in the end.

John Sergeant, who was impatient with practical details and also too easily imposed upon, requested my father soon after we came to Stockbridge to take over the management of the clothing and supplies which arrived several times a year from the Commission of Indian Affairs in Boston. This was a task my father enjoyed, sorting over the goods and doling out to the Indians the shirts and blankets and hatchets and pigeon-shot and tobacco and kettles. There was always a quantity of the cheap woolen cloth called stroud made up in black or red, and for the women gaitering and worsted hose and calico and ribbons, all shoddy and bright-colored. My father kept an accurate account, controlling the portioning with a tight hand to make sure no Indian got more than his due, not bothering that this increased the resentment they had shown toward him almost from his first coming.

Before long, as a matter of convenience, he was taking orders from the English families as well, adding from time to time on his own account items which he thought his neighbors would fancy once they saw them. He seldom made a mistake. By the time I was twelve years old he had taken over the lower two rooms of a small house on the Plain where he stored his goods and carried on his transactions. Everyone called it the Williams store, and though it would be some years before the enterprise justified that title, it grew, like all father's ventures, into a flourishing business.

By the time another month had passed and the pack horse loaded with panniers came over the trail again, I had forgotten the disturbing moment in Abigail's kitchen. Only as I helped my father to count out the orders did I suddenly remember.

"What pretty cloth!" I opened the bolt a width and smoothed

my hand over it. It was a fine tight-woven grogram of a clear blue.

"Hmm," commented my father, coming to look over my shoulder. "The girl knows what she wants. But the Lord alone knows how John can pay for it."

"You mean it's for Abby?"

"She ordered it. The finest, she took pains to make sure right on the order, And she's got it. At the finest price, too."

"Can I take it up to her?"

"Wait till I make out a bill to take with it. And she needn't be rolling her eyes at me. Family is one thing and business is another. If she wants goods like that from my store, she pays for them."

Abigail's fingers trembled as she unrolled the bolt of cloth. "I couldn't have done better had I gone all the way to Boston," she exulted. "And I've worked out the pattern down to the last buttonhole. A skirt like the one Anna Jones' sister wore when she visited here last fall. And the neckline like my dove-colored lutestring. Even if it's not the latest thing, it looks well on me. And the sleeves —"

"Father sent the account along with it." I nudged it under her elbow.

"He would. I'm afraid to look." She did look, hurriedly, and crossed the room to toss the slip of paper into the fire. "Best get rid of that before John sees it," she said briskly.

"Won't he have to see it?"

"No, he won't. I'll speak to father about it. He's the one who manages the fund."

"The commissioners' fund? Does the dress come out of that?"

"Yes, it does," said Abby, closing her mouth tightly as though she realized she had said too much.

"But that is just for the Indians."

Abby whirled on me. "Look here, Liza. This is none of your business. You ought to be in my shoes for one minute. It's a fine thing for rich men off in London and Boston to send money to feed and clothe the heathen. What about their minister with barely enough salary to keep the roof over his head? Do they ever think what his family is wearing? We're supposed to set an example for the Indians. If Mr. Hollis wants me to set a good example he can pay for it for once. And you needn't look so horrified. I've more than earned that money in ways you don't know anything about. And if there's a Mrs. Hollis, I know she'd back me up."

I told myself that she was right. I said it over and over in my mind, especially on the Sabbath when Abigail walked into meeting in the blue dress, the week after John had made what everyone reported was a splendid sermon in Springfield. I saw the looks some of the women exchanged from one pew to another, looks which said as plainly as words that some people thought themselves too fine for Stockbridge. Watching that slender erect figure with its proud lift of head, I was filled with pride for my sister. Abigail *was* too fine for Stockbridge. At least she had something that none of the others could touch. I looked at the thick slumped bodies of the Indian women in their shapeless hodge-podge of garments, at the dresses they embroidered with such care and skill and then indifferently soiled with grease and smoke, and I looked back at Abigail, as fine-cut and polished as a precious stone. Truly, Mr. Hollis would have delighted in Abigail's example.

Yet whenever I stepped into Abigail's house I was ashamed of the questions that nagged at me. The new brass warming pan. The little white kid shoes for Electa. The cone of clear hard sugar. Had John put the bills away in his desk with his patient sigh? Or had he seen them at all? It was none of my business, as

Abigail had told me. But I had learned now that the small things I had taken for granted all my life did not come over the trail for the mere ordering. One way or another they had to be paid for.

4. To THE END of his days my father prided himself on his piety; it was forever a satisfaction to him that he had reared his family by the gospel. Each morning of our childhood he read aloud from the Bible at breakfast, allowing none of us to be absent. He made it a rule that Moni and Candace leave their work to stand just inside the door to listen. Each evening he brought us all to our knees. Every Sabbath, when the first blast of the conch shell bleated from the Plain, he expected us to be dressed for meeting; the only exception he ever made was rarely for Judith. So fixed was the pattern he established, I would have said it could never be broken.

I did not really dislike the Sabbath meeting. John Sergeant's voice sometimes lulled me into such drowsiness that it was anguish to hold up my eyelids; at most times it served as a gentle curtain behind which I could pursue my own thoughts. After my thirteenth birthday a change took place. Intermittently now the smooth curtain of sound was broken by isolated words thrusting through to my attention. I began to listen for them and to sort over like colored pebbles the words I gathered, each word, like a pebble, possessing its individual feel and texture.

The word Grace was smooth and warm as though it had lain long in the sun. Grace was the immeasurable gift of God, freely and generously bestowed upon us all, even the Indians, available as the sunshine itself to which we had only to lift our faces.

Sin was an uncomfortable word, in my childhood small and

sharp, recalling a sweet that should have been left on the shelf, or a falsehood that should have been left unspoken. Imperceptibly it had grown, becoming now too large to hold in my hand or mind, monstrous as the killing of one man by another, troubling as the secret thing which happened between a man and a woman. It was the formless evil that crept out from the deep rocky place or lay coiled in the brush where a whip had fallen.

Hell was another disturbing word, though John did not use it often, finding it perhaps as grating and repellent as it seemed to me. Sometimes he reminded us of danger, but always gently. In our meetinghouse the threatening smoke of hell was quickly dissipated in the sun-filled sky.

Though I had parroted the catechism from the time I could talk, I found my way into religion by way of the Indian sermons, which by the time I was twelve I could follow quite easily. Though the Hill families sat through these resignedly, only bringing back their attention in time for the two-hour English sermon, I discovered that John habitually pursued the same theme throughout a Sabbath morning, and that if I gave the Indian version my careful attention I could safely let my mind wander during the elaboration prepared for my elders. When father took a notion to test our memories at the dinner table I could acquit myself at least as well as Judith, who honestly tried her best to concentrate on the long sermon. Though my glibness sometimes provoked her to tears, I kept my secret, for it would have been of no use to her, but eventually I took pity on Elijah and passed it on to him. There were disastrous times when I realized too late that John must have delivered quite different sermons. But Elijah and I tacitly understood that father's loud suspicion often concealed an uncertain recollection, and that if we stuck firmly to our statements he would let the matter drop. We never questioned his sincerity; I would not question it even now. Though he had no fondness for theological discourse, my father knew what he believed, and his stubborn Calvinist convictions made up one of the secure walls of my childhood. Up to the time of David Brainerd's coming it had never occurred to me that a single word of Christian doctrine could be a matter of debate.

The new missionary came over the trail late one evening and spent the night with John and Abigail. I did not see him. Abigail came in much dispirited as the family was finishing breakfast next morning and sank wearily into the chair Eph pulled up for her. The visitor had kept them up half the night and had insisted that John set out with him soon after dawn to show him the way to Kaunameek. He had taken with him to serve as interpreter John Wauwaupequunanut, who had acquired an unpredictable knowledge of English.

"John tried to persuade Mr. Brainerd to rest for a day," Abigail told us. "He wasn't fit to go on. But nothing would do but he had to get to Kaunameek. You'd have thought every Indian there would be snatched straight down to hell if he waited an hour."

Eph chuckled. "You've something to learn about Enthusiasm, my girl," he informed her.

"Well, I don't care for what I've observed of it," Abigail said. "I wonder what help he's going to be to John. He looked half sick to me and much too excitable."

"An Edwards man," father put in. "I could of told you he'd be New Light the minute I knew Edwards had a hand in hiring him."

"He was expelled from Yale," Eph said thoughtfully. "He made the mistake of saying that his tutor had no more Grace than a chair, and then refused to make a public apology. You've got to admire him for sticking to his principles when it cost him a degree."

"Nothing to admire about it," father contradicted. "Plain damnfool impertinence. I've heard since Tennant preached in New Haven the students have got completely out of hand. Now I suppose this young whippersnapper is thinking to put ideas into those Indians' heads."

"That's just it," said Abby. "I don't want him putting ideas into John's head either."

"I shouldn't worry about John," said Eph. "Your husband is a very sensible man. But I agree with father, I can't stomach New Light preaching. I've heard revival meetings that were nothing short of bedlam. When Whitefield preached in Boston there was a disgusting spectacle. Women shrieking and dropping over cold, grown men grubbing on their knees or stretched out staring like corpses. Give me a good Indian powwow any day."

"Well, we'll have none of that in Stockbridge!" My father's fist on the table set the plates jumping. "Enough to make a man puke. If I had my way, Jonathan Edwards would have nothing to say in this town, committee or no. He's one of the worst of 'em. Drove one man in Northampton to cut his throat. You tell your John to warn this young Brainerd, Abby. I won't stand for any damned revival nonsense around here."

I knew better than to ask a question at table, and I sat looking from one to the other of them, bewildered. How had this new missionary set them all against him in one night, especially father, who had not even laid eyes on him? The familiar words they were using were distorted out of all meaning. Why should women scream at a sermon? And to say that a person had no more Grace than a chair seemed a childish thing, rude indeed, but scant cause for a man to be expelled from college.

"What is a New Light?" I demanded of Abby, following her to her house.

She looked at me with amusement. "You're like me in one way at least," she commented. "I can't bear to have the men talk about something I don't understand. Take Abby Woodbridge, now, when Timothy and John get into one of their arguments her eyes just go blank and you can see her mind is off somewhere, planning what she's going to cook for supper, I suppose. I listen, even though I always get furious at Timothy, he's so unreasonable. John explains afterwards when I ask him, but I honestly think he'd rather have me like Abby. Take my advice, Liza; for women to use their brains just makes men uncomfortable."

"Did John tell you what a New Light is?" I persisted.

"He probably did. All I know is, I'm thankful John isn't one. He follows the Half-way Covenant.

"And you'd know what that is," she said, reading my obstinate silence, "if you'd just listen to something besides the Indian sermons occasionally. Any properly trained girl in New England could tell you, long before your age. I was admitted to this church on the Half-way Covenant, and so will you be when your time comes. It simply means that because father and mother are members, and because they had us properly baptized, we can be admitted without a test of our conversion. This is what Timothy Woodbridge can't agree to, and he's always bringing it up. In the church he came from, the deacons decided every case individually, and if they weren't satisfied they could refuse to admit a person. Can you imagine having to stand up before Timothy and that ridiculous Peter What's-his-name to let them decide whether or not you can take the Lord's supper? I'd sooner stay outside for the rest of my life."

Then, with a sharp look that took in my confusion, Abby slowed her rapid steps, and in the few moments between our house and hers she gave me so compact and logical a lesson in theology that I have never forgotten it. Oversimplified it was, for I am sure that at the time she herself had had scant instruction

in the controversy which throughout New England had already
filled thousands of printed pages and hours of preaching and debate. But she had always possessed a mind which cut straight to
the bone of any matter, and often in the years since, when I have
had more than my fill of argument, I have wished that others,
and Stephen among them, could have had the benefit of her
logic, for it seems to me that they mistake the trees for the forest.

All ministers, she explained to me, did not believe, as John did,
that God's Grace is free to all. Odd that they should have been
termed New Light, the old-fashioned ones who insisted on going
back to Puritan ways and who would admit members to the
church only after satisfactory testimony. The preaching of
these men was all to one purpose, to bring about the experience
of conversion, and their method was to rouse in their listeners the
realization that they were hopeless sinners, utterly powerless to
help themselves, and in instant danger of hell. The great Jonathan Edwards preached like this, Abigail had heard. She herself
had never heard such a sermon, but John had, and he said, like
Eph, that when the fear and despair became unbearable, people
groaned and shrieked aloud and sometimes fainted. Then, in
their remorse and hopelessness, to some of them came a sudden
conviction that they had received Grace and were saved. To
some, but not to all. Only to those whom God had chosen to
save, long before they were born.

Yes, Abigail answered, at my horrified questioning, the New
Lights believed that only a few were elected to be saved. All the
rest were doomed, predestined to eternal punishment, no matter
how they repented or pleaded.

It was as though she had told me there was a country in which
the sun did not shine.

John did not hold with this, she said; he was too kind-hearted.
Even though they accused him of heresy, he could never believe

that God would deny his Grace to anyone who longed for it, and so he would never shut out from the Lord's table any who asked. And furthermore, he did not believe that one man was qualified to judge another and to decide who had been truly converted and who had not. That was why he would never give in to Timothy Woodbridge. She wondered now about this Mr. Brainerd. From what she had overheard he seemed to be still fearful that he might not be saved himself, for all he was going to save the Indians. John had tried to reassure him, dear John, who could not bear to see anyone troubled. Yes, John himself had had some experience in his youth, something that had made him certain once and for all, but he did not insist on it for others. And a good thing for us all, she added. She herself never had, nor had Eph, and could you imagine father? It went against the grain, somehow, for a Williams.

She was so logical. I was a Williams too, and I should have been satisfied, but I was not. Abby's words revealed to me for the first time how insecure was the ground of my faith. That morning I began a winding journey from which I would not return for half a lifetime, and then never, in all the years ahead, to the unquestioning trust with which I had listened to the Indian sermons. I had scarcely more than heard his name, but already David Brainerd had shaken a firm wall of my childhood.

5. ONE MORNING Mr. Brainerd stood in John's place to preach the Lord's Day sermon.

He was ludicrously tall and thin, his wrists knobbing out below the sleeves of his coat as he spread his papers on the lectern. His cheeks were sunken, the bones of his jaw and temples outlined harshly. I had never before been conscious of the shape of human bones under the skin, and I shivered at the reminder of an Indian skull Elijah had once found in the meadow. The skin that stretched tightly over this man's bones was waxy pale, and his eyes stared out from shadowed hollows. His mouth, wide and thin-lipped, was angular with nervousness, and a peaked Adam's apple moved constantly in his long thin neck.

Then he opened the Bible and began to read. At his first words some nerve deep within me jumped in response, the same nerve that quivered when the Indians sang. Mr. Brainerd's speaking was a sort of singing. And with the words a transformation took place. His nervousness dropped away, his eyes glowed, and the wide angular mouth took on a peculiar beauty. He looked straight at the men and women before him, and between them and himself he began to weave a link of words. Gradually I felt the rope of them twisting around me and drawing tighter, so that I was constrained to breathe deeply against its pressure. I am not sure I listened to what he said; I had never heard a musical instrument, and the rich cadences of this man's voice satisfied some unrealized need. A long time later, looking for a moment away from his face, I marked that the sand lay quiet in the bottom of the hour glass. Two brilliant patches of red burned now in his cheeks. There was a radiance all about him. It came to me suddenly that an archangel must look like this.

When he concluded his sermon, the line slackened across the meetinghouse with an audible sigh. Dazed, almost unaware that I walked at all, I followed my family out into the noon sunshine. Near the door John was presenting the young missionary to each family, and as Mr. Brainerd took my hand in turn, my flesh shrank from the naked feel of the long bones. I looked up into his face and forgot to curtsy.

No, he explained to us all with a diffident smile, he could not

share the noon meal with anyone. He seldom ate any meal between services; he needed to stay alone and prepare his mind for
the sermon to come. As he went back into the meetinghouse the
buzz of comment began.

"What is your opinion, Mr. Williams?" Timothy Woodbridge approached my father. "It seems to me I have never
heard so eloquent a statement of the incarnation."

Why did it have to be Timothy Woodbridge? Watching
them, I knew in advance what my father must say. He had never
seen eye to eye with the schoolmaster since the night we had first
arrived in Stockbridge; it seemed to me sometimes that my father
would be compelled to point out a cloud if the young man so
much as mentioned that the sun was shining. And whenever Mr.
Woodbridge attempted to parade his learning, my father invariably took pleasure in displaying his own lack of it. I winced now
as my father's voice, deliberately uncouth, caused heads to turn
on every side.

"I wouldn't know what fancy words like that mean," he
drawled. "Enthusiasm, I call it. If you ask me, there was a sight
more heat than light. I like a sermon with more meat to it."

So the lines were laid out, and all over the Sabbath house they
took sides. There were those who would agree with my father if
he said the grass was red. There were others who kept silent,
their looks sliding toward each other, who would later, out of
hearing, support Mr. Woodbridge. It had little to do with the
man they were judging. Seeing the neighbors nodding at father,
I felt a lump tighten in my throat. They had listened to a man of
God, to a messenger whose tongue was touched with holy fire,
and now they shrugged and dismissed him with one word — Enthusiasm.

I could not touch the cold beans and white bread my mother
unwrapped; obstinately I shared the fast of the lonely man who

had stayed behind in the meetinghouse. As a consequence, the gnawing of hunger and the excitement that tensed the muscles of my stomach were indistinguishable as we walked back for the afternoon meeting. I dreaded a disappointment, yet I was not sure I could bear a repetition of that morning. When Mr. Brainerd began to speak, the line looped about my heart once more and drew taut. I saw that it did not matter what my father said of him, or how many failed to hear. He was not trying to win their favor; he was compelled only by his God.

In spite of my father's reservations, he was obliged by his position in the town to invite the visiting preacher to supper. For me this was an almost intolerable prolonging of the tension that had held me since early morning. As I slid onto the bench beside Judith I was afraid I would disgrace myself and have to bolt. When John Sergeant waived his right and gave to the visitor the honor of pronouncing the blessing, I clenched my hands in my lap, trembling. Afterward, raising my head, I looked directly into Mr. Brainerd's eyes, and as I did so their grave intensity was warmed by a smile of such simple friendliness that my nerves went suddenly limp like a released bowstring.

My father, who could be an admirable host when he pleased, applied himself to his plate without a word. John plunged into the awkward silence.

"The most immediate need is to persuade the commissioners to finance a school at Kaunameek. I believe your interpreter is reasonably qualified to be its master."

Mother intervened, astonishingly, for she seldom forgot her place. "Let him eat first, John." Quietly she replenished a plate that had been almost instantly emptied. I felt a rush of love for her, and suddenly, looking at the visitor through her eyes, I too saw not an archangel but a very boyish and uncertain young man, and much of my awe of him dropped away.

"It is very good, ma'am," he said, with his surprising smile. "I can't remember when I've had such a meal."

"I can well believe it." Mother smiled back. "Have you found even a place to sleep out there?"

"I intend to build something of my own in time," he answered. "Just now I'm lodging with a Scotchman, about a half a mile from my Indians."

"I hardly thought there'd be a house."

"I don't think you'd call it a house, ma'am. He is a very poor man, and he has only a log hut of one room. Our beds are heaps of straw on the bare earth. Please don't think I'm complaining. He willingly shares all he has."

"Does he give you proper food?"

"We have Indian meal to make cakes. Any bread we have has to be fetched ten or fifteen miles, and we can't often spare the time to go so far. If we try to keep any quantity of it it turns sour and moldy."

"I shall make up a packet for you to take back with you," she promised. "And you must come to eat with us whenever you can." In the face of my father's silence this was a bold invitation.

"Thank you," he said gravely. "I trust you are sincere, ma'am, for I am very much afraid that I will take up your offer."

Abigail laughed, and under her laughter I sensed her relief that the burden of entertainment had been lifted from her shoulders. "There's nothing mother likes better than putting a little fat on someone's bones," she told him. John smiled his gratitude. My father looked down the table at mother from under his eyebrows and kept silent. He would never let it be said that he lacked hospitality. For myself, I was all at once content.

John could spare scant time for eating; it was too rare a pleasure to have someone equally absorbed in the task nearest his heart. Did Mr. Brainerd intend to begin with the catechism? he inquired. He himself had found it useful. Of course, with any method one must be prepared for endless digressions . . . Presently the two ministers had forgotten both hunger and manners and were deep in a discussion that had no meaning for the rest of us. Father, with a grunt of exasperation, finally pushed back his chair, pulled it nearer the hearth, and lighted up his long pipe. Mother and Abigail, taking this for permission, rose too and cleared the table. When the bread and meat had been wrapped, we settled down to our knitting. Father sat staring into the flames, ignoring the talk that went on behind him. For a time his fingers moved on the arm of his chair, counting over some calculation, and presently a long snore announced that the tally was completed. Mother rose quietly, took the pipe gently from his fingers, laid it on the mantel and resumed her knitting. She and Abigail began to murmur, dropping into their never-ending talk about the babies. This time I had something more engrossing to listen to.

"I must spend more time on the language," Mr. Brainerd was saying. "Speaking through an interpreter is intolerable. How can I know what he tells them? I do my best to lay before them the infinite love of God. And then I must wait and force myself to stand silent while this ignorant youth translates for me. And their faces do not change. I search them in vain for the slightest hint of understanding."

"John is a good boy," John Sergeant answered. "He will do his best for you. The difficulty is that the Indian language is so meager. Not only that, there are no equivalent concepts. That Christ should have died for them, for example, is incomprehensible. I have spent hours with some of the Indians, trying to find some way to explain it to them. It is no use to refer to civil law, which means nothing to them. That a man should stand surety in place of another — they have never heard of such a thing. In their code each man stands for himself. And that Christ should have given up his life? An Indian would be willing to die for a son, or for a father, rarely perhaps for a friend. But to die for a stranger would seem to him laughable. Courage they admire. They respect a Christ who suffered on the cross without begging for mercy. But there is no way to make them see that the suffering paid a debt for them, for us all. Or even that a debt needed to be paid. The hardest problem of all is to stir in them any sense of sin."

Mr. Brainerd's voice trembled. "Not to know that they sin? When every moment they are in mortal danger? Why then their souls are in utter darkness!"

"They are like children," John explained, in his mild reasonable voice. "Remorseful when they have done something to displease us. They know it is wrong to get drunk. But when they have not been drunk, when they have not harmed anyone — except of course an enemy — or stolen anything, or taken another man's wife, then they cannot see why they are sinners. There are no words with which to convey to them the fact that every mortal man shares the fall of Adam."

"Oh, I should not be here today!" The missionary's voice seemed to burst out in torment. "What right have I to take these moments for my own selfish pleasure when even while I sit here their souls are sinking into the flames?"

"On the contrary," John said firmly. "I think you should come here more often. I shall teach you all I have learned of the language, but it is not easy. You will have to work at it as you have never worked at anything before. But if you care enough to make the trip, I will set aside regular hours for your instruction."

How could John doubt the man's caring, seeing his face so haggard and full of pain? Yet there was a quality in the caring that made me uneasy even then.

6. In spite of our urging, Mr. Brainerd did not come often, which was perhaps just as well for father's patience. He had left the Scotchman, he reported on one of his infrequent visits at our table, and was living in a wigwam while he built a small house of his own. He seemed far more cheerful. He enjoyed the solitude for his study. He had planted a garden, and his beans and corn were doing well, except that in reckoning his own needs he had forgotten to allow for the toll the rabbits and groundhogs demanded. This was the nearest to humor we ever knew him to venture. Seeing the way his eyes lighted up at each new dish, I was compelled to fast so that there would be more to put into the packet mother always wrapped for him. I would sit through the meal in a daze of hunger and sanctity, exalted by my own sacrifice.

All of my life seemed to be spent in this heightened state. At times I was seized with a trembling and a terrifying feeling of imminence. Some unfathomable experience seemed to wait just beyond my reach, and I became convinced that it must be conversion. I did not know what to expect, and there was no one to ask, for Abigail had admitted that our family had never made its acquaintance. I began to give earnest attention to John's sermons, listening for some hint; finally, impatient with his familiar assurances, I poked among his books on the pretext of dusting the study. There a name on the cover of a leather-bound volume attracted me, that of Jonathan Edwards, so despised by my father. I took it out into the fields under my apron, and for long hours I puzzled over its pages, finding that the simple lessons Judith and I had learned had prepared me poorly for such reading.

I can understand how the children and young people of the Northampton church were driven to their knees in those revival years. Jonathan Edwards' written words brought tears of longing to my eyes. It was my first contact with the two-edged sword of this great man's preaching, and the words sank deep into a heart peculiarly vulnerable.

People have made much of the dread and terror that attended his sermons, and indeed in those pages hell opened at my feet, and I glimpsed for the first time its infinite horror. I woke sometimes in the night and could have screamed aloud with sudden fear of it. Only the practical Williams strain in me kept me from despair. Oh, I am sorry for children. I have tried to urge upon Stephen that he temper his sermons to the young who sit in the pews. Do they recall his words in the dark, shaking with terror in their beds? But though he too pities them, he holds with Mr. Edwards that he would spare them at their mortal peril. Remembering, I cannot believe he can be right.

For it was the other edge of Jonathan Edwards' sword that cut deepest, and I marvel that those who recall his hell have not felt more keenly the power of his heaven. In that first book, long before I ever heard him speak, I caught something of his own wonder. He made the Grace of God surpassing sweet. The manifestation of beauty, he called it, a vital indwelling of the heart, the spring of all delight. Such words filled me with a yearning close to ecstasy. I thought that nothing else on earth would ever matter if I could obtain it.

I remember how I searched their faces. My father, who night and morning prayed aloud before us, addressing so confidently this God who could at any instant thrust him into everlasting flames. Mother, whose uncertainty and ease were traceable only to my father's moods; she did not have the strength to stand in awe of God's as well. And Abigail. Had Abigail ever acknowledged any submission? John stood safely beyond the flaming sword, having had his "experience," and it made him, to me at least, unapproachable. Eph, who might have helped me, was seldom in Stockbridge that year. I could think of only one person who would understand. How I was so sure of this I could not have said, but I knew that out in the forest David Brainerd woke alone in the night and knew both my fear and my longing.

7. *Make a joyful noise unto the Lord, all ye lands —*
That October the hills shouted and sang. I woke to the flame of the maple outside my window and went out into a world where every tree flung out its thanksgiving with scarlet and wine and bronze and gold. All day I breathed in color with great gulps till I was dizzy, yet never surfeited.

What recognition does the earth possess, that at the very dying of summer it is so expectant of joy?

One morning Abigail arrived at our house early, carrying Erastus, with Electa toddling behind.

"Can you take them?" she asked mother. "I've no time to watch them. Mr. Brainerd came in last night with scarcely the strength to crawl over the doorstep. John and I got him into bed, and none of us had a wink of sleep all night. I've come for some of that syrup. I don't see how his body holds together the way he coughs, and I know he's raging with fever."

"I'll come with you." Mother was already bundling together a clean apron and her medicine box. "The children can stay right here with Liza. Judith, start some of the gruel, will you dear? It's easy to keep down and he'll need some nourishment." Her step along the path had the confident spring that a bedside summons always invoked. I had a sharp longing to run after them, a conviction, illogical as I knew it to be, that it was I more than Abigail and mother who had a right to be there. For the first time in their lives I looked at Abigail's children with resentment.

I was charged with them for three days. On the fourth day mother reported that help was no longer needed, that Mr. Brainerd was mending, his fever had dropped, and he needed only to recover his strength.

"I don't think the boy takes the slightest care of himself," she scolded, forgetting her respect for the clergy in her concern for a patient. "He's nothing but skin and bone, and his clothes are in a shocking state. I brought home his shirt to mend, but it's so thin I'm not sure it will hold a patch."

"I'll mend it for you," I offered, taking the shirt out of her hands. It had a queer live feel under my fingers and I did not want to set it down. I found a piece of new linen in the scrap box and spread it carefully across the worn area where I could almost see the mark of hunched shoulder blades. I took pains to set my stitches carefully. When I had finished the patch, I snipped and rolled the frayed edges of the neck ruffle; then I washed the shirt, spread it in the sun to bleach and dry, and heated up the iron on the hearth. In the end I was pleased with my work, actually uplifted. For was I not serving God when I waited on his servant?

"I wouldn't know it was the same shirt," mother commented. "Why don't you walk over and give it to him yourself?"

Mr. Brainerd was sitting in a chair just outside Abigail's door in the Indian summer sunshine. He looked more thin and pale than usual, but his smile as I came nearer was warm, his pleasure no adult feigning.

"They tell me you've been minding the children so your sister could mind me," he greeted me. "I've been a sore trial to you all, but I thank you."

Tongue-tied, I laid the shirt on the doorstep beside him. He looked down at it.

"I can't remember when I've had an ironed shirt. A pity to ride home in it. I ought to save it till I preach in your meetinghouse again." He was so much more at ease with himself here than at my father's table, and somehow, having submitted to inactivity, less driven.

"Next time you come to preach I'll iron it for you again," I said.

His quick smile at once transformed my offering into something of worth. "Sit down for a few moments," he said. "I'd welcome your company. I'm not accustomed to being idle."

He had, he told me when I sat down with my legs crossed Indian fashion on the dry leaf-strewn grass, another thing to thank me for. He had noticed me — *me!* — that day when he first preached at Stockbridge.

"You were listening," he said. "'Not as the others were, waiting to pounce upon the slightest error, shutting their ears to the spirit. I saw that you were open to the word of God and that strengthened me. I thought I should tell you so."

I could only look up at him, speechless. He seemed to be studying my face. "Miss Elizabeth," he said at last, "you have a gentle spirit."

I looked down at the square tips of my shoes below the hem of my calico dress. My lips were stiff with embarrassment.

"You have all been so good to me," he went on. "There are moments, and today is one of them, when the sweetness of God seems so close, and I am so rapt in it and enfolded that everything in the world seems clear and beautiful. There are other times — I pray that you may never know about such times."

"I do know," I whispered, so low that I do not think he heard me.

"But how should you know? There is a transparency about you, and a quietness. But I also am at peace today. God withholds his wrath and his scorn, and his love surrounds me. May he bless all of you for your goodness."

8. IT WAS NOT only my inner world that was shifting that autumn of my fourteenth year. I was confused by change everywhere I turned. Catherine had moved ahead of me into the adult world. The long carefree rides in the forest were over; when I visited her now I found her always at work. She never complained. She would look up and greet me with a smile, and after she had brought me something to eat, a ceremony I could never persuade her to forgo, she would take up some task again and only rarely allowed me to help her. Mother and Abigail scolded me once for my sunburned skin and rough hands; when I confessed that I had turned the green ears of corn as they roasted over a fire in the field, and cut my fingers on the splints as I helped to weave the storing baskets, they found added chores for me on the Hill, claiming, with justice, that since I wanted to do such work I might better be helping my own kin. I saw Catharine less often, and I spent more time in Abigail's kitchen.

Eph had been appointed representative to the General Court, a matter of pride to us all. Father deferred to his opinion as he would to no one else's, and when Eph rode into town that autumn they sat long evenings over their pipes. Sometimes they were joined by one or two of the Hill neighbors. There was nothing jovial about these meetings. Hours would go by without the accustomed roar of male laughter that had formerly punctuated my sleep.

At the same time, father took a sudden interest in John Sergeant's plans for his new school. For more than a year we had been hearing about the new building which was to accomplish all that the mission had so far failed to do. It seemed that, no matter what the conversation, any topic in the world reminded John of the school, and he never noticed the glances of resignation and amusement which attended his eloquence. I hope that Abigail sometimes heard him out, for the rest of us seldom did. When father not only began to listen but to nod his head in agreement, I could scarcely believe my ears and eyes. When he suggested that the Stockbridge families take up a collection for the school, even Abigail's suspicions were aroused.

"What is father up to?" she demanded of Eph one afternoon. She was happy and flustered that he had dropped in for tea as he so often used to do. When I offered to run home and leave them, she laughed and on an impulse brought another cup from the cupboard. I suppose she had no idea that for me that teacup was a rite of initiation, as much a symbol of my coming of age as an Indian boy's new name. I sat holding it gingerly, terrified that I might drop the fragile thing and be banished again to childhood.

"Father has never paid the slightest attention to John's plans," Abigail said to Eph. "Now he not only wants to contribute money but he insists everyone else has to. John is overjoyed of course, but it has a strange smell to me."

Eph looked at her with a pleasure and admiration in his blue eyes that I would happily have walked over live coals to provoke. "A man's mind," he said. "I always said so, and in such a pretty little head."

"Don't be silly," she answered, pleased nonetheless. "It's not hard to see that something's behind all this."

Eph stirred his tea, his handsome face looking more sober. "You're right of course," he said. "Though perhaps it's just as well not to share your suspicions with John. The fact is, your husband may have a much more important part to play in Massachusetts colony than he has any notion of, and one reason for it will be that the Indians know he has no hidden purpose in his mind."

"And father has?"

"Not the mercenary one you suspect. And scarcely hidden, since it's discussed freely at the Court sessions. The way we look at it, this school of John's may prove to be of considerable value. The Mohawk's friendship is essential to us, and a few Mohawk children living and being educated in our boarding school could have an influence out of all proportion."

"Why the Mohawks? John says our Indians fear them."

"All the more reason. They happen to be the nearest and the only one of the Six Nations we can hope to influence. Not so powerful as some, but their word carries weight with all the others. The French are bringing all the pressure they can on the Iroquois up north, with every sort of bribe. If we can offer a little persuasion on our end —"

"So John's school is to be a political bribe?"

Eph shrugged. "Call it what you will. It won't matter to John, will it, if he gets his boys to teach?"

"I suppose not." Abigail frowned. "I don't like the thought that you and father and the others are just using John. If he realized, I think it would hurt him. It makes all his work seem somehow unimportant."

"On the contrary, it makes the mission exceedingly important. It could even be that all our lives might depend on it here in Stockbridge."

"You think there's real danger?" Her voice was sharp, and Eph did not answer till she repeated her question insistently

"We've got to be prepared for it," he said finally. "It may not seem of much concern to us that Prussia and Austria are at war. But France and England have chosen to support opposite sides. King Louis sees this as a chance to get back the Netherlands, they say, and King George will not sit back and watch that happen. The rumor is that one of them is certain to declare war on the other, may have done so already."

Abigail sat with a line of worry between her eyes, and her happy mood of a few moments before entirely snuffed out. I was child enough to feel only a faint thrill at the thought of war, more of curiosity than fear.

"Holland is a long way from Stockbridge," said Abigail, speaking my thoughts.

"It seems so to a lot of people. But war anywhere on the continent of Europe is bound to affect us. It always has. The French in Canada will use it as excuse. The moment France and England are at war we can expect raids along our borders again."

"Our Indians would never turn against us," I spoke up. From the anxious looks they exchanged I knew they both regretted that they had allowed me to stay.

"This isn't to be discussed, Elizabeth, outside this room," Eph reminded me. "Particularly with Catharine. You understand that, don't you?"

"Of course I do." I was offended.

He nodded. "And you're right, Liza. We can count on the Stockbridge Indians. Furthermore, they're a good example to the other tribes. The Mohawks can see for themselves that our Indians have advantages worth bargaining for. A few Mohawk boys enrolled in John's school might go a long way toward winning their friendship."

On Thanksgiving Day a special fund was pledged by the English families of Stockbridge, one hundred and fifteen pounds, ten shillings. Looking back, I doubt that John was so naïve as to believe that this money came spontaneously from the hearts of his parishioners. He could hardly have ignored the rumors of war that stirred the town in recurring gusts like the first winter wind among the leaves. I think that the reasons for the generosity were of less importance to him than the school that he could now see almost within reach. I doubt too if he ever shared Abby's sensitivity about father's purpose. To him the alarm of war might well have been another of the mysterious ways in which God moved.

Just before Thanksgiving, when the ground was hard and bare and the nights came on early, Mr. Brainerd began to ride into Stockbridge once a week to study the Indian language with John. He no longer spent the nights at the Sergeant house, however.

"I was willing when he was a stranger," Abigail explained to me. "Even when he was sick all those days I didn't complain. But I've no mind to make a habit of it. He can see for himself that the house is too small."

"The Woodbridge house is much smaller," I pointed out, and knew that I had made another of those "unnecessary" statements that so annoyed her.

"It's not the same thing. They're used to being crowded. Moreover, it's not fair to John. Just an extra bed is one thing, but Brainerd wants to talk all night. There's no stopping him, he gets more and more excited the later it is. And then those morbid spells when nothing John says will bring him round. No, I'm not going to have it. This house is John's refuge after working all day, and I'm not going to have it spoiled for him."

I thought of the passageway where, securely barred from the house, the Indians sat in silence waiting for their minister. I remembered the feeling I myself always had, that I must not linger overlong after John had come home. Perhaps she was right. I liked the thought of a house being a refuge; it would be a lovely thing to find one's refuge at home instead of searching for it somewhere outside.

Yet of all the people I had ever seen it seemed to me that Mr. Brainerd needed a refuge most, and he would never find it in the smoky Woodbridge cabin. I was filled all at once with hurt

for him. Or was it in part my own hurt? For with Mr. Brainerd
spending the night down on the Plain and riding off at daybreak
I had little prospect of ever seeing him at all.

9. THE WINTER OF 1744 was a mild one in which we were
housebound far less than in any year I could remember. I
was able to ride every day till close to Christmas, when the first
heavy snows set in. There would be plenty of snow to make up,
everyone promised, and true enough there was one blizzard on
the heels of another through January. Then early in February
there came an unseasonable thaw with heavy rains which washed
the snow from the ground except in the deep woods, where it lay
in patches criss-crossed with the tracks of small animals.

Some said the thaw was unhealthy. At any rate, many of the
children on the Plain and some of the older folk as well took
sick with throat distemper. Mother, her hands full, was compelled once more to enlist my help. Judith too was given the
tedious chore of shredding and pounding the dried herbs and of
stirring and straining the pungent brews. But when mother set
off down the path it was understood that I alone went with her.

In most cases mother's simple remedies were sufficient. She
had great faith in saffron tea. With a bit of snakeroot added, it
seemed to hasten the red eruptions that appeared about the sixth
day of the illness, and though this rash was hot and itching and
frightening to a child's parents, mother always observed it with
relief, assuring them that the sickness was working its way out.
Sometimes, in spite of all her efforts to keep a patient in a sweat,
the rash failed to appear, and then the dreaded sores broke out
within. I would sit, hour after hour, keeping a reeking mixture

of herbs and brandy at a scalding point near the fire, wringing out a flannel cloth and laying it against a swollen throat. Yet I think the most valuable remedy that mother taught me during that time was her calmness. Though she was often perplexed and anxious, she hid her uncertainty behind a smile, and who knows but that smile accomplished more than all her potions?

For three weeks the distemper raged through the town. Timothy Woodbridge closed his school and the white families kept their children indoors. In the end all of the English recovered, but among the Indians two children and one young woman died. Then, when it was about over and the children were out again, shouting and splashing in the mud, Electa, who seldom saw another child, whimpered all day with earache and was feverish by night. Two days later the Woodbridge baby came down with the same complaint. John had taken advantage of the bared trails to ride to Connecticut on behalf of his school, taking Timothy Woodbridge with him, so they both were spared the sleepless nights their wives endured in their absence. Just as Electa was beginning to display the peevish temper that was a sure sign of recovery, mother and I found Abigail shaking with chills. Fortunately she had the mildest of cases, but for a week mother moved into Abigail's house and I went alone the rounds of her nearly recovered invalids, carrying instructions and doses and feeling capable and important.

When Abigail was back on her feet, father, who had been remarkably patient, announced that mother was going with him for a holiday to visit my brother Thomas while the road to Deerfield was still open. He was blasted if he could see the sense in filling the house with servants when all the good it did was to give her more time to wear herself out in other people's houses. So, reassured that all danger was over, mother rode off with him, looking both guilty and pleased and very tired. They promised to be back in a week's time.

The week was almost up when Mr. Brainerd's Indian interpreter rode into town. I was sitting by Abigail's hearth with Electa when she opened the door to him.

"Mr. Brainerd very sick," he told her. "Cough all time. Sometime can't get breath back. Very big fever."

Weak tears of distress sprang easily into Abigail's eyes; I was not sure whether they were provoked by the news or by the muddy moccasins on her threshold. "Get the cough syrup, Liza," she said to me. "You know which bottle it's in."

The Indian was not satisfied. "Mr. Sergeant he better come," he said. "I go schoolmaster's but him gone."

"So is Mr. Sergeant. They went together. Just take the medicine back to him. It made him well last time."

"More sicker now," the boy insisted. "Him talk all time to people not there."

I spoke without even thinking. "I can go, Abigail."

My sister wheeled around. "To Kaunameek? Are you out of your mind?"

"Someone has to."

"I don't see why. John should be back tomorrow. He'll find someone to send, if it doesn't snow before then. Look at that sky. Or maybe Josiah would go, if you can find him."

Josiah might be anywhere, going the round of his traps. If I found him there was no predicting the mood he would be in.

"I'll get the medicine," I said, pulling on my clogs. Abigail watched me uncertainly. If she had been herself, I am sure she would not have let me out of her house. She would have known that my mind was made up.

The Indian boy waited outside my father's door, refusing to step inside, while I set about in a frenzy. I found the heavy glass bottle of cough syrup. I snatched corn bread and wrapped it in a clean linen napkin, shook out a measure of fine flour into another napkin and tied it snugly by four corners. I found the brown package of fever medicine in the chest. Mother had never allowed me to touch this, for it contained not the garden herbs that we ourselves had prepared but a powder of antimony that Thomas had sent her, but I took it now without hesitation.

Judith, puzzled by all this bustling about, watched me from over her embroidery. It was not till I pulled down from the wall a pair of Josiah's long woolen breeches and began to drag them on under my skirt that she suspected my intention.

"Elizabeth — where are you going?"

"I'm going out to Kaunameek. Mr. Brainerd is very ill."

"Kaunameek! You must be crazy. Mother would never let you."

"She probably wouldn't. But there's no one else. When she gets home, tell her to send someone out. With some more medicine, too. There isn't much in this bottle."

"You can't ride out there by yourself. You'll get lost."

"Of course not. His helper is waiting to show me the way."

"You're going off in the woods alone with an *Indian?*" Judith's voice rose frantically.

"Don't be silly. He's Mr. Brainerd's schoolteacher."

Judith burst into tears. "It's going to snow. Josiah said there'd be a storm before night, and suppose father and mother don't get home. You can't leave me all alone here."

"There's Moni and Candace, and Elijah will be back for supper, probably Josiah too. For heaven's sake, Judith, what can happen to you here?"

"I might have a spell," she wailed, her voice already catching threateningly.

I stopped pulling on the trousers and glared at her. "Don't you dare to!" I said, so fiercely that she did not say another word. I pulled on my heavy cloak, tied a woolen shawl under my chin and gathered up my bundles. "Anyway, Abigail is just across the field." I slammed the door behind me, shutting off her ascending protest.

When he understood what I meant to do, the Indian too was alarmed. "You not go," he said flatly. "Mr. Williams he not like."

"Never mind Mr. Williams," I said. "Come and help me saddle Nip. Hurry!" I urged him, as he stood shaking his head.

"He blame me."

"No. I promise you. Oh, for goodness' sake — why is everyone so *stupid?*"

The Indian boy led the way along the trail. I had never ridden Nip so deep into the forest before, and she moved hesitantly, twitching her ears as though to question me. Perhaps she sensed my own dismay. The day had been cheerless enough on the Hill; here in the woods, at midmorning, there was a thick damp twilight. The snow that lay in the hollows concealed quagmires where the mare's feet sank deep, and she stumbled often. The Indian had continually to rein in his own horse and wait for me. We had been riding for about two hours, I judged, when the first flakes of snow drifted through the skeleton ceiling of branches.

Nippe hesitated, lifting her head, waiting for the signal to turn back. How willingly I would have given it now! "It's all right," I told her. "Go on, Nip."

It was the sort of fine dry snow that begins with deceptive quietness. It dropped so gently that I was surprised how rapidly the floor of the forest whitened. When, after another hour or so, we came out on an open stretch, I saw what the thick woods had concealed, that this was indeed the blizzard men had predicted. Here gusts of winds blew a heavy curtain of snow in gigantic folds. At times the Indian, riding a few feet ahead, was completely shut off from me. Nip moved at a dragging pace, her head lowered against the ceaseless stinging assault. Presently she jerked to a stop; she had almost collided with the Indian's horse halted before her nose. Then out of the white the boy appeared, trailing a length of vine. This he tied to Nip's bridle, and then to his own, and we went on. Nip, reassured, kept a steadier pace, and no longer having to strain my eyes to make out the way, I wrapped my face deep in the shawl and bent my head.

After an endless time the boy shouted and I saw him pointing, and made out a dark shape ahead. I don't know what I had expected of Mr. Brainerd's house, but my father would not have sheltered an animal in such a place. My heart sank as I slid off the mare and stumbled through John's tracks toward the cabin.

Inside it was fully night and as cold as without. I could see nothing at all, but the stench of sickness shocked my frozen nostrils. A few feet away a single orange coal winked in the darkness; the Indian went down on his knees and blew upon it till it flared and revealed a shallow hearth. He lighted a pine knot and stuck it into a chink in the stone chimney. "I fix wigwam for horses," he said, and went out into the snow.

There was a table with a half-burned candle in a knot of wood, and beyond the table a jumbled heap of skins and blankets. My icy fingers clumsy, I managed to light the candle at the pine torch and moved closer, filled with dread at what I might see. The face half buried in the blankets was totally unfamiliar, darkened with beard, the eyes closed, breath escaping with an uneven sound from the sagging mouth. As the candlelight fell upon him, the man moved his head and the eyelids opened.

"John," he said hoarsely.

"It's not John. It's Liza — Elizabeth Williams. I've brought you some medicine."

"We are lost," he muttered. "Without hope. Not one of us can escape his wrath."

I backed away, appalled now at my rashness. How could I

know what to do for a man as sick as this? I put down the candle
and stood wringing my hands, shaking with cold and terror.

The Indian boy came into the room with wood and almost at
once had a fire blazing; gradually my body began to thaw and
with it my confidence. He carried out a pail and brought in
snow, dipped some into a small sooty kettle and hung it by its
chain from the wooden lugpole. When the steam began to rise he
went out again to fetch small green hemlock tips, which he
dropped into the boiling water. Presently he poured some of this
brew into an earthen cup and held it out to me. The aromatic
steam heartened me before the cup touched my lips; the Indian
tea, even without sugar, was sweet and strength-giving. When I
handed back the cup, he filled it again and drank from it. Then
into the same cup, for there seemed to be no other, I measured as
large a dose of the fever powder as I dared. When I carried it to
the bed, the sick man was asleep again, far too deeply to hear my
timid whisper.

I appealed to the boy, who watched. "We have to make him
drink it. You'll have to lift him up for me." I had often helped
my mother do this, but never with anyone so ill. John came
silently to the bedside, and with a gentleness and competence
that astonished me, he raised the sick man's shoulders and supported his head while I put the cup to his lips. Mr. Brainerd's
eyes opened and he stared at me. "John," he said again. He did
not seem to mean the Indian.

I choked, and tears of helplessness blinded me. The Indian
boy took the cup from me and pressed it against the man's lips.
The liquid ran down into the stubble of beard, but some of it
was swallowed in painful gulps. When he handed the empty cup
back to me I was shamed.

There was nothing to do now but wait. After a time I realized
that some of my weakness was due to hunger. I unwrapped the

corncake and held it out to the boy, but he shook his head; I could not persuade him to touch it. As I broke off a piece for myself, he drew a pouch out of his belt and shook out a handful of parched corn which he tossed into his mouth and munched noisily. Watching the way he carefully closed the pouch and replaced it, I dared not eat more than a few bites of the bread. I wrapped it again, and not finding another cup, I poured a little of the heated water into a wooden bowl and sipped from it.

Then I sat down near the fire, dragging my knees up under my chin, my whole body tight against the cold which steadily advanced on the flames. I realized that in spite of the dark it was not yet night, that the hours before daylight would be endless. The boy made me uneasy; I wished he would go away. But instead he lay down on the floor in front of the door, rolled over with his back to me and appeared to sleep. Twice he got up and put new wood on the fire, poked it to bright heat and went back to his place. After a time Mr. Brainerd roused and began to mutter half-formed words, and I prayed that I might be able this time to give him the medicine alone. But when the cup was ready, the Indian came silently to lift the man's shoulders. Had he really been asleep at all?

The snow beat in a constant savage attack against the walls. In the occasional brief silences the fire hissed from the flakes that sifted down the smoke hole. An evil procession of shadows slid in an endless nightmare along the log walls. As the night came on, the man on the bed became more restless, heaving the blankets wildly and uttering hoarse sounds, half groans, half meaningless words. Now and again a single word leaped out with clarity: God — vile — sin — beast. He seemed to be praying, inploring God with a despair that filled me with horror. I thought of the pictures I had seen of the damned souls in hell. Such souls must plead with God like this. He would sink into silence for a time, and I would wait, shuddering, and my flesh would shrink as it began again. "Blessed God — vile — worthless — merciful —"

At the next medicine he woke more fully and stared at me and muttered something I could not understand. The boy was instantly beside me, carrying a bucket made of bark. "Go," he said. I understood, feeling the hot blood in my face. I went over to the fire and stood with my back to them. "A fine nurse I am," I told myself with scorn and shame. But I no longer wanted the Indian to go away.

Against my will I slept, and finally I came achingly awake and saw that the cabin was filled with grayness that must be daylight. I could distinguish now, dimly, the objects that had loomed as threatening masses in the night, the coat hung against the wall, the axe propped in a corner, the shelf of books. No longer menacing, they looked merely shabby and pitiful. I went over to the bed and watched the sick man. His face was far more frightening in the gray light; it struck me for the first time that he might actually be dying.

The Indian boy had gone out while I slept, and he returned now, his arms full of wet logs, bringing with him the chill damp. Behind him through the door I saw the gray curtain steadily falling. In the half light I fumbled about the cabin in search of food. Literally sick with hunger, I found only a half loaf of bread, black with mold, and a gourd with a handful of dried beans. The beans would take most of the day to cook, but I added them to water in a pot and hung it on the lugpole. I unwrapped the corncake, thinking with a lurch of my stomach of my mother's larder. How could I have come away with so little? I held out the cake to the boy, and once again he refused it, so I bit off a small piece, trying to chew it slowly, and drank more of the hemlock tea.

With the flour I had brought I mixed a gruel, boiling it slowly as mother had instructed me, and together we managed to spoon a few mouthfuls into the restless man. The wildness of the night had abated. He no longer prayed, but now, between the racking spells of coughing, his stillness alarmed me even more.

With the passing hours I knew for certain what I had in fact known on first waking. No one would come from Stockbridge. My parents could hardly have returned; mother would have turned back to the nearest inn at the first flake of snow. Judith would not have ventured out even to tell Abigail I had gone, and Josiah was often away for days at a time. But a new strength came with certainty. The cabin no longer terrified me. A second night would be only a little darker and longer than this day. If an Indian could be content with a mouthful of corn, then surely I could make do with the cooked beans.

Then I remembered with shame that I had not even asked if Nip had been fed.

"Hay gone," the boy told me. "Your horse eat. My horse strong, she go without. Mr. Brainerd, his horse very bad."

"Can you get them something?"

"Long way. You alone."

I insisted that I could manage without him. He would come back, he promised, and vanished into the twilight, leaving me with the sick man.

I had been wrong. The second night was a hundredfold worse than the first. The fever and delirium increased. I could no longer make sense of the hoarse sounds that alternated with the dreadful coughing. Try as I would, I could not get him to swallow more than half the medicine. I could feel with my hand the swelling in his neck that made it impossible. Not having linseed, I kept plain snow water boiling, tore off a strip of my linen petticoat, and laid it folded against his throat again and again, wringing and replacing it every few moments.

Deep in the night he slept, and I dared not disturb him further. I was shaking with exhaustion and could not get warm. The firewood the Indian had left for me was wet and burned un-evenly; whichever side I turned toward the fire, the cold clutched at the other. I sat upright in the one chair as long as I could endure it. Then I went over and stood looking at the bed, shaking. After a time I knelt down and lifted the edge of the blankets and eased myself under them onto the straw mattress. Cautiously I stretched my legs down and pulled the blankets up to my chin and relaxed into the blessed warmth. As I did so, Mr. Brainerd moaned and turned his head and put the weight of it against my shoulder, not waking. I could not sleep for the hot heavy feel of it, the rough hair under my cheek, the breath so close that my own lungs ached with each heavy rise and fall. I lay still, and my fear was mingled with a strange, inexplicable joy.

With the morning I was aware of an intense stillness. The snow had stopped, and the wind. When I went out to the privy I had to flounder through drifts waist high, and though I peered in every direction I could make out no sign of a trail. The horses in their tight pine shelter stood close together. Nip whinnied and pushed her nose against me when I tried to comfort her. As I struggled back to the cabin I saw the Indian boy coming be-tween the trees on snowshoes with a sack over his shoulders.

When he came into the cabin he had a fresh-killed partridge. I waited hungrily while he plucked it and speared it with a stick and roasted it over the flames. I could have cried like a child when the flesh shrank to almost nothing.

The third night was almost upon us when I thought I heard a shout. As I pulled open the door I could distinguish two figures coming slowly through the trees. I watched them come nearer, and then I ran out into the snow to fling myself against the near-est.

"Eph — oh, Eph!" He was the last one I had thought of and

instantly the one, the only one, who would of course have come. Behind him John Sergeant was unstrapping his snowshoes.

"I told them you'd be all right," Eph said. "I knew you had sense enough to ride out a storm."

"John kept the fire going," I said shakily. "He did everything. Eph, did you bring some food?"

He laughed and unstrapped the pack from his shoulders. Before he was out of his coat I had dumped the contents on the floor and bit into a chunk of bread half unwrapped.

John Sergeant stood looking down at the bed, and Eph went to stand beside him. When I joined them I saw what I could have sworn had not been there a few moments before — in the candlelight there was a thin line gleaming above Mr. Brainerd's upper lip, and a glistening on his forehead. And as he looked up at the two men, there was the first wavering of recognition in his eyes.

John Sergeant felt his friend's forehead. "The fever is definitely breaking," he said. "You've done well, Elizabeth." He took the sick man's wrist in his hand and was silent a moment, counting. "Your mother couldn't have done better."

For the first time in three days I burst into tears. "Can we go home now?"

"Not on your life," said Eph. "We've come nineteen miles on those barrel tops — started long before daybreak. Now we sleep."

We all slept, each of us watching by turns, and I was so deep in slumber that Eph had to shake me hard to raise me.

"Bundle up all you can," he advised. "The parson will stay here for a few days, but it's my duty to get you home, even if my legs are stiff as pokers."

There was no question of taking my mare. Under his pack Eph had carried a light pair of Indian snowshoes, which he strapped to my feet. "You won't find this any picnic," he told me. "But the float we made yesterday is frozen over, and ought to hold us up. And thank the good Lord you're a husky wench."

Husky or no, it was the longest day of my life. I plodded behind him, clenching my teeth to keep from asking him to go slower, neither of us wasting breath on words. Every hour or so, when I could scarcely set one snowshoe ahead of the other, Eph would mark my dragging and would stop, strip off some fir boughs, and make me sit or stretch out flat on them, but he never allowed me to rest long enough.

"Is father very angry?" I asked once, when he helped me to my feet.

"They're sufficient anxious. We all were, or I wouldn't be making a trip like this two days in a row. It didn't seem like you, Liza," he added, leading off again, "to dash off half-cocked like that. I gave you more credit."

"Somebody had to take care of him."

"Did you make any effort to find someone a little better qualified?"

I thought back, remembering my frantic haste to get away before anyone could stop me.

"You know someone in the town would have gone," he said. "And you knew John was expected back."

"Suppose he had died?"

"People don't die as easy as you think. From what I hear, Brainerd is pretty used to this sort of thing. He's weathered quite a few bouts by himself, and he would probably have come through this one."

I could not have been more chastened. I was prepared to meet my father's wrath. But to be told I had never been needed at all — and by Eph!

He must have sensed my misery, even behind his back, for he called back more encouragingly, "To be honest, I'm not so sure he would have this time, now that I've seen him. Mind you, Liza, I'm not blaming you. In a pinch all any of us can do is what we think is right. Not many girls would have had the courage.

"Now look here," he said at last, when, late that night, we came, stiff and frozen and weary beyond describing, to our doorstep. "You gave them a scare. Don't forget that. Just keep your chin up." He gave me a quick hard hug and stood me on my feet.

Still, he had not prepared me for the welcome I received. Mother embraced me tearfully, but backed away at once to stare at me, her eyes brimming with not only reproach but question. Father stood across the room, and the look in his ice-blue eyes was not so much anger as a cold censure. It was up to me to break the silence with a stumbling plea for forgiveness.

"That all you have to say for yourself?"

"It seemed to me someone had to go," I said lamely.

"Did you have a single thought to your family's reputation?"

"You mean mother?" I was puzzled. "I did only the remedies she's taught me."

"That is not what I mean. You're not a child, Elizabeth. Do you have no shame at running off to spend two nights in the woods with a man you scarcely know?"

"Wait a minute, sir!" Eph came stamping in behind me and he looked red and angry. "Brainerd couldn't lift his head even this morning."

"Who in the town will know that? One thing about our family. No woman in it has ever given the slightest cause for gossip. Now the minute I leave home —"

"Let the child alone!" Eph shouted. "Can't you see she doesn't know what you're talking about? She may have saved Brainerd's life."

His angry words followed me as I stumbled up the stairs. In

my own room I twisted into a tight knot on the bed, heedless of my snowy leggings, and pressed my face against the quilt. Eph was wrong. I did know what they were talking about. What did it have to do with me or with Mr. Brainerd? How could they think it did? Yet a sick shame scalded my frozen body.

I can never face him again, I thought.

In a few moments mother came behind me into the room. "Now," she murmured. "Don't cry any more, Elizabeth. You meant to do right. Eph said you nursed him real good. It's just that girls have to be careful always to think what people — But there, 'tis over, and we're not going to talk about it any more."

With the gentleness I had so often watched, she eased off the stiff wet woolens and pulled a clean linen nightrail over my head. She brought a bowl of hot soup and combed out my matted hair, and finally helped me between the sheets. But she did not touch my icy spirit. Her solicitude had come too late. In the moment when I had needed her, she had sided with my father.

She left me to sleep and I lay wakeful. I had indeed been a child, and my father's words had stripped away the last wall of my childhood. I knew in my heart that on one count he had been near to the truth. I had not gone to Kaunameek out of duty. And I must be shameless, for given the choice I would go again, no matter what the cost.

Father's tempers were always short-lived. When I came downstairs at noonday, I was once more in my family's good graces, and when John Sergeant rode Nip home a few days later I found myself as near a heroine as I have ever been in my life.

"We owe a great debt to your daughter, sir," he told my father in my presence. "She showed both courage and skill. In my opinion, Mr. Brainerd may well owe his life to her."

The scar on my own spirit would be a long time in healing, but the easement began with John's next words.

"He has no memory of those days," he went on. "He did not

even realize that Elizabeth had been there until he came out of the fever, and when he first recognized her he thought she had come with Ephraim and me. In his delirium he thought that his brother John, who is nearest to him of anyone on earth, had come to care for him. He sends his deep gratitude and begs me to ask forgiveness for the anxiety he caused."

So Mr. Brainerd would never know that through half a night his head had lain on my shoulder. I was the more confused that I was not altogether thankful.

10. IN APRIL David Brainerd received a call to establish a mission among the Indians on the Delaware River in Pennsylvania. This was the work to which he had first been called and which had been postponed the spring before because of the uneasiness in that territory. The news was a shock to me, for I had never heeded the fact that the mission to the Kauna-meeks was a temporary one. Much to my father's disgust, the Kaunameek Indians, about thirty of them, agreed to move into Stockbridge and attend our meetinghouse and school. Still, I did not grasp at first the full import of Mr. Brainerd's new mission. With scant knowedge of distances, I remembered that John had traveled to the Delaware and returned. So, I reasoned, would Mr. Brainerd, though of course less frequently than from Kaunameek.

We were all concerned that he was not yet well enough to go. On the last Sabbath in April when he sat behind the pulpit with John Sergeant, he was exhausted and ill from a week of riding through Connecticut, and there were times during his two long

sermons when his body shook so violently that we wondered
how he could continue. He rode away two days later, and returned to Abigail's house at nightfall, having turned back in
weakness and distress after riding for hours in a driving rain. It
was a week before he could set out again. I did not see him during all those days. Though mother used every obvious ruse to
keep me from Abigail's house, she could have saved herself the
effort. My scars were still too fresh, and I had no wish to talk
with him.

Then, four months later, in September, without warning he sat
again in the pulpit, and with a dizzy lurch of relief and joy I
realized that through the whole summer I had been waiting for
just this. I twisted my fingers tight in the folds of my dress, and
by the time he rose to speak I had my breath under control. I
tipped back my head and held my gaze on his face, and felt his
words winging straight to me in a flight so direct that it seemed
they must mark a visible course through the meetinghouse and
that everyone present must see it plainly. Then the meeting
dropped away, and I sat alone on a peak of a high mountain, the
words beating in the air around my head. Yet when I trembled,
just short of some unspeakable joy, the words ceased and the
beating died away. The promise still eluded me.

Toward the close of that day, on the doorstep of Abigail's
house, I confronted him alone, not altogether by accident. Now
that the fire of his preaching had died down, he looked seriously
ill. If anything he was thinner than when he had left us in the
spring, and without the red color that flared in his cheeks when
he spoke, his pallor was disturbing.

"I searched out your face when I first began to speak," he said
to me, with an effort at his old smile. "I would I had someone
like you to encourage me in my congregation on the Delaware.
You cannot imagine what it is like to preach and to search the

faces before you and find not a solitary one in which the spirit seems to be present and heeding."

"Perhaps they do," I answered, troubled. "Indians don't show what they are thinking."

He looked down at me, a cloud blotting out the smile. "My intrepreter is not even a true Christian," he told me. "It is very discouraging. A hideous and desolate country, and I am entirely alone in it."

My own thoughts could never be hidden, and now, even in his distracted state, he saw my distress.

"Why should I speak so to you?" he asked. "Your sympathy makes me forget myself. God has upheld me through all these trials, and I know he will sustain me in this place where he has called me."

"Will you come again?" I asked him, unable to think of any comfort.

"When I can. It renews my strength to meet again the friends who have been so kind to me." Then, as if he sensed that this did not meet my need, he looked down at me earnestly. "How is it with you, Elizabeth? Have you experienced the joy of conversion?"

"No," I faltered, looking away.

"I believe it is closer to you than you realize."

He was the one person who would understand, and in a few moments he would be gone. I must say, before it was too late, what was so heavy on my heart. "I wish — sometimes it seems so close that I could almost reach out my hand. When you are preaching it is like that. But then it goes away, and it is so long before you come to preach again."

I saw that without intending I had brought him the comfort he craved. His smile transformed his face. "How generous you are," he said. "I would like to think that God has made me his instrument for your salvation, even as he sent you to help in my illness. But God's Grace is not dependent on me, or on anyone at all, even on you yourself. In his own time, through his abundant mercy alone, he bestows it on those he chooses."

The underlying fear I never dared to face welled into words. "I am afraid that he has not chosen me."

"Then you must give the throne of Grace no rest," he said seriously. "And I will pray for you. And you also, will you pray for me?"

That he should ask this of me swept me beyond all thought of my own salvation. Looking down at me he seemed startled. "Elizabeth —"

But John Sergeant came through the hallway in search of him, and I have never known what he meant to say.

II. THAT AUTUMN I, who had never been moody, was puzzled by moods I could neither anticipate nor understand. Aloneness was not new to me, but the sense of it had become intensified. There were days when I walked altogether alone, in a world made up of prayer, of thoughts of Mr. Brainerd and of a strange sense of waiting. My family, my books, our dinner table, the burnished hillside and the distant mountains were all unreal, and often I scarcely knew what I was doing. A quick rebuke would jerk me back to remembrance that my hands held a pen or a skein of wool or that the bread scorched in the toaster near the fire. There were other times when my awareness of all these things was painfully heightened, when the monotonous words in my lesson books suddenly took fire like bits of dry tinder, lighting up the corners of my mind, when a single flaming tree or the fragrance of a snuffed bayberry candle or the lavender of an evening sky was a sweetness almost past toleration. There were mo-

ments when I looked at my family and felt some veil of habit
swing aside, and I knew in my own bones Judith's listlessness or
Josiah's impotent rebellion. It was in one of those unexpected
disclosures that, looking at Abigail and John Sergeant, I glimpsed
what it might be to love a man.

I spent a good deal of time in Abigail's house. I was happiest
there, and I think in truth that it was Abigail's energetic common
sense and the plump demanding bodies of Electa and Erastus that
held me fast to the everyday world and helped me to shake off
the dragging cobwebs of my own moods. I think too that it
pleased Abigail to have me with her, especially during John's ab-
sences. It was during one of these that I sat with her toward
dusk, companionably carding wool. There was a stamping of
feet outside the door, and John stood on the threshold, unexpectedly, for he had planned to be away all the week. Electa moved
first, like a darting chickadee, with chirps of delight. With one
hand on her curly head, John looked across at Abigail.

"We left two days earlier than we planned," he said, with a
sort of shyness. "Can you find some supper for a ravenous
man?"

Abigail had not spoken, and for one uncanny fragment of time
I had the illusion of being inside Abigail, looking out through her
eyes. In an instant I was back in myself, startled and shaken by
what I had seen. The carding combs clattered to the floor as
Abby moved almost as swiftly as Electa, almost before John
could reach out to her.

I had planned to stay for supper, but as Abby and I bustled
about to hurry a meal to the table, I changed my mind. Something in the room wanted me gone. They both urged me to stay,
but they stood in the doorway, their arms around each other's
waists, and watched me set off across the field, unable to hide the
relief in their faces.

I would have sworn I had forgotten before I crossed the field, but a week or so later I had a dream. Vivid dreams have been a constant part of my life, and I have never attached much importance to them, but this one I remember clearly to this day. In the dream Abby and I were sitting together, as we had on the evening of John's return. I heard again the stamp of feet outside the door, and the creak of the hinge as the door swung open, and I turned with my heart in my throat. It was not John who stood in the doorway, but David Brainerd, and he smiled and held out his arms to me.

Before I could move, the gray light struck through my opening eyelids and blotted out his face. I lay without moving, struggling to find my way back into the dream. Like a shattered bottle of essence it sent over me waves of sweetness. I groped for it, knowing that it was gone, knowing that it had contained the moment I had waited for so long. And then at last I woke fully and came upon the truth and recognized it for what it was. I was not converted. It was not salvation that had been close to me all these past weeks, waiting just beyond my reach.

I felt a thin needle of terror. Had I blasphemed? Would God strike at me in wrath for my wickedness? But instantly I knew that nothing so right and beautiful could anger God. If he did not hold my sin against me, I would spend the rest of my life in recompense. For now David Brainerd's work would also be mine, and I would go beside him wherever God willed us to go. I belonged to David Brainerd, as Abigail belonged to John.

In the days that followed, the dream walked with me every waking moment. I had no impatience, for I knew that I was still too young. I was not unhappy at the thought of the miles of wilderness between Stockbridge and the Delaware, or at the months of waiting before he could come again. It was enough that we lived in the same world.

12. You CAN'T KEEP any one thing in life separate from the rest. I would have sheltered my love, perfect and apart, but it altered everything I touched, just as a pomander ball hidden in the linen cupboard insinuates its fragrance into every fold and seam.

"You've changed, Liza," Abigail commented. "You used to be such a difficult child. You know, I really think you're getting to be quite pretty, too."

When her back was turned I ran to the murky little mirror over her chest. I could see no change in my plain round image, save that perhaps my no-color eyes looked larger and brighter, and her words had set a trembling in the corners of my mouth. Like everything that came to me of late, Abby's words had only one relevance. Would he think I had changed? Would I seem pretty to him?

Confirmation came unwelcomed from an unexpected source as our family left the meetinghouse on the next Lord's Day.

"He's coming over to speak to you," Judith whispered with a little giggle.

"Who is?"

"You know perfectly well who."

I didn't. I was emerging slowly from a daydream so engrossing that I would have trouble accounting for a word of John's sermon.

"He stared at you every minute of the meeting."

Following my sister's glance, I saw that she had to mean Sam Brown. He was the only male who seemed to be approaching, and with a purposeful smile that penetrated only slightly my abstraction.

"Miss Elizabeth," he greeted me. "And Miss Judith. 'Tis a warm morning for this time of year, is it not?"

I did not bother to answer. Miss Elizabeth indeed — when it was no more than a year or so since I had stopped playing stone-tag with him, and beating him at that. He walked beside Judith and me all the way up the hill, making the same kind of nonsensical conversation, till I lost my patience.

"For heaven's sake, Sam," I snapped. "What's got into you? You sound like an imitation of Mr. Woodbridge."

The abrupt red that spread even to his ears surprised me even more than his new manners. "Well, you've changed too, you know," he stammered defensively. "I was only trying to please you."

"Well, stop then," I said. "I like you better the old way."

He laughed, shedding Mr. Woodbridge's manners with relief like an overwarm coat. "Maybe you haven't changed so much after all," he said. "You puzzled me with those new airs of yours."

"I didn't know I had any airs," I said honestly.

"Well, you're different, whether you know it or not. And I like it. I'd like to come and see you, Liza."

"You see me all the time."

"I mean — hang it all, you know what I mean. I know I'll have to ask your father first. But would you mind? This evening maybe?"

At last he had my full attention, and I felt a blush beginning that must outdo even his.

"I'll ask him now," he said, his masculine confidence restored by this first sign of maidenly shyness. He left us, taking the blush for an answer.

"I don't see why not," mother said at supper time, looking at me with obvious relief. "At your age Abigail was —"

"I'm not Abigail," I countered stubbornly. My father's jocular announcement to the whole table had drowned me in consternation. "I don't want any — any —"

"Beaux," Judith supplied. "I do. I wish he'd asked to call on me. You always have all the luck."

If she called this luck she was welcome to it, I muttered fiercely.

"Now Judith," mother said with surprising firmness, "you will have your own beaux presently. 'Tis Elizabeth we have to think of right now, since it has happened this way. Perhaps my lace collar on her blue lutestring —"

Abigail was no help to me. "I should think you'd be pleased," she said. "Goodness knows there aren't many chances in this place. What fun is it sitting all alone on a Sabbath night?"

"I'd rather be alone."

" 'Tis time you woke up. At your age I'd had at least three proposals."

The sheer horror in my face only produced further amusement. "You don't have to marry him, Liza. Nobody's going to make you."

I thought of an argument at last. "If I'm not going to marry him, then it isn't proper to let him call on me," I said righteously.

"Nonsense," she said. "You're both children. He's not sixteen. It won't do any harm for both of you to learn how to behave."

How must I behave? I groped back in my memory to the Abigail of Newton days, a birdlike creature with quick provocative smiles and sidelong glances under her lashes, and always the twittering applause of other girls. It was a different world; it had nothing to do with me.

Yet how could I make a scene in the face of all their pleasure? Spinelessly I let them take me in hand. At sundown Judith stationed herself behind the parlor curtains to watch for Sam's arrival.

"You stay with us every minute," I ordered her. "He's really coming to see both of us anyway." It wasn't hard to make her believe this.

I can't go through with it, I thought, when after five minutes the conversation about the drought and the day's sermons had come to a halt. Even the ticking of the great clock in the corner seemed to have slowed to half time, so that at the rate the hands were moving the hour would never strike. Here he sat, this boy I had raced barefoot and climbed trees and shot arrows with, dressed now in a tight woolen coat and stout boots, the knuckles of his hands scrubbed raw. He looked so uncomfortable that I suddenly felt sorry for him. "We could pop some corn," I suggested helplessly.

I soon reaped the consequences of my weakness. Sam overstayed the proper hour, and when he left he took it for granted that he would be back on the next Sabbath. As the door shut behind him, Judith threw both arms around me. "I never had so much fun in all my life," she rejoiced. "And if we hint, perhaps he'll bring Jo Woodbridge with him next week. It will be almost as though we lived in Newton."

So I entered upon an uneasy duality, telling myself that it was for Judith's sake. For as the Sabbath nights continued, Jo Woodbridge did come with Sam. I cannot deny that the long winter evenings passed agreeably, nor that I was gratified that my mother, Abigail, even my father treated me less as a child. Moreover, to my bewilderment, the girls on the Hill opened their tight circle, and I who had always been outside, on the simple merit of having a beau, was now included. I was invited to sewing bees and tea parties; I was offered advice and whispered confidences. I was even given a new name, for the girls declared they did not care for Liza and would call me Betty; some of them still call me so, though the name has always sat uncomfortably. For a brief time all this went to my head, and I confess I did my best to be one of them; I failed not only because I found their concerns and expectations still remote from me but because I was shamed by my own duplicity. When Jemima Woodbridge linked her arm in mine, I turned stiff and unresponsive, knowing myself for an imposter.

Judith's confidences especially filled me with guilt. It had never occurred to me to wonder what she thought about, sitting indoors as she had to do so much of her time, and so often lying in bed. Now she revealed to me a secret life, a network of day-dreams more complex and fanciful than anything I was capable of devising. Where had she found the material from which to weave such fancies? Yet I should have recognized that she had found it exactly where I had found my own. For Judith, as for me, Abigail had provided all the romance her imagination re-quired.

One afternoon, as six of the Hill girls sat together around a quilting frame, the others laughed at some foolish thing I had said, and Keziah Jones reached over to pat my arm. "I do like you, Betty," she said. "You're not at all the way I thought you were."

"I don't think I've changed," I said awkwardly.

"Then maybe we never really knew you. We couldn't very well, could we, while you were spending all your time with that Indian girl?"

Jemima Woodbridge looked across the frame at me with a gleam of something like malice in her eyes. "Some of the girls were afraid to invite you at first for fear you might bring her with you. But I knew you wouldn't." She laughed knowingly.

A cold lump settled in my chest. I sat looking down at the quilt, the little diamond patches slanting sickly before my eyes. In a few moments I clumsily gathered my needles and scissors into my pocket and made some excuse to leave them. Dressed as

I was, in my thin slippers, I went straight down the hill to Konkapot's cabin. There was no one there; in the village they told me that Catharine had gone out with the Indian women to gather ginseng root.

By the time I saw her again, weeks later, I had wondered too long what I could say to her, but she did not seem to notice my ineptitude; her smile was free of question or reproach. She had little time to spare; her days were filled now with work which I could not share. Vaguely resentful, unhappy, I went back to the Hill.

I was in truth separated from them all. For underneath all that I did and said the steady reality of my life ran like a quiet river that waited for the tide to turn. Sometimes it seemed to me that nothing I spoke was altogether true, and yet the truth could not be spoken. I hoped that when the time came they would forgive me — Judith, Catharine, Sam and the others. For in time David Brainerd would come back, and then all of them would understand.

13. THAT NEXT SPRING, one year after England and France declared war on each other, Eph received the commission of captain. It was, I am convinced, the opportunity he had been biding his time for ever since he had come home to Stockbridge. As I have said, Eph had never worked very earnestly at anything, his only visible occupations being the representing of our town at the General Court and an occasional job as surveyor. Now, overnight, his life was filled with purpose. I remember that in late winter, when there came news from Boston of a great fleet about to sail against the French fortress at Louisbourg, he

talked of joining it, but I think his cousin Israel Williams in Hatfield dissuaded him with promises that were soon fulfilled. As
Eph had predicted, the remote war in Europe had its echoes close
to home. Along the borders of New Hampshire province and
farther to the north in Maine, sudden raids and burnings kept the
settlements in constant terror. Along our own western border
was a line of new forts stretching from the Connecticut River to
New York, and of all these forts our Eph was to be in command,
having his headquarters at Fort Shirley and riding out from there
to supervise the others.

He wore his responsibilities as easily as he did the scrupulously
tailored new scarlet coat. When, rarely that summer, he rode
into Stockbridge, his eyes sparkled with cheerful vigor. He
talked importantly of drilling his men, spoke of them all as his
friends, boasted that he could throw any one of them in a wrestling match. Word came to us that he was enormously popular
at the fort, and we could not doubt it. When news reached us
that the French citadel of Louisbourg had surrendered, he was
confident that a march on Canada would meet the same quick
success. He was certain of Indian support, for the Iroquois, even
though the Six Nations had agreed to remain neutral, had grudgingly promised to aid the English in the event of such an attack.
Optimistic and impatient, Eph would have set about recruiting
at once.

Yet as I remember him, it seems to me that he had still the air
of a small boy parading in his father's boots. He was no more
ready to settle down than he had ever been. His house, when he
came back to it, was frequently filled with guests in scarlet coats;
candles blazed till morning, and uproarious male song and laughter were flung into the night from a suddenly opened door.

He had brought a new guest with him last night, I reported to
Abigail one morning in September. An important one, I gath-

ered, from my father's tone of voice, a Brigadier General and a judge as well.

"Father was offended that they didn't ask him to have supper with them," I told her. "This General Dwight fought in the battle of Louisbourg. Father is itching to meet him, and I think it was mean of Eph to leave him out. If he knew King Hendrick was there all the evening, he'd be furious."

"How do you know about Hendrick?" Abigail inquired.

"Elijah saw him. Hendrick comes quite often, you know, when Eph's home."

Abigail looked as though she preferred not to know. "Eph uses him to get information," she explained. "It's Eph's business to know what the Indians are up to."

"Perhaps," I agreed. "But they both enjoy it. Eph told me once that Hendrick was as good company as any white man he knew."

Abigail started to lecture me, then, diverted by a more immediate concern, went to peer into the round wall mirror. "I'd best do something to my hair," she said, "and put on a fresh bonnet. Eph might take it into his head to bring over this friend of his. Cut some sugar lumps for me, will you Liza dear?"

She should have blessed me for my warning, for she was prepared when the two men stepped into her hallway. Certainly the like of General Dwight had never crossed her threshold before. Considerably older than Eph, he possessed a suavity and distinction Eph would never attain. The swing of his stiffened coat skirts, the exquisitely embroidered buttonholes of his waistcoat, the fit and polish of his boots were all impeccable. His heels made a discreet click as he bowed low enough for me to see the top of his freshly powdered wig.

Abigail led him not into the kitchen but into the parlor, where she had had time to arrange the china cups and the thin silver spoons, not obviously in readiness but quick to hand. General Dwight would see that we were not barbarians here in the wilderness, she had said to me. While they talked I brewed the tea as she and Eph liked it, skimmed some of the new cream into the pewter pitcher and carried the tray into the parlor to set it on the little table beside Abigail. She did not offer me a cup, but I did not leave before I had taken a good look at this visitor. I couldn't help but think how much alike they were, he and Abigail. He reached to take the cup from her hand the way the Indians sometimes played their games, observing each small rule scrupulously. I thought that he knew very well how gracefully the linen ruffle fell away from his long elegant hand. Abigail was a match for him, in simple flowered calico that clung snugly to her ribs under her breasts, with the soft muslin ruffles at throat and elbow. She lifted the teapot with a sort of deliberate pleasure, the way she had done so many small tasks in the first year of her marriage, her head slightly tilted, her eyelashes lowered. From the kitchen where I minded the children I heard her delicate Newton laughter.

Afterwards, when the door had shut behind the two men, I went back into the parlor. Abigail was standing by the window watching them walk along the path, and she did not notice me. All at once she clenched her fists and beat them against the sill.

14. "WHY DOES IT have to be my house?" Abigail's anger was rising.

"There's no other house in the town could accommodate them, and you know it." At times my father's fleshy weather-roughened face and Abby's fine-cut features had a curious resemblance. It was in the set of the lips and the quick chill of the blue eyes.

"Sixteen soldiers! You know what they'll be. Ill-bred louts, or worse, riff-raff out of some jail. I won't have it, father."

"Look here, my girl." Father's voice was losing its indulgence. "You built yourself the biggest and handsomest house in the town. When it comes to claiming you can't put up a few soldiers you haven't got a leg to stand on."

"I've got children to think of, whether you think of yours or not. I won't have them exposed to vile talk."

"Rather see them scalped?"

Abigail drew in her breath. "That's nonsense," she said, shaken nevertheless. "I don't believe there's that much danger. Honestly now, Eph?"

Eph, who had been letting them argue it out, deliberately tapped the ashes from the bowl of his pipe and reached for his pouch of tobacco. "We're not bringing in soldiers for nothing, Abby," he said finally. "Nor does the legislature vote one hundred pounds for them without good reason. You know yourself that Stockbridge is as vulnerable as any town on the border."

"What about your new forts?"

"We can count on the forts to block a full-scale attack from the north. But a fort fifty miles away is no protection in a sudden raid."

I sat listening, the snake of fear stirring again in my stomach, actually I suppose still more curiosity. Eph had come down four days ago from Fort Shirley and for the nights past he and father and sometimes one neighbor or another had talked in this room. I had waked in the darkness above in what must have been the deep of the night and heard their voices and sat up in bed to see the bobbing torches the men carried down the path on their way home. In Stockbridge the war still seemed remote.

Accustomed every day to seeing our own Indians going quietly about their business, we felt secure.

"It's better everyone understands," Eph was saying now. Father shrugged. Though his policy was to issue orders without explanation, he knew well enough that Abigail would not budge without knowing why.

She had an argument ready now. "John swears the Mohawks will never attack us."

"He's probably right. As I've told you before, the question is will they let the French Indians come through their territory? It's more a question right now than ever before. Someone's been stirring up the Indians in the Mohawk Valley. Just recently an alarm went through the tribes that the English were marching out from Albany to destroy them, and the redskins swarmed out of their villages like deer in a forest fire. Fellow by the name of William Johnson who lives out there managed to quiet 'em down. Now they've sent a delegation to Montreal to confer with the French, and there's no knowing what they'll agree to. When it comes to dealing with Indians, the French can outsmart us. The English governors don't begin to understand the way an Indian's mind works. Clinton is the worst, thinks all he needs is to hand around a few presents. If those men in Albany knew how the Indians laugh at them. Hendrick regards them as children, says outright that grown men so gullible deserve to be fooled."

Eph had taken on a good deal of authority in these months at the fort; my father kept silent as he went on. "The thing these men can't get through their heads is that the Indians have no intention of fighting this war for us. Why should they? Isn't it logical to an Indian that the more white men, English or French, who kill each other off the better? Take this business of scalp bounties, for example. Got to be done, I suppose, but it's bad policy. Every French scalp we pay for makes our own hair sit less easy. Hendrick tells me scalping was a rare thing in the old days; it's the white men who've encouraged it, offering bounties. You mark my words, the Indians will bring in French scalps, maybe English, but you won't see them turning in many scalps of their own kind."

"You set great store by your friend Hendrick," Abby said. "He may just as well be gulling you. What makes you so sure he won't take a fancy to your scalp some night?"

"It's a possibility," Eph agreed calmly. "Depends on the circumstances. When Hendrick comes to my house and sits over a mug of rum, he comes as a friend, and I'd trust my life with him. But Hendrick as head sachem in his own council — yes, he could become my enemy. The Indians will only fight for reasons of their own, and if the French can give them better reasons they'll fight with the French."

"What better reason?"

"Confidence, for one thing. The Indians think the English are all talk. The French know how to get their point across. I heard one story that the French invited the Senecas to a war feast. They not only stuffed the Indians with good food, they joined in a war dance themselves, even carried bloody wolves' heads and shouted that soon they would be dancing with the heads of Englishmen."

Instantly he saw that he had said too much. Judith put an end to his lecture with a gasp that brought mother rushing across the room.

"Told you there was no sense in this talk," my father growled. "No need to get everybody roiled up. Abby's a grown woman and she's got common sense."

"I suppose I have to take the soldiers, if that's what you mean by common sense." Abby's voice was sulky. "I can't do the cooking for sixteen men, though. The other women might as well understand right now that they're going to help."

15. THE SOLDIERS CAME, and everyone breathed easier to have them there. Our town was so widely scattered on the Plain and the Hill that in a sudden attack we could scarcely have gathered all in one place. But everyone felt that the very presence of a garrison would discourage an Indian raid.

Once having accepted the total disruption of her household and the burden it placed on her shoulders, Abigail set her chin, and I never heard her speak another word of complaint. She packed away her fine china and drew her plans as carefully as a general, dictating where the men would sleep and eat, portioning out the necessary labor, and managing somehow to preserve a part of the house forbidden to the soldiers where John and the children could dwell with a measure of peace. I don't think there was ever a doubt in anyone's mind as to who was the real officer in command of that garrison.

Every morning Judith and I helped with the other women to prepare the incredible amount of food that was needed to fill sixteen soldiers. As Abigail had predicted, they were an unattractive and troublesome lot. Two were middle-aged, thin-mouthed men with little to say but what was plentifully spiced with oaths. The others were young, and their constant boisterous laughter could be heard as far as our own house, sounding like the noise of crows in a cornfield. But somehow within a few days Abigail had cowed these men as firmly as she had the Indians. When they filed into her kitchen for a meal, their voices were subdued, their clumsy bodies stiffened, they pulled their caps off their heads and said yes ma'am and no ma'am like school boys. Even so, I did not like to wait on them; the small kitchen could not comfortably contain so much maleness. At the third meal, as I leaned over to put a platter of mush on the table, I received a pinch that hurt through my skirts and petticoats. I was too shamed to let anyone know, but the next day Judith ran crying to mother, and after that we went home the moment the food was prepared and the men took turns waiting on each other. When mother voiced a tearful concern for Abigail, Abby only snorted and said she'd like to see them try any tricks on her. I thought secretly that I would indeed like to see it.

More serious than this, the soldiers were contemptuous of our Indians. The two older men said often, taking good care some Indian was in hearing, that redskins and wolves were meant to be wiped off the face of the earth. The younger ones ordered them about. If an Indian happened to be passing, some soldier would shout at him to tie up a horse or fetch some water and be quick about it. They couldn't seem to get it through their heads that the Indians weren't our slaves, and when John explained to them patiently that the Indians were freeholders and equal subjects of the King, they winked behind his back and went on lording it around the town. They strolled about on the Plain eying the Indian girls till Catharine told me the fields had to go untended because the women preferred to stay inside the wigwams. It was not beneath the soldiers' dignity, however, to trade with the Indians; every man in the garrison soon boasted good beaver skins hidden in his pack, and certainly there was more rum than ever before in evidence on the Plain. Some ugly incidents that flared into blows were stopped by John Sergeant just short of serious trouble. Altogether it was a trying winter.

16. WITH ALL WE had to do, it was easy to forget that of us all the war weighed most heavily on John, for it meant the ruin of all his plans. Just as his new boarding school had been almost within reach, it had vanished like a drifting bubble.

Weeds and grass had overgrown the foundation of the new building; the influential men in Boston had more important claims on their attention. The money he had hoped to raise in Massachusetts had been poured instead into forts and cannon; the men who would have worked to raise the schoolhouse had been recruited for the Berkshire County contingent. John had not abandoned his vision, but I think he must often have despaired.

It seemed to me that my father and John Sergeant moved ever farther apart in those years. I understood that much of the news Eph brought back, news which my father and the neighbors pondered with serious faces, was never intended to reach John's ears. I don't know whether John was aware that he was deliberately excluded from their discussions. "He's too touchy," my father said once. "Upset at a mention of his Indians. There's no talking sense to him." I was beginning to see that my father's idea of sense could never be reconciled with John's. Loyal to the King as he was, and uncomplaining about the burden the garrison had imposed on his household, John still had no real concern for the issues father saw at stake in this war. He had no interest in trade; he could not understand the English need for undisputed possession of the wilderness. He was unmoved by the gusts of alarm that shook the town, for he had no thought of personal danger and utter trust in his Indians.

The money which still arrived faithfully from Mr. Hollis in England weighed on his conscience. This good Christian gentleman must, I think, have possessed a nature even less practical than John's, and being at that great distance he could not understand why his money was lying idle merely because of a war. He was John's most generous supporter, and should he decide to withdraw his funds, all hope of a new school would collapse. In desperation, John entrusted his plan to a Captain Kellogg, a retired soldier from Connecticut then living in Stockbridge, who agreed to take into his house a few boys and to teach them farming and some reading. I am sure John could not have been satisfied with this arrangement; Mr. Kellogg was a rough, ill-spoken man, a haphazard farmer and certainly no scholar, with but two qualities in his favor. Having been captured by Indians in his youth, he had a fair knowledge of the language. And he was willing. Pressed by the need to put Mr. Hollis' money to use, John made a tragic choice, but how can he be blamed that there was no one worthier of his trust?

17. TWO OF THE younger soldiers stood out from the rest for quite different reasons. The youngest of them, a greenhorn if ever I saw one, kept to himself a good deal, sitting on a stump and polishing his musket. One day as they all shambled out after dinner, he stopped by the dresser and opened the cover of a book John had left there. The next day he worked up the courage to ask John if he might read it, and thereafter, encouraged by John's real pleasure, he read straight through one book after another, sermons, theology and all, sitting engrossed and unconscious of the jokes that glanced off his bent head. But though he seemed not to notice anything that went on around him, he twice laid down his book and came to help me carry water from the well. Once he shyly asked my name and told me that his own was Benjamin Niles.

One morning when Judith had stayed at home to rest, I carried the last basket of apples to the doorstep and sat in the thin spring sunshine. Presently Benjamin came across the yard and stopped in front of me, and then, without asking my leave, he sat down with the basket between us, took out his knife and began to pare apples with quick capable hands.

"Got a letter yesterday," he told me, after a time. A pack train of provisions had come into town the day before, and most of the men had heard from their families. "Would you want to read it?"

I was amused, but looking over at him I saw that he had pulled the letter from his pocket and was fingering it and that he was aching to share it with someone. "Of course," I said quickly, and reached out my hand for it.

"It's from my mother," he explained. "Pa learned to write some when he was young, but I guess he's out of practice."

The letter didn't say much, only that his pa had had to borrow hay to get the animals through the winter and that his grandpa's bad knee was bothering him again. At the end it said that Emily asked every day when he was coming home, and I knew that this was what he had wanted me to read.

"Tell me about Emily," I said, handing back the letter, and from that moment he did not even notice that I quietly pared and cored the whole basket of apples while he talked.

I learned a great deal about Emily in those long months, and about the farm in Brookfield and his younger brothers and sisters, and about Benjamin himself. I never heard from him after he went away from Stockbridge, and I suppose he and Emily may well have great-grandchildren by now. I hope they had a fine houseful of their own; he would have been a good father to them.

The other soldier, Luther Binney, stood out because of his lean good looks and his own conviction that he was cast from a different mold than the others. Luther managed through the winter to wear very lightly the admiration of all the Hill girls, implying with an easy gallantry that though he found them all charming they could not hope to compete with the girls he had left behind. With the soft spring days he made it plain that he had taken a fancy to Judith. This was not surprising; at seventeen Judith was exceedingly pretty, and her delicacy gave her added appeal and set her apart from the rest of us. The change in her now was so immediate and so remarkable that I wondered father did not notice and interfere. There was color in her cheeks, and sometimes her eyes, slanting from under her lashes, seemed almost as blue as Abigail's. She was like a reflection, not quite clear or true, of the Abigail I remembered in Newton. There was no doubt Judith was remembering too and that the tinkling laugh was a deliberate echo. You can't imitate laughter that sounds in one's memory like drops of sunlit water. With Judith it came out more often an ascending giggle. I was uneasy, and finally I spoke to Abby about it.

"What a prude you are," Abby said. "It won't do Judith a bit of harm. She's been eaten up with envy since Sam Brown started paying you attention. Let her have a little fun now."

But I was disturbed, coming suddenly out of Abigail's rear door, to see Judith standing under the trellis with Luther Binney. She was leaning against the wall with her head tilted back, looking up at him. He stood with the sort of easiness and arrogance our Stockbridge boys never possessed, and I knew that he was well used to seeing that look in a girl's eyes. I disliked him suddenly and intensely, and I was rude to Judith when she caught up with me on the path. When she asked me if I did not think him handsome I said nothing at all, only kicked at the pebbles in the path and hated her high little giggle.

But when, a few days later, I saw his blond head moving through the fern along the path that led to the spring, and was certain I caught the flicker of her skirt beside him, I waited for her and blurted out what I thought.

"You look like a solemn owl," this new Judith said scornfully. "I wonder sometimes what Sam sees in you."

"If it were somebody like Sam," I insisted. "Juda, you don't know this man at all."

"What of it? Abby said we had to learn, and what better chance is there likely to be?"

"He's not good enough even to practice on. He's just what Abby said they'd be — riff-raff. And it's gone to his head to have a girl like you —"

Judith's face suddenly twisted. "You're jealous!" she flared. "You're just trying to be mean. What do you take me for? Do you think I don't know as well as you what's wrong and what isn't? All I want is to have a little fun the way girls do in other places. If you say one word to mama or to Abby or to anybody, I'll hate you as long as I live."

I promised miserably. Perhaps I was a prude. Perhaps I would have thought Luther Binney handsome, if I had not had etched on my heart a face as different as light from dark. I might have thought this boy's jokes were clever, if I had not known a man so bent on the work of God that he had no time for joking. I felt years, a lifetime, older than Judith, and I knew that this pleasure of hers was counterfeit. But how could I tell her that?

So like a coward I said nothing, and a week later I found her hunched on our bed, sobbing wildly and almost out of her mind. Filled with panic, I shook the truth out of her.

"He — I tried to run and he came after me. He's so strong. I couldn't even breathe. I thought I was going to faint. And then he let me go, so sudden I fell down. And he swore. And then he said go along, it wouldn't be worth it. And when I caught my foot in my skirt trying to get up he stood there and laughed. He kept on laughing all the time I was running along the path."

I was shaking between relief and anger and a rage to strike at

his laughter with my own hands. But at the same time I was helping Judith out of her clothes and trying to shush her so that
mother wouldn't hear. There were purple marks already on her
arm, and she went on babbling and sobbing, unable to stop herself.

"I always thought it would be nice to have somebody kiss me.
It was horrible. I almost choked. Liza — don't ever let anybody kiss you, not ever!"

At last I got her into bed and got the warming pan and poured
out a measure of brandy and made her drink it, and finally she
stopped shivering and went to sleep. I picked up the dress and
smoothed it out as best I could and tried to think of a story to tell
mother. It was only a scare, I kept telling myself. She'll get over
it. Tomorrow it won't seem so bad, and she'll be able to laugh
about it.

By tomorrow Judith had a fever and an attack of asthma that
lasted for three weeks, and after that she was poorly for a long
time. All that summer I wanted to cry whenever I looked at her,
and it seemed to me I would have given anything in the world to
hear that silly high giggle again.

18. THE GREAT BEAR in the sky was wounded, and his blood
fell on the forests, staining the leaves. Very soon he must
be overtaken and slain, and the white oil of his body would drip
down upon the earth. In the spring the oil would melt, making
sap for the trees, and with the summer the great hunt would
commence again. But now one must grieve for the stricken bear.

It had been long since I had seen Catharine, when on a warm
afternoon I rode through the red-gold woods to Konkapot's
cabin. She was outside, bending over a wooden frame, scraping

with a sharp-edged stone to clean the hair from a doeskin she had stretched taut. Her smile held no tinge of reproach; she brought me one of the small maple-sweetened cakes she knew I loved and went back to her scraping. I sat on a stump and watched her, wondering why I had stayed away so long, enjoying the sun and the slow downward drift of maple leaves and the comfortable silence she never needed to fill with chatter.

"There is much work," she said presently. "I am going to marry."

I sat up, startled. "Who?"

"Yokon Yokon. It is arranged a long time. He wait while I care for my brothers. Now, because I cannot leave, he come here to live with us."

"He is an old man!" I did not mean to be rude, and she was not offended.

"Not very old. Indian girls do not marry young men like white girls. Young men hunt and make war. They have no time for wives."

"Catharine — do you want to marry him?"

She shrugged. "It is time," she said.

"Do you love him?"

A short while ago the derision plain in her eyes would have silenced me. Now I believed myself wiser than she. "It is not right for you to marry if you don't love him," I insisted. "Your father should not make you."

"My father does not make me," she said proudly. "It is my own wish. Yokon is a brave hunter. He will have brave sons. Then perhaps I will love him."

"Do not look so sad," she said, when I did not answer. "It is good for a woman to have a man of her own to work for."

I sat trying to find some word to say, sick at heart. She had never looked lovelier, slender and fine-boned, her skin smooth and warm, her heavy braids shining with lights like a grackle's wing. Would Yokon be good to her? Would he make her work for him till she was bent and stiffened like the older Indian women, her beauty coarsened and eroded by wind and sun? Would she thicken and grow fat with bearing her brave sons?

"You too," she broke my silence. "Will you marry soon?"

"No," I said, "not for a long time."

"There is English man who loves you the way you say."

"How do you know?" I asked, feeling the startled red in my cheeks.

"In the Sabbath meeting he eats you with his eyes. Indian would never do that. He would be too proud."

"Oh — him!" Sam Brown had been far from my thoughts. "He's only a silly boy. I'm never going to marry him."

Then on an impulse I told her, because all of us at times must speak to someone. She stopped her work to listen with grave soft eyes. When I finished she did not rush into swift words as an English girl would have done. She stood silent, pondering. It occurred to me that she was as troubled by my confidence as I had been by hers.

"The missionary is a good man," she said finally. "He has a strong spirit. But it is like an eagle in a cage made of grass. I think he has a sickness."

"I will take care of him and make him well."

She bent over her work. "I think Indian way is better," she said, not looking at me.

"What do you mean?"

"The other one, the one you think you do not love, he would give you strong sons."

"You don't understand at all," I cried. "You don't know what it means to love someone."

"Do not be angry," she said. "We are friends."

I was not angry, but hurt and disappointed, as no doubt she had been and given no sign. Each of us was aware of the shadow between us.

We were still friends, but never quite the same. Nevertheless, it was after that that for the first and only time in our lives she asked a favor of me. Not on her own behalf, but for one of the least deserving of her tribe. She was waiting one morning at the bend of the road not far from my father's store. I don't know how many days she had waited there, but I was instantly sure that had I not happened to walk that way that morning she would have waited for me the next day and the next. She never came to our house. I was glad to see her and walked with her to the bridge. She talked politely for a few moments, and then spoke, with no emphasis, of a slight matter, making it easy for me not to recognize that this was why she had come. Nomshoos was about to lose the portion of the Indian land he had cultivated, she told me, because he had not repaid the money my father had lent him. The Indians knew that my father had no ill will toward Nomshoos, and that he did not wish to do him harm. But Nomshoos was not a gifted speaker; he had not been able to make my father understand the reasons why he could not repay the money. When my father understood, the Indians knew, he would keep the chain of friendship bright between them. He would allow Nomshoos more time.

I went directly to my father. He sat in the corner of our parlor at the table he used for a desk. His ledger was open, and his broad hand, clenched around the delicate quill, was poised just above the inkpot.

"I am busy, Elizabeth."

That I had chosen a poor time put me at a disadvantage, though I had little hope of ever being certain of a right time. I pleaded my case poorly.

"Why are you telling me this?" he interrupted at last.

"I knew that if you understood you would give Nomshoos more time."

"What right had you to make such an assumption?"

"I knew it must be a mistake. The Indians don't understand about money."

"Nomshoos understands all right. He came to me for that money three years ago, and every six months since he's come to the store and explained why he can't repay a penny of it."

"He has been ill."

"Intoxicated, you mean. And bone lazy like all the rest of them. There's no reason I should suffer for it. It may interest you to know that the General Court of Massachusetts has approved my buying a small portion of Indian land at a fair rate. Nomshoos doesn't own it. You know as well as I do the Indians hold all their land in common."

"It is the portion Nomshoos has cleared to plant."

"Then let him clear another section. There's land going begging. Any Indian would rather sit and howl that he's been cheated than lift a finger to help himself."

"That's unfair!" I burst out.

Instantly I saw that I had lost any chance of a further hearing. "You are being impertinent," he snapped. "Do I have to spell out my business affairs to a child?"

When I tried to speak once more, he laid down his pen and turned about in his chair and looked at me, and my tongue went dry in my mouth.

"Wait a minute, young lady." He stopped me at the door. "I've been too patient with this friendship of yours. I've never favored it, any more than I favored Eph's giving you that horse. I'd advise you now to let it drop. You're a Williams, and it's high time you began to act like one."

There was nothing I could explain to Catharine, for I saw that whatever I said must be disloyal to my father. So I said nothing and let her think I had not understood. She never spoke of it again, but the shadow between us was more palpable. I was miserable that I had failed her, but obscurely I held it against her that because of her, in some indefinable way, I too had been betrayed.

My father was right, I suppose. To be fair to him, he did not claim the land for several years, and in all that time Nomshoos never planted the acres, nor did he ever clear any new land. Henceforth he was one of John Sergeant's most grievous problems, and I rarely saw him sober.

Catharine did not marry. That winter she fell ill of the same malady that had killed her mother. I went as soon as I heard she was ill, and through the last days I sat beside her, not talking, only feeding her a mouthful at a time, raising her head when she could not breathe, loving her, and knowing that even if I could save her we could never go back. I would look up, sitting there, and see the blue beads still hanging where they had always been, blinking in the firelight.

19. THERE IS A day in those years that I have not yet faced, preferring to veil it with other matters. It is the day that David Brainerd returned.

I know that not a Sabbath had passed in that year since he had come back to visit Stockbridge that I had not wakened with a lift of hope. I understood that endless stretches of wilderness must lie between our town and the Delaware River. But visiting clergymen were no rarity in our meetinghouse. They seemed to think little of days on horseback, and conventions drew them readily from great distances. Moreover, John Sergeant was the magnet who would surely draw back the young missionary who had leaned on him for support and encouragement, for I was certain these were as greatly needed in the Delaware as they had been at Kaunameek. But Indian summer went by. The glory of the hills faded day by day, the scarlet dimming to bronze and the bronze to brown, and finally the first November winds blew the leaves in whorls across the paths, and the gray and black lacework of branches edged the distant hills. Soon the snow would put an end to my hopes for months to come.

Then without warning he was there, standing in his old place to read the scripture. In the first dizzying shock of joy I could scarcely see his face; when my sight cleared I was struck with horror at the change in him. He was older, years older. His emaciated body no longer stood quite erect, weariness blurred all its outlines. His cheeks were sunken, his dark eyes enlarged by heavy shadows.

When he rose to preach I held my breath. His anguished look moved slowly over the congregation, found my gaze that never left his face, stopped for a long heartbeat and went past me. Then he began to speak, and the fire sprang up in him as hotly as ever. He was no longer a green young preacher, uncertain of his reception. The words flowed from him confidently in a tide of eloquence that caught up not only me but every man and woman and child in the house. His shoulders straightened, the red sprang into his cheeks, his eyes were brilliant. He did not look my way again.

He does not need my help, I thought, with both pain and a fierce pride. God had granted him the power he had prayed for. But I remembered suddenly Catharine's words — an eagle in a cage of grasses. It seemed to me that the spirit that beat against that frail cage must shatter it altogether.

Before he had finished speaking, my mind was made up. He

had followed the call of God; now my own call seemed as clear. Age and modesty and patience were foolish trifles before the loneliness that spoke from his eyes and voice and before the full unquestioning tide of faith and love that rose in my own heart.

I had only a handclasp and a brief smile before he retired to be alone as was his custom between services. I was content with these through the long afternoon service. But I was dismayed, as we came from the meetinghouse, to see that he had not stayed to greet us but was already slowly walking toward the Woodbridge house, and that Timothy Woodbridge and John Sergeant walked one on each side, closely, as though they might be needed. Soon after we reached our own house, an Indian boy delivered to my father a brief note from Mr. Woodbridge stating that Mr. Brainerd was too ill to accept the invitation to supper but would call later to pay his respects to us.

When the knock came, however, it was Sam Brown who stood on the doorstep, and I had to sit through the long evening with him, straining my ears for a footstep, marking each quarter hour as the clock struck. After Sam had gone I watched at the window till I saw John's lantern moving along the path, and I ran out into the cold without my hood. John swung up his lantern to light my face, and there was surprise in his own, but he answered me calmly, taking for granted as he always did in any situation only a simple goodness of intent.

"He meant to come, Elizabeth, but even putting on his coat was too much for him. We could not allow him to ride up the hill. He must save his strength if he is to leave in the morning."

"Leave — is he well enough?"

"I doubt he is often well enough. He goes in spite of it, and he believes the riding to be good for him. He was very foolish to come so far north this time. He was called to Long Island, but he wanted to talk to me."

"Can I go down to see him?"

"Tonight? It is late, my dear, and I think he was about to sleep. It would be kinder not to disturb him."

I went back into the house and packed a few warm clothes into a bundle which I hid under the bed Judith and I shared. I lay beside her without sleeping. If once or twice in the deepest hours, when I think doubt must fill the strongest heart, I wavered in my purpose, the gray chill before dawn found me steady again. I dressed and combed my hair in the darkness, making no sound. I wished that I could kiss Judith goodbye. I would miss her, and this room as well. Downstairs in the hall I had hung my heavy cloak on the peg nearest the door, and I took it down and lifted the latch and let myself silently out into the winter dawn. Nippe was not surprised, for we often rode early; she whinnied softly as I strapped on her saddle.

I waited so long, shivering, where the trail crossed the river, that I thought with despair that he must have left in the night, or perhaps had been too ill to leave at all. Then I heard hoofbeats and slid down from Nippe's back to wait for him. I had put out my lantern, and the gray outlines of the houses on the Plain were sharp in the thin light. Yes, it was he, and he was alone.

"Elizabeth!" I had startled his horse, and for a moment he had his hands full with her. "What are you doing here?"

"I am going with you," I told him.

"That is kind of you," he said. "Mr. Woodbridge offered also to see me on my way, but I would not allow him."

"I mean I am going with you to the Delaware."

He looked very ill. It seemed to take a long time for my words to reach him.

"My dear child —" he said finally.

"I am not a child. I am fifteen years old."

When he did not answer, I hurried on. "I would have liked

my father to marry me, but I have thought about this carefully. It is better for us to leave here now and find a justice of the peace in some other town."

"Elizabeth," he said, "this — it is impossible."

I moved nearer and looked up straight into his face. It puzzled me that there was no joy in it, only pain.

"Haven't I proved that I can care for you?" I asked him.

"Yes. You have more than proved that."

"Then there is no use in this waiting. You need me now."

"My dear," he stammered, and this time he did not call me child. "I cannot. It is impossible. I — there is a reason which I cannot speak of now."

It was his tone more than his words that reached me, a finality that pierced below my thinking and made me step back out of his path. He looked down at me with tenderness.

"I thank you with all my heart," he said. "God be with you, Elizabeth."

No, no matter what we say, we would not really be young again. I know now it would have been better if he had told me outright. Yet I do not blame him. I know he meant to be kind, that it was only my own stubborn blindness that I misread his kindness. I went back to waiting, because though waiting was no longer a joy it had become the pattern of my life. I wept in the night, but I never really doubted. I knew that when this obstacle, whatever it might be, was removed, he would come back. It is hard to believe now that I waited so for two more years.

The Ice Glen

1746

I. My FATHER came up the hill at midmorning and stood in our kitchen. Sweat drenched his face, and his eyes looked as though they were being pushed outward from behind.

"Are you ill?" my mother asked quickly.

His answer was harsh. "Fort Massachusetts has been attacked."

Mother's clasped hands pressed against her mouth. Eph had moved some time since from Fort Shirley to the new fort at Hoosac. "Indians?"

"French and redskins together. That's all the rider knows. They burned the fort."

"Eph?" The word was squeezed from her throat.

"He didn't know, I told you. It happened days ago. He said the fort surrendered. He thinks some of them died, and the rest were taken captive."

He sat down in his chair slowly, like an old man. "Thomas was at the fort too," he said.

I wanted to run to him, but I was past the age for that. Like mother I stood helpless, ice cold and shaking.

"They never took Eph alive," father said to the wall, as though it had accused him. "By God, they never did. Not Eph."

Abigail came running along the path, tears on her face. "John told me," she gasped. She went straight to father and put her arms around him, as mother and I had been unable to do. Then she sat beside him and held his hand.

"Eph wouldn't have surrendered," she whispered, and I saw the half-blind grateful look he turned upon her.

"You don't need to tell me." His voice was unsteady. "They never took him alive."

How many times he repeated those words, and every time they twisted like a knife in my chest. Yet he seemed to find his only comfort in them. We sat in the parlor, the whole family, our hands empty. From time to time some neighbor came, his face awed, his voice lowered. There was nothing to talk about. The post rider had known no names, no destination for the captives, only that the fort had surrendered. I would have preferred to go away by myself, but I stayed, caught with them all like pigeons in a net. Though my eyelids burned, I could not find release as Judith and mother did perhaps in their steady weeping. The morning dragged on. For the first time, the war became real, in the only way it would ever be real to us here on the Hill. I do not know what men vision when they think of war. For women it is waiting, and the tight net of fear.

At noontime Abigail broke from our numb circle. "I'll come back," she promised. "John must have his dinner and so must the children."

"No need to stay here," my father fretted. "May be days before more word comes in."

"I'll get some food on the table myself," mother decided. "Some hot tea anyway. It isn't good for us to just set like this."

Slowly we took up the work of the day again. But in the evening, when Abigail returned, we were all there in the parlor, sitting as though we had never moved. So we all were late that night when Eph himself rode into Stockbridge. There was a shout outside, and then he came stamping through the door, alive, solid, clean-shaven and beautiful.

Abigail reached him first, flinging herself at him with quick sharp sobs. Abruptly, he disengaged her arms.

"The heroics are wasted, Abby," he said. "I never heard a shot."

My father, halfway across the room, stopped.

"I wasn't there," Eph said to him. "My damnable luck after all these months."

"Thank God!" Abigail cried. "Oh, Eph!"

We were all upon him then, wanting to prove his wholeness in our arms and hands and fingers. All but my father. He still stood in the middle of the room, and it was to him that Eph spoke, over our heads.

"I was ordered to Albany to confer with Governor Clinton. I had no way of knowing anything was brewing. The French have a fiendish system of intelligence. They waited till I had gone. They even watched Thomas go out."

"Thomas?"

"He wasn't there either. When Hawks got the first alarm, he sent Thomas with fourteen men to get help from Deerfield. The Indians must have been hiding all around the fort when he went out. They let him pass right through them."

"How many were left in the fort?"

"Twenty-three. I admit it wasn't enough, and to make it worse, fourteen of them were sick."

My father sat down heavily, leaning with his hands on his knees. Head bent, he looked up at his son, the struggle plain on his broad face. Relief, thankfulness and something else that Eph was not slow to read.

"I had no way of knowing," Eph repeated. "Of course I should have left a stronger force. There were seven hundred of the French, and they waited three days, thinking we were stronger than we were. When they came on, Hawks did his best. He held them off for two days till his bullets gave out. If I know him, he'd have gone on fighting with nothing but his bare hands. But there were women and children, and the sick men. If I'd been there —"

My father looked at the floor, his head bent still further. "Yes." He cleared his throat. "Yes, of course."

There was a silence now as we all remembered. Everyone in the town must know how he had sworn that Eph would never have surrendered.

I could not endure it. "What's the matter with everybody?" I cried out. "Was it Eph's fault he was ordered to leave?"

Eph patted me on the shoulder. "Thanks, Liza," he said. He faced us all, his customary cheerful open face oddly blurred, as though his father's image had been stamped upon it. "I understand," he said harshly. "It's awkward for me to come home with a whole skin. What will people say?"

Abigail spoke up, her voice sharp and emphatic. "They'll say precisely what we want them to say," she announced. "That if you'd been there the French wouldn't have dared attack at all. And that you've been half out of your mind because you weren't."

Eph turned and looked at her. "Very handsome of you, Abby. You'd actually perjure your soul for my reputation?"

She flushed. "It's true, isn't it?"

"It will be, I can see that, before you're through. But let's have it clear between us. I wish I'd been there. If I had, I think I'd have held my end up. None of us knows that till the test comes. But I'm not broken-hearted. I happen to prefer to be alive, and it's my opinion I'm more useful that way. If you think I'm going to apologize to this town because they aren't celebrating my burial, you can think again. And I'm damned if I'll stay around and listen to you apologizing for me. I'm starting for Shirley before daybreak. You can tell them what you like."

In the morning my father went back to his store on the Plain, and Abigail let her own work wait while she visited from house to house on the Hill, spreading the joyful news of Eph's safe return. Sympathy and rejoicing echoed in every household. While the English families respected Eph's grief at not being in the fort to stand with his men, they all took his absence for a sign from heaven that he had been spared to be Stockbridge's chosen protector. From that time on he was more than ever their favorite. But he came home less often to enjoy it.

As one surprising consequence of the burning of Fort Massachusetts, my father came to share the military honors in the town. He enlisted for active service, was commissioned a major and assigned the task of supervising the rebuilding of the fort. With a vast deal of fuss about a new horse, a new uniform, and the stocking of food, tobacco and the ingredients for his indispensable lime punch, and leaving behind a disheartening list of reminders for us all, he rode out of Stockbridge to take up residence in Hoosac. When the new fort was completed in June he was given the post of command there.

2. THAT LONG SUMMER of 1747, in my father's absence, the strain of waiting was heavy on us all. Rumors filtered through to us now and again that Indians had pounced somewhere along the northern border, leaving some poor farmer's house in flames, perhaps his children slaughtered. But the threat of a French attack never materialized. All the talk of the vast march our colonies were to make against Canada also seemed to come to nothing. Some of our Stockbridge boys returned from Albany, their terms of enlistment run out, having seen no more of war than a pestilence-ridden camp.

My father, accustomed to having a finger in many pies, chafed

at the monotony of life at the fort, complaining at the same time
that he missed the peace and quiet of his own house. In his heart
he was not a soldier but a farmer, uneasy about his hay and his
young fruit trees and his animals. He would appear in the yard
unexpectedly, berate anyone in sight for laziness and neglect,
shout a new volley of orders, which likely as not contradicted
the last set, gorge himself on mother's cooking and ride off again,
each time more openly loath to go.

Josiah had his own house on the Hill now, and we saw little of
him. Elijah was restless and continually in trouble; Mr. Woodbridge complained that he was an indifferent student, the fact
that he stood too easily at the head of the school making him
careless and impertinent. He was popular in the town, leader of
an unruly group of younger boys. I began to wonder if I had
done right to cover up his misdeeds as I so often had to save him
a thrashing. That summer it was clear to me that he needed his
father's hand.

Judith waited too, I think, though she no longer confided in
me. Immersed and seemingly content in her feminine world of
embroidery and gossip, she yet had about her a vague discontent,
perhaps only the reflection of mother's anxiety.

Abigail waited for her third child, plagued, as she had been
with the other pregnancies, by spells of sickness, melancholy and
resentment, this time with good reason, for there seemed to be no
prospect that the soldiers would soon depart from her house.
John was constantly overtired, his cheerfulness often clouded;
we still did not know how seriously he was in debt, and to a man
of his simple honesty the burden must have been intolerable.
Erastus had begun to study under Timothy Woodbridge, but
Electa was demanding, her eager mind needing more novelty
than any of us could provide. Perhaps because the waiting had
been more filled with difficulty than ever before, when her son

was born in October, Abigail claimed him with a passion and a possessiveness she had never shown toward her other children. She insisted that he be baptized John.

As for myself, I was close to seventeen and no longer able to content myself with waiting. In the two years since David Brainerd had visited Stockbridge I had rarely heard his name. John Sergeant told us once that the harvest of souls had been miraculous in the Delaware. So he had come into his own, he no longer had need to come to John for guidance, and I rejoiced for him. I never doubted that he would come, not for John this time, but for me, when the time should be right for his coming, when the obstacle between us had been removed. But the certainty that we belonged to each other, which was the air I breathed, was not enough to nourish me as it so long had been. I needed the certainty of sight and touch.

For a long time now I had discouraged Sam Brown from calling; we were no longer children to enjoy popping corn of a Sabbath night, and I knew he should be finding a girl he could properly court. Yet it was not easy to extricate myself without explaining from this tangle I had slipped into so weakly. The girls on the Hill still talked openly about my dowry; I could not so much as help my mother with a bit of sewing without suffering their knowing glances. Judith and mother approached, in a thousand circling ways, the question they did not dare to ask. Abigail, shrewder than the others, suspected that Sam had not yet come to the point, and she tried to give me advice. Increasingly I strained against my deception and sometimes came close to ending it.

Abigail was right, Sam had not come to the point. I hoped he never would, but in the end I could not prevent it. There came a night when Judith could not attend the singing meeting, and Sam walked home with me in the twilight.

"You've been making it plain enough," he said, detaining me at the last turning, out of sight of the house. "You've always put me off. But I'm not going to let you go for lack of one more try. I want you to listen this time, Liza."

So I had to hear him out. "It would never work, Sam."

"What makes you so sure it wouldn't?"

"You don't know me. You don't really know what I'm like at all."

"What do you mean by that? I've grown up with you. I've been courting you for going on four years."

"We've never really talked to each other."

For just an instant I saw a doubt in his eyes; an acknowledgment that for him too there had been a lack in those Sabbath evenings. But he rushed past it. It never occurred to him that there could be someone else.

"I'd be good to you. I swear, Liza, I'd give you anything you wanted."

"I know you would. I've always liked you. But liking isn't enough."

"I never said it was. It's a start. Lots of couples start with no more than that. How do you know about the rest? You've never let me come within three feet of you. Liza —"

I could have prevented him, but I stood still. After a time he let me go, and backed away while we both got our breaths.

"It's no use, is it?" he said, when I did not speak. "Maybe I was wrong. I swear there's a real woman behind those cool eyes of yours. I was fool enough to think I could flush her out of hiding."

I reached out my hand to him. "I want to go now," I said. "Please, Sam."

"All right," he said, in a voice stripped of excitement or hope. "But just think about it. You're the one I want, always have wanted. But I'm not one who holds there's only one girl in the world. I mean to get married. I want a home of my own, and I mean to make my wife happy. You or somebody else. I don't intend to wait forever."

I thought, whether I wanted to or not. Sam had been right; there was a woman there, and though he thought he had failed, he had indeed flushed her out of hiding. For the first time in my life I had seen her clearly and recognized her for what she was. From now on I could not pretend that she was not there; she would have to be reckoned with, not just that night but over and over again. But she did not have to be yielded to. In the morning I wrote a letter to Sam and sent it to him by Erastus. Within a week he was courting Lydia Willard.

It was after this that the waiting seemed at times to be more than I could bear.

3. ON THE SABBATH night of little John's baptism in October, the first time that Abigail felt strong enough to leave her house, we celebrated at my father's table. We were all there. My father had returned to us, having had his fill of military life, and our world once more revolved on its proper axis. Eph had just completed a tour of the forts and had a night's leave. He had brought with him a bottle of French brandy, and at the end of the meal he rose to make a graceful toast of welcome to the new member of the family. John sat unsmiling, more abstracted than was his custom, his face thin and exhausted. Abigail tried to rouse him.

"You are the proud father," she prodded him lightly. "Can't you make a proper reply?"

Still John did not smile. "I'm afraid not," he said. "I beg your forgiveness, Eph, but my heart is too heavy tonight."

"Is something wrong?" Abigail asked quickly.

He hesitated. "I did not want to spoil the celebration," he explained, as we all waited. "I suppose I must tell you. The Lord giveth and the Lord taketh away. I received word this morning of the death of our good friend David Brainerd."

A whirlwind roared in upon me, lifting me from among them. From its still eye I could see them all sitting about the table, their faces filled with shock and pity; their voices came to me from a vast distance. Abigail said something sharply about his never taking care of himself, and mother murmured about the dreadful wilderness. Then John's voice reached me clearly.

"He had left the Delaware," he said. "He came to Northampton last spring and died at Mr. Edwards' house. He was betrothed to Edwards' daughter Jerusha, and she tended him."

Their voices receded as the whirlwind carried me away into a roaring icy darkness.

I woke in the night alone in the bed. There was a candle burning, and mother sat in a chair dozing, her head tilted down. I lay still, sensing an unspeakable terror that waited beyond the circle of light, straining to identify its form. Then suddenly from the dark corners grief advanced upon me, and I cried out, bringing mother to my side. But over her shoulder I glimpsed in the shadows a merciless paling holding grief back from me, and I understood that I never could claim it for my own.

They told me afterwards that I had a fever of the brain. There is little I remember of that time, but I recall that Thomas came from Fort Massachusetts and that he applied leeches. I suspect the horrid creatures drained my strength as well as the fever, for after my head was clear again I seemed to have no power over my body.

I believe now that it was the denial of grief that prolonged my illness. Somehow the need for concealment, the knowing that I had no right to my grief, left me helpless under its weight. Useless to ask myself now why I was so desperately compelled to silence. I remember weeping that Catharine was not there, but I wonder if, had she lived, I could have spoken even to her. Why could I not find the words to reach toward my mother, who blamed herself for allowing me to work too hard at the nursing? I once overheard Abigail say to Judith that Sam Brown was not worth it, and I suspect that to this day she believes that Sam's turning to Lydia Willard was the cause of it all. In their own ways they tried to make up to me by waiting on me and urging me to rest. Their efforts dimly touched and shamed me, wrapped as I was in a tight cocoon, only barely transparent, through which I was helpless to break. I yielded to them because I could do nothing else, and I was a sore trial to them all for a long time.

Gradually I began to go back to Abigail's house; cautiously she gave me small tasks to do, and found me once more worthy to lean upon. Rata's sober questions, Electa's wren-like darting and prattling, and little John's warm solid body, these were the only things that were real to me, and through that winter I clung to them.

4. Eph's visits were brief flashes in the dullness and good for me, but he had little time to spare. In the spring he took over the command of Fort Massachusetts which my father had vacated. It was not an enviable post, as my father had discovered, being poorly paid and monotonous, but that summer, unexpectedly, it gave him a second chance and the opportunity

to vindicate at last my father's boast. In August the fort was again surprised by a force of Indians and French, this time Eph was in command, and within two hours the attack was repulsed. Word came back to Stockbridge that he had acted decisively and with coolness and courage.

Eph himself wrote a report of this encounter, a copy of which in due time reached my father's hands. When the ambush of Indians near the fort was discovered, there was, he wrote, some disagreement among the men as to whether they should march out and surprise it at once. Eph wisely insisted on a planned attack later in the day. But during his careful preparations four men, without his knowledge or consent, undertook a sortie of their own and ran into more than they bargained for. To rescue them Eph had to go out with a hastily assembled force of thirty men, and they had no more than left the fort when the concealed French army rose on either side and threatened to cut him off. By quick thinking and hard fighting Eph managed to get his men back inside the fort, losing only one in the retreat. From within the fort they drove back the attacking enemy.

My father showed us the report without comment. It was evident that Eph had indeed shown courage. But I could not help but wonder as I read, from what little I knew of army discipline, how four men could have left the fort unnoticed, or by what reasoning thirty more should have been ordered to rush after them into the ambuscade. When we had all read the letter, my father folded it thoughtfully and put it in the pocket of his coat. I do not think that anyone else in the town ever saw it.

Almost on the heels of Eph's triumph, rumors reached Stockbridge of a possible peace between the European powers. The men began to straggle home, since it was apparent that no major offensive would now be planned. While here and there along the border small bands of Indians, unaware of any talk of peace, burned and scalped as savagely as before, the people in our town felt more secure. It was nearly Christmas, however, before official news arrived that the war in Europe was over. The soldiers garrisoned at Abigail's house at last marched away, and the whole town was thankful to see them go.

As the first rejoicing quieted, grumbling grew louder. News filtered through the woods bit by bit, and the town men, meeting in clusters after the Sabbath meeting, standing about in my father's store or sitting at his hearth in the evening, debated with uncertain faces. As far as the colonies were concerned, nothing had been settled by the treaty signed in October at Aix-la-Chapelle. Worse than that, after all the cost and labor that had gone into the siege of Louisbourg, England had now handed it back to France in a lordly gesture, callous to the fact that some of the best blood in the colonies had been sacrificed for its capture. This treaty was not the final reckoning, the men said. Not while the French still coveted land that belonged by right to Englishmen.

To one person besides myself all this meant nothing. John Sergeant was free now to build his school. He at once wrote a long letter to the Indians who lived along the Mohawk River in the colony of New York, urging them to bring their children for instruction. He promised that in the summer he would visit the Mohawk country and speak his invitation to them in person. In the meantime, he flung all his energies into building the schoolhouse. By April, with the walls and roof completed, Mr. Kellogg and twelve boys took occupancy. A barren structure it was, the interior still uncompleted, but to the man who had raised it with prayer and unwavering will, it was a visible sign of the advance of God's forces into the territory of darkness.

"May our gracious God direct and succor our endeavors," John said from his pulpit. "May we continue to enlarge the kingdom of our glorious Redeemer."

"We will gradually acquire a stock of sheep and cattle and

hogs," he would say to anyone who would listen. "Then we can take in girls who will churn the butter and cheese and work the wool and flax. In a short time we will be entirely self-supporting. And by the time they are twenty years of age, the boys will be ready to commence farming on their own land. The virtue is that they will begin young, and grow up in the way of industry. They will never have any temptation to fall back into idleness."

How clear and logical it must have seemed to him, this prospect of neat farms spreading across the land, tilled by a gentled Christian folk indistinguishable from their English neighbors except by their darker skins. Each industrious Indian family would have its English frame house, its barn and yielding acres, its spinning wheel and loom. The vision beguiles me even now. I cannot explain what is the flaw in it. Yet I think that John knew in his heart that it would never come about in his own lifetime.

5. "Liza should have a holiday," Eph said to the family without consulting me. "I'd like to take her with me to Albany. She can rest and wallow in luxury at the inn while I dispatch my business, and after that I can show her the sights. What do you say, Liza?"

I could not rise to a decent thanks. The opportunity which would once have sent me into ecstasies seemed an intolerable effort. I was not sure I could endure several days on horseback; I shrank from new faces. But the family was for once united and shamed me with their concern for me. Father brought from the store a little cap of plaited ribbon, mother sat up for two nights to make over a dress and Abigail pressed upon me a new pair of mitts and a fan. I allowed myself to be prinked and bedizened and helped up onto the pillion behind Eph and waved on my way, and I knew myself for a wretched ungrateful girl.

The journey was pleasant, after all, with Eph undiscouragedly cheerful, the countryside a tapestry to which I could not altogether shut my eyes. I remember the little sloop with its wing-like sails that carried us up the Hudson River, and my first glimpse of the serrated Dutch roofs of the city of Albany. Yet it was all too much after the thinness of my accustomed fare. I did not know how to wallow in luxury, and I saw the sights through a haze of weariness.

On the way home, when we were nearing Stockbridge, Eph announced a change of plans. "We're going to spend the night at Kaunameek. You've never been there, have you? Well yes, so you have," he recalled at my sudden stiffening. "I mean the Indian longhouse."

"I didn't know any Indians still lived there," I said. "Most of them moved to Stockbridge."

"They keep their longhouse at Kaunameek for councils and feast days," Eph told me.

I was surprised. "Does John know?"

"He knows. He's wise enough not to take much notice. He has never tried to stamp out the old customs altogether. It does the Indians good to get away from us once in a while and be themselves. I happened to learn from the Mohawks that they're having a council today."

"Will they want us bothering them?"

"As a matter of fact, they invited John. He has sometimes attended their feasts, but he couldn't spare the time for this one. They would like, just once, to welcome Abigail, but I suppose it will never happen. So tonight we will serve as their substitutes."

I was longing now for my own bed and solitary room, but Eph gave me no chance to refuse. As he turned his horse away from the traveled road into a barely discernible path, my indifference was pierced by a thin shaft of feeling, whether of pleasure, pain or fear I could not distinguish. It had been five years since I had ridden through the blizzard to this place. Would there be any sign of the man who had lived here? Did the Indians ever remember him, or had the path he had hewn out for God grown over with superstition and ignorance so that it might never have been? With resentment I felt my nerves tight again. They had relaxed a little on this holiday; now I would have to be on guard the more to keep from betraying myself in this place.

In the deep woods, twilight was only an intensifying of the leftover dimness of the night before, held in all day by the interlocking branches overhead. It was close to dark when we rode into a clearing. The longhouse, the first I had ever seen, was no more than a giant wigwam, the same dome-shaped, bark-covered structure, higher and lengthened to perhaps thirty feet. I counted five separate columns of smoke rising from the roof.

An Indian came from the doorway nearest us, his smile white in the dimness. "Brother, I greet you," he said in English. "New house ready for white brother."

Eph slid stiffly from his saddle and lifted his arms to help me down. The Indian led us to the far end of the longhouse and beyond for a short way into the woods, to an ordinary small wigwam, and he held back bark curtains for me to enter. It smelled of fresh-cut wood; here and there a new-peeled branch gleamed white, green leaves clung to projecting twigs, and the moss chinking was damp and velvety. I had an impression that the wigwam had been constructed especially for our entertainment. A fire burned in the center of the room, and by its light I saw clean new blankets spread on the narrow shelf along the wall. I sat down on them and waited, not sure what was expected. Almost at once a woman came soundlessly through the curtains with two small bowls which she handed silently to Eph and to me. This I understood; it was the first formality, which must be observed before any conversation could take place.

"Eat lightly," Eph warned me softly. "They are waiting the feast for us."

I sipped from the carved wooden spoon. "This is all I want," I protested. "Must we go to the feast?" My body wanted only the soft blankets.

"Of course we must. That's why I brought you here, and you may never have the chance again."

I combed my hair and washed my face in cool water from an earthen basin. Eph watched me with a troubled look I could not interpret.

"I hope I've done right," he said at last. "White people seldom have the opportunity to see a true Indian dance. But for your first one, the Feather Dance would have been a better choice. Tonight will be — somewhat different."

"A dance? I thought you said it was a council."

"That wasn't quite accurate. It is really Keutikaw, the Dance for the Dead. They hold it every autumn for the members of the tribe who have died during the year. The spirits come back for this one night to watch the dance."

I could not cover up my horror. "Eph! What would John say? These are Christians."

"They were Indians first. It's not blasphemous, Liza, I promise you."

The feast in the longhouse, at which they gave us an honored place, lasted for a long time. Before my tired senses it was a blur of smoke and shifting color, of jabbering voices, and a succession of platters heaped with meat and corn, for which Eph tried to show appreciation enough for us both. When finally it was over, the Indian women raked away all but one of the fires, leaving clean hard earth. There was a general moving back to make a cleared space, the men seating themselves along the sides, the women standing behind them. Some little boys, unable to see, scrambled up the poles and clung there to the bent rafters. All talking ceased, and an expectancy settled like the smoke about the silent figures. Fear quivered through me. Feasting they had seemed like old friends; in this prolonged silence they had become alien. Above the familiar choking stench of food and grease and sweat, some new element seemed to rise and thicken the air till it was difficult for me to breathe; it was something primitive, eluding perception.

As the silence grew more intense I had a compulsion to run from the longhouse. I sensed in Eph the same troubled indecision I had noticed in the wigwam. He too was aware that we were foreign, and I knew he was doubting again that he should have brought me here. But he sat without moving.

From time to time an Indian glided to feed the single fire. Finally an ancient chief stepped forward, one whom I had never seen before. He stood in silence, and when even the children were motionless beside their mothers, he began to speak in a dialect slightly different from that of the Stockbridge Indians, but one which I could understand sufficiently.

These many days, he said, a great darkness had been spread over their fireplaces. Now, according to the custom of their ancestors and with the help of the Great Good Spirit, he would remove these dark clouds. He entreated them, his brothers, that they would wipe away all tears from their eyes, that they would remove the obstructions from their ears that they might hear distinctly and clear their throats of all bitterness. He would raise their heads which had been hung downwards and set their hearts right again so that they might understand.

He waited for a long time, and then he began again. He

would recite to them the names of those who had gone the long trail. He began to speak the names slowly, with a long breath's silence between each one. There was no sound in the waiting that followed. Listen again, he told them finally, for there was one more name, that of the white brother who had lived among them. His spirit too had returned to their fireplace where he had taught them. Tonight they would wipe away their tears for their brother David Brainerd.

An animal fear thrust up through my body, impaling me so that I could not move. I was shaken by the beating of my own heart; it swelled, rhythmic, in my temples, in my throat, in my womb. Then I realized that it was not my heart but the gourd rattles, shaken softly, sounding just at the threshold of hearing. Above them there sounded now a single high-pitched note, which came from five women sitting near the fire and was sustained, unbroken, excruciating. Sickness rose in my throat, but I forced it back; the spasm passed, leaving me wet and cold.

Then the dancers came, soundless as shadows, women dressed in wraithlike ragged garments drained of color. They twisted around the red center of the fire, stooping down and straightening slowly. The single anguished note shifted from one indefinable level to another, and underneath was the unbroken throbbing of the rattles.

Now from the ranks along the walls the first shattering wail broke out, and at once women around me began to sob. The wreathing figures did not quicken their pace; the singing did not escape its rigid control. But an intensity of grief mounted in the spectators. Their cries flailed me like whips. I think I passed beyond all conscious thought; when the first sob was wrenched from my own throat I barely distinguished it as my own. In the darkness I put my hands over my mouth and gave way to a ragged wild weeping that almost tore me apart.

I do not know how long I wept. It was as though I were

drowning in a dark river. The common pain of every man and woman in the place flowed over my head, mingled with the wailing. Far below the surface I was gathered into it, my own identity flowed away from me, and deep in the blackness I came upon a shining current of joy.

After a long time I rose to the surface and drifted weightless, till I felt the earth beneath my feet again. The dancers still moved, the music and the weeping went past me, and I was remote from it. I could scarcely remember what they meant. I was aware again of Eph beside me. Perhaps I made some motion, for very quietly his arm came about my shoulders. Like a child I let my weight relax against him and I fell asleep.

I woke to a dim filtered daylight with the rough knots of branches under my hip and shoulder and the scratchy warmth of a blanket against my cheek. Overhead were the withes of the roof, stuffed with bunched grasses. I remembered uncertainly that Eph had carried me here and laid me down, and that the blanket he had drawn over me and the barely interrupted sleep that flowed back were one and the same. I was fully awake now and sharply hungry.

Eph, lying on the opposite shelf with his arms under his head, turned lazily to look at me. "About time," he said. "We've got to be on our way."

I sat up, trying to straighten my dress. Eph had not even taken off my shoes. "I can go now," I said.

It might have been a ghost camp, except that we were forced to step around several very real and snoring Indians.

"They'll sleep through the day," said Eph. "They kept it up all night long. How they do it is beyond me." He held out a piece of corncake, laughed at the way I snatched at it and handed me another.

We talked little on the long ride home. Exhaustion possessed me so completely that I barely kept my hold on Eph's belt. But it was a weariness totally unlike the heaviness of the past months. The weight was gone; I was empty, scoured thin and smooth and clean as an ancient shell from the bottom of the river. Eph did not look round at me, and there was no need to speak or to think, even to feel.

At home I slept almost around the clock. "What on earth did you do to the child?" mother fussed at breakfast. "You promised to let her rest." Across the table Eph winked at me, exactly as he had on the first day he had come home, so many years ago.

Neither Eph nor I ever spoke of that night in Kaunameek. Did he take me to that place deliberately, knowing? I wish now that I could ask him, but as it is I will never be sure to my dying day.

6. ON A SABBATH morning of early summer Abigail overtook us as we walked down the hill to the meetinghouse. "I'm worried about John," she told us. "When it was almost time to go I found him sound asleep at his desk, and his forehead felt hot to me. He says it is only a cold in his throat."

Through the morning service we watched him anxiously. Not by a sentence did he shorten his prayer or his two sermons, but a perceptible hesitation and a nervous swallowing betrayed his discomfort. At the noon meal he could not eat.

Abigail pleaded with him. "For this one day, can't you dismiss the afternoon meeting?"

He shook his head impatiently. "This is the Lord's Day, not

mine. His strength will be sufficient." But by the end of the last sermon his voice almost failed.

"You must try to make him rest," mother said to Abigail that night. "He's grown dreadful thin this past spring."

It was impossible for John to rest. His fever hung on, the hoarseness increased and a painful canker in his throat restricted his food to sips of warm milk. Yet every morning he rose and stood at the breakfast table to read aloud to his children the customary chapter of scripture. Urged back to his bed, he sat up to work, propping his books against his knees. Every afternoon he dressed and went the round of schoolhouse and Plain, and all day long the passageway was never clear of Indians waiting to talk to him.

On the next Sabbath, John's hands clenched the sides of the lectern. The Indian sermon went haltingly, the grinding syllables a torment. In the midst of it he paused, and when he began again I felt a prickling along my scalp. Instead of continuing his argument, he was speaking directly to them, with a strange sound of entreaty in the words.

"Some of you," he told them, "have not shown any gratitude for all that God has done for you. I am afraid that God may send you a heavy judgment to show his displeasure.

"It may be," he said, "that God will take me from you, and then my mouth will be shut and I shall speak to you no more."

A woman's sob broke the stillness behind me, then another. Abigail looked round at us with question and terror in her eyes. John's sermons had never caused the Indians to wail like this. He waited quietly until there were no more sobs, and then he went on to finish his sermon. He came to the end at last and shifted his papers to begin the English sermon. Then instead he bowed his head and was silent for a long moment. When he looked up, his face was gray and wet with beads of sweat — or could it have been tears? His voice was no more than a whisper, the sound of which was to rasp all our nerves raw in the days to come.

"God knows what is in my heart to say to you," he told us. "But I must submit to his will. The service is ended."

Weeping broke out again among the Indian women, this time unchecked. The English families filed out of the meetinghouse, embarrassed and uneasy, and stood in nervous clusters on the grass outside. John, wavering in the doorway, surrendered weakly to Abigail and allowed her to lead him past them all and past the distraught Indians, who fell back before her fierce prohibiting face. My father had his own horse unhitched and helped to boost the exhausted man onto its back. Timothy Woodbridge walked beside him, holding him in the saddle.

As soon as John slept, Abigail sent Electa to fetch me. "What did he say to them?" she demanded.

I looked away, not knowing how to answer.

"Tell me!"

"He said they were not grateful enough for God's blessings. He said he was afraid that God might send some punishment upon them."

"That was not all. Tell me exactly what he said."

I told her as best I could. Abigail gripped the chair back till her knuckles were white. " 'Tis the fever," she said. "It's not like John to be dramatic. He shouldn't have gone this morning, but I can't — oh Liza!"

For once it was I who held her and comforted her, but after a few seconds Abby drew away. "I'm as bad as the Indians," she said, blowing her nose. "But now I won't break down before John. It's just that he's never been sick before and I can't reason with him."

John did not leave his bed next day or the days that followed, but the compulsion of unfinished work still drove him. Abigail and I both tried to intercept the Indians at the study door. But no matter how low our voices, he somehow overheard and insisted that they come in. Abigail was forced to break her ten-year isolation and to let them into the bedroom, even to watch them touch his bedclothes with their unwashed hands. She did not deny him, and she stood by helplessly while in his rasping voice he patiently untangled some foolish misunderstanding and pleaded with them not to forget the things he had taught them. As he grew weaker and at last had to admit, with tears of defeat, that he could not speak to them any longer, he insisted that she hear what they had to say and bring him a full account and take back his answer. She tried to do this, but faced with her strained accusing face the Indians forgot the little English they knew and shuffled away with their questions. They stopped coming to the door, gathering instead a little distance from the house. More of them came every day; some did not leave all night long. They simply sat, without speaking. On the third Sabbath they assembled instead in the meetinghouse and remained there all day.

The thought of his schoolhouse never left John. When Abigail tried to tend him, he caught at her hands and whispered urgently the things that she must not forget to do. She must write to Mr. Hollis and to Dr. Colman. She must arrange for new shoes to be made for the boys. She must make sure there was sufficient flour and that the hay was thoroughly dried before it was stored. Everything he asked she promised desperately.

In the middle of July Josiah rode to Deerfield to fetch Thomas. The first sight of him brought us all fresh hope. But when he came from John's bed, his carefully controlled face was somber.

"Don't worry, Abby," he said on the doorstep. "I've seen much worse cases. I wish he had more strength, but we'll manage. I told my wife not to expect me for a few days. I'll stay as long as John needs me."

He was still there two weeks later. Eph too had come and

stayed, making himself useful. He took the burden of the Indians at once into his own hands, meeting them outside the house,
responding seriously and with good humor to their endless questions. They liked and trusted him.

Thomas never altered the imperturbably cheerful manner on
which we all leaned even while we recognized it as his stock in
trade. The actual words he spoke were evasive. We could all see
that John was steadily weakening; only Abigail refused to speak
of it. She allowed herself to be deceived by the unabated activity
of his restless mind. She would not admit he could be in danger
when he could still compose a diplomatic letter to Dr. Colman or
ponder the best Christian name for an Indian's new grandson.
But after so many weeks of broken sleep, her nerves were
strained beyond endurance by his continual hoarse whispering.
One morning late in July, as Thomas and Eph and I walked toward the house, she came bursting through the door as though
she were running to escape.

"Can't you give him something to make him stop talking?" she
cried out to Thomas, in a jagged high-pitched voice I could
scarcely recognize. "I can't stand it. He never stops. Now he's
preaching to me about my soul. I don't care about my soul! I'd
pledge it to Satan himself if I could make him well! He wants me
to bring the children, even baby John. I can't do it. I can't listen
to it any more."

Thomas shook her, not gently. "Stop this, Abigail. You are
only making it harder."

"Listen to me, Abby," Eph said sternly. "You must let John
have what he wants. Don't you understand even yet? John
can't die like the rest of us. Even his death must somehow serve
God."

"Don't say that!" she screamed at him. "He's not going to
die!"

She looked from one silent pitying man to the other. "Thomas!" She flung herself against his chest.

"You'd best take the children in as he wants," he told her wearily.

She slid down on her knees and wrapped her arms about his legs, babbling, pleading, blasphemous. Eph pulled her up.

"Abby! Thomas has done everything he can. Now you must help him to die as he wants to."

She quieted. "I can't," she whispered.

"Yes," said Eph. "You can. Get the children."

Eph and I waited in the room below while upstairs John prayed with his wife and children and took leave of them. What I will never forget is the Indians. They sat in a circle all around the house, silent, unmoving, hour after hour, the intensity of their grief somehow pressing against the walls. In the late afternoon John died.

7. EVEN NOW some folks hint that Abigail recovered from her husband's death with undue haste. Those who would have pressed broth and sympathy upon a prostrated widow were repelled by her lifted head and brilliant dry eyes. But their talk angers me, for after John's funeral mother sent me to live in Abigail's house, and day after day I watched her drive herself without mercy. Her first act after the week of mourning was over was to scrub the back passageway, the walls, even the ceiling, and to bolt fast the side door to the house. Then in a fury she set her house to rights. All day she heated kettles of water and scoured and pounded the bed linens. She dipped candles

on the hottest day of late August. She harvested the beans and corn from the back garden and dried and stored them for winter. In the evenings she cut up John's shabby clothing, piecing out carefully the cloth still strong enough to make trousers and coat for Erastus. I did not try to stop her, and I helped where I could, but sometimes it seemed to me I could see pain in the air all around her, as though it welled like heat from her slight body. She would stop suddenly in the midst of a task, and clench her hands at her sides, her face twisted. Then she would tighten her lips and draw up her ribs sharply and set to work again. I never saw her weep.

She was battling more than grief, for without even a decent interval the creditors came like vultures. Who would have dreamed that John could have accumulated a debt of seven hundred pounds? And she had to fight my father as well when he offered to take her and the children into his house.

"I am going to stay here and bring up my children," she insisted. "This is my home; I'm not going to leave it."

"I could get you enough for it to pay off the whole score. Some of those bills go back to when the house was built, and no man is going to wait forever."

"They'll get their money, every last penny, I promise you. But they'll wait. I won't be hetcheled."

"What will you live on?" my father asked.

They faced each other in her kitchen, and I saw the respect in his eyes. He knows she is the only one to inherit his will, I thought, watching them. Did he really believe that at twenty-nine she could return with three children to be herself a child again under his roof?

"I have one hundred pounds," she told him. "It came to John from England a fortnight after the funeral."

"For the school, wasn't it?"

"No. It was sent through Governor Belcher of New Jersey, specifically for John's personal use. What better use could there be for it now than to care for his children?"

My father scowled. "You sure of this, Abby? Certain people are bound to say it belongs to the school fund."

"Do you think I'm lying about it?"

"You know I don't. There's some who might, however. Is there proof? Some letter that would settle the matter?"

"There was a letter from Governor Belcher, but I've let Rata use the backs of letters to save paper. Perhaps the Governor would remember if I wrote to him."

"I'd advise you to write, then," my father said. "I think Woodbridge is out to make trouble."

"It wouldn't surprise me," Abigail said, "and John always counted him his closest friend."

"Well, he's no friend of mine. He never misses a chance to turn the Indians against me. Tells 'em I'm a bad influence. Course, he may not hold it against you."

Abigail was silent, and I knew she was remembering that Timothy Woodbridge might have other matters to hold against her. "I'll write to the Governor," she promised.

"Another thing," my father went on, settling his bulk into John's chair in a way that told me he would stay till he had spoken his mind. "Woodbridge has been mighty free with his remarks about John's boarding school. He claims Kellogg is good for naught as a teacher."

"I've never understood John's hiring him," Abigail admitted. "I consider him stupid and contemptible."

"Don't imagine John had much choice. I'd say he's good enough for the Mohawks. Thing is, I'd like to take a look at John's figures on that school. You been keeping track of things?"

"I haven't had time even to sort John's papers out. Timothy

keeps asking for the school account books, but I can't bring my-self to it."

"You let me take a look first."

She hesitated. "Why?" she asked him directly. "What is the boarding school to you?"

"It's town business, isn't it? If you remember, when the fami-lies in this town took up the collection I was the biggest contrib-utor."

She went into John's study and came back with a hasty jumble of books and papers. "Take it." She thrust them at him. "I never want to hear the wretched school mentioned again. If it weren't for that school —" She stopped, biting her lip.

"Can't say I blame you," my father said mildly. "But you can't avoid it. Looks like it's what you might call a necessary evil."

"Necessary for what? The war is over."

"That remains to be seen. Nothing's settled that I can see. Just as well to keep on the good side of the Mohawks. Most important thing about the school right now is it brings in a good income from that Mr. Hollis. No sense letting good money slip out of our hands."

"Why should he keep sending the money? I've never under-stood it. He's never seen an Indian in his life."

"Probably trying to buy off a guilty conscience with charity. That's not our concern. Our business is to see his money keeps coming, and to do it we've got to make sure there are twelve boys in that blasted school. If there aren't enough Housatonic boys want to live there, then we've got to get Mohawks, though I never did think it was the smartest thing. We'd be better off getting rid of Indians, not bringing in new ones."

"How can we get rid of them?" she asked wearily. "Stock-bridge is Indian Town. It belongs to them."

"Aye, that's where the mistake was made at the start. Finest piece of property in this corner of the world thrown away to a passel of mangy Indians. There's one thing been proved here in America, Abby. Land belongs to them as can use it. It makes my blood boil to see this good farmland going to waste. I won't rest easy in my grave till it's a fit place for my grandchildren to be raised in."

"Without Indians?"

"Sooner or later it's got to be. That's one thing John never could understand. No offense, Abby, but you know how he was. Indians and whites don't mix; they know it well's we do. But right now, with the French crowding us in, we need 'em, and we've got to make sure they stay. A town full of praying Indians' as good as a fort and a lot cheaper."

Protest leaped up in me. He would never have dared talk this way when John was alive. Nor would Abby ever have allowed it. I was appalled that not one word of protest came from her lips. I drew a quick breath to speak out, and then I remembered the day I had pleaded for Nomshoos' land, and I kept silent. It is only his way of talking, I told myself, for habit is strong. And his next words reassured me.

"Don't you worry about the school, Abby. I'll handle it from now on. It's no job for a woman, and you've got your hands full. I've been considering it would be a good thing if they put me on the Board of Commissioners, seeing I'm handy to look after things. Eph knows the right men to speak to in Boston. Don't you bother your head about it. And meanwhile, don't forget what I said about coming to live with me. I'm figuring on building a new house come spring, and you could have a hand in planning it the way you like."

After he was gone I was ashamed that I had not spoken, even knowing how useless any words of mine would be. Who was there now to speak for the Indians?

8. My QUESTION was soon answered. The Indians found a voice in Timothy Woodbridge. They had always trusted him, recognizing his simple unshakable honesty, which even my father never questioned. He was a good man, what I think the Bible calls a God-fearing man. He should not be blamed that somehow his uprightness lacked the persuasion of John Sergeant's. For one thing, he did not have John's indiscriminate trust, and he did not have John's springing optimism. I believe that for many years Timothy had been corroded by suspicion and bitterness. Now the Indians found him all too willing to listen to grievances that John had always managed to smooth over.

For it was apparent to us all that the resentment of the Indians was not a new thing, that it must have been present almost from the beginning. How many of those exhausting conferences in John's study had been devoted just to preserving the peace? And how much of John's weariness had been due to standing as a buffer between the Indians and his wife's father? For there was no doubt now, it was my father they resented most. Timothy Woodbridge stepped forward to champion them, and some of the newer English families took their stand behind him, having perhaps their own reasons for resentment, while the old Hill families held with my father. The crack had been there for a long time, but because John had refused to recognize it he had kept it from splitting straight across the town as now it did.

Timothy Woodbridge wrote out with his own hand the Indian petitions that went to Boston, most of them concerned with the land in the town. Actually they were slight matters; in John's time they would never have been taken to Court. In most cases the Indians needed only to have someone explain to them, in words they could understand, that in truth my father had not defrauded them.

In the beginning the Indians had agreed that out of the tract of land six miles square granted them by the Court of Massachusetts, the four English families should be allotted one hundred and fifty acres each. They had been willing that the families should choose the acres they preferred. Only when my father began to increase his holdings did they grumble. And I could not doubt my father's word that he had purchased fairly every additional acre, since in each case the purchase had been confirmed according to law by the General Assembly, and the Indians could produce no evidence to the contrary. The fact is that the Court upheld him in every instance. He is not to blame that the Indians did not understand a deed of land, that they were still puzzled by the Englishman's need to own land for himself apart from the rest and that to them a court decision was a meaningless tangle of words and therefore trickery.

On the other hand, my father never understood in the least the Indians' complaints, nor, to be honest, ever troubled to. John Sergeant had tried to encourage them to clear more land, and had promised them free seed for sowing, and a few of them had gone to great pains to do this, clearing and fencing in a portion of the common land. Unfortunately they chose a plot that lay directly between two lots owned by my father. He made the mistake of allowing them to proceed for a time, and when he finally put a stop to the work the Indians claimed they had already spent one hundred days cutting and drawing timber. He paid them ten pounds for their labor and offered them in trade eight acres of meadowland near their own settlement. Though the Court confirmed all this, the Indians never got the matter clear in their heads, as they had never understood about the land he had purchased from Konkapot or the grist mill which he had built, for their use as well as his own, out of mission funds.

There were complaints that had nothing to do with my father. Sam Brown Senior, by an error in surveying, had built his house on Indian land. He willingly paid them for the nineteen acres in question, but they continued to grumble. Mr. Jones likewise agreed to pay for the grass he had cut on what he had assumed to be common land. The Indians held my father accountable for every grievance they held against the English families. In fact they now held it against him that some of the English were there at all, claiming that they had agreed in the beginning to only four families and that now English houses were going up wherever they looked. Did they think, my father argued, that one man could hold back the course of nature? He himself was convinced that the Indians still had more land than they knew what to do with. He said they were too lazy to develop a tenth of it, and that they had no right to raise such an almighty howl when a farmer with an honest need for a few more acres tried to buy them. Furthermore, he claimed that Timothy Woodbridge was at the bottom of all the trouble, that the Indians were perfectly well off until he began to stir them up.

I know that it is true that my father could not have held back for long, even had he desired to, the steady encroachment of the English on Indian land. About this time the General Court revised the ruling which had provided for all the Indians' land to be held in common. It was argued that each Indian, being a true freeholder, should henceforth own his individual acres, and the land not claimed by the English families was now fairly portioned out to the Indians. Perhaps there were some who sincerely believed this measure to be to the Indians' advantage, but in the long run it has proved to be their undoing. They have never understood nor shared the English respect for property, and the more ignorant among them were easily persuaded to trade land for some immediate benefit. The next step, some years later, would be another law allowing an Indian to sell his land in payment of debt. It does not require much astuteness to run an Indian into debt, and there are some in our town who have chosen to forget how they acquired their pleasant holdings.

9. THAT YEAR MY father built his new house. Someone — Abigail claimed it was Timothy Woodbridge, though I think it sounds unlike him — termed it the Castle, and the name, whether meant as flattery or epithet, has stuck fast. I am too fond of it to care. It is a beautiful house, solidly built, with white-painted clapboards, dormer windows set in its sloping roof, and a graceful center doorway. The appearance of a fortress was not so much in the house as in the moat with which my father entirely encircled it. By intention too father placed the foundations squarely over our old well, so that in the event of a siege there would be water enough for half the town right in his own cellar.

Impregnable though the Castle might have been against an Indian attack, it could not withstand the animosity which rose like mist from the Plain and seeped through the heavy walls of black oak. More and more my father was losing favor in the town. When he went out from his Castle these days, he had the grimness of a man riding out to do battle.

His loosening hold on the town goaded him the more because it must have seemed that his family also was escaping from his control. Eph was rarely in Stockbridge, won over altogether, between duties at the fort, by the lively society of his cousin Israel Williams' house in Hatfield. Josiah had his own farm and was still mulish about any advice in the running of it. And that year both Elijah and I left home.

Elijah went first. It was a never-ending gratification to my father that Elijah was admitted at last to the College of New Jersey, for he had set his heart on seeing his youngest son respectably educated. It was only through the intervention of John Sergeant's brother Jonathan, treasurer of the college, that this had been possible. Elijah, though he has a good mind, has always had an amiable aversion to overtaxing it. But that year the prospect of the independence he would enjoy in distant New Jersey inspired him to a brief spurt of diligence which carried him safely through the examinations.

What would become of him, I wondered, looking at him with sharpened fondness on his last night at home. I remember how he pushed back his chair and tilted it cockily on its back legs, immune from reproof on his last meal with us. How like father he was, cast from the same mold, as was Eph, handsome and inclined to fleshiness. But it was as though with each casting the mold had lost firmness; none of his sons had my father's sinew, Elijah least of all. A hint of masculine swagger made me wonder again about those rumors I had so indignantly scotched. Undeniably, Elijah had the Williams charm; perhaps college would give him some discretion to go with it.

Every time he had visited us since the war ended, Eph had talked about my going away to Boston to a school for young ladies. This was quite a different matter from a few days' journey to Albany, and neither my father nor mother, nor I myself, though I was not consulted, could see any advantage in it. Abigail had at first agreed with him; I knew she was concerned that I had thrown away my chances with Sam Brown and that I was so plainly a misfit in the feminine society on the Hill. I would doubtless have been bundled off long before if John's illness had not put a stop to all such talk.

As for me, I had no thought beyond the day just ahead. After so many years of waiting, I had come to terms with the truth that there was nothing now to wait for. I clung to my accustomed life as a rabbit crouches against the brown leaves, risking no slightest move. I knew I was of help to Abigail and that at times she truly needed me. Her growing children gave a seeming purpose to my life, and in her youngest child, then two years old, I found a measure of true happiness. I loved Electa and Erastus; John was like my own.

10. EIGHT MONTHS AFTER John Sergeant's death we had still found no one to take his place. Occasionally Mr. Hopkins, minister at Sheffield over the mountain, rode the seven miles to hold a service for us. Even more rarely we gathered in the meetinghouse to listen to Timothy Woodbridge expound the scripture. This was a situation my father could not tolerate for long. It was enough to take all the religion out of a man, he said, to hear the schoolmaster presume to address the Lord. The man was already puffed up enough with his own importance now that he had the Indians truckling to him. If something wasn't done soon he'd think he was mayor of the town. Still, when the meetinghouse doors opened, my father took his accustomed place, for he felt a responsibility for the other Hill families who followed his lead.

In March a letter arrived from New Haven recommending Mr. Ezra Stiles, son of an eminent preacher, a tutor at Yale and recently licensed to preach the gospel. Even Timothy Woodbridge, suspicious on principle of anything my father suggested, could find no immediate objection to inviting the young man to spend a week in Stockbridge in order to deliver the sermons on two successive Sabbaths.

Mr. Stiles came in April, and as was only fitting, he stayed in the house of the former minister. Since Abigail was distressed at this breaking in upon her mourning and resentful of the extra cooking it would involve, once again mother sent me to help. But I think Abigail was disarmed the moment she opened the door to him. As she led him into her parlor that morning, I recognized in her smile, in her voice, in her very walk the first tenacious flickering of a spark that could never be totally extinguished.

"I am more than grateful, Madam," I heard him say. "I realize what an intrusion this must be. But for me it is the greatest honor to be in the home of a man I admired so fervently." His voice was energetic and assured; his straight narrow nose and fine mouth were aristocratic, his brilliant dark eyes direct and searching under sweeping brows. He impressed me as a man who knew very well what he wanted from life and had every confidence of getting it.

The Hill families were charmed with him at sight. On the first Sabbath he preached to us, with sincerity, a familiar and reassuring doctrine. At supper in my father's house he entertained us all with the latest New Haven opinion. I think there was no question in all our minds but that providence had sent the right man. But throughout that week Timothy Woodbridge withheld his judgment.

With the first meal at her table, Abigail and Mr. Stiles discovered a like-mindedness that astonished and delighted them both. Every evening at his return they took up again their apparently inexhaustible dialogue. For me that week was a bitterness.

Mr. Stiles was young, much younger than Abigail, probably little older than myself. Yet in his presence I felt myself a child, dismissed once more to insignificance. Beyond a good morning and an abstracted word of thanks when I passed him a platter at table, he rarely spoke to me. He was not a man to accuse of rudeness; I had to acknowledge the fault to be in myself. In the evenings, when we three sat about the hearth, I might as well have been the neglected flax wheel or the cat asleep in the corner of the settle for all either of them remembered I was there. There was nothing novel in this, except that for the first time in my life I found it galling.

Yet to be truthful, had they ever turned to me and asked for my opinion, I would have been confounded, for they moved almost at once beyond my depth, into the confusions of theology. They began by speaking of John Sergeant. Mr. Stiles' admiration was no empty praise; he was already acquainted with John's Springfield sermon, and he had requested on the first day that Abigail allow him to read more of John's unpublished work.

To my surprise, his words brought a glistening of tears to Abigail's eyes. "If you knew what your approbation means to me," she said to him. "No one in Stockbridge ever really appreciated Mr. Sergeant. And now you, who never saw him, have realized what he was truly capable of doing."

"I should have known even had you not shown me his writings," Mr. Stiles told her. "There is something in these walls, in the spirit of this town, even more, if you will forgive me, in you yourself, that bears witness to the man your husband must have been. A rare and saintly man of God. In these days I'm afraid it is inevitable that he should have been misunderstood. Voices such as his, moderate, rational, have been all but drowned out in New England these past years."

"John believed in moderation. There were some, one in particular, who even accused him of heresy. I don't mind telling you it was Mr. Woodbridge, who was supposed to be my husband's friend. He said behind John's back that he was Arminian — that he preached salvation by good works rather than by election. My husband was hurt by it."

"Yes," said Mr. Stiles, unsurprised. "There are many today who use Arminianism as a convenient term to strike at anyone whose thinking differs from their own."

"John had no time to spare for controversy," she said. "But he could never bear to forbid anyone, especially an Indian, from coming to the Lord's table. Is that being Arminian?"

"I doubt very much that your husband was an Arminian. I am sure that he would never have held that by his own works a man can win his way to salvation. In all his writings he clearly acknowledged that by God's Grace alone we are saved." He hesitated, then went on. "Yet if, in spite of this, they would accuse him, I wonder what they would make of me?"

She looked up quickly from her sewing.

"They called my father Arminian also," he said. "They were enraged because he would not admit that they could tell with certainty who of the parish were saved and who were not. He believed no man could speak so freely for God, and I know he was right. How can we know the mind of God? How can we even know that we ourselves have been chosen?"

In spite of myself my own curiosity was stirred, for he had touched on the old question which had never ceased to trouble me. His honesty seemed to give Abigail increased courage, for now she appealed to him.

"There are some things," she said finally, "that I never said to John. They would have shocked and hurt him. But since his death I have had no one to talk to, and they are heavy on my conscience."

"I would be honored if you would speak to me," he said seriously.

"Is it a sin to question? If it is, then I am wicked and unregenerate."

"What do you question?" His eyes had a special brilliance.

"If God has already chosen — then what does it matter what any of us do? Suppose he has already chosen to save some barbarous Indian who doesn't understand the meaning of the word? Or suppose that my husband, who wore out his life in service, is not one of the elect in the end? It seems to me cruel and unjust."

"I knew it!" he burst out. "I think I recognized from the first moment I saw you that you were a kindred mind. You call yourself ignorant, yet in one moment you have gone straight to the vital perplexing center. My dear Madam Sergeant, if you are unregenerate, then I am also. I have scarcely dared confess this to anyone. But I have studied all their arguments and I am not satisfied. It is just as you say. If God has already chosen — if each of us is predestined long before our birth to either heaven or hell, then of what avail is reason or morality? More than this, if a man is not to be rewarded in the future world for his virtue, then is there any reason why he should be punished for his vice?"

They stared at each other, awed by the heresy they had spoken, awed even more, I think, by the audacity of sharing it.

"You can understand now," he continued more quietly, and even more seriously, "why I hesitated to come to Stockbridge. I am reluctant about my whole future. Do I have the right to be a minister at all? How can I preach the gospel to others when my own heart is so filled with doubt?"

"Yes, doubt," he repeated, at her startled look. "For almost two years now I have been lost in it. It is strange that I can confess this to you when I have kept it hidden from the friends who know me best. How can I make myself clear to you? It is not disbelief. Never, never for one moment have I questioned that God exists, that he is all-good and all-powerful. It is the scriptures that trouble me. If they are the word of God, why do they contain the difficulties that I find insuperable? If I find that one word contradicts another, then must I conclude that the whole Bible is a fable and a delusion? I search continually for a final proof, for a demonstration that these words were in truth inspired by God."

"You have comforted me," Abigail murmured. "I thought it was only my ignorance that made me uncertain."

"Ignorance is no bar to certainty," he said wryly. "The New Lights are proof of that. Mr. Pemberton, for example. He preached at Yale that knowledge is a hindrance and is esteemed by God no better than foolishness. I consider that ingratitude. Surely God has given man reason and the freedom to use it in the pursuit of truth. Yet I concede that the more one studies the more one questions. Those who are afraid to question had best be wary of education."

"I envy you your education," said Abigail. "Learning is not considered suitable for a woman, I know, and a woman's life doesn't leave much time for it. But it seems to me unfair. I should like to have gone to Yale — does that shock you?"

He looked at her with delight. "Wait a moment—" He seized a candle from the table and strode with his firm quick stride up the narrow stairs. He was back in a moment with a thin leather volume in his hands. "This is one of the books I most admire — Alexander Pope's *Essay on Man*. I have committed pages of it to memory. If you have time you may want to read some of it. Mark the passages that strike you, and tomorrow evening I will show you my own favorites."

She turned the little volume in her hand, smiling.

"It is very late," he said. "But one thing more I must tell you. It may even help you. I long to believe. I long for a certainty of salvation. I am not sure that this unspeakable joy they tell of will ever come to me. I have faced the probability that I may not be one of the elect, that I may even have been predestined to ever-lasting misery. Yet even so, I cannot help but believe that if I earnestly pray, if I resolve to keep myself from sin in so far as I possibly can, then the misery must surely be less than it would be if, being without any hope, I gave myself up to sin. Surely if a man thinks and acts rationally in this world, then there must be some improvement in his lot in the next."

"I am sure John would believe this," she assured him.

"I am resolved to live by it. It seems to me that this is the surest, indeed the only way to live happily."

After we had bade Mr. Stiles goodnight and left him in the parlor, which was also the guest chamber with its canopied bed, Abigail banked the waning fire in the kitchen, snuffed out all but the last candle and, carrying this with her, went up the stairs and moved in the accustomed ritual from one child's bed to another, tucking in an outflung arm, drawing a bed curtain closer. Dulled with all the talk, wanting only to sink down and shut out all sound and thought, I marked with wonder that she was brightly awake, her eyes sparkling, an almost feverish flush in her cheeks, as though some wave were still rising, suspending her on its crest.

This was the pattern of that week. I believe now that those eight days were a turning point in both our lives, Abigail's and mine, even though when Mr. Stiles rode away from Stockbridge the old pattern flowed back and there was no discernible change in either of us. For Abigail the shackles of grief and loyalty had been loosened, and in a far more subtle way than the Hill women, with their sharp questioning glances, ever surmised. That Abigail was still a beautiful woman and still able to set a man's pulses racing, she had not needed to be told; had Mr. Stiles attempted the slightest acknowledgment she would have despised him. Instead, while he had never, by a single word or so much as a flicker of his candid gaze, forgotten the respect due a bereaved widow, he had paid her a far more heady compliment. He had recognized her intellect.

Why was it, I wonder, that John, who worshipped her, was never able to realize the craving of her mind? It seems to me now that throughout their marriage John both stood in awe of Abigail and underestimated her. I don't think he ever quite trusted his own great fortune or felt deserving of it. Perhaps her beauty and the perfection of the home she made for him were all the riches he could grasp. And if he had understood her need, when had there ever been time for the leisurely hours of discussion of the week just past? Here in Stockbridge John had sacrificed scholarship, along with other things, to the immediate needs at hand. No money to buy books, no time to read them. His sermons, I realize now, grew less and less scholarly, never fulfilling the promise he had shown in Springfield. At the end of his life I think John's theology had been winnowed to a simple unquestioning trust, which is perhaps the reason why his is the only preaching I have ever truly comprehended.

Eph had known that Abigail's thoughts leaped beyond the cage of domesticity. "A man's mind," he had said of her more than once, and in his offhand way he had fed it with tidbits of masculine conversation. Now Mr. Stiles had gone further; he had opened for her a door into a new world, and without hesitation she had recognized it and claimed it as her own.

As for me, I had wasted my opportunity. I had sat with them every evening, and the learning that had set Abigail's mind ablaze could just as well have started a small glow in my own had I not smothered it with resentment. It is a sad truth, that all my life I have never been able to keep my mind from wandering in a theological argument, and that week I was more than ordinarily wrapped in introspection.

For Mr. Stiles, unintentionally, had given me a quite different revelation, and mine was exceedingly unpalatable. His pleasant unregarding eye had chilled me. Not because I had any aspirations to his attention — he was too far removed from the image still grooved in my heart — but because it made me understand, finally and clearly, how I had deceived myself. I realized now that David Brainerd had never really seen me either, that on that last morning he must have been as stupefied as Mr. Stiles would be should I so shockingly compel his attention. More than that, I saw now that in all my life only two people had ever really looked at me, Catharine, and sometimes Eph. I was twenty years old, and I was invisible. I had always been so, and there was no reason now to expect that I would ever be anything else.

But for the first time something, perhaps it was the Williams in me coming awake at last, rose up in protest.

II. WHEN MR. STILES left Abigail's house I don't think there was much doubt in either of their minds that he would soon be back again, or that for him she was the most persuasive argument for his return. They must both have recognized that the Stockbridge mission and Abigail were now part and parcel, and that in accepting the call to one he would unmistakably be declaring his eventual intentions towards the other. She showed me, with a delicate smugness, the letter in which he thanked her for the pleasant week spent at her house. I remember that it referred to "sorrow which itself appeared beautiful," and to "virtue in distress which struck the mind with delight and surprise."

Yet though Abigail had tried to warn him, he must somehow, in spite of his caution, have betrayed to Timothy Woodbridge's alert ears a hint of the uncertainties he had confessed to her. For the schoolmaster, standing stubbornly in the face of the combined Williamses, managed week after week to make sure that no definite invitation went out from the Stockbridge church. When we learned that he had written an inquiry to the comissioners in Boston, my father made a special trip to New Haven to warn Mr. Stiles, and when he stopped by her house on the morning of his departure, Abigail penned a hasty note while he lighted his pipe.

The report my father brought back to her a few days later was far from reassuring. Mr. Stiles appeared to have little taste for battle.

"The commissioners have already asked him to appear before them in Boston," my father told us. "I warned him of what he's like to meet there. Stiff-necked Calvinists, especially Dr. Sewall. It might help if you wrote again, Abby. He seemed mighty pleased with that note I handed him."

I don't know what Abigail wrote to him, but that summer scarcely a mail bag arrived at my father's store but contained a letter from Mr. Stiles to Madam Sergeant. Yet in the end it all came to nothing. In October we learned that on the advice of his father Mr. Stiles had decided not to accept the Stockbridge invitation. My father cursed Timothy Woodbridge for a meddling fool. But Abigail blazed at Mr. Stiles for being too cowardly to face the Boston commissioners. If she knew a deeper disappointment, she gave no hint of it, even to me. If she was wounded, it was in her pride alone; I think her heart had not been touched.

So Stockbridge was still without a minister. Timothy Woodbridge and his supporters now moved swiftly. The candidate they proposed was Mr. Jonathan Edwards, recently dismissed from his pulpit in Northampton.

That Mr. Edwards, the preacher whose name must surely be familiar to every man and woman in New England, whose powerful sermons and writings had been in large part responsible for the great revival of religion that had swept across the provinces in these last years, should condescend even to visit our wilderness pulpit seemed to me a remarkable honor for our town. But no one in my family shared my awe.

"You must be able to do something!" Abigail berated my father. "How can you possibly allow a thing like this to happen?"

My father flushed, not missing her implication that he had lost his grasp. "I've about shot my bolt, Abby," he confessed. "This time it's not just Woodbridge and his toadies. We're up against the whole Commission. They've got a big fish in Edwards, and they don't know what to do with him. Settling him here in Stockbridge would get him off their hands."

"If he's such a big fish, why should he be willing to come here?"

"It's the best offer he's likely to get. His own church has barred him from preaching in Northampton. He's queered himself everywhere with his notions, and he's too stiff-necked to back down. It's a fact he's got a claim on this mission. He was a member of the first committee that planned this town and hired John to come here."

"I know. I also know he's a stubborn bigoted man, and that Cousin Israel Williams and Solomon Williams as well have had trouble with him for years. Isn't there someone you can appeal to?"

"Seems not. Particularly with Dwight behind him."

"Dwight? *General* Dwight? What does he have to do with it?"

"Court's just voted him onto the Commission. He carries a lot of weight, and he's a friend of Edwards."

Abigail's patience broke out of control. "So you're just giving up, are you? You're going to let this man come in and stir up the same trouble he made in Northampton?"

My father scratched his head, still affable. "Now Abby, just hold your horses. Looks like we can't stop Edwards from coming. As to giving up, that's another matter."

"Once he comes what can you do about it?"

"I'm still the town moderator. Edwards spends most of his time writing. Shuts himself up alone most of the day, they tell me. And he's not a one for figures. Don't even know how many head of cattle he owns, or like as not how many children he's got — though he took his head out of a book long enough to get a houseful of 'em. So long as business here in town runs along smooth enough, he's not likely to go looking for trouble. That's one thing we can see to, Abby."

Abigail looked at her father thoughtfully and seemed satisfied with what she saw. But I did not like what I had heard.

"If Mr. Edwards is so busy with his writing," I spoke up, "what about the Indians? Can he speak Mahican? Will he have any time for them?"

My father stared at me. "You've scored a point, Liza," he said slowly. "Damned if you don't have a head on your shoulders after all. Edwards is the wrong man for the Indians. They ought to see that."

Abigail turned her shrewd blue eyes on me as she fastened her hood under her chin.

"I'll have another try at the commissioners," my father promised her. "And I'll write Eph to put a word in their ears when he's in Boston. I doubt it'll do any good now, but if it don't, we'll see. We'll see."

12. THAT AUTUMN WHEN Eph came home for a visit, he renewed his arguments about my going away to school. He made frequent trips to Boston on military business; he could conveniently take me with him, see to all the arrangements, even keep an eye on me from time to time. When Eph put his mind to it, he seldom lost an argument. Won over completely, my father magnanimously offered to send Judith as well. But Judith shrank from the very thought of it; she was absorbed in the quilting bees and the singing lessons and the invitations to tea. But thanks to Mr. Stiles, this time I began to pay some heed. I had been badly shaken in these past months. In the night the old dream of the Ice Glen sometimes returned. Worse still, even in the daylight the notion that I was invisible kept coming back to plague me. It was as though I had walked through a spider's web and, unable to rid myself of the soft loathsome strands, I knew a sharper dread that the spider might still be clinging to them. *Was the fault with the others that they did not see me? Or was there in truth no one there to see?* Now, listening to Eph, the fearful hope grew in me that in Boston I would discover the answer, if I could summon the courage to try. Faint-hearted, shilly-shallying from one day to the next, I agreed to go.

On the morning I left Stockbridge behind Eph, with a satchel of new clothes strapped to the saddle, I wanted nothing more than to stay. I could not even laugh when Abigail remarked that I reminded her of the way the Indian girls had set out long ago to live in Northampton. She added that she hoped I would cheer up and be more sensible. Indeed, I knew that I would, for I must. There would be no walking home from Boston, and the combined generosity of my family had laid an obligation upon me.

All my misgivings were justified. Had I been less ignorant I should have known that Miss Richardson's School for Young Ladies could differ only in degree from the little group of girls on the Hill. It was a feminine world intensified, the girls prettier, gayer, wittier, and so all the more removed from me. Having failed on the Hill, how could I possibly have hoped to succeed in Boston?

Here I would have given all I possessed to be invisible. I was a country girl, my body inept with self-consciousness, my good clothes still not fashionable, my speech too plain, lacking the modish phrases. What a pity, I thought often, that Abigail could not have come in my place. How she would have delighted in it, and how they would have loved her. Mrs. Richardson would have found little to teach her, could only have held her up to the others as that finished product, a lady to her fingertips. But the wilderness, which had never touched Abby, had set its ineradicable mark upon me. Often, sitting with my back achingly erect, my fingers cramped from shaping the delicate spidery letters of some meaningless exercise in penmanship, I thought with pity of the Indian boys. Surely our Stockbridge schoolhouse must have seemed to them just such torment.

"It won't hurt you, my pet," Eph said lightly, when on his first visit to the school I poured out to him a woeful recital of rebuffs and failures. "You don't really want to stay a barbarian all your life, do you?" And he chucked me under the chin like a child and took me out to a sweet shop to buy sugar almonds.

This snubbing from Eph, more painful than any the girls could inflict, I took to heart. I think it was the one thing that kept me in the school. Thereafter I set myself to learn, steeling myself to remember that the very fact that the education was so painful proved how much I needed it, as mother used to comfort the children when she spread salve on a hurt finger. I learned to

sit and to stand properly, and to murmur ridiculous phrases I
would never in the future bring myself to utter. I constructed
wax posies and painted ferns and flowers on glass. I labored over
an embroidered chair cover which was no more than a glorified
version of the hated sampler of my childhood, except that this
time I had my way. Instead of copying the unnatural roses of
the patterns, I worked the figure of a small spotted black and
white dog who resembled Adam, and for good measure a young
antlered stag such as Catharine and I had so often surprised in
the forest — quaint and rustic, Mrs. Richardson pronounced
them with raised eyebrows. I could follow the steps of the cotil-
lion and the minuet, though I had little expectation that I would
ever be invited to dance either one.

The next time that Eph came I did not rush helter-skelter
down the staircase to greet him. I came down slowly with my
hair powdered and piled high on my head, and I tilted my cum-
bersome hoops to show just the embroidered band of my petticoat. I still remember his long slow whistle of surprise. I never
told him again how much I hated the school. I am glad to recall
this, wishing only that he could know how many times in these
past years I have blessed him. That I have not failed altogether
in my task here in Stockbridge I owe to him.

I was never reconciled, however. I used to wake early, an obstinate habit that betrayed my country breeding, and I would lie
rigid lest I disturb one of my five roommates a moment before
the rising bell. I could never get over my urge to push open the
window, which was tightly shuttered against the night air, winter and summer. Even when the room was so cold that my
breath went up in smoky puffs, it was still stuffy, and I longed
for the fresh wind east from the harbor and salt-laden which I
relished on our brief excursions on Boston streets. I would lie
trying to imagine the ocean, which I had never seen though I
knew it lay less than an hour's ride away.

Eph's visits were my one claim to distinction at Mrs. Richardson's school. When he waited in the hall in his scarlet coat and the white wig he always wore in Boston, there was a rustling and twittering all along the upstairs bannister. I would go out with my hand tucked in his elbow, knowing very well how any one of them would have liked to take my place. On these visits I gathered desperately the news of home that I would hoard and count over and over in the weeks to come.

Important things had begun to happen in Stockbridge the moment I was no longer there to see them. Mr. Edwards had come in January, and out of necessity Abigail had taken him to board. Every minister who had ever visited the town had found welcome in John Sergeant's house, and moreover, she could not forfeit the money he would pay for board and for pasturing his horse in her field. She deserved the money she earned from him, Eph said. In Eph's opinion, Mr. Edwards was a proud, overbearing man, stiff, taciturn, and his effect in any roomful of people was chilling. In addition he was frequently in poor health and limited to an austere and inconvenient diet. From Eph's account I fancied that this time there were no pleasant evenings of conversation by the fireside.

"There's one thing Abby's not going to find it easy to swallow," Eph said. "Edwards' wife will be coming soon. He's arranged to buy John's old house on the Plain, though God knows how all those children will fit into it. A come-down from that fine house in Northampton. But from all I hear, Mrs. Edwards is a real beauty."

Mr. Edwards had not, so Eph told me, shut himself up with his books as my father had predicted. On the contrary, he was poking his nose into everything. He visited both the schools every day, with Mr. Ashley as his interpreter. He insisted on hearing the English boys read, he questioned them in Latin, he examined their copy books. He had complimented Timothy Woodbridge,

but he had virtually insulted Mr. Kellogg. How could he expect
the Indian boys to answer? Eph reasoned; that scowl of his
would scare every thought from their heads. To Abby's disgust
he had re-established John's old custom of conferring with the
Indians, and she had to endure their coming to the side door at all
hours with their ceaseless whining.

The boarding school had limped through the winter. A number of Mohawk families had finally accepted the invitation
which John had sent out almost two years before, and had
moved into Stockbridge, set up their bark wigwams at the edge
of the town and brought their children to be educated. The
Stockbridge Indians regarded their coming with suspicion and
jealousy, unable to forget that the fierce Mohawks had been,
only a short while before, their bitterest enemies. Even the boys
of the two tribes did not mingle, each attending a separate
school. But Eph regarded it as a triumph that Hendrick himself,
partly because of his long friendship with Eph, had come to
Stockbridge to spend the winter and had entered his own son in
the school. Hendrick's presence was a guarantee of friendship
which no one, Eph insisted, not the commissioners in Boston, nor
the Governor at Albany who thought he had the Mohawks at his
beck and call, nor the Six Nations nor the French Governor himself could ignore.

Something must have gone seriously wrong, however, for in
the summer Eph reported that Hendrick had departed, taking
with him his son and several other Mohawk families, and Eph
confessed that there was little left in the way of a boarding
school to satisfy the commissioners who came to inspect it. Mr.
Edwards had himself gone to Albany to try to persuade the Indians to return.

Presently Eph, from his vantage point in Boston, discovered
that Mr. Edwards had written directly to the commissioners.

"He described all sorts of changes he wants to make in the boarding school," Eph told me. "He aims to take it out of Kellogg's hands, and I suspect out of father's as well. He wants three trustees appointed who will handle all the funds. You can imagine how that's going to set at home."

I looked at him silently, wondering if he suspected as I did that the financial record of these last months might not bear close inspection.

"He even suggests the three trustees he'd like. Only one of them likely to go out of his way, as I see it."

"Who is that?"

"General Dwight. He's a friend of Edwards, but he's a sensible choice. The man has a good head. He's done some surveying in the neighborhood and knows Stockbridge."

"I remember him," I said, thinking wryly that though General Dwight had come several times for tea at Abigail's house he would not have the faintest memory of me. "He didn't look to me like a man to bother with an Indian school."

"He had a good law practice, but he gave it up during the war. Also, he lost his wife a while back, and he's left with five children. Edwards may be trying to make a place for him in Stockbridge. But I rather suspect the parson knows he's going to need some support for himself. He wants Dwight made a resident trustee. I don't like the sound of it. I don't think father is going to put up with it, nor Abigail either. It gives Edwards altogether too free a hand."

13. DURING INDIAN SUMMER of that first year in Boston, I had one brief holiday which blooms in recollection like a single exotic flower on a thorny scraggle of vine. At my father's solicitation — how else? — I received an invitation to the wedding of my cousin Mary Williams in Connecticut. I had never seen Mary nor any of my Wethersfield cousins. To make their acquaintance now seemed an unnecessary ordeal, but I had no choice. The invitation came quite properly to Mrs. Richardson, who, impressed by this belated evidence of some social connections, ignored my hesitations and capably saw to all the preparations. She found an elderly friend who was traveling to Hartford and would take me under her wing. She supervised my packing and added to my qualms with instruction and advice for every possible misadventure. My roommates astonished me, anticipating my journey with far more delight than I could manage, and showing a rush of generosity I did not deserve. On the night before my departure, they showed me, by the cautious light of a single candle, how to roll my front hair in curl papers, and before I closed my satchel they tucked among my serviceable garments a little collection of their own furbelows. I went away bewildered, wondering for the first time if perhaps I had been mistaken about them.

We sailed from Boston harbor, and to my joy I proved to be a natural sailor, as Mrs. Richardson's friend did not. Having done all I could to relieve the bad-tempered woman, I left her groaning in the cabin and escaped to the deck, where I leaned to watch with rapture the glassy bank of water forever sheering back from the prow; I thought I could never tire of it.

We were ten days at sea and nine more moving with a capricious wind up the green-bordered Connecticut River. When we tied up at Wethersfield, my cousin Ezekiel was waiting, and I felt at once that I had known him all my life. He was a farmer, a sensible young man with a tanned face and capable hands. He helped me into a smart little riding chair, the first I had ever set foot in, with two high, freshly painted yellow wheels and a leather-covered seat, and we rode away from the river toward a church spire rising among the treetops. Wethersfield was a pretty town, just the sort of town, I thought, that Abigail would have liked Stockbridge to be, with a wide, tree-shaded green, flanked on either side by comfortable houses with green grass and flower gardens, and with nowhere anything so untidy as an Indian wigwam.

I felt at home from the moment I stepped into my cousin Elisha's house, different as it was from any home I had ever known. Head of the house was Elisha, a lean, deep-voiced young man whose scholarly seriousness could vanish in a smile reminiscent of Eph's. He had a wife, Mehitable, soft and appealing as a kitten, and a one-year-old baby, Anne, who staggered laughing straight into my arms. My cousin Mary had made her home with her brother since her mother's death a year before, since my uncle Elisha was still in England on military business. It was a young household, lively with a bewildering mixture of visiting second cousins and cousins-once-removed. After the first night I never bothered to untangle our relationships, accepting with my inevitable blush their teasing assurance that they were all kissing cousins.

So easy and delightful their life seemed to me. They took for granted the things that father and Abigail were still contriving to bring, one by one at long intervals, over the wilderness road. There were fine Chinese porcelain and English china, dozens of pieces all of the same pattern; Abigail would have gasped to see us drinking our breakfast chocolate from the egg-shell cups. We walked on soft woolen carpets, red- and blue-dyed, and the walls were covered with wallpaper from France so that indoors as well as out there were green leaves and flowers. There was a harpsichord in the parlor which gave off thin sweet melodies under Mehitable's fingers. On many evenings Ezekiel followed her melodies with his flute. Of all the beautiful things in that house, I coveted only the harpsichord. To be able to make music still seems to me the rarest of delights.

Yet this was not a wealthy household, and we were not idle. Except for an elderly African who pottered about the kitchen indulged by them all, there were no servants. All the preparations for the wedding, the mending and polishing and baking, were accomplished by the cousins, speeded by deft fingers and unending chatter. When the day's work was done, we strolled arm in arm about the green in the cool twilight, coming upon friends who included me in their greeting. For I was visible; no one in this place ever seemed to question it. There was much visiting from one house to another, and a round of festivities as the wedding day approached. The night of the wedding, when Ezekiel offered me his arm and led me across the shining uncarpeted floor to dance the minuet, I blessed Mrs. Richardson for the first time, and Eph for sending me to her.

At home, in my father's house, I had been a child, even when I knew in my heart that I was an aging spinster. In Wethersfield, for a few short weeks, I knew what it was to be young. I went away in love with them all, with my head ringing with their voices, and my heart foolishly warm with their reminders that I had promised to come again. That visit has come down through all the years with its perfection untarnished. I suppose there must have been, even there, the human anxieties and vexations that plague us all, but I was blind to them. I saw only that they were simply, uncomplicatedly happy, and that they were content with themselves and with each other, even with me. In my memory they have remained always the same. I cannot think of them without sunshine and laughter.

The school itself seemed different to me when I returned, for I saw it in a new light, appreciating at last some purpose to all the discipline, comprehending that the girls were not all vain and frivolous but, like my cousins, only young and lighthearted. Had I stayed, I might even have come to be happy there myself.

Stockbridge

1752

I. I suppose I should have been prepared, but I was completely taken aback when Eph told me that Abigail was to marry General Dwight.

It was on the day just after Thanksgiving that he finally took me to see the ocean, as he had long promised. To my delight, he hired a carriage, and drove me to a hill that looked down over the harbor, a gray wintry emptiness not at all as I had dreamed it. And there he told me about Abigail.

He chuckled, not noticing my silence. "Everyone's saying she deliberately set her cap for him, and perhaps that was true at the start. I swear all she intended was to charm him away from Edwards. But Dwight is no man to be led around by the nose. I think he turned the tables on her."

"How *could* she?" I cried out. "Oh — how could she?"

"She's doing damned well for herself," Eph replied shortly.

"He — he's not good enough."

"Come now. He's a judge. Excellent family, graduate of Harvard. He distinguished himself at Louisbourg. It seems to me our Abby has overreached herself."

"Overreached — after John Sergeant?"

"Ah — he's not a minister. That's it, isn't it? You're one of those girls who think there's only one breed of man fit to marry?" There was a harshness in Eph's voice I had never heard before. "I'm fed up with having the clergy thrown in my teeth. They depend on the rest of us for their keep, don't they? Without us they wouldn't have pulpits to preach from."

Whatever had caused this outburst, he checked himself at once. "Forget what I said, Liza." His voice was once more his own. "It happens to be a sore point with me just now." Though I waited, he did not explain. "Look at this from Abby's point of view," he said instead. "It hasn't been easy for her, you should know that. Would you really want to see her go on the way she has for the last two years, scrimping to keep a little food in the cupboard and trying not to let us know?"

I looked down at my gloved hands, struggling to be fair. At last I said, "I can't bear for Abigail to marry just to — to keep food in the cupboard."

"As a matter of fact, I don't think that's the case at all. What I've been trying to tell you is that, whether she intended it or not, your sister shows every sign of being in love."

He saw that to me this made it even more shocking. "Be reasonable, Liza. Abigail is only thirty. And she had the short end of that first marriage. She's not the sort of woman to be always giving way to God. Jo Dwight may not be a saint, but if I don't miss my guess he'll be considerably more of a husband."

I did not like the laugh he gave when he saw the blush that came up past the prim collar of my dress.

"Grow up, Liza," he said. "You look like a spinster aunt."

"I am one," I answered. "But I happen to know she loved John."

"Yes. I'd be the last to question that. It's possible to love more than once. You don't believe that, do you? It's true, and I hope you'll find out for yourself before long. Don't shut your mind to it when it comes." He picked up the reins and we drove away from the sea, which had become of no importance. The gray stretch of water only mocked the turbulence within me.

I did shut my mind to it. I could not be reconciled, remembering Abigail's wedding and the marriage that still seemed all that a woman could ask for short of heaven. I was not such a spinster aunt that I had not understood what Eph was saying. I had understood a long time ago, ever since Sam Brown had made it plain to me. But I had determined never to give in, and I was hurt and ashamed that Abigail had done so. I thought that if I could, for even a few years, have had what Abigail had possessed, it would have sustained me for the rest of my life.

2. IN MARCH I rode home with Eph for Abigail's wedding.
As we came out of the woods to the Plain, I clung to Eph's back with inarticulate joy. A light snowfall in the night had rounded the wigwams to clean white hillocks and softened the harsh outlines of the houses. The frozen river was a smooth untouched highway, and along its banks the dry brown spikes of goldenrod were tufted with pure white wool. Umpachenee's grandchildren, scuffling in the roadway, stared, then came running to greet me. Their shouts brought a girl to a doorway, and nothing would do but I must dismount and follow her into her house to admire the new baby suspended in its cradleboard on the wall.

"What is there about this town?" I asked Eph, as we rode up the long hill. "It even has its special beautiful smell."

He laughed. "You're a Williams."

"That's odd, when you think of it," I said. "Not one of us was born here, but I feel as though my ancestors must have worshipped the mountain from the beginning of time."

"You're all alike. Take Josiah. After all those years when he couldn't wait to get away, now he's dickering to buy an extra field from Sam Brown. Even Elijah will come back to settle, I'll lay a wager on it."

"You say *we're* all alike. Don't you include yourself, Eph?"

"Yes, I do. I could succumb to it like the rest of you, but I don't aim to. I want to put down my own roots somewhere new, where the mistakes haven't already been made."

"I don't," I said, too content with greeting every familiar stump and rock to trouble myself about mistakes. "I want to stay here forever. Don't make me leave again, Eph. Please don't."

Neither Boston nor Wethersfield had diminished my father's house. It welcomed and warmed and reassured me, and I loved every corner of it as much as father did. Inside its walls, however, there were changes which chilled even the first moments of greeting. Or had the months away given me keener vision? My father had taken on weight, and the high flush that had always given him a look of bluff good health was overly heightened. There was something new, a defiance against some threat of loss. It showed itself in a temper shorter than ever and in a more insistent boastfulness. Mother, in contrast, had receded still more; it was harder than ever for me to see a sharp image of her. And to my distress Judith was taking on the same vagueness. Perhaps she had been recently ill; her face seemed blurred by fatigue and fretfulness.

In spite of Eph's warning I was not prepared for the change in Abigail. From his words I had anticipated a girl gone back to the days I remembered, young again, and pretty, and in love. Abigail had not gone back; she had moved far ahead. She was a woman, too thin to be pretty, but tautly beautiful and aware of her beauty. There had always been an air of royalty in Abigail; now she was all queen and to me unapproachable. My affection glanced back from her as from new-polished silver. As for Gen-

eral Dwight, he was exceedingly handsome, his manner had a
perfection I was now able to appreciate and he was exaggerat-
edly devoted to Abigail. I could find no fault in him, and I could
not like him.

On the first Sabbath after my return, when I came downstairs
dressed for meeting, I discovered that my father had gone to the
barn and that my mother was obviously not intending to stir
from the house. When I pleaded with Judith, she waveringly
consented to go with me and hurried into her good dress and
bonnet.

"I've missed meeting," she confessed, as we walked down the
hill. "The week just isn't right without it."

"Why don't you go alone then?" I asked her.

"You'll see," she said nervously.

I did see, the moment we took our places in the Williams pew.
Neither Abigail nor General Dwight nor any of their respective
children was present. It would require a stouter heart than Judith's to endure alone the icy spatter of stares and whispers I
could feel against my back.

I confess that my own anticipation made me somewhat obliv-
ious to the sensation we had caused. I could think only that I was
about to see with my own eyes the last man who had talked with
David Brainerd, who had tended him and preached the last sermon over his grave. Whose daughter — But she whom I would
have most yearned and dreaded to meet must remain forever a
shadow. Jerusha Edwards had died a year after the death of her
betrothed; her grave, scarcely grassed over, had been left behind
in Northampton.

Just before the service began, Mrs. Edwards walked into the
meetinghouse, leading a very small boy by the hand and followed by six girls and two more boys. As she stepped serenely
into the minister's wife's pew, in which Abigail had sat for so

many years, I felt a pang of compassion for my sister; it could
not have been easy for Abigail to yield her place to another
woman, most certainly not to this woman. Yet it was difficult at
first sight for me to admit Mrs. Edwards' reputed beauty. The
thin aristocratic nose and the firm mouth had too much strength;
she was at least fifteen years older than Abigail, and her dark hair
was streaked with white at the temples. Though there had been
gossip in Northampton that the minister's wife was extravagant,
the plain serviceable dress showed no evidence of it, nor of any
special care in its donning, the black ribbon fluting of her bonnet
being badly in need of ironing. Then as she turned to supervise
the children's seating, she glanced for an instant in my direction
and I received the full shock of her magnificent dark eyes. And
as she seated herself, composed and erect, she lifted her face toward her husband, who was ascending the pulpit, and there lay
open on her features such pride and beauty that I winced at the
sharp tightening of my own desolation. How could Abigail have
borne it?

Having so long anticipated Mr. Edwards' preaching, I was left
puzzled by it. He stood in the pulpit, a solemn, arresting figure
with a pale ascetic face. He did not speak directly to his congregation. He fastened his eyes on a point somewhere above our
heads, and he spoke in a voice so low that it compelled our ut-
most attention. He read first his text from Romans: "Therefore
hath he mercy on whom he will have mercy, and whom he will
he pardoneth." He went on to expound his doctrine of the sov-
ereignty of God in the salvation of men, laying one logical relentless argument upon another, till my mind was overwhelmed
by their weight. His sermon stirred again all my own confusion.
Six years had passed since I had confessed to David Brainerd my
fear that God had not chosen me, and nothing in all this time had
given me any reason for hope.

The Stockbridge congregation followed his words intently. That they admired and respected and agreed with him was evident on all their faces. Yet as we left the meetinghouse I saw on a few faces my own uncertainty reflected.

"Yes," said old Mrs. Pixley, greeting me outside the door. "Yes, I'm sure he is very fine, though I always lose the thread of it long before he's finished. It's never been the same for me since Mr. Sergeant. The dear man always sent me home on a Sabbath feeling so *comforted*."

The Indians filed out of the church and moved silently down the hill to their houses. They too had had a sermon. Mr. Edwards had preached to them in short careful sentences, as though addressing small children, pausing between each admonishing sentence for Mr. Ashley's translation. It was the most they could hope for; many of them would never again in their lifetime hear the word of God spoken to them directly in their own tongue.

At the noon meal we were subjected to such sarcasm on the matter of family loyalty that Judith left the table in tears.

"It wasn't her fault," I told my father. "She went because I begged her to. I didn't realize the family had stopped going. Truly, father, I don't quite understand why."

"It's plain enough. This Edwards is an outsider. He should never of come here, and he had fair warning. As long as he stays, I want none of this family setting a foot in meetinghouse."

I was not quite his child again. With the foolish courage born of my year of independence, I ventured to reason with him. "Why don't you give him a chance?" I asked. "He might not do anything so dreadful."

He was about to roar at me, but something changed his intent. I think he remembered that he needed support, even mine. "I've given him every chance," he told me. "I agreed at first to go along with him. He's the one hasn't let well enough alone. Why didn't he stick to his preaching and book writing? What right did he have to meddle with the school finances?"

"Perhaps the commissioners asked him to."

"I don't believe it. The commissioners in Boston have always left everything to me. They never haggled over a few dollars. All they want is to keep the Indians here, and they know I'm the man to do it. They know what a time they'd of had finding anybody else to come out here and sweat his guts out while they sat back in Boston. Believe me, my girl, what I've done here is worth a pretty penny to them. If I've managed a little profitable business of my own on the side, that's my own concern."

"I know that, father. We all do."

"All right then. What I want to know is, are you going to stand by me? My own flesh and blood? Who do you think I'm worrying about if it's not you children? I'm an old man, and I ought to step out and let somebody else fret about this town. But when I die I want to know you're well fixed here. What else does a man have to live for?"

I was torn between affection and dread. "You're not an old man," I protested, reassuring myself. "You're not ready to talk about quitting."

"Things'd be in a fine mess if I did. I've been here from the start, and I know what's good for this town. And nobody, not Edwards, nor Woodbridge, not the devil himself is going to rule this roost while I'm on it."

I was seriously alarmed. The muscles below his temple had knotted into bunches, and the veins of his face were a startling purple. "Father — please —"

"All right. All right. I just want one thing understood. You're having nothing to do with this outsider. You're a Williams. Do you understand that?"

I did not go to meeting again.

I had wanted only to placate my father, but I soon discovered
that whether I would or not I must take a stand in the town.
There was bitter division everywhere. Timothy Woodbridge,
who had always blocked my father when he could, had increasingly gained prominence since John's death. Now he had ranged
himself with Mr. Edwards, as had a number of the English families. Opposing him, my father had a powerful new ally. For a
newcomer, General Dwight had acquired surprising influence.
He had come to Stockbridge as Mr. Edwards' friend and supporter. Since his betrothal to Abigail he had turned against his
friend, had joined my father and was now Mr. Edwards' open
enemy.

The bone of contention was Mr. Hollis' boarding school and
the money that had supported it. The irony was that much of
John's dream seemed about to be realized. One hundred and
sixty pounds came regularly each year from Mr. Hollis. There
was also, with the settlement of the Mohawks in Stockbridge, a
very real possibility of diverting some of the royal funds allotted
to New York for the support of the Indians. But whereas up till
now only a few boys had benefited, only recently a Mr. Paine in
England had offered to support a female school for the Mohawk
girls, and the Massachusetts legislature had already voted five
hundred pounds for the building of a second schoolhouse. Yet at
the very point of realization, John's plan had somehow been
twisted awry.

Perhaps it had been too trusting of him to invite boys from the
neighboring tribes, but I believe that through sheer faith he
would have persuaded the Stockbridge Indians to forget their
ancient hatred. Without him, at the coming of the Mohawk
families our Indians had withdrawn their sons, so that everyone
now spoke of it as the Mohawk school. Much of the failure too
lay in John's inability to find a proper teacher. Mr. Edwards
had perceived at once that Mr. Kellogg was unqualified in every

way, that the Mohawk boys were idle and unruly and had learned almost nothing at all. My father refused to admit this; since Mr. Edwards had taken it upon himself to secure a new schoolmaster, my father was obliged to uphold Mr. Kellogg.

I felt sorry for the earnest young man who had arrived in February, appointed by the commissioners as schoolmaster to the Mohawks. Mr. Gideon Hawley was devout and optimistic, with much of John Sergeant's dedication but little of his persuasiveness, and he had come with no suspicion of the hornet's nest that awaited him. Mr. Edwards welcomed and advised him; my father ignored his existence. General Dwight, who as resident trustee had taken over much of the management, allowed him no authority. Mr. Kellogg continued to walk in and out of the schoolhouse as though he owned it, giving orders to the boys and constantly interrupting the classes. Between them all poor Mr. Hawley must have despaired. The Indian boys were confused and the Mohawk families suspicious and hostile.

And in the center of the battle stood Abigail. Nothing had prepared me for this. I was confounded by her audacity. I had thought that like me she had submitted to my father; instead she had wrested the lead from his hands. I think that Mr. Edwards was never deceived. I know that he took up the fight reluctantly, having had enough of fighting in Northampton and hoping only for a sanctuary in Stockbridge where he could write his books in peace. But when he finally became aware of the fury around him and took stock of his position, I believe that he recognized at once that his chief adversary was not my father but Abigail. From that time on, while the other antagonists shouted threats and insults, Mr. Edwards and Abigail advanced to fight in single combat. He was the first man she had ever encountered, perhaps the only one, who stood completely unmoved in her path, as she stood in his.

This was an Abigail I had never seen before. She was determined to be the mistress of the new female boarding school. I
could not believe my ears when she flaunted that old sewing class
to prove her competence, for her memory of it was plainly far
different from my own. She even broke her long-established
precedent and visited the Indian houses and literally coerced a
few children into studying with her.

She was possessed; there is no other word. A demon seemed to
be shaking her, and it was some time before I understood. I had
known that Abigail had resented the boarding school from the
start. I remembered the helpless anger in her face that day that
she had crumpled John's letter and flung it into the fire. She had
grudged the strength John had poured out on the school, feeling
that she and her children were cheated of their right. After his
death she had hated it almost as though it were a living thing that
had taken John from her. Now it seemed, with a sort of savage
fury, she had risen up and taken this hated thing into her hands
and was determined to make it serve her.

To do her justice, she had a need. General Dwight, though
everything about him bespoke an easy flow of money and a confidence that this was the natural order of things, had apparently
no certain plans for the future. If she were to keep her house in
Stockbridge, and I believe no other plan was even thinkable to
her, then some source of income must be discovered for them
both here in the town. Together they would have eight children
to provide for. I would have said there was little in a small Indian school to content for long a man like General Dwight, but I
was mistaken. Together they glimpsed in it possibilities never
dreamed of by John Sergeant.

Just what part Eph played in all this I could never determine.
In his amiable way he listened to them all, or simply got up and
walked away. He remained on good terms with everyone in the

town. He was a friend of General Dwight's, he exchanged a courteous good morning with Mr. Edwards and I knew, if the rest did not, that he frequently visited Hendrick in his wigwam. Now, in spite of his seeming detachment, he agreed to intervene for Abigail in Boston and to propose her name as head of the female school. I could not keep silent; I followed him out to the stable one day and demanded to know why.

"For the love of God," he snapped at me. "Don't you start too. Can't you stay out of it?"

"I wish I could. But I can't see how you could possibly have let Abby wheedle you into this."

"When your sister has set her mind on something, it takes a better man than I am to refuse."

"You know she wouldn't do at all. How can you possibly tell them she would?"

"Don't underestimate her. Abby can do just about anything she has a fancy to."

"Perhaps. But it wouldn't be fair to the Indian girls. They've always been afraid of her. Abby has never wanted to have anything to do with the Indians. And neither has father. Now all they can think of is John's school."

"I've explained all this before," he said patiently. "The school has a political importance. The Iroquois —"

I interrupted. "I don't think that's the real explanation, and neither do you." I gathered my courage. "There's another thing. Eph, is it true that father is selling rum to the Indians at his store?"

He looked squarely at me, and for a moment I saw, not for the first time, the just-perceptible reflection — or was it presage — of father in his face. "Liza," he said, "you ask too damned many questions. Leave father alone. No man wants someone poking into every corner. God knows I don't. Can't you ever learn to look the other way once in a while?"

That I was no longer a child to be put off by a quick hurt was in good measure his own doing. "Is that your answer?" I asked him. "To look the other way?"

"I don't consider it my business. And right now I have other things to think about than this infernal school." He slapped a length of harness against the wall in exasperation, but I refused to be put off.

"If you don't care about the Indians, don't you care about father?" I persisted. "Can't you see how this is harming him?"

"Arguing only makes it worse. Don't think I haven't tried. I'd be as thankful as you would for a little peace."

"You could at least not encourage Abigail."

He hesitated, then turned back to me. "The truth is, I can't stomach Edwards myself. I was opposed to his coming here from the beginning, and I told him so. You blame father. You say Abby would be bad for the Indian children. Can you honestly tell me one thing Edwards has done for them?"

"He hasn't had much time. At least he seems to listen to them. He isn't just — just using them."

"How do you know he isn't? There's more than one way of using people. To my way of thinking, the missionaries' way isn't much preferable to father's."

I stood trying to be sure I had heard him correctly.

"All right, you're shocked, aren't you? But listen with your mind open for once. These missionaries come here to teach the Indians. Do they ever consider that the Indians might be able to teach them something too? I don't mean such things as how to trap beaver. The Indians have a Great Spirit of their own, and moral laws that they hand down to their children. The Six Nations have an extraordinary system of government. Does this mean anything to the English? We must root it all out, simply because it's Indian. Do you think the Indians don't resent it? They're willing to learn from us. They want to send their children to our schools. They'll listen to our preaching. But they don't want to crawl in the dirt to do it, and the missionaries expect them to. When these preachers look at Indians, do you think they ever see human beings with brains and livers and feelings like themselves? Not by a long sight. They see heathen creatures, wallowing in sin and darkness, who've got to be saved for God's glory — or for their own salvation, if they admitted the truth. Even John Sergeant — I know, I know, don't stop me — he was as fine a man as ever lived. But still, he called them his children. You've heard him, time and time again. Damn it, Liza, they're not children, and they're not creatures. Those miserable heathen redskins are men, and they want to be treated like men. Anyone who doesn't understand that is using them, no matter what name you give to it."

He stopped suddenly, rubbing the back of his head, his face now wholly his own. "Don't wonder you look baffled," he said ruefully. "That's always been my curse — never know which side I'm arguing on. Matter of fact, the redskins are a troublesome lot. Only one Hendrick in a hundred thousand. They're simple as children right enough in some ways, and crafty as devils in others. And make no mistake, they're using the white man, English or French, for everything they can get. How can you expect me to take a clear stand one way or the other?"

3. IF OUR FAMILY's enmity troubled Mr. Edwards, he gave no sign. As we walked through the town, he bowed meticulously to English and Indian, friend and foe, and seemed equally disinterested in us all. He was like a rock, firmly anchored in the midst of a spring flood, unmoved by the sticks and

pebbles hurtling past. His wife and daughters too kept to themselves. It was said that inside that tiny house they labored not simply as the rest of us did at housekeeping but to add to Mr. Edwards' small salary, and that the mysterious bundles which went out by the post rider contained the paper fans they had fashioned and painted. Even so one wondered how such a large family managed at all, and if the hundred sleigh loads of firewood annually doled out by our parish were enough to keep them from freezing.

The girls, the youngest of them, had a certain proud carriage and an independence that repelled both curiosity and friendship. Yet they had certainly not inherited their father's coldness. One sensed a warm solidarity and an extraordinary liveliness; I remembered that even in that first Sabbath meeting I had caught them sharing some secret amusement in a single gleeful nudge. In the town I think much of the censure was pure envy.

Once we heard that there was serious illness in that house. My father was not at home, but his hold was so strong upon us that mother actually whispered when she drew me into the kitchen.

"I know your father wouldn't want me to go," she said. "But I can't bear to think of their needing help. I've made up a bowl of calf's-foot jelly. It goes down easy on a sore throat and is real nourishing. And they may not know about my cure for quinsy. You go, Elizabeth, and your father just doesn't need to know a thing about it."

When I knocked on the door of Mr. Edwards' house, Lucy, the middle daughter, let me in with a natural greeting as though I came every day in the week. She had a woolen scarf fastened about her neck, and the house seemed to me wretchedly chilly. It was true about the fanmaking; the table and floor were littered with snips of paper. Chiefly I noticed the books everywhere, on chairs and tables and leaning in untidy piles against the walls.

Lucy took me straight into the bedroom, which was dark with shutters closed and stuffed with bits of rag to keep out the drafts, and heavy curtains drawn about the bed. I could see well enough, however, the sunken hollows under the eyes of the woman who struggled up from the pillow to look at me. I bent over the little girl in the trundle bed beside her, and put my hand on the hot forehead, and I explained to Lucy what mother had taught me about the care of a fevered child.

"Thank you for your kindness," said Mrs. Edwards, and even in her hoarse whisper and white strained face there was a remnant of queenliness. "Be sure to come again, my dear, when we are about once more. It will be a pleasure." She knew that I would not, and I think she knew that I was wishing with all my heart that I could.

4. ABIGAIL AND Mr. Dwight were married very quietly in the parlor of our house. Father spoke the marriage lines as he had before, with only our family and a few friends from the Hill gathered to listen and to eat the simple and elegant supper that Abigail had planned. Later in the evening, without any of the merriment that ends most weddings, Abigail took her husband's arm and they went out into the soft May night to walk alone the short distance to her house. A few wishes followed them through the darkness, and then in the sudden silence through the open door the sound of the peeping frogs came sharp to my ears. I had not called after Abigail. I stood shaken by the look on her face. It was a look that set stirring all that I had tried to forget.

"Two husbands," said Judith, as together we began the clearing up. "And I don't suppose you and I will ever have even one."

If the empty punch bowl or a turned-about chair had suddenly spoken my own thoughts aloud I would not have been more shocked. Embarrassed, I tried to pretend that she had spoken lightly.

"How do you know? We're not so old as all that."

"I'm twenty-three," she said. "Lots of girls are married by sixteen. And I never meet anybody. Elizabeth, don't you ever worry about it? How are we ever going to meet anyone in this town?"

She stood twisting a linen napkin between her fingers, her pale blue gaze fixed on me. I suppose I should have been touched that she had found the courage to push through her own diffidence, but I was not; I preferred not to see. My own thoughts were all that I could manage; I wanted to go on thinking that Judith's thoughts were as placid as the flat surface of her days. I busied myself with scraping up a gobbet of candle wax that had melted down onto the tablecloth. "Abigail met both her husbands in this town," I said briskly.

"Abigail would meet a man in a desert. Anyway, I wouldn't want General Dwight."

"Eph thinks he's a very good catch."

"I didn't mean he wasn't, for Abigail. I don't know how to talk to a man like that. I feel as though he's laughing at me. You know, Liza, I don't think he is a really good man."

I stared at her. She dipped her head, her lips working. "I mean — I guess he's no worse than most others. They're all alike. I just keep hoping I might meet a man who is different — one who wouldn't care about — about —"

I could not laugh, for I saw she was in dead earnest, and that painful as it was for her, she was determined to go on. I don't suppose any of us ever picks a sensible time for confiding. Something wrenches the latchstring, or a chance wind blows open the door, and we never stop to wonder whether anyone cares to listen. Judith was not stopping now.

"I thought for a long time — after the soldiers were here, you remember — that I wouldn't ever care again about marrying. I don't want to have any children. Abby Woodbridge says it's terrible, she suffered something awful every time. I don't think I could stand it. And I'm not good at tending them like you. I'm not strong enough to get up in the night and all the smelliness makes me feel sick."

"If you don't want children," I said, "why should you think about getting married?"

"I don't want to be an old maid. I don't want to live here at home all my life and just be the Williams girl even when I'm eighty. It's as though I'll never be anybody at all. There must be some man who isn't like Mr. Dwight. Someone who just wants to have a wife to keep house for him and to look after him. I'm sure there must. Someone who is kind and unselfish and cares about higher things. A minister, like John."

"John wanted children," I said helplessly. I did not say that Mr. Edwards had had eleven.

"Well, of course, I know that. But Abby wanted them too. I don't think Abigail knows what it is to be afraid of anything. I meant perhaps an older man, maybe a widower, with children who were grown up and didn't need caring for."

Why couldn't I have put my arms around her and found something reassuring to say? I wished that I had, when later I lay aching with pity for her. At the moment I wanted to shake her. I was appalled at what I had glimpsed — the same Judith, locked in helplessly with her daydreams, only now too old for dreaming, and with phantasies even more implausible.

"Are you shocked at me?" she wavered.

"Of course not," I lied. "I — I'm just sorry, Judith."

"I shouldn't have said all that. I never have anyone to talk to. I guess it was the wedding. There's something about a wedding that makes you feel so — left out."

"I know," I said.

"Do you really? You never say how you feel about things. I never understood what happened about Sam Brown. I couldn't tell if you ever even thought about being married."

"It isn't much use to think about it," I told her. "I just don't think I ever shall be. But maybe it will work out for you. I hope you meet your minister, and perhaps you will if you keep thinking so. Look at Abby. When she wants something she never has a thought but what she'll get it, and she always does."

"It doesn't work for me," said Judith, picking up a heap of spoons. Her voice had lost its urgency and had fallen back into its sighing tone.

Nor for me either, I thought, brushing up the cake crumbs. I shouldn't have encouraged her. Better not to want anything so much. Yet why is it that some people only have to ask, and others have no right to ask at all? Better not to think of it, certainly not to speak of it. Or to think about the look on Abigail's face.

5. ABIGAIL'S MARRIAGE was a great satisfaction to my father. Not only had he gained a son-in-law who was everything he admired in a man, but just when his own hold on affairs was threatened he had been joined, for the first time in his life, by a man whose ambition matched his own. I am sure he saw in Jo-

seph Dwight the strong right arm he had hoped to find in Eph. Leaning on this promising support, my father could delude himself that his power in Stockbridge was still invincible.

The wedding was but the briefest lull in the conflict which was to darken our summer as a distant forest fire sometimes fogs the air under low-hanging clouds. Abigail's happiness, undeniable as it was, only seemed to sharpen her desire for battle. Together the three of them worked out a plan the details of which are too complex and wearisome for me to trace. As a resident trustee, General Dwight now held in his hands the funds of the boarding school. The London society had paid Abigail a year's salary in advance as mistress of the girls' school soon to be erected. She had chosen for its site a corner of her own land to be purchased from her at a generous price by the legislature of Massachusetts, and the proposed building would necessarily be large, since for Abigail to perform her duties it would be expedient for the combined families to move into it. Her children and stepchildren would thus receive a free education, and as soon as Mr. Hawley could be removed, Joseph Dwight's eldest son would replace him as schoolmaster to the Mohawk boys. All provisions for the two schools would be ordered and dispensed through my father's store, in which Mr. Dwight was now a partner. There were other details, all contributing to a logical and reasonable plan. I refuse to believe that any of the three intended any real dishonesty; it was simply a plan to which Mr. Edwards could not possibly subscribe.

He fought them all with his arrogant rectitude, and I heard little else all that summer. We never had a meal free of it. I did not know then that Mr. Edwards had worked out a plan of his own; I doubt that he ever presented it to my father or to General Dwight; I learned of it only a few years ago when Lucy Edwards found it among his papers. I was astonished that it was sensible and orderly and showed a knowledge of the Indians' needs which none of us ever gave him credit for. What struck me as most remarkable was that Mr. Edwards had discovered the single weakness Elijah had detected on his first day at school but which none of our elders had ever taken seriously. The Indian boys learned to read by memorizing English sounds and letters. Given a passage of scripture they could sound out the words quite creditably, but the words they pronounced were meaningless to them. Even Timothy Woodbridge had never seemed to grasp the fact which Mr. Edwards presented so clearly, that unless the words made sense the reading was profitless and that the children must learn first to speak and understand the English language. It is useless to wonder now what might have been accomplished had Mr. Edwards had his way, for by the time the school was in his hands the Mohawks had departed and the Massachusetts legislature no longer cared whether an Indian could read so long as he could shoot a musket or bring back an enemy scalp.

Father and General Dwight and Abigail were convinced that Mr. Edwards was the stumbling block; they were determined to bring about his removal by one means or another. General Dwight rode off to Boston to see what could be done through influential friends. My father stayed at home, his frustration compounded by a savage attack of gout. Week by week I watched the anger mount in him. He was actually a prisoner in his own castle. Deprived of his dignity in the church, for he would no longer set foot in the meetinghouse, helpless as a moderator with the majority of the town ranged against him, snubbed on the town road where once every man and woman had been flattered to pass the time of day with him, he shut himself up and became a tyrant in his own household. He stumped about the house whacking the feather beds with his cane and summoning us to witness how the dust flew up. He fussed about the kitchen, lifting the pot lids and complaining that yesterday's soup had been nothing but wishwash. He roared abuse at poor Moni, and he filled his prayers, morning and evening, with reminders to the Almighty of the ingratitude of mankind.

I am sure his anger had much to do with the frightening illness that came upon him suddenly in May, an attack of palsy so severe that we were all terrified for his life. For four days he lay almost helpless, his left arm useless, his speech thick and unintelligible. When very gradually these faculties returned, he was weak and constantly discouraged. He was never the same after that illness. The buoyancy, the love of life was gone; the old fires could be stirred now only by anger.

I often wonder how we would have lived through that summer without the cribbage games. On father's last trip to Boston someone had introduced him to the game, and he had procured for himself a pack of playing cards, surreptitiously, for there was a heavy fine on the sale of them and no reputable storekeeper would handle them openly. Eph, who was well acquainted with the game, was his favorite partner. Whenever Eph came home, my father insisted on having supper served early, so that they could set up the little tilt-top table and cribbage board. Our knitting would be punctuated by his grunts of disappointment or his sudden snorts of triumph. Mother kept a nervous eye on the path; had an unexpected caller observed the playing cards there would have been one more black mark against father's name. But there were few callers these days. Sometimes I would stand behind Eph to watch over his shoulder, fascinated by the innocent-seeming bits of pasteboard which Mr. Edwards would have considered the property of Satan himself. One night Eph remarked, "Better teach Elizabeth how to play. She can hold up my honor when I'm gone."

Half expecting that God would strike me down on the instant,

I picked up the hand he dealt me. To tell the truth, to this day I do not understand what was so wicked about those cards. I would like to ask Stephen, but I cannot bring myself to confess to him that I have held them in my hands. Or worse, that I enjoyed them. Every evening through the long summer, and often on hot afternoons when his swollen foot and the intense sun combined to keep him indoors, father and I sat at the little table. There was more to the game than the simple rules suggested. Father threw himself fiercely into every match, and he could not endure to lose. I learned not to observe when a peg was slyly advanced an extra notch or so, and I developed some cunning of my own in playing on cards which would give him a likelier chance to score, though he was suspicious of this and furious if he caught me at it. I discovered too that an occasional victory on my part, even though it brought on an hour's sulk, made his next day's triumph the sweeter. He would greet me at breakfast with still-lively glee or an uncomfortable nudge in my ribs. "Licked you good last night, didn't I? Guess your old man is still smart enough so his children don't get the best of him!"

Those games of cribbage did much more than keep father's mind occupied. For me they drained my heart of every trace of awe or terror. When I looked at the man across the table, I no longer saw either a god or a tyrant. I saw my father, his heavy red-veined cheeks sucked in with scowling concentration, or his blue eyes gloating under his shaggy brows. I loved him, if not just as I had loved him in childhood, at least as I had never been able to do in the years between.

6. I COULD NOT expect that so flimsy a defense as cribbage could hold back for long my father's gathering wrath. I was uneasy, I did not sleep well and my healthy habit of waking early became that autumn the ordeal that has plagued me ever since. Father also woke early, and wandered about the house as soon as it was light enough to see, taking note of the things we had neglected, so that we were greeted every morning with a list of faults which must be remedied at once. So on the particular morning in October when I heard him clump down the stairs before dawn, I paid little notice. At last it seemed to me that his rummaging had more a sound of purpose than was usual, or some sixth sense warned me; putting a rail over my nightclothes, I went down. He was sitting on a kitchen bench, fully dressed, pulling on his heavy boots.

"Can I fix you some breakfast?" I asked. He had not bothered to stir up the fire but he had unwrapped some leftover cornbread and poured out a mugful of cider, spilling it in a long smear across the tabletop.

"Time for that when I get back."

"Are you going out? It's still dark."

"I don't loll in bed all day like you young ones. Thing to do is get them early, before they start chores."

"Get who?"

"Dave Pixley, for one."

"He won't even be up yet."

"He'll get up fast enough." He lifted his head and stared at me; his face, red from the struggle with his boots, had a purplish tinge from the stubble of beard. I had never known him to go abroad without shaving.

"Father," I asked, uneasy now, "what are you going to do?"

"None of your affair," he growled. Then, "I'm going to buy his place, that's what I'm going to do."

"Does he want to sell?" I had never heard him mention Mr. Pixley's property.

"He'll sell. Him and all the rest of 'em. Ain't a man anywhere won't sell if the price is high enough."

The sweep of his arm knocked over the mug. He stood up, wiping his sleeve across his mouth.

"Wait!" I was truly alarmed. "What do you mean, the rest of them?"

He turned on me the icy glitter which had always quelled me. "I'm buying them out," he said. "Every last one of 'em."

I could not think fast enough.

"They'll see who has the last word. You mark what I say, girl. By noon today I'll have this town in my pocket, if it takes my last penny."

I gasped. "You can't do that. You know you can't."

I thought he would strike me. His fist crashed down on the table top instead. "Don't you tell me what I can't do. I've done as I pleased in this town for fifteen years. I've made this place what it is. Now he comes in here acting like God Almighty himself. There's not room for both of us in this town, and it's not me that's going. I'll see us both in hell first."

I watched him go. What else could I do? Then I went shivering up the stairs to where mother and Judith, in their nightrails, cringed on the landing. I went past them into my own room and began to pull on my clothes. If only Eph were in town!

Abigail was already up, heating milk with her dark hair streaming down her back. She heard my incoherent account through silently.

"He must have lost his mind," she said. There was annoyance in her voice, but I could not detect the fear that was shaking me.

"Why didn't he say something to me? It's an insane idea. They'll never sell."

She bit her lip, following some thought of her own. "On the other hand," she said slowly, "you never know. He might buy out just enough of them to tip the balance."

For the only time in my life I almost shook her. She came swiftly to some secret conclusion. "There's not a thing in the world we can do," she said reasonably. "Go on home, Liza. You look like a scarecrow. Father can take care of himself."

I was far from believing that he could. I waited in the front window all the morning. Toward noon I saw him coming slowly, and I clutched the window sill to keep from running out to him. He walked past me as though I were the stair post, dragging his bad leg as he went up the stairs. The dull creak of his door shutting announced his defeat to all the house.

Toward supper time Josiah came in, stamped up the stairs and turned back when father refused to answer his angry knock. We extorted from him all he knew. Dave Pixley, taken by surprise, had actually signed a bill of sale; he was the only one. After the second unsuccessful attempt, word had gone ahead of my father through the town. At his last call three neighbors had been waiting.

"He went too far this time," Josiah said. "I heard they threatened to tar and feather him."

"How could they? There's no law against trying to buy land!"

"If folks get riled up enough they don't need a law. Just see to it he stays in this house till things calm down. If any of them come here, don't let him talk to them. One oath out of him will be all the excuse they need."

Only Abigail was admitted to father's room, and she was there for a long time. She came out looking sober and tired. "He's not well," she said. "Not himself. He wants to go away for a while, and I guess it's the best thing. If you'll help him pack, mother, he wants to start before daylight. And be sure Josiah rides with him for a way."

In the hallway she looked back up the stairs. "He's frightened," she whispered to me. "I can't believe it. Oh, poor father!" That was the way it always was with Abigail. I had to forgive her for this morning, because now there was pity in her eyes.

For a week we were frantic with worry about him. Word came back from unexpected sources; we heard that he rode first all the way to Wethersfield, then back to New Haven, and then even to Boston in all sorts of weather, feverishly pursuing some will-o'-the-wisp of his past influence. Then, like a runaway colt whose willfulness has run itself out, he came back, not to us but to Thomas in Deerfield, and there he stayed. He died there two years later without ever seeing Stockbridge again.

He vowed over and over that he had shaken the dust of the place from his feet, but I truly believe he died of homesickness. Though in one final renunciation he sold the house and land and slaves and animals to his sons, principally to Eph, he could not get them out of his mind. He wrote to us to send him a cheese and some apples — he could find nothing to taste like his own. He reminded us that the swamp must be flowed over before winter, and the horse's shoes removed and sharpened, and instructed us to graft a new shoot to the little cherry tree close to the bee house. In every letter he begged us to visit him, and I rode to Deerfield as often as I could. In those two years I watched him age two decades. It still wrings my heart to think of him, asthmatic, hobbled by rheumatism, palsied, querulous and purposeless. He of us all belonged in Stockbridge; to die in exile was a heavy price to pay for his sins.

By the time he died there was no schoolhouse to quarrel over, for it had caught fire mysteriously one night and burned to the ground. Mr. Gideon Hawley, discouraged, had departed on a long journey to Onohoguagua territory to establish there a new mission. Abigail and Joseph Dwight had been forced to retreat, not at once nor easily, before an adversary they had underestimated, and Mr. Edwards held the affairs of the mission, what there was left of it, securely in his hands.

It is fruitless now to ponder the lost opportunities for our Indians, for the Six Nations and for the glory of God. And I have dwelt too long on that sorry conflict; it does no credit to our family. I know that Mr. Edwards had the right on his side, much of it at least, but he was a cold stern man, and in such a man the right sometimes repels us; we choose the wrong for its own illogical merits. Father spoke truly that Mr. Edwards should never have come as missionary to the Stockbridge Indians. I believe he failed them as surely as those who wronged them openly. His great intellect meant nothing to them. They sensed his rectitude and cast themselves upon it, and he did at last take up his pen in their defense. But they found little comfort in him. His failure was that he was not John Sergeant. Neither, in truth, is Stephen. Nor young John. In the end must we believe that even John Sergeant failed them by offering them an image of the white man which they could never hope to realize again?

And Abigail? Remembering, I am confounded by shame and admiration. For she was magnificent, mistaken as she was. She was of the breed of Deborah and Jael, but unlike them she fought a titan armed by the Lord. Had she chosen instead to fight by his side, could they have made of Stockbridge a Promised Land? Yes, if there is to be a reckoning, I know that the heaviest of the blame must rest on the Williamses. On all of us. I have lived with the memory of the blue beads for thirty years, and I will live with it till I die.

7. WE WERE ON the threshold of war again, and the men were all agreed that it was inevitable. I have never had a mind for politics; I could not understand why two powerful nations must kill and maim for the sole right to land which seemingly was wide enough for all. Eph tried to explain to me that the wilderness was not so infinite as I supposed, and that a line of French forts stretching down from north to south along the Ohio River would be like a prison wall to the English colonies, so that men like my father, risking the western forests to find new acres for their families, would someday have no further place to go. I could readily agree on one thing, however, that we could not go on living in constant fear of the Indian raids along our borders.

For us in Stockbridge the war began early in the spring of 1754, though the French and English colonies were still uneasily at peace. The brush fire of panic was lighted by a single small incident. At least to the General Court, long toughened by news of whole villages in flames, it must have seemed a trifling thing that one Indian was shot in an argument over a horse. He was not one of our Indians, but from the Schaghticoke tribe just to the north, and the white men who killed him were strangers to us, passing on business through the town. But the Stockbridge Indians, suspicious from their own grievances, were incensed at what they took to be outright murder. They sent emissaries with wampum and messages of sympathy to the funeral of their brother, and then they waited to see what the English would do.

The two strangers were discovered and brought to trial in the court in Springfield. They convinced the court that it had all been a misunderstanding and that they had shot the Indian in what they believed to be self-defense. One man was acquitted, the other received a small fine.

To the Indians this was no settlement at all. An Indian death must be paid for, justly by another death, but acceptably by a payment of money to the bereaved family. Some would call it barbarous, this willingness to accept money in payment for a life; actually it is an insistence on a man's worth, and at the same time a very sensible way of avoiding repeated bloodshed. It is a pity that the learned gentlemen of our courts have never bothered to understand an Indian's way of thinking. In Stockbridge we knew what must be done, but it required several entreaties from Timothy Woodbridge, an urgent letter from Mr. Edwards and finally a petition signed by half the English men in the town before the General Court sent a letter of condolence and a gift of six pounds, nowhere near enough to wipe the tears from the eyes of the grieving family or to mollify the Stockbridge Indians.

For a month rumors stirred like snakes in a thicket. Then in July vengeance came down on, of all possible victims, the Chamberlains, new to our town, innocent of every past injustice, guilty only of building their house too far from help on the northern slope of the Hill. The Schaghticokes struck in mid-morning on the Sabbath, and the news was carried screaming into meeting. The Indians had tomahawked the three-year-old boy on the path outside the house and had snatched the baby from its cradle to dash it against the mantle, before a passing neighbor had frightened them off. Mrs. Chamberlain was unharmed, and so was Mr. Chamberlain, who, poor man, never lived down the memory that he had hidden under the bed with his two little boys and that his wife owed her life to the hired man. This brave Mr. Owen was carried all the way to our house that morning, but there was nothing that I could do even to make his dying easier. It is the only time in my life I have seen a scalping. I have remembered through two wars, watching the boys ride away in their stubborn courage. For how, once they have looked upon such a face, can they ever again rid themselves of fear?

Even before Mr. Owen died there in the back kitchen, I was aware that the house was filling up with people. Their shrill voices jangled in my ears, and their scared faces showed briefly in the doorway and retreated from what lay on the floor. When I finally went out, I found they were coming not only straight from meeting and from all over the Hill but from the settlement of Yokon and from as far away as Pontoosuc, for the Indians had also killed a man on the road to Yokontown. These people meant to stay, putting their trust in father's oak walls that were built for trouble, but some families had gone over the mountain to Sheffield. Abigail had been seen hurrying the girls ahead of her, and little John trailing after without even shoes or stockings on his feet. Down on the Plain, they said, everyone was making for Mr. Edwards' house. There was no knowing what would happen when night fell.

From that day on fear clogged the air again, draining the taste from the food we ate. We were not to be free of it for nearly ten years. Though our town lay exposed in the very path of the enemy, this war, like the one before, passed by our fields and houses. But it struck to our hearts. Scarcely a single family in the town, English or Indian, was not somehow made desolate in those bitter years. I am grateful that my father did not live to see it.

That first night passed and the days, and then the weeks. I don't know which is harder to bear, solitary terror or a houseful of frightened relatives and friends. I know I barely held my patience till the promised soldiers arrived and the last of the families straggled back to their own houses. I was resigned to an allotment of soldiers this time, and the burden seemed slight when I learned how the Edwards family had suffered. During the worst of the panic they had sheltered at least twenty people in that already crowded little house, and now the town voted, unfairly it seemed to me, that his house should be the one fortified on the Plain and that most of the soldiers should be garrisoned there.

8. AFTER MY FATHER's death mother stayed with Thomas in Deerfield. She could never bring herself to face the Stockbridge families who had turned against her husband, though I think they would have welcomed her without rancor. After a time Judith and I went back to the meeting again; we had missed it, and it gave a semblance of order and purpose to days which had little to distinguish them one from another. On the first morning that we attended, Mrs. Edwards greeted us.

"I am so happy to see you both," she said, her dark eyes warm and brilliant with the sympathy she knew we would not want to hear. "My dear," she added to me, "I have always remembered your mother's kindness and your own and hoped that you might come again. Would you have tea some afternoon, both of you, with me and the girls? On Wednesday next, perhaps?"

So Judith and I went to the enemies' house for tea. Why should we not? I urged Judith, who vacillated between curiosity and flattered eagerness and the doubts that persisted in spoiling her pleasure. To me the old quarrel had always been meaningless, and in truth, since the afternoon when I had visited two years before I had always wanted to go back.

For Judith that Wednesday afternoon was not a success, complicated as it was by so many remembered loyalties. "I still don't think we should have gone," she said afterwards. "Even if mother did send medicine, she would never have called. It's not respectful to father's memory. Besides, I don't like them. The girls are too — bold. Lucy was laughing at me, I know she was. And it's not polite for them to discuss things we don't understand."

In a way she was right, yet it was precisely the things she complained of that drew me back again and again without Judith, despite her injured looks and silences. I was helpless against the quality of life I recognized in that house. They were not bold, but I could not find a more accurate term. Perhaps "alive" was the word, for Judith and I were not alive as the Edwards girls were. Life flooded through those crowded rooms; the narrow walls and the low rafters were shaken by it; the whole family seemed carried along on its swift tide; and I was stirred as I stood cautiously on the shore. They never stopped talking. It was quite true, as Judith said, they talked about people I had never met and books I had never read. They talked about whatever came into their heads, an impulsive enthusiasm sweeping them beyond the bounds of politeness. It did not matter to them if someone interrupted, and as time went by that someone, to my surprise, was sometimes even I myself.

I could not begin to envision what the house in Northampton must have been, with eleven of them growing up together. There were only five in the house on the Plain that year; they all spoke constantly and regretfully of how few they seemed at table. Sarah, the eldest, now Mrs. Parsons, also lived on the Plain, not too far away to be frequently in and out of the house with her baby daughter. Esther had been married two years before and lived now in Newark, where her husband, the Reverend Aaron Burr, was president of the College of New Jersey. There was another married daughter still in Northampton. Of the girls still at home it was Lucy who had most distressed Judith, for undoubtedly the current of life ran most swiftly in her; there was gossip in the town that she was keeping young Jahleel Woodbridge on tenterhooks. Besides Lucy there was Sukie, just turned sixteen, with a head full of romantic notions; Eunice, half-child, half-woman; and Betty, who had been the sick child in the trundle bed and who had never wholly recovered from that illness; I sensed that underneath their teasing they all watched and protected her. It was a houseful of girls. Timothy was away at the college in New Jersey, and young Jonathan, only nine years old, had ridden away with Mr. Hawley into Indian territory to learn the language more perfectly. I was astonished that they would let him go in such uncertain times. Of the three boys, only four-year-old Pierrepont remained at home, precocious, spoiled by his sisters, chattering in Indian with the boys at Mr. Woodbridge's school and reminding me of Elijah the year we had come to Stockbridge.

In the center of this household, its very heart and spring, moved Mrs. Edwards. Without ever raising her voice, she exacted an obedience that was extraordinary, for the family standards were not easy. Mr. Edwards expected his children to be familiar with Latin and Greek and well-grounded in the scriptures, and the girls were not exempt even though they must learn in addition the practical skills of the household. It was Mrs. Edwards who carried out these exacting requirements, and she did so without ever troubling her husband with the stress and occasional rebellion they produced. The children and Mr. Edwards too adored her, they leaned on her, they drew from her strength. Yet in spite of the warm love that enveloped them all, there was about her something apart and untouched and serene. She seemed to possess a special knowledge, as though it had been granted her to look through some secret rift of life and to see the meaning beneath and beyond. If this is the Grace of which they speak, then I have seen it in a woman's face, and I know it to be precious beyond reckoning.

On one of my visits to the Edwards house, I saw on a table a book I had never noticed before. The name leaped at me unexpectedly with such violence that I stood shaking. *An Account of the Life of the Late Reverend David Brainerd, Missionary to the Indians.*

"Oh," Lucy exclaimed, looking quickly from the book to my face. "Did you know him? Of course, you must have. He had a mission near here, and he studied with Mr. Sergeant."

"I did not know there was a book about him," I stammered.

"Father wrote it. Most of it is taken from Mr. Brainerd's journal, in his own words. He stayed with us, you know, for four months before he died."

I could not take my eyes from that name printed in gold. "A journal?" I repeated finally, taking in her words slowly. "A journal that he kept himself? Does your father have this?"

"Father destroyed it. I think Mr. Brainerd asked him to, but he gave him leave to choose first the parts to be published. Working on this book was a sort of labor of love for father. He was very fond of Mr. Brainerd. But more than that, I think it was father's way of grieving for Jerusha too."

I had grown accustomed to hearing Jerusha's name without wincing, for they spoke of her often, as though she had perhaps only gone away for a visit, though always I detected a subtle change in their voices. Now suddenly the name held its old searing hurt.

"She was betrothed to David Brainerd, you know," Lucy said.

For a moment I could not speak. Then a terrible need surged up through my body, finding its own words. "Was she beautiful?" I whispered.

Lucy considered. "No, I don't suppose she was. Not the way mother must have been, or even Esther. But there was something — have you ever seen a paper lantern with a candle burning inside? Jerusha was like that. She was quite different from all of us. She never seemed to want anything for herself, or even to think about herself.

"You know," she went on, "I've always wondered if Mr. Brainerd really understood what Jerusha was like. He was so wrapped up in his own thoughts, in his religion. I know he loved her — how could he help loving her? But I'm not sure how it would have been if they had married. How could he have taken care of her, when he never took the least care of himself? She would have gone with him gladly, to those dreadful places, but I wonder if he would have realized if she was hungry or ill or didn't have warm clothes.

"Oh dear," she said, not understanding my silence. "I shouldn't talk like this. Father would be angry with me. But it is important, you know it is, Liza. Father seems absent-minded, but he notices in an instant if anything is wrong with mother. You see, that's how Jerusha was different. I would want a husband to take care of me, but Jerusha never would have had such a thought in her head. She nursed Mr. Brainerd when he was ill; at the end she hardly left his room. It's strange. They say you don't catch lung fever, but she came down sick of it so soon after."

I did not know how I could endure it, but I wanted her to go on. I wanted to know everything; bearing it would come later. But Mrs. Edwards came into the room.

"What are you talking about, Lucy?" Her keen eyes had not missed her daughter's quick discomfiture.

"Elizabeth was asking about father's book. She knew Mr. Brainerd."

Mrs. Edwards turned her warm intense regard on my face. "Would you care to read it, my dear? You are welcome to take it with you."

I was terrified of those kind eyes. Did the woman even understand that I was helpless to reach out and touch the book? For she lifted it from the table and put it into my hands. "If he was a friend of yours," she said, "perhaps you would like to keep his journal. Please take it; I am sure my husband has some copies to spare. Mr. Brainerd was a rare and devoted Christian. All of you here in Stockbridge must have honored him."

That night, when the house was still, I lighted a candle and took the book from under my mattress.

Mr. Edwards wrote in his preface: "There is one thing easily discernible in the life of Brainerd, which by many may be considered an objection to the extraordinary evidences of his religion and devotion — that he was, by his constitution and natural temper, so prone to melancholy and dejection of spirit." Dejection of spirit! I cannot say what other eyes have found between those covers; what I found there was the record of such agony of body and spirit that I thought my heart must break anew, this time not for my own grief but for David Brainerd's.

It was the story of a lonely boy, early set apart from normal companionship by the call of God, yet never able to still the doubts of his own worth. There was the pitiful account of the disgrace at Yale, which I had never understood, now quite clear — a few rash words spoken by an ardent student, and on both sides that stubborn maintaining of principle no matter what the cost. I saw how he had brooded, alone in the cabin at Kaunameek, on the refusal of the college authorities ever to relent and grant him a degree. I believe it caused much of his sickness, and I wondered as I read if sometimes, in his confusion and despair, he saw in the God who denied his frantic prayers only the enlarged image of those obdurate men in New Haven.

I had thought the agonies of spirit I had witnessed were the phantoms of fever; I learned now that they were the constant torment of his solitude, forever threatening to destroy him. They pursued him through all the years after he left us, taunting him at Crossweeksung while he struggled against indifference and cold and hunger. I could have beaten my fists against the pages.

And how few, how pitifully few, were those who listened to him. What did they think, those Indians he had gone to save, of a frail sick man at times scarcely able to stand? Pleading humility to a race of men who respected only a strong body and a defiant spirit, how could he have hoped that they would listen?

Yet finally, at Crossweeksung, when he had almost lost hope, God saw fit to grant him one recompense. On a Lord's Day the Indians were suddenly stirred; a melting spread through the congregation; their hearts were pierced, he wrote, and they were moved to tears and bitter cries. By his own account, the power of God seemed to descend upon the assembly like a mighty rushing wind. Old men and women who had been drunken wretches for many years, even small children were swept by the irresistible force. A surprising day of God's power, he called it; to him it was a miracle. And from that moment the heathen in that place began to be saved in great numbers, coming from afar, bringing their families, and building cottages to be near him. Children crowded the schoolroom. "What amazing things has God wrought," he rejoiced in his journal.

Though he had his victory, his strength was too spent to sustain it, and he left the Delaware soon after. And in the end there was Jerusha. I had thought to hate her, but I loved her instead. I blessed her that she had been able to bring him some comfort, and I knew with a wrench of pity how little of it she must have eked out for herself. Because in the end it was his brother John whom he called for, just as he had cried out for him in the cabin at Kaunameek. Oh, Jerusha, I thought, how did you bear this bitterness which even your father never suspected? Would it have helped to know that there was another girl, exactly your age, who had drained the same cup? Are you with him now, beyond all need of my comfort and all reach of my envy?

I read straight through two candles, until the gray light from my window made it possible for me to see without one. When the sun reached my bedpost I turned the last page and put my head down and wept. I forgave Mr. Edwards everything I had ever held against him, his coldness, which was a disguise, for the man who had written this book was not cold; his obstinacy toward my father, which I knew in my heart had been forced upon him; his fearsome hell which carried with it such visions of glory. I must be forever in debt to the enemy of the Williamses. Everything Jonathan Edwards had taken from my family he had repaid to me in full measure.

9. EPH NEVER STAYED long in the Castle of which he was now master. He spent much time on horseback, riding to survey the line of forts which were his responsibility, and often visiting Boston on business for his cousin and commander, Colonel Israel Williams. In addition to his military tasks, he was absorbed in the planning of a settlement near Fort Massachusetts, where some of the permanent garrison had set up homesteads with their wives and children. Eph had received from the General Court a large tract of land surrounding the fort itself, and on it he had built a gristmill and a sawmill for the use of the men stationed there. He had leased the farmlands in Stockbridge to Josiah to work. The house on the Hill was to be our home, he insisted, as long as we chose to live there, and Judith and I, with Elijah returned from college, shared its management and kept it ready for Eph's visits.

In the spring of 1755, when the attack on the Chamberlain household was still fresh in our memories, we learned with relief and hope that the colonies were uniting in a decisive move against the enemy, and that one of the three plans of action was designed to rid the New England borders once and for all of the death and destruction that kept us in constant terror. That spring Eph came home with orders to recruit a new regiment which, it was widely known, would join the expedition against the French fort at Crown Point.

Tanned, vigorous, trimmed of his excess pounds by the constant riding, a new hardness in his eye and jaw, Eph was handsomer than ever, and seemed to me — how shall I say it? — more whole, his energies gathered now into a single purpose. I did not doubt the rumors that his men worshipped him. I know that when he beat for enlistment in Stockbridge even the wives and mothers proudly surrendered their men. Virtually every ablebodied man we boasted, English and Indian, enlisted from the town. Certainly the Williams family rallied to his support. Josiah went with him as ensign, Thomas rejoined as surgeon and there were several prominent Williams cousins from Pontoosuc and Longmeadow proud to serve under him. Elijah reluctantly stayed behind, obeying orders to share in the defense of the town.

We watched our men march away, knowing they would not soon be back. For almost six months we were to wait in uncertainty, never knowing where they might be or whether they had yet engaged the enemy. Out of that blur of waiting, one July day still leaps, clear and perfect. It might have been yesterday.

Eph appeared without warning at noontime. He was riding to Albany, he explained, with a company of thirty horses, and since they had been pushing hard he had ordered a halt just outside Sheffield and given the local men a night's leave to visit their families. I was alone in the house with the slaves when he came, Judith having ridden with Abigail that day to visit friends, and for the whole golden afternoon I had him to myself. We walked slowly across the fields, and Eph, more relaxed than I had seen him for a long time, stopped to examine the grafted cherry tree, the wool from the shearing and the two new calves. Finally we reached the great rock at the crest of the hill and rested there, looking down through the treetops to the winding river and beyond to the mountain, hazy lavender in the slanting afternoon sun.

Eph looked at me with his old teasing smile. "You still haven't noticed," he said.

"Do you lack for girls to tell you how handsome you are?" How could I not have noticed the new red coat, so fine of fabric and so meticulously fitted to his new military figure?

"Look again," he said.

"Do the epaulettes mean something special?" I asked after an inspection. "Don't laugh. I know I'm a nincompoop."

"They merely indicate that I'm a colonel."

"Eph! How splendid. What a stupid I am. Does that mean you're to be in command of this expedition?"

"Hardly. Not even second in command. I'm serving under General Johnson. He's no soldier, but he's a good man, an Irish trader who knows the Mohawks like his own two hands. He's been adopted into the tribe as a blood brother, and he's married, in a manner of speaking, to an Indian woman. The Mohawks will follow him anywhere. I'd a sight rather serve under him than under a pig-headed Britisher like Braddock. I've been lucky so far to keep clear of that one. I couldn't stomach his contempt for our provincial troops. Do you know he refuses to admit our best officers as having equal rank with his own?"

"I don't blame you. Eph, I'm terribly proud of your being a

colonel, but it frightens me too. This marching north. I know you can't tell me much, but will there be — I mean — ?"

"Will there be shooting? It's quite possible. I doubt this new coat alone will scare the French into a run, for all it cost me a fortune."

"I don't like it," I said, refusing to joke about it.

He reached for a daisy and sat plucking off the petals one by one. Perhaps the old charm was not in his favor, for he threw it away abruptly. His face looked sober, even strained.

"Matter of fact, I don't relish it myself," he said. "Maybe it's this hot weather. I've been hankering for a look at this farm, and now that I've had it I'm not sure I'll be any the better for it. Days like this it's right for a man to be out in a field breathing in hay dust instead of gunsmoke. I've come to the conclusion I'm not much of a soldier."

"Everyone says you are. A born soldier. I don't know how many times I've heard father say so."

"Maybe I've said it myself. I like working with the men. At the fort it was a good life on the whole. And I don't claim to be more of a coward than most. There's a sort of excitement once the fighting starts that passes well enough for courage. But I'm not itching for a tussle the way some of them are. The thing is I don't hate them. Indians or Frenchies, the ones who hate their guts make the real fighters, but it doesn't make sense to me. They tell me once you've seen one of your own kin scalped you don't have any trouble hating, and it's probably true. But we've encouraged the scalping offering bounties. And when it comes to the French, I keep thinking that the one I'm like to pick off is some scared kid who never had a musket in his hands before."

I was silent, not really from surprise, for this fitted the Eph I knew, but because it was the first time in my memory that he had talked openly about himself.

"The truth is, Liza, I'm bone lazy. All I really want is a stretch of peace where I can build a house for myself and read some books and perhaps even raise some children. Not a world-shaking ambition, is it?"

"I don't know a better one," I answered him.

"Though as a matter of fact, I do have one other ambition. I'd like to start a town. Take those men out at the fort. Some of them have their wives and families living with them, in any sort of shelter they can throw together. It's no place to bring up children, there's no school for them. I'd like to see a real township there, and know I had a hand in making it, and that it would go on after I died. Don't laugh. I'd even like to have it named for me. There's this much of father in me at least. He wanted his own town too, and he made a mistake when he got tied to this mission. He was a damned capable man when he had the reins, and he never really had them here in Stockbridge. If he'd been free of the mission and never had to tangle with a bigot like Edwards, he'd have died respected in his own house."

"I suppose that's true," I said slowly. "But there were mistakes he did not have to make."

"There are some things in my own life I'm not proud of. Things I expect you couldn't understand. For all you're so soft-hearted, Liza, there's a hardness in you. You judge us. Father. Abigail. Me."

"Not you, Eph."

"No?" he asked, and saw my flushed cheeks.

"The trouble is," he said, "you're too honest. You're the only one of us all who has never compromised."

I remember distinctly how I bent my head to watch an ant zigzagging along the rock surface, pulling a bit of something that was too heavy a burden, slipping back from an infinitesimal mountain, darting to find another way. "It seems to me," I said, "that everything I have ever done has been a compromise." I was not able to keep my voice steady.

"We've all let you down, haven't we? You've compromised for us, not for yourself. I've always had the idea that you were holding out for something. Is it love?"

"No," I said. "That is all over."

He sat silent, looking out, his eyes squinting toward the distant mountain. "You and I," he said finally. "The unlucky Williamses."

"*You?*"

"Don't tell me the word didn't get back to Stockbridge?"

I hesitated. There had been a good deal of talk about his attentions to a girl in Hatfield. "I didn't really listen," I said truthfully. "Somehow I always thought — there would be a girl wherever you happened to be." I could feel my cheeks hot again.

"So there has," he said thoughtfully. "So there has. But just one I was biding my time for, waiting for her to grow up. I fancied I was Jacob waiting seven years for Rachel. It was pretty near that long. But Jacob got his reward in the end, probably because in those days Rachel couldn't speak for herself. This girl could, and she did it very plainly just before I left."

"You mean she refused you?" Looking at him, I could not conceive that any girl could be so benighted. "She must have been out of her mind."

"I thank you for that," he said shortly. "But she was altogether too possessed of it. For eternity, I'm a poor risk. She wants a husband she can be sure of not only in this world but the next. She concluded that I'm not saved, and she's probably right."

"How dared she?"

"I made the mistake of trying to explain to her some of my

ideas. She was shocked to the very depth of her little regenerate soul."

"Then she's not worthy of you," I said hotly.

"You're judging again, aren't you? The shoe is on the other foot. I suspect she's a saint. It's a strange thing the way we Williamses are drawn to saints. We never learn from each other's mistakes."

He may have meant only Abigail and John. It did not seem to matter. My own grief was far behind, and his hurt was fresh and here beside me.

"Your — saint. How can she be so confident that she is saved herself?"

"She was converted when she was thirteen. Fainted dead away in the middle of a sermon. She can't accept my salvation without some proof, and I've none to offer."

"Why is it," I asked, "that none of us, not one single one, has ever had any proof? Why should all of us have been denied this thing that the others — the saints you call them — hold so important? Are we so terribly wicked?"

"We're too practical, I'm afraid. Do you care that much, Liza?"

"Yes, I do," I admitted. "I've cared for years. I think it must truly be the pearl of great price. But whatever it is that is supposed to happen never has. Does this mean that God has not chosen — any of us?"

"No," he said, without hesitation. "I refuse to believe that. I've thought about it too. God knows I've thought about it this summer, what with one thing and another. I always come back to the same place. I can't believe that God has judged a man — or a woman — and condemned him utterly without hope before he was born. It goes against all we know of justice. I could not worship a God like that."

To hear him say it, straight out, was such relief that I turned weak. A knot which had held tight all of my life was unloosed and thankfulness flooded over me.

"I don't believe that we can know in this life whether we are saved or not," Eph went on. "I think we have a right to hope. Anyway, I don't believe for one moment that the fact that a girl fainted in meeting when she was thirteen years old is any indication of salvation."

"Did you tell her that?"

"Yes, fool that I am. That's what she can't forgive. To her it's the final proof that I'm totally unacquainted with Grace. Mind you, if anyone was ever saved, she is. She has a goodness that's transparent. It's the *sign* I object to, and her putting so much faith in it."

"Eph," I urged. "She must be very young. I can't believe she means what she says. Give her a little more time. When you come back — "

"Yes," he said, and there was a flatness in his voice that I had never heard there before. "When I come back. Yes." He sat looking off at the mountain, and there in the warm sunshine a small icy snake uncoiled itself within me. Then he got to his feet. "We'd better get back. If we can get some water heated up, I'd like a bath. No knowing when I'll come by the next one." But he stood still, looking slowly around the field, at the line of birches along its edge, at the solid slant of our roof beyond. Then he said, on a long breath, "You've done me good, Liza."

How like him. I had done nothing at all, while he, though neither of us was aware of it, had given me his third and finest gift. In years to come I would remember his words, and I would lean my full weight upon them, and they would be sufficient for the rest of my life.

After supper we all carried our chairs out of doors, and friends from the Hill came to join us. Eph was at his best; his ringing laugh must have carried clear down to the Plain, and you would have thought he was starting out on a summer outing in the woods. Once or twice it seemed to me, in those sudden silences that fall upon a company of people, I caught a reflection on his face of that odd melancholy, so unlike him, but it may have been only the shadows of the house and the ancient elms. We held our ground against the mosquitoes until the first fireflies starred the bushes. Then we went inside and lighted the candles and Eph searched the cellar and came up with a dusty bottle of father's Madeira for us to drink him a toast. When he rode away next morning, with a brisk confidence that forstalled tears, I could persuade myself that I had imagined. But I had not. He came home that day to say goodbye.

There is still talk, but never to my face, about that battle in September. General Johnson, marching north against Crown Point, had left some of his men encamped on the Hudson River and had moved on with the rest to the body of water now named Lake George. There he received warning that a force of French and Indians were marching south to cut between his two forces, and not knowing which camp would be attacked, he sent Eph at the head of one thousand men to make a reconnaissance. It is said that Hendrick warned they were too few. It is also said that Eph failed to take proper precautions, that he neglected to send out advance scouts and that he marched head on into an ambush. Josiah, who was with him that morning and received the wound which caused his death four years later, swore that this was not true. Josiah was convinced that Eph and Hendrick, who led the advance guard of Mohawks, had a secret plan. Hendrick had his own means of communicating with the Iroquois who fought with the French army. It was a band of these Iroquois who made up the left flank of Baron Dieskau's forces and who moved ahead and were the first to encounter Hendrick's Indians. According to Josiah's theory, and admittedly it is no more than that, though Thomas is much in agreement, there was a secret understanding that the Iroquois would desert and would stand aside with Hendrick's Mohawks. Josiah had no way of proving this, and when later he tried to convince General Johnson he was cursed for his pains. If there was a plan, it failed, for a shot, perhaps never intended, struck Hendrick down.

Eph, advancing just behind, met the French right flank. He did not try to take cover; they could scarcely have missed him, and he died in the first moments of fighting. The main columns of French and English never engaged at all. Our militia fled, in confusion and panic, and managed to regain the shelter of the camp they had just left. Dieskau hesitated just long enough for General Johnson to rally his men at the camp. The beating back of the French was regarded as a great victory, and Johnson was knighted for it, even though no ground was gained and he never reached Crown Point at all.

I don't pretend to understand battle plans, but I have pondered Josiah's account and it seems reasonable to me. Eph had confidence in Hendrick, and his confidence was returned. Yet balanced against this explanation is the shadow on Eph's face that last day, and the fact that before he left Albany he made out his last will and testament.

It was a fair and generous will, remembering us all. With it he made two requests. The first, not in the will itself but in a letter to Israel Williams, his executor, asked that the affairs of the Stockbridge Indians left in charge by his father should be settled from his own estate so that they might not be wronged in any way. The second asked that the township near Fort Massachusetts, for which he bequeathed funds for a free school, should be named Williamstown.

10. ALMOST A YEAR after this fatal battle England and France declared the war which was to last for seven years. This time General Dwight persuaded Abigail to leave Stockbridge, which we all knew could scarcely be defended, and he built for her a new house in Sheffield, larger and handsomer than the one John Sergeant had built, but never I think as beloved. I saw her seldom, and young John even more rarely. Elijah and Judith and I stayed on in the Castle. I do not know what would have become of me in those years if there had not been work to do. There was much illness in the town. The sick, like the poor, we have always with us; there were many more families now and still no physician nearer than Sheffield. Without mother I was forced to rely on my own wits and memory. Thomas sometimes sent me advice and new drugs, but mainly I raised herbs as mother had taught me, rue and saffron and tansy, and pounded and ground and steeped them to make the old concoctions, dandelion for the liver, peppermint for heartburn, saffron tea for the jaundice.

I fear that often my ministrations did little good, not from any lack in the remedies but because the one ingredient I could not manufacture was the cheerfulness with which mother had always administered them. Much of the time my hands and feet went about their business while my mind drifted on a tide of emptiness. In the nights the old dream of the Ice Glen came back with such terror that it shadowed the days as well. I almost lost myself in it. I am sure now that the one strong tie that held me from despair was the friendship of Sarah Edwards and her daughters. If their hearts ever quailed at my unsmiling approach, they showed me only a never-failing warmth and welcome.

Their house has always been for me the pattern by which, given another destiny, I would have created a home for a family of my own. It lacked the golden tranquillity which has always veiled the memory of my cousin's house in Wethersfield; the war years were too heavy for that. There was illness in the Edwards household, and anxiety and the daily scrimping to stretch what was meager enough for seven to provide for the unexpected traveling clergymen who so frequently sat at their table. Yet all this was seasoned with a cheerfulness and laughter which warmed me, for there was none such to be found in our house on the Hill, nor ever had been.

In the Edwards house the fear which spread like an evil fungus over everything in the town was never mentioned, except for the brief time when lovely Esther Burr, who had never known our Stockbridge Indians and was utterly terrified of them, journeyed from New Jersey to visit her father. I can remember her wringing her hands and wailing that she had not slept a wink since she had come. Though her sisters laughed at her, I do not suppose they were immune to fear, any more than I was. We knew that Stockbridge was vulnerable. The soldiers who came to guard us were a careless lot, the best men being of course reserved for active duty. Our guards took off the moment their terms were up, not caring whether or not replacements were on the way, so that for weeks on end we were left totally unprotected. A breath of rumor could send the whole townful of whites packing into the garrison, at any hour of the day or night, where they must be fed and bedded down till some equally unreliable rumor gave them courage to go home. No one knows why an Indian attack never came. But I believe that John Sergeant's trust was indeed justified, and that it was our own faithful Mahicans whose presence shielded us from harm.

I think it was my recognition that fear, not only of physical danger, but of that God of wrath whom Mr. Edwards preached, was so remarkably lacking in his own family that finally prodded me to heed more carefully his Sabbath sermons. I confess that up till now his words had found scant room to enter a mind so filled with selfish concerns. He was not a comfortable preacher. His congregation in those war years was a dismal one-sided affair, the singing a plaintive sighing of pigeons without the undergirding of male voices, but Mr. Edwards did not temper his sermons to the timorous feminine remnant.

The women, most of us, responded scarcely more than the Indians who sat like gnarled stumps through the long meeting. Mr. Edwards did not speak our language any more than he did theirs. He was like a hunter who pursues his quarry so single-mindedly that he does not notice the rabbit or the quail crouched under a bush. Or like a man who can point out the tall pine on the top of Bear Mountain and cannot thread a needle in front of his own nose. I think Mrs. Pixley spoke all our minds one morning when Judith, coming out the meetinghouse door, tried to make some polite comment. "I just don't listen, dear," she said, fixing on us her dim, apologetic gaze. "I know I am a wicked woman, but if I stopped to think about it I just wouldn't have the strength to go on. And I'd be shamed to be fretting about my own soul with my son Jonathan and his boy Reuben sleeping on the damp ground somewhere with maybe no food in their stomachs."

But I began to see that my judgment of him was far too limited. I realized now that behind the awful wrath which he preached, Mr. Edwards himself was acquainted with a God of indescribable wonder. Sometimes the radiance of his vision shot through the harsh words like lightning, revealing an unearthly beauty. The God I had glimpsed years before in Mr. Edwards' book was still present in his spoken word, if I chose to listen.

I regret now my deafness, and I am ashamed too that I have never read the books which he wrote while he lived among us. Stephen and Mr. Hopkins speak his name with reverence. *The*

Freedom of the Will, they believe, is a work of genius, greatly promoting Christ and His Church. I am glad to think that here in Stockbridge, after his long battle with the Williamses, he found a measure of peace in which to accomplish God's purpose, which lay far beyond this town and mission. It is a vast pity that so soon he was taken from us.

When at the death of his son-in-law, President Burr, Mr. Edwards was called to be the new President of the College of New Jersey, many of those who had been indifferent to him must have been surprised at their sudden feeling of loss. I do not think that he wanted to go. They say that when the council of ministers whose advice he sought decided that it was his duty to accept the new call, he wept before them all, though this is hard to believe. But he accepted their decision and went away, taking Lucy with him to Princeton and leaving Mrs. Edwards and the other children to wait in Stockbridge until he had found a house for them. Three weeks later word came that he was dead of an attack of smallpox, a victim of inoculation designed to prevent the disease.

Almost at once this loss was made more terrible by further news that Esther too had been cut down by the same infection. Lucy came quietly home. Mrs. Edwards went about the work of her house; she sat at meeting, she welcomed all who called upon her, her head as proud and high as before, her eyes as clear and serene. But she grew very thin, and there was a transparency about her, through which one could almost glimpse the hard bone of her will. In the fall she insisted on making the trip to New Jersey to bring back Esther's two orphaned children. She died on the way, only a few days from Stockbridge.

Before such an enormity my mind staggered, and my own grief was annulled. How could one reconcile such waste? Yet the Edwards girls, whom I longed and was powerless to help, did not need my comfort; to my shame it was they who comforted me. For I was with Lucy and Sarah and the younger girls day after day, and I saw beyond any possible doubt that their father's pitiless God, who had visited this grief upon them, was also strong and merciful to uphold them.

II. WHEN THE Reverend Stephen West came to take Mr. Edwards' place the next year, the way was made smooth for him from the beginning. He had no battle to fight, and people were little disposed to find fault with him; indeed there was little they could have found. "He puts me in mind of John Sergeant," the older folk said, the highest praise they could offer. The children, whose names Mr. Edwards had never been able to recall, responded to this young man's genuine concern. At the close of his first sermon it seemed to me that the entire congregation relaxed almost audibly. There was to be no more terror and brimstone; Stephen preached to us a benign God whose demands would not disturb the noonday meal. The Indians sat quietly as always, accustomed now to hearing their sermon through the voice of an interpreter, no longer expecting that any minister would speak to them in their own tongue.

He was young, only four years out of Yale, quite handsome. The way he carried his shoulders, a hint of the military in his walk, gained perhaps in his year's chaplaincy at Fort Massachusetts, made one forget his lack of height and his delicate stature. There was indeed something of John Sergeant's warmth in his dark eyes, but none of John's boyish spontaneity. Everything about Stephen, his careful tactful speech, his fastidious dress, his meticulous powdered wig and the orderly pattern of his days was as controlled as his deliberate handwriting.

Unlike Mr. Edwards, Stephen delighted in social calls. He soon established a pattern, undeviating from week to week, predictable to the very striking of the clock, equitable in its respect toward every family, with quite properly the balance tipped only slightly in favor of the Hill. On Tuesday afternoons he drank tea with "the Williams sisters." It was flattering the way in which he could dignify such a simple occasion by the ritual he made of it. I could predict to the second the lifting of his napkin from the tray, the deft manner in which he would open it one fold and spread it at a precise angle across his knee, the exact number of times he would stir his two lumps of sugar before delicately laying down the spoon. Judith thought it irreverent of me to mention such things; she could see nothing amusing about them, and that should probably have warned me at the start.

Once these initial formalities were over, the teatime would progress very pleasantly. If we were lucky enough to hit upon some congenial topic, Stephen could lose himself in his own flow of thought. He talked well, brilliantly, but he showed even then the special gift which has won and held his host of friends all his life. He listened. One of his students once said that he could pull ideas out of a block of wood. Certainly at this time in my life my own mind was little more, yet in spite of me Mr. Edwards' sermons had stirred my thoughts so that far below the surface they had begun to move like sap in late winter. Now, under the springtime of Stephen's encouragement, they began to run. Where Mr. Edwards' sermons had left me troubled, Stephen's reassured me. His views were moderate, and I thought that Eph would have agreed with them. I began to store up questions against the next Tuesday, and when he took them seriously I felt new questions rising up behind them. The first time I burst out with an involuntary contradiction I broke off, appalled at my

own impertinence, and was astonished by his delighted smile. I
know now that he welcomes argument from his pupils; opposition, instead of rousing anger or stubbornness, seems to be the
climate in which his mind functions most profoundly. I even
began to believe that at this late date it might still be possible for
me to join the church.

I suppose I took all this too seriously, as Eph always said I did
everything. At any rate, it was many weeks before it dawned on
me that my own tardy education might not be the most important issue on these weekly visits. I looked away one day from
Stephen's face and saw Judith's. She was leaning forward in her
chair, her pale blue eyes blinking in her rapt following of his
words. There was a faint pink along her cheekbones, and her lips,
slightly parted, were soft and somehow defenseless. She looked
so young and pretty that I was startled out of my selfish questions.

No interest in theology had made Judith look like that. How
could I have forgotten, or thought that Judith had forgotten her
daydreams? A minister, a man of God, mild, tenderhearted, fastidious — and unmarried. Even handsome, which was more
than she had asked. It seemed at once so inevitable and so right
that I could not understand why I had not seen it from the beginning.

Neither Judith nor I ever spoke of it. Those days she seemed
to tread very lightly, as though whatever she touched were made
of glass and might shatter at a touch, and the look on her face
stilled my tongue. I was truly happy for her, and I never questioned that if we went on, exactly as we were, all would come
about in due time, until the night when, as we were washing up
the teacups, Judith suddenly began to cry.

"Nothing," she insisted, and for a few moments her sniffling
filled my perplexed silence.

"It's just that I was so embarrassed," she burst out then. "The way you kept interrupting Mr. West."

Had I interrupted? I tried to remember, but I knew it was a rudeness I had never outgrown. Either I could think of nothing at all to say, or my thoughts came too fast for decency.

"You never let him finish. And why do you have to ask so many questions, anyway? Why should you think he only comes to talk to you?"

I tried, that next Tuesday, to hold my tongue, and the afternoon was uncomfortable for us all. Judith did nothing on her own behalf. Stephen was baffled by what must have seemed our rudeness; we were all relieved when the striking of the clock released us. That night I came to the only possible conclusion; whether I talked or kept silent, by my very presence I was ruining Judith's chances. No girl can be her best under a sister's watchful eye, especially a girl as shy as Judith. The only thing was to go away.

Where? Thomas would take me in, of course, but his household was full. Perhaps at last it was time to visit the Williams cousins in Wethersfield, as I been urged repeatedly to do. I sent out a letter the next day, and within two weeks had the answer I had been confident of receiving, a warm assurance of welcome to stay as long as I liked. Not surprisingly, Judith was pleased for me.

As the day approached, I knew increasingly that I did not want to go. There had been times past counting in these years when I had dreamed of Wethersfield, where the sun was gentle in a cloudless blue sky, where one walked on woven carpets or on springing grass to the sound of laughter and a tinkling harpsichord. I had wept with longing to see it all again. But nine years is a long time. Mehitable had seven children now to claim her attention. The affectionate baby Anne would be a grown child with aloof eyes. Ezekiel was married to a strange girl. My uncle had brought home a new wife from England to be mistress of his house. The gay careless neighbors who had strolled on the green would all have changed or disappeared, the men marched away to fight, the women marked with days and nights of waiting. As for me, the years might as well have been fifty. I felt immeasurably old, a country woman, fixed here on the Hill with roots too deep for transplanting. I had forgotten how to dance the minuet, and I had no heart to learn.

Even so, the visit was set and I went about my preparations. I was sorting out my clothes cupboard, packing away the garments I would not need, the day that Stephen West came unexpectedly to our door. It was not a Tuesday, for Judith would never have gone to Sheffield on the day of his regular call; knowing now that he is a man who never leaves anything to chance, I suspect he must have seen her riding away. He apologized for coming unannounced and suggested that instead of having tea we walk out across the field in the afternoon sunshine. He seemed unlike himself, constrained; it occurred to me that he wanted to ask me about Judith, her health perhaps, and I searched my mind to have ready an answer both honest and encouraging. We walked to the end of the west field and stood by the fence looking out over the pasture, the September sun pleasantly warm on our shoulders. I remember that autumn flames already smoldered among the trees, erupting in an occasional branch of maple and dogwood.

"I did not mean to speak of this so soon," he said at last. "But when yesterday I learned that you were going to Wethersfield I knew I must not wait. Please reconsider, Miss Elizabeth. Must you go away just now?"

I looked at him and waited, uncomprehending. And then he asked me to stay in Stockbridge and to become his wife.

"Are you surprised?" he asked, when I could not speak and he could see beyond a doubt that I was not pretending. "Surely my intentions have been plain enough."

Plain? I had accepted long ago that I would never in my life hear again the words he had just spoken.

"Why?" I stammered.

"Why do I want you to stay?"

"Why do you want me to marry you?"

"What a strange question," he said with amusement in his voice. Then, seeing that I was truly confused, he hesitated, choosing his words with care. "Because I admire you with all my heart. Do you know what they say about you in this town? That you have never refused to go to anyone who called, no matter what hour of the day or night. That just to see you walk into the room gives an ailing person new courage. I like to think that we could serve this parish together, you to minister to their bodies and I to their souls. Our Lord thought that both were important."

I was shaken, for I had not known that anyone in the town had such an opinion of me. But he had spoken of marriage.

"I am older than you," I said slowly. And bigger, I thought, looking at the fine-boned hand that rested on the bark rail close to my own.

"Would that matter to you?" he asked gently. "It would never be of the slightest concern to me.

"It was your goodness that first appealed to me," he went on. "I recognized your spirit the first time we met. Then you cannot imagine my delight when I found that the interpretation of the scriptures was important to you. It seemed to me too great a fortune that I had found all this in one woman, that there was someone who might come to share all the deepest purposes of my life."

Could he possibly imagine how unnerving such words could be to one so unaccustomed to praise?

"Think about what I have said, Elizabeth," he said at last, when I still could not raise my head. "I see that I have distressed you, and I did not mean to do this. If your father had been living — perhaps I should have approached your brother first?"

Even at this moment, at the thought of his asking Elijah for my hand I choked back laughter that was close to hysteria. "No," I said, managing a firm hold on myself. "I am old enough to make my own decisions. I — I am very grateful, Mr. West. I will think about it, I promise you. Only —"

I stopped, leaning on the rail fence and looking away over the fields I had planned to leave. It was very still. There was a humming of bees in the goldenrod and a blue-winged dragonfly trembled almost against my hand.

"There is something else," he said hesitantly. "You see, I have observed you more than you know. I have seen that you are fond of children and that they respond to you. This also we share. I will confess to you. I have committed my life to the service of God, to work for his glory, and I have no right to ask anything in return. But if he should in his infinite bounty give me children to teach and to bring up in his way, I could desire no greater joy. I have never met a woman who seemed more fitted to be the agent of his loving kindness."

At his words a trembling I had never experienced began deep within me and spread down into my legs and up till it reached my throat. The field blurred green and gold before my eyes, and my hands clung to the solid wooden rail.

It was not too late. *I could have a child.*

"Forgive me." I heard him through the roaring in my ears. "I am disturbing you. But you have promised to consider, and I will be content with that."

I looked at him then, and he must have read in my eyes the decision that had already been made without my willing, for he reached out and laid the palm of his hand against my temple, resting it there for a moment on my hair. Then, walking lightly and swiftly across the field, he left me alone.

I came to my decision deliberately, or told myself that I did. In the level hours between night and morning there was no confusion and no trembling. Surprise is short-lived. I understood now that, incredible as it had first seemed, Stephen had chosen me. But I also knew that if I went away he would marry Judith. Stockbridge was a small world in those years, with not many marriageable women in it, none at all, in spite of our age, possessing the assets of the two remaining Williams sisters, assets which would not have shone very brilliantly in the world outside but which could be exceedingly helpful to a young minister — a small inheritance, unquestioned rank on the Hill and an imposing house which could be purchased reasonably from a brother who did not relish the burden of it. It was evidence of Stephen's delicacy that he had not hinted at all this, nor at the benefits he could offer in return. He must have been fully aware that this would be, for either Judith or me, a match far beyond anything we could any longer anticipate. A favorable marriage, advantageous from whatever side you viewed it. I had not been so dazed as not to notice that Stephen had made no mention of love.

Yet how needless all this reasoning. My body had made its decision, not from any longing of the flesh, which I had long ago learned would obey my will, but from a fiercer need which made self-denial a child's fortress of twigs. Stephen's words, which had given the decision an independent life within me, had provided me also with its justification. Judith did not want children; she had said so herself. Like my father before me, like Abigail, for I was after all a Williams, I reached out and took what I wanted and told myself that it was for the best.

I had overlooked the fact, as we all did so often, that Judith too was a Williams. I think that telling her was the hardest thing I have ever had to do, and even now, with all that has gone between, I flinch at the memory. She did not speak a word of reproach. For one single moment I read in those widened pale blue eyes the full measure of my treachery, and then I saw the Williams pride veil them with ice. She went into her room and stayed there alone all day while I paced the floor and walked the fields and knew that even now I would not weaken. Next morning she told me with dignity that since I would be there to oversee the house she would ride to Deerfield, as she had long wanted to do, to visit mother and Thomas. So it was Judith who went away from Stockbridge and the Hill, and her visit was prolonged until the first snow delayed her return indefinitely. When the time came for my marriage, mother sent word that Judith was suffering a spell of asthma and that it would be impossible for either of them to make the long journey. Abigail too was away on a visit to Boston, where her husband was engaged in military affairs.

It was perforce a simple wedding. I was not, after all, a young girl to come out bride the Sabbath after with bridesmaids carrying flowers. I had a seamstress in Sheffield make me a new dress, a silver-gray satin with a gray pelisse of velvet lined with the rich red of autumn sumac. On the day we had chosen, Lucy Edwards stood with me, and Jemima Cooper baked a wedding cake. Stephen's brothers, Eleazer and Peletiah, came from Connecticut to look over the unlikely bride he had found in the wilderness; I don't know what they thought of me, but they were so charmed with Stockbridge that they shortly came back with their wives to settle here. We were married in the front parlor of our house, which was now Stephen's by right of purchase, and since we did not have to walk or ride away, we stood together in our own doorway and bade our guests goodbye.

12. How VERY STRANGE are the ways of Providence. A year later, in Deerfield, Judith met her man of God, minister of the Ware River Parish. She brought him home to be married in our house, with that sense, so strong in all of us, of the fitness of our own rooftree. I was taken aback at my first sight of him, having presumed he would be a much older man. The Reverend Ezra Thayer was, I suspected, younger than Judith, overly thin and stoop-shouldered, with a scholarly anxious face and prematurely thinning hair. But the more I observed them both, the more it seemed to me that he did indeed fulfill Judith's exacting requirements. His speech and conduct were mild, his natural kindness was obvious to us all, and he worshipped Judith from his faintly puzzled near-sighted eyes.

"I suppose he's as much as Judith could hope for at her age," Abigail commented in the pantry, ignoring the fact that my own wedding was little more than a year past. "If you ask me, they make a pair. He looks as if he'd oftener need a nursemaid than a wife."

"I like him," I insisted. "He seems altogether right for Judith."

She gave me a sharp glance. "Quite true," she said, so shrewdly that I realized I had betrayed Judith by that simple answer. "Judith was always timid about everything. I doubt she'll have much to worry about with him."

Ezra Thayer and Stephen sat up half the night before the wedding discussing the doctrine of original sin. After the ceremony Stephen, with his methodical courtesy, complimented the bride not on her beauty — though Judith really did look lovely on her wedding day — but on her husband's sound theology.

13. How DID IT come about that the gentle man I married became known, as I said at the start, as a lion in the pulpit? I must recount the change in him, though it has always been to me, and is to this day, unaccountable. It was a strange darkness of the soul which came upon him, out of which he struggled at length to a radiance I cannot comprehend.

Stephen was Arminian when he came to us, believing that any man who earnestly desires it may hope for God's Grace. Though a few in Stockbridge, and Timothy Woodbridge among them, were minded to complain, they had had enough of controversy, and he pleased them in every other way. As for me, I found myself at last at peace with the church. Soon after our marriage Stephen asked, without insistence, if I might find it in my heart to enter into communion. At thirty years of age I was still only a halfway member, and I realized well enough that it was unseemly that the minister's wife should not partake of the Lord's Supper. I was troubled, wanting to please him yet knowing myself still far from any experience of conversion. Since that last afternoon with Eph I had shut my doubts and my longings into a cupboard of my mind and turned the key upon them, aware from time to time that they still waited there, unappeased, but always too occupied, perhaps too cowardly to face them. Had I not married Stephen I might never have opened that door again, but now, with his gentle encouragement, I forced myself to do so and to reveal to him my failure. To my relief I saw that in his eyes it was neither dreadful nor irredeemable.

"I have often found," he said reasonably, "that in young persons who have been raised in the truth there is no single transforming moment of conversion, only a quiet assurance of Grace. I am sure that is true in your case. Surely, Elizabeth, you can confess that you love God."

I hesitated, for this time I wanted no shadow of compromise. "I believe in God," I said at last. "I am grateful for his goodness and mercy. But how can I love what I cannot comprehend? I only know how to love people."

Stephen laid his hand over mine. "And to spend yourself in service to them," he said, smiling. "My dear, don't you see that it is the same thing?"

So I became a communicant, as I might perhaps have done under John Sergeant but never under Mr. Edwards, who had insisted upon a test of conversion which none in Stockbridge attempted to meet during his ministry here. Elijah, who like me had remained without, though never I am sure with my uneasiness, came into the fold on the same day. So simple and natural a thing Stephen made it for us both. How could it be then that, soon after, Stephen himself, my reasonable, enlightened husband, became lost in the Ice Glen?

Despondency was so unlike him that I thought at first he must be ill. I noticed first his manner of reading. Contrary to his orderly temperate habits, he began to read far into the night, and not in his usual methodical way, giving close attention to each word and at the proper time setting a slip of paper to mark the page. Now he turned the pages feverishly, as though he had lost his place and must with desperate urgency find it again. Once when I ventured to remind him that the hour was late, the look he turned on me was abstracted, almost dazed. "I cannot stop reading while the word of God is concealed from me," he said. "Go to bed, Elizabeth."

I have always blamed this on Mr. Hopkins, though I acknowledge that the cause may lie much deeper, and how do I dare deny that it was, as Stephen claims, the prompting of God? Clearly the spells of discouragement were much worse after Mr. Hopkins' visits. They had become close friends, having much in common, and very frequently Mr. Hopkins would ride over the mountain from his parish in Sheffield for supper with us and a long evening of the theological reasoning that delighted them both. Or had until now. Increasingly of late such an evening left Stephen gloomy and distracted.

By custom I stayed in the same room with them, occupied with sewing or sometimes sitting at the small table in the corner to pen a letter to mother or Judith. I seldom bothered with their talk, which was over my head. I could not miss, however, a change in the climate of those discussions, the unwonted agitation, even pleading in Stephen's voice, and the unyielding censure in Mr. Hopkins'. Finally one evening I laid down my pen and listened.

"One who merely thinks himself a Christian," Mr. Hopkins was saying, "is willing enough to be poor and despised, even to suffer great pain, if it may work for his good and God will make him eternally happy at last. This is not real resignation. It expresses nothing but selfishness in making God a tool to answer our own ends."

Stephen's voice was troubled. "Is it not right for a Christian to pursue his own salvation in order that thereby he may glorify God?"

"It is not right to make any condition," Mr. Hopkins replied. "A true Christian gives himself into the hands of God saying, 'May God be glorified, let what will become of me.'"

"A Christian should not hesitate to do so," Stephen agreed, "knowing that God's will is infinitely wise and good."

"Yet," said Mr. Hopkins sternly, "we know that the greater part of mankind has been and still is eternally lost. God has revealed it to be his will that some men shall sin and be punished forever. You know not but you are one of them. Suppose he feels it most for his glory and his infinite benevolence that you should be damned?"

"I cannot believe —" Stephen attempted.

Mr. Hopkins stopped him. "It is impossible to believe any-thing else. If one loves God supremely and desires his glory above all things, then one cannot will or choose anything else but to be damned, if this should be most for God's glory. One who cannot do this is the enemy of God."

"I cannot reconcile your sentiments with my own." Stephen's voice was muffled, as though his hands had covered his face.

"Then indeed," said Mr. Hopkins, "you must be damned."

I had to grip the table edge to keep from jumping to my feet. How dared he say such a thing — to Stephen of all men? Yet I kept silent, knowing it would only shame my husband for me to fly to his defense.

Only when Mr. Hopkins had gone did I speak, trying to hold back my anger and concern, to sound as reasonable as Stephen himself would once have done. "You must not allow him to trouble you so," I urged. "He has no right to set himself above you simply because he is older. After all you have studied —"

Stephen did not look up to meet my eyes. He had picked up the paperbound tract that Mr. Hopkins had left behind on the table, and I knew that he would not set it down for hours. "Suppose he is right," he said slowly, "and I am mistaken?"

"You can't believe that! How could any sane person rejoice at the thought of being tortured by flames for eternity? Even Mr. Edwards would never have said —"

"Mr. Edwards would have said it," he cried. "All his logic leads irrefutably to just this."

"Stephen —"

"If they are right," he almost groaned, "if I have been mis-taken, then I am indeed damned. There is more hope for the lowest creature that crawls on this earth." He went heavily into his study and the door closed behind him.

When I heard the clock strike three I went down the stairs and opened the door. He was at his desk, hunched forward, head down, his forehead pressed against the page. When he raised his head I was struck cold by the torment in his eyes.

"How can I go on preaching?" he whispered. "I am a blind leader of the blind, a worse sinner than any of them."

He would not hear what I tried to say.

"All these years God has watched my foolish pride. It is only by his infinite mercy that a thousand times already he has not plucked me up and hurled me into the flames."

I went down on my knees on the floor beside him and pressed my face against his coatsleeve. He went on as though he did not notice me.

"I could bear his judgment for myself. But how many other souls have been lost because of me? I am a Judas who pretends to espouse his cause only to betray it."

The words were an echo that jerked me from my pity. My head went back. "Stephen!" I cried out sharply, as one would to a distraught child. "Those are not your words or your thoughts. They sound like — like Mr. Brainerd."

He looked down at me. "Yes," he said. "How did you know that I have been reading his life, only today? It gives me hope. It was he who showed the true light to Sam Hopkins, years ago at Yale. Perhaps now he may be God's instrument for me. Leave me, Elizabeth, I beg you. I must wrestle with this alone."

When finally I slept, the old dream came back and I woke trembling, thinking of David Brainerd. I had believed once that I could comfort him and hold him from despair. What a child I had been.

Much later Stephen came up the stairs, treading softly, snuffing out his candle at the door and undressing in the dark so as not to disturb me. I knew it would only add to his distress if he thought he had wakened me. I lay, not moving, until almost dawn, when finally he turned and laid his head against my shoulder and slept.

He has often told me that he could not have come through this time without my help, but it seemed to me that I could do nothing at all. Though I could see him stumbling, I could not reach him. I could only wait, never really doubting that with his natural goodness he must find his way in the end, seeing to it that the house was calm and orderly and that the spare diet he has always allowed himself was exactly to his liking, smoothing out where I could the petty concerns of the parish and of the Indians that would disturb his day, and putting my arms around him in the night. I wish I could have given more cause for his gratitude.

I cannot explain what happened, nor can I deny. Months later, alone in his study, Stephen received a conviction of Grace. His conversion was manifest not only to me but to his entire congregation. He stood in the pulpit one morning with the shining face of an angel, and his voice had new authority and power as he announced his text: The Impotency of Sinners with Respect to Repentance and Faith. I sat in disbelief as the terrible echoes of Jonathan Edwards thundered in our ears.

"Your husband looks mighty happy all of a sudden," whispered Mrs. Pixley, giving me a sharp poke as we crowded together through the door. "Could it be his wife has good news for him maybe?"

"Nothing of the sort," I snapped at her. Would they never stop needling me?

Mrs. Churchill was more perceptive. "Mr. West is like a new man," she proclaimed, with the far-reaching voice of the hard-of-hearing. "A new man. I could tell it the moment he began to speak this morning." Stephen, standing in the doorway to shake the hands of those who passed, overheard her and turned his head and smiled radiantly at me.

It was true, he was a new man. From that morning he preached a new doctrine, or rather the old in its most uncompromising form. Unbelievably he was reconciled — no, more than that, he was surrendered without condition — to the awful God of Jonathan Edwards and Mr. Hopkins, and in this God he found a comfort and serenity which has never deserted him. I was thankful for his sake, but I did not understand, nor do I now.

14. JANUARY WAS A barren month when the icy ground, slick under a thin powder of snow, and the wind, sweeping unmeshed across the hilltops, made the hurrying from one house to another a gauntlet to be dreaded. I carried a footstove with live coals to the meetinghouse and wore my muff through the service as well, but the place was cruelly cold and the bread froze on the plates before Stephen finished his sermon. In the middle of that month a letter came from Judith.

"I am expecting a child in June," she wrote. "Liza, do you remember those ridiculous things I believed once about having a baby? I never felt so well in all my life."

I put the letter in my pocket and carried it about with me for a week before I could bring myself to show it to Stephen. We had been married for nearly three years, and I was shamed that I could not at first rejoice at her news.

Early the next September, when Judith's daughter Abigail was three months old, Stephen, knowing how I longed to see them both, and hearing that Erastus was to ride to Deerfield to study medicine with his uncle Thomas, persuaded him to ride an extra day to keep me company to Ware River, telling me I should stay as long as I pleased. It was a good visit. Ware River was a comfortable settlement, and Ezra Thayer's farm a prosperous one with a fine view of rolling acres, the house shaded by ancient elms. During my stay there Judith and I were more sisters than ever before in our lives. She had not forgiven, I think, so much as actually forgotten all that lay between us. She had changed beyond belief; her old frailness had disappeared in a soft plumpness that became her; she hung on her husband's every word with a girlish dependence that was at once appealing and possessive. She had reason for pride; he had gained stature in every way and was much honored in his parish. She went back to the cradle a dozen times in a morning to marvel that its occupant still breathed. "I always said I'd be a bad mother," she said complacently. "I expect I shall spoil her to death."

"It just goes to show," said Thomas, who rode over on the last day of my visit with mother behind him. "Your mother and I were both set for trouble, with her history and all, and she dropped that young one like a husky wench of sixteen. As for you, Liza, I'd have predicted two pairs of twins by now.

"Confound my fool tongue," he added instantly. "I didn't realize you were taking it so hard. There's no need to, you know."

"I'm thirty-three," I said.

"Just last month I delivered a woman nine years older than that. Her first child, and a strapping boy. Don't give up hope. You've been away for three weeks now. It's an odd thing, but sometimes a separation like that —"

Three weeks had been longer than I had intended, but I was forced to wait for the post to come through so that I could ride with him to Stockbridge, having promised Stephen that I would not travel alone. I would gladly have set out on my own, for the days were beginning to drag. I am not one to be content save in my own house, and I was not really needed in this one. It was a relief to start off at last on a fine clear morning, even with the weathered, hard-bitten man who was none too pleased with my company. Once he discovered, however, that my mare could easily keep pace with his heavier mount, and that I did not need to rest, he tempered his disapproval by an occasional grudging comment.

"Rain on the way," he said in mid-afternoon. I looked up, surprised, for the sun was still shining. But following his squinting gaze I saw that the wind had shifted to the east and was flipping up the leaves of the trees so that their undersides flashed silver. The dust from our horses' hooves was blown up in quick spirals. I hoped he was mistaken, but in the night I woke to the ominous rattle on the roof of the inn room where I slept.

"What you want we should do, ma'am?" the man had the courtesy to ask me in the morning. In the southwest corner of the inn where we stood the panes were clear and the drumming less urgent, but outside I could see the bushes and the orchard trees huddled and bent all one way.

"What would you do if I were not with you?"

"I'd ride. It's my business."

"Then we'll go on," I told him. " 'Tis not my place to delay the mail."

He gave me a dour suspicious look which made me wonder if he respected me the less for my unwomanly hardihood. "Perhaps it will clear," I said.

"Not likely." He added, unnecessarily, for I knew it well enough, "Northeaster like this is good for three days."

It was one of those September storms, coming after a long dry month, when the heavens seem to pour down with vengeance all the moisture for which the farmers have prayed. Drenched and sodden we pushed through it all day, exchanging scarcely more than three sentences in as many hours, our horses moving at an ever slower pace as the dust turned to a thick mud that sucked at their feet. Twilight fell a good hour before its due, and when we came upon a dubious-looking ordinary at a crossroads, much short of our goal, we turned into the yard and dismounted without a word.

Fortune was with me, however, there being so few travelers on the road that day, and allowed me a room to myself with a small fireplace. A frowzy serving wench came with a shovel of red coals, and never had the sight of flames curling about a log been more welcome. She brought me also a harsh linen nightrail and a bowl of steaming venison stew, and I sat half the night before the fire, feeding the flames from the woodbox and turning my soggy garments this way and that. I could not have slept anyway from the masculine revelry that rose through the cracks in the floor, evidence that my companion was not morose by nature.

In the morning he hailed me with the first real cheerfulness he had granted me. "Might as well make yourself comfortable," he advised me, taking his own advice and not rising from his seat. "Bridge is washed out. River's up two foot already and still rising." He and his companions of the night before had already set up a table before the fire on which one of them was dealing out a pack of dingy cards.

After making certain that my mare was sheltered and fed, I went back to my room, which had lost by day the slight comfort my extremity had lent to it the night before. My disappointment was so sharp I could have wept like a child.

I cannot account for what happened that afternoon save perhaps by the long day of inactivity, a luxury I have seldom known and do not care for. When there is no work for the hands to do, the mind seems to elude its customary channels. Toward evening, wearied by the steady fall of rain outside the window, by the nagging plop of water dripping through the plaster in the corner and by the beating of my own thoughts within, I sat on the low stool in front of the fireplace and stared at the flames. All day long the thought of Stephen had grown in me till now it pressed against my chest and ribs like a bodice too tightly laced. The prolonging of our separation was all at once intolerable, the distance magnified by the glassy rain till it might have been half a continent. It was as though the flooding river had washed away the connecting ground between us, stranding me on some island beyond all reach of him. I was shaken by the realization that I had never really known before what it meant to miss another person — I who had lost so many that I loved. When Stephen I had neither really lost nor really — ah, how could I have been so blind!

Then, just as surely as though he had come to me there in that room, I felt the touch of his hand, laid as it so often had been against my cheek and hair, in a gesture that was the essence of himself, undemanding, comforting and simply deeply good. For a long moment I felt it, more real than any dream, more real even than actuality, because all of my being was gathered with intensity into that one sensation. Then it was gone, and I was left shaken by a question. Was it Stephen who had reached out to me, across the miles of rain-soaked fields, across the greater distance of our passionless, courteous, reasonable marriage? Or had the reaching out been altogether my own?

Four days later the post rider and I came straggling into a Stockbridge green and glistening under a late afternoon sun. My mare had lost a shoe somewhere in the clinging mud, so for hours we had had to ride slowly with frequent rests. Unwilling now to take her up the long hill, I rode straight to Mr. Nash, our blacksmith, left her with him and went home on foot. Weary as I was, in my dragging muddy clothes, I went up the hill like a girl, and when I opened the door of my house — Stephen's house — I was trembling.

I stood for a moment in the hallway, letting its coolness and its order settle like silk against my skin, weak with relief at the sight of Stephen's silver-headed cane and hat and gloves laid out on the table. Then I went through the parlor and opened the door of his study, and only at his shocked face as he stared up at me did I realize how I must appear to him.

"I'm not a ghost," I said foolishly.

He laid down his pen carefully; did I imagine that his hand was shaking? "I wasn't expecting — Elizabeth — you came through the storm?"

I was never able to wait for the seasonable moment. Always I have had to know *now*. "Stephen," I said, my breath caught tight with the need of knowing, "on the second day of the rain — on Thursday afternoon — what were you doing?"

He considered in his careful way. "It was my day to drink tea with Mrs. Willard," he said slowly. "But for some reason I was uneasy and I excused myself early."

"Just as it began to be dark — do you remember where you were?"

"I remember very well. I was sitting here in this room, at this desk, writing a letter to you."

When I did not speak, he pushed back his chair and stood up. "I wrote to you to come home," he said.

We stood and looked at each other. I don't know what he saw in my eyes, but I saw a light grow in his, gathering slowly until under its brilliance my tears came, blurring his face.

"My dear," he said. "Oh, my dear." And at last he came across the room to me.

15. BY LATE WINTER I knew for certain that I was with child.

I have come to believe that one cannot ask more of life than to have known a single interval of time from which one would not sacrifice even the smallest perfection of a crystal of snow caught and held against one's sleeve. That springtime my cup overflowed.

I recall, however, that I was often ill, so that when I first noticed the bleeding I was not alarmed. Then one morning, as I was drawing water from the well, I collapsed against the stone rim. I remember old Candace running from the house with her skirts flapping, and crouching over me making clucking noises of pity. After that there was pain and nausea and fever streaked with the old dream, and after hours — days? — of this there was the doctor from Sheffield bending over the bed and forcing a spoon between my teeth, drowning me with some bitter drug.

When I finally woke to a clear mind, the room was still and Stephen was beside me, and I had a distinct memory that he had been there all the time. The sheets were dry and clean and my body felt scoured. I moved my hand, and Stephen's dear hand came instantly to meet it, and we looked into each other's faces.

When the doctor came again I was stronger, strong enough to send Stephen away. "At my age is there still a chance?" I asked, when he was out of hearing.

The doctor looked at me, his blue eyes fierce, and gave me the truth I demanded. "I'm not saying you won't conceive again. If you did once you could again. But I hope you won't, because there is not a chance of your carrying it more than a few months. There is a deformity —"

"Does Mr. West know?"

"Yes, I told him. I don't believe in wives keeping such things to themselves."

When he had gone I lay with my face to the wall. It was not Judith I had wronged after all, but Stephen, my husband. She would have given him children.

When Stephen was with me there was courage in his hand; when he was not there there was no courage. Knowing this without my saying, he seldom left me alone, until sufficient of his strength had gathered in my body and my will so that I went back to managing my house and to sitting in meeting, and to all the small necessary tasks that have filled the years.

16. I WOULD BE ungrateful to God if I did not admit now that they have been good years, most of them, and that they have passed swiftly. I will not dwell on the years of war just ended, for they were not good, no matter how worthy the cause for which we fought. It is over now, and everywhere in this new meetinghouse today is evidence that we have taken up our lives again and would forget. Perhaps our lives will be different, now that our country is an independent nation; it is too soon to tell, though we are isolated here by the mountains and change does not come easily.

Once again Stockbridge escaped the ravages of battle, but we had our full share of fear and waiting and grief, of boys marching away and of hearts breaking. Our town acquitted itself with honor. Less than one day after the news of the battle of Lexington reached us in 1775, the first regiment of Berkshire men was on the march, and for eight years thereafter the same pitiful scene was played over and over again. There are sounds I pray I may never hear again — the dread booming of cannon carried on the wind from the north, the early morning signal of guns summoning the men, the stamping and neighing of horses, the roll of drums and the tremble in Stephen's voice lifted in prayer over the impatient shuffling men and the silent wives and mothers gathered to watch them go.

The men came back, when they could, to plow and plant and harvest; in their absence the women carried on the labor in the fields and still redoubled their work at the looms to provide coats and blankets, doing without and praying and growing old beyond their years.

The Indians were persuaded once again to take the warpath in a struggle from which they had nothing to gain and which they never really understood. Most of them had for a lifetime been taught that they were loyal subjects of the English king; they were bewildered now that they must fight against him. General Washington, they say, was similarly perplexed as to what to do with them, for they knew only their old ways of warfare, they despised army discipline and they were too often defeated before the battle by their constant enemy rum. Nevertheless, on every battlefield, north and south, which was stained with the blood of Stockbridge men, Indian blood was mingled with the white. After the war was ended, General Washington himself sent money to our Indians for a great feast in commemoration of their service. I wonder, did it wipe the tears from their eyes?

I start even yet when I hear people speak of Colonel Williams. They mean Elijah. Though he came through the war honorably, being Elijah he did not do it without stirring up talk and trouble, and some in the town have never forgotten that he was first a Tory. As a matter of fact, here on the Hill we were most of us inclined to support King George at the start; Elijah simply clung to his British principles after the others had seen fit to abandon them, and he suffered for it. Treachery was an easy word to bandy about in those days, and patriotism was confused with violence everywhere. Three times poor Elijah was thrown into prison, once in Northampton because some overwrought citizens claimed that our local jail was not secure enough to hold him, once in a loathsome common jail in Boston and a third time when he went in chains before General Gage under threat of execution. Each time he talked his way out, but there is no denying that he was in the beginning a reluctant patriot. He enjoyed his tea and his small luxuries, and he must have been loath to trade his handsome scarlet coat for the plain continental blue, having always a preference for velvet and satin and gold braid.

So many times I wondered if Elijah would ever settle down. His debts were scandalous. I shall never forget to my dying day the morning that impertinent girl sat in my parlor and stared me in the face and told me she was carrying his child. In spite of all I could do, she took the suit to court and Elijah had to pay her an exorbitant settlement for the support of a child he disclaimed, for it came out in the trial that he had been infatuated enough at one time to order for her a gold necklace from Paul Revere in Boston.

Has Elijah ever been moved, I wonder, to see this child of his indifferent making? How many times in secret I plotted how I would go to that girl, rehearsing our meeting, choosing and re-choosing my words, weak with fear at one moment, at the next fierce with determination to snatch from her what was ours by right. What was it that held me back? Stephen would have accepted a child not his own, even, I think, a bastard. But suppose he bore as he grew older, as I think he must, the unmistakable Williams stamp? What people think is of much concern to Stephen. Or was it uncertainty, remembering Elijah's cynical, "She sued me because I had more money than the rest of them." Or was I afraid that she might laugh in my face? Perhaps after all she wanted him and has cared for him. I would like to see him once. He would be as old now as Elijah when he came home a man from the College of New Jersey.

Fortunately Sophia Partridge did not hold this affair against Elijah, for she has been exactly the wife he needed. I still tremble at times lest he do something rash and foolish, but I remind myself that a family man, and a justice of the peace, has reason to be prudent, and that Elijah is no longer young.

In the end Stockbridge has gathered in "the Williams girls." In 1765 Abigail came home, a widow once again, and she has lived in her old house here on the Hill ever since. Her son Erastus, after a time at the College of New Jersey and three years of study with his uncle Thomas, was ready that same year to set up a practice of his own; it was high time that Stockbridge had a physician, and Erastus has more than filled the need, being greatly loved and trusted. Three of Abigail's children have houses in the town, and from her bedroom window she can watch each morning, for she also wakes early, to see the smoke rise from their chimneys and know that all is well with them. At the beginning of the war Judith too came back to the Hill, Ezra Thayer having died in the forty-third year of his life.

Stephen and I still live in the house that my father built on the Hill; I have never wanted to live anywhere else, and I expect I shall die there. We have not had to live alone in it, after all, for Stephen has had his pupils. When his sermon on Moral Agency was published, it brought him the fame he deserved, and young men came from as far away as Boston to study with him. Up until the war there was scarcely a day in all those years when there were not young voices in the house and young faces at the table, and now they are beginning to come again. His former students write to him from parishes all over New England; they name their firstborn after him, and they speak of this house in Stockbridge as home.

And I have had young John.

17. I SWORE TO Abigail that I did not influence John, and I
would hold to this still for I know I never had any conscious intent. But I admit that when he came to his decision
something deep within me was satisfied.

Always I was drawn to young John of all my nieces and
nephews. He was not really an appealing child, having inherited
neither his mother's charm nor his father's warmth; he was not
affectionate like Electa nor clever and studious like Erastus. The
truth, I suppose, is that he was the child I had been, plain, untal-
ented and always lonely. He was but two years old when his
father died, and for a long time his mother was distracted with
grief and burdened with debt. In his stepfather's house he was
very soon a middle child, too old for the coddling the new babies
demanded, too young to compete with the older children of both
families, who quickly joined forces. He was alone a good deal,
reading, riding the country, and like me he turned to the Indians.
He did not, as his brothers and sisters did, merely tolerate them
goodnaturedly. He was at home with them, and some of them
he came to love.

I don't remember just when he first asked me about his father.
I think he must have been about ten. I am sure that he must
have gone first to Abigail, but it was painful for her to talk about
John. At any rate, he came to me.

"Do I look like him?" he asked. I could not honestly say he
did, nor like Abby either. Again he was more like myself, square-
built and sober.

"Tell me about him," he would insist. What could I tell?
Could I speak of the marriage that had brought him into being,
when every day he witnessed his stepfather's devotion and his
mother's delighted response? Instead I turned to what I could

speak of without confusing him, his father's mission to the Indians. How they had loved and trusted him. How he had labored to translate his sermons and prayers so that they could share the meeting and understand. How they had waited patiently all day to tell him their troubles, and sat for those last three days outside the house, only asking in the end, humbly, if they might someday be buried in a circle around his grave. Was I wrong to tell all this to John's son?

Was I wrong to let him have the journal? I found it on the shelf of the library of Abigail's new house, when she had gone with General Dwight for a short trip and I had offered to mind the children. "Have you ever seen this?" I asked him, without thinking. "It is the record your father kept of the first years of the mission." Surely there was no betrayal in this. John had specified in his will that his books were to go to his sons, and besides, this was not an outpouring of the heart as David Brainerd's journal had been, only a factual account of the school and church. How could I know that Abigail would find it, years later, worn threadbare, packed among the provisions he brought back from that bitter winter at Fort Ticonderoga?

I believe it was only his father's example that kept John at his books, for he was not gifted by nature and Latin came hard to him. I suspect he was as unhappy at Princeton as I was at Miss Richardson's school in Boston, and after two years he came home to Stockbridge to study with Stephen. It was then that I gave him Mr. Edwards' edition of David Brainerd's journal. I should have known, had I stopped to think, that it was heady nourishment for a boy already too susceptible.

John was ordained at length as a minister of the gospel. Then, quietly, he set about doing the only thing he wanted to do. He spent all day with the Indians, visiting them in their houses, teaching the things that had been left untaught for years, listening to the complaints that had been dumb for so long, speaking in their own tongue to comfort the women who sat beside their dying children and to rebuke the men who found in drink their only forgetting.

Abigail came to Stephen actually wringing her hands. It is the only time since the day of her first husband's death that I have seen that imperious self-control shattered.

"There must be something you can do," she pleaded. "He will listen to you. He can't throw away his life like this. I won't tolerate it."

"My dear," Stephen tried to calm her. "Are you not proud that your son wants to carry on his father's work?"

"Don't mouth words at me, Stephen West," she blazed. "I can't stand it. You've never been one for martyrdom yourself. You know as well as I do there's nothing in this to be proud of. He'll be poor and tired and overworked and discouraged till the day he dies, and no one will ever hear of him."

"They heard of his father. John Sergeant's name is honored everywhere."

"It was different then. This mission was a novelty and they pinned all their hopes on it. Not one of them knew what the Indians were really like. That's finished. Who cares any more what happens to Indians? Who do you think is going to honor John's son or even pay him the slightest respect? He'll be a no-body, a failure."

Poor Stephen was terribly distressed, not so much from her words, I sensed, as from the fact that in his heart he agreed with her. Still, he tried. "It is God's work," he said. "John will be carrying out his will."

"I can't believe that any more. God knows I tried to for years. If it had been God's will that the Indians should be saved, why has he thrown every single factor against it to make it impos-

sible? You believe in predestination. Tell me — what indication
have you ever had for thinking the Indians were elected to be
saved?"

Stephen was shocked now. "It is not for us to judge whom
God has chosen," he rebuked her. "And even in this world he
would not want any of his creatures left in such wretchedness.
Have you no pity, Abigail?"

"Of course I pity them. I'm not heartless. But I'm not foolish
enough to sacrifice my son for pity. There's nothing anyone can
do now. We can't go backwards. The Indians had their chance;
they haven't the faintest conception what it means. They don't
understand kindness or decency or even cleanliness."

"Abigail!" I broke in, for Stephen stood helpless. "You've
never been fair to them. Most of them are good Christians. Two
of the Indian boys have gone to college. It takes time and patience and —"

"You!" She turned her withering fire on me. "It's all your
fault anyway, all of this. Filling his head with your impossible
sentimental ideas from the time he was a little boy. What do you
know about it? I don't see your husband wearing himself to skin
and bone. They killed John. They sucked out all his strength,
and if he'd gone on living they'd have broken his heart. And
now they'll do the same for his son. It's all waste — nothing but
foolish sinful waste!"

I honestly meant to do what I could to dissuade young John,
realizing that there was much justice in what Abigail had said,
even in her blaming me. And it is true that Stephen's real calling
has never been with the Indians. But the days went by without
my finding the right moment, and when the moment came of
itself I could not rise to it.

Often John called on me in the night, for though the Indians
trusted Erastus, they have known me all my life and sometimes

they want a woman. On this particular night I sat with John all night beside the mattress of a dying Indian child. We had done what we could; there was no need of our staying, but it was the only thing we could offer to the silent man and woman who sat on the other side of the mattress. It was the fourth and last time these two would wait like this; there were no more children in the wigwam. Such tragedy is not uncommon — scarcely more than half the Indian children live to their tenth years, and some families are more susceptible than others. Erastus says their chests are weak by nature, for the adults too seem to catch cold easily and to go at once into consumption. But I wonder sometimes if bitterness can corrode the lungs as rust eats into iron, if it is not that hope has already died in their houses. Erastus would call me a superstitious old woman.

Almost as soon as we realized that the child had gone, the wailing began outside the wigwam. We left them, to make way for the women. Though John would conduct a Christian burial next day, they still have their own ways which it is better not to question.

John insisted on walking home with me though it was close enough to dawn so that I could make my way easily. The slaves were not yet up, so I fed the fire to a blaze and heated water for coffee, and we sat at the bare table too tired to speak. My body was stiff and painful from sitting so long in the damp wigwam. I could think only of stretching out in my bed for the hour or so that remained, but the coffee made John suddenly talkative.

"At least," he said, "the child was baptized. When I think of those that die every day without the slightest hope of salvation, I feel accountable to God that I ever stop to rest."

I looked across the table at him, thinking how sorely he needed to do just that, startled too that his words might have been read aloud from David Brainerd's journal.

"Mother has been talking to Uncle Stephen, hasn't she?" he went on. "He has offered to recommend me for a new parish north of Pittsfield."

"Are you sure it might not be the best thing?"

"You know better than that. Uncle Stephen tries to please everybody, and he's never understood the mission anyway. You always have. You can't side with them now."

"If I side with anyone it will be you," I told him. "I honestly don't know that it is right for you to stay here."

"Do you remember what my father wrote in his journal when he was first called to this place? He said he would be ashamed to own himself a Christian or even a man if he refused. I feel the same way."

"I know you do," I said, pulling my weary thoughts together. "But you must remember that the situation isn't quite the same. The Indians themselves invited your father here. Konkapot and many of the others were very eager for Christianity, even Umpachenee then, for all he was skeptical at times. Nowadays this new generation seems to be indifferent."

"They still have the need, whether they recognize it or not. That is what determines our mission."

"I suppose so. But I wonder — those women tonight, for example. The wailing and the black ashes on their faces. After all your father's labor, do you think they have ever really given up their old beliefs?"

"Not altogether. They have taken some of his teachings, the parts they could understand, and scrambled it all together. Perhaps that is all my father hoped for. When I study his sermons I see that he didn't trouble them with much theology. He tried to give them simple faith and to make them repent of their sins. If we can achieve that, the rest will come in time."

"Will it?" I questioned. "Sometimes they seem to be set

against learning anything from us, even such a practical thing as using manure when their soil is so thin they can barely make anything grow in it."

"That's something else again. They won't face the fact that they've got to become farmers. I don't know why they refuse to see it. They complain there's not enough game now for them to live by hunting, but the old ones would still rather let their families go hungry than work in the fields. They still want to raise their sons to be warriors, but the war is over and there are no hostile tribes to fight any longer. So they are idle. It's the idleness that's responsible for all their troubles; my father knew that in his day. Even for the drinking. There is only farming — it is their one hope."

"We have taken away everything they lived for, haven't we?" I asked. "How can they believe that if they farm the land they will be able to keep it for their children?"

John leaned forward across the table. "Aunt Elizabeth, can't you see there is one thing we can give them that nobody can take away? If they have a knowledge of God, of his love, if they have salvation —"

"Will it make up to them for all we have taken?"

"What is this life compared to the glory of heaven?" His young voice was stern. I could not answer.

"It is all I have to give them," he said, his voice less certain. "You see, don't you, that I can't leave them? They are my children, and I must stay with them."

"John!" I spoke sharply, remembering. "Eph said something to me once. He said the missionaries — even your father — spoke of them as children. He said that they were men and that they must be treated like men."

He looked at me blankly. "But they *are* children," he said. "They are the children of Satan — what else could you call them? And they must be saved. Without us to help them they are utterly lost for all eternity."

His face was haggard in the light and I was stabbed with remorse that I had only distressed and confused him. I laid my hand on his head for a moment as I bent to fill his cup.

"Your father would be proud of you," I said, because it was the thing he needed desperately to hear said. But my heart misgave me. He had set himself to his father's task without his father's faith that the task could be accomplished. Whether this makes him a lesser man or a greater I cannot say.

The year that the war began, Stephen, with what secret relief I can only conjecture, surrendered to John the ministry to the Indians, with the small salary which still comes from the Society for the Propagation of the Gospel. Since that time the Indians have met on the Lord's Day in their own house of worship, and John preaches to them in the Indian tongue. Abigail has never forgiven me, though we Williams sisters have come close again in these last years. I doubt I had much to do with John's decision, which must surely have its place in God's design. But I find it hard to meet her sharp blue gaze, for I know that often I have not been able to remember that John is not my own son.

EPILOGUE

1784

THE DEDICATION SERMON must be nearly over; Stephen's voice is beginning to tremble. He has forgotten to turn the glass and the sands have run through how long since? In a few moments the ghosts will have left us, fleeing before the bustle of congratulation.

See, I plead with them, the Indians are still here.

The ghosts do not relent. They see that the Indians sit together in this new meetinghouse like strangers, aloof, wrapped in their stubborn differentness, that they listen with courtesy, understanding little, knowing that the words were not prepared for their ears. If ever the chain of friendship was bright between us, it is broken now; they are remote from us, immured in their own Ice Glen.

They will have to go, John says. It will take a little more time before they can accept it, but next year, or the year after that, they must move farther west. The Oneida tribe has invited them to share the tract of land in New York State set apart for Indians by the Congress.

When they move, John will go with them. They will take the great leather Bible with the gold letters which was sent to them long ago as a gift from England, and they will build a new meetinghouse and a new school. God grant it will work out for them. That they will forget the free forest and be content to till the land. That they may be allowed to keep the acres they have tilled. That there will be no store where they can buy rum. That in this new place they will stand as men. That John —

He will fail! I cry out to the ghosts. Just as you failed.

Yes, they answer. He will fail.

Then Abigail is right. It is all waste. All the love, all the suffering, only waste.

The ghosts deny it. They strain forward as though they would shout aloud, as though they had come here today for this one purpose, to deny it.

There is no waste, they tell me. The rain falls on the just and the unjust. It sinks into the ground and rises to earth again through living root and hidden spring.

I look from one to the other, and it is Konkapot, who long ago came to deliver me, who makes me understand.

We must find each other in the Ice Glen, for there is no other way for God to reach us there. Some must go alone into the dark, not blindly stumbling but clear-eyed, searching, even though they find only one insignificant willful child. How else could any of us ever hope to escape? No, the waste is not in the searching. The waste is in all those who wait without hope for someone to come.

Heads turn abruptly; I must have sighed aloud like an old woman. Stephen is beginning his benediction. The formless re-membered guilt focuses sharply into a single sin: I have not heard one word of my husband's dedication sermon.

I bow my head.

Acknowledgments

ACKNOWLEDGMENTS

THERE ARE many accounts of the early years of Stockbridge, Massachusetts, but for carefully documented history four volumes are indispensable: *Historical Memoirs Relating to the Housatonic Indians*, by the Reverend Samuel Hopkins (Boston, 1753); *Stockbridge, Past and Present*, by Electa F. Jones (Springfield, 1854); *Origins in Williamstown*, by Arthur Latham Perry (New York, 1896); and *Stockbridge, 1739-1939, A Chronicle*, by Sarah Cabot Sedgwick and Christina Sedgwick Marquand (Great Barrington, 1939).

From a long list of biographies I would mention especially: *An Account of the Life of the Late Reverend Mr. David Brainerd*, by Jonathan Edwards (Boston, 1749); *The Gentle Puritan*, by Edmund Sears Morgan (Yale, 1962); *The Life of Jonathan Edwards*, by Sereno Edwards Dwight (New York, 1830); *Jonathan Edwards*, by Ola Elizabeth Winslow (New York, 1940); and *Sketches of the Life of the Late Reverend Samuel Hopkins*, by Stephen West (Hartford, 1805).

In my fictitious portrayal of Elizabeth Williams West, I have been guided by the description of her character presented in the address delivered at her funeral by the Reverend Alvan C. Hyde.

The conversation of the famous ministers who appear in these pages has been based on, and in some instances quoted from, their own diaries and letters, and this is especially true wherever they are concerned with theology. For this purpose I have borrowed freely from the works mentioned above, from the letters of John Sergeant to Dr. Colman, from the *Literary Diary* of Ezra Stiles, edited by Franklin Bowditch Dexter (New York, 1901), and from the unpublished letters of Jonathan Edwards.

The discussion between Stephen West and Samuel Hopkins was based on *A Dialogue on the Nature and Extent of True Christian Submission*, by Stephen West (Hartford, 1805).

For the suggestion of a secret plan for the battle at Lake George, I am indebted to *Colonel Ephraim Williams, An Appreciation*, by William A. Pew (Cambridge, 1919).

I owe a debt to the many people who have helped me to recreate the past, but I acknowledge with special gratitude the generous assistance of Mrs. Graham D. Wilcox, curator of the Historical Collection of the Stockbridge Public Library, of Mrs. Raymond Leslie Buell of Richmond, Massachusetts, owner of the Dwight Collection, and of the Beinecke Library of Yale University, where I was permitted to examine the Stockbridge papers of Jonathan Edwards.